LETHAL HORIZON

JASON KASPER

SEVERN RIVER
PUBLISHING

Severn River Publishing
SevernRiverBooks.com

ISBN: 978-1-64875-577-4 (Paperback)

ALSO BY JASON KASPER

American Mercenary Series
Greatest Enemy
Offer of Revenge
Dark Redemption
Vengeance Calling
The Suicide Cartel
Terminal Objective

Shadow Strike Series
The Enemies of My Country
Last Target Standing
Covert Kill
Narco Assassins
Beast Three Six
The Belgrade Conspiracy
Lethal Horizon
Congo Nightfall

Spider Heist Thrillers
The Spider Heist
The Sky Thieves
The Manhattan Job
The Fifth Bandit

Standalone Thriller
Her Dark Silence

To find out more about Jason Kasper and his books, visit
severnriverbooks.com

To Logan Ryles – Thanks for walking the trail with me.

The gigantic challenge is the magnitude of the individual differences in the optimal set point for "good stress." For one person, it's doing something risky with your bishop in a chess game; for someone else, it's becoming a mercenary in Yemen.
-Robert M. Sapolsky

Welcome to Project Longwing.
-David Rivers

1

Aden, Yemen

The empty city streets were a world of green shadows through my night vision as I followed Worthy alongside a low building, inhaling warm night air that bore aromas of spice, lingering car exhaust, and saltwater from the nearby Sea of Aden. As the pointman crossed an alley outlet to our left, I heard multiple dogs barking in objection to his presence. I broke into a run and raced to the corner ahead, fearing that after everything my team had been through in the past couple years, it would be a pack of stray mongrels that got us killed.

We'd been dropped off in civilian vehicles ten minutes earlier, choosing our insertion point just outside the ring of an early warning network in the structures surrounding our target building. Since then we'd utilized meandering alleys and narrow back streets to approach our target, avoiding main thoroughfares along a route that had been meticulously chosen to evade CCTV and law enforcement.

Aside from a few encounters with the peripheral glow of flickering sodium-vapor streetlights, we'd been successful in infiltrating undetected, but that was all about to go out the window if the damn dogs woke up anyone in the surrounding buildings.

The barking continued as I reached the corner and lifted my suppressed HK416 assault rifle from beneath a shawl draped over my right shoulder. Pivoting to face the alley, I flipped the selector lever from safe to semi-automatic—four dogs were advancing in a tight pack, the largest in the lead.

I fired twice into the alley, and the dogs went silent and fled as a duo of subsonic bullets cracked into the pavement a few meters ahead of their alpha male. They scampered out of view while I conducted a tactical reload, stowing my partially expended magazine into a dump pouch for later use and transmitting to my team.

"Warning shots, we're good."

A quick rearward glance assured me that Ian, Reilly, and Cancer were keeping pace, and by the time I faced our direction of movement, Worthy had already continued slipping alongside the building ahead. Pulling the shawl over my weapon, I hastened to follow him.

Our armored plate carriers and their attendant pouches of magazines, grenades, and medical equipment were concealed by black thawbs, traditional Yemeni robes that hung down to our ankles and had been modified with access cutouts and Velcro seams for hasty removal. Combined with the shawls around our heads and necks, the local attire provided some degree of discretion for any cursory observers, and if necessary, we could remove our night vision to blend in more fully.

But it appeared we wouldn't have to: the good news about a nighttime raid was that every civilian from the lowliest street urchin to the highest-ranking politician in the displaced government was currently sleeping off the effects of their afternoon high from chewing the stimulant leaves of khat, an otherwise benign flowering plant whose use in Yemen exceeded epidemic proportions.

I followed Worthy another few meters along the back street when my night vision glared with a sudden flash of light, and I was in the process of maneuvering my HK416 from beneath the shawl when my radio earpiece crackled to life.

"*Freeze,*" Reilly transmitted. "*Suicide, right above you.*"

By the time he finished the message, it was redundant—I held my rifle at a near-vertical orientation, aligning the suppressor with the metal grid of a balcony floor twenty feet overhead.

A man stepped onto the balcony, the profile of an AK-47 appearing in stark relief against the interior lights flooding the open doorway behind him.

He'd clearly been summoned by the barking dogs, but I couldn't make out any night vision over his face. Functioning streetlights were in short supply in Yemen, and I was certain the rest of my team had already tucked themselves into the deepest shadows they could find. In the meantime, I steadily aimed my HK416 at the intersection of the guard's legs. If he spotted one of us, I was a few trigger pulls away from ruining his night: some of my subsonic rounds would ricochet off the balcony floor, but the rest would inevitably find their way through his pelvis at the most tragic angle possible for any man.

He scanned the street beside us, and I waited for him to look between his feet to initiate my opening salvo.

But he fumbled for something in his pocket instead, a new spark of light appearing as he lit a cigarette. After blowing a single smoky plume outward from the balcony, he returned inside and closed the door.

The world beyond my night vision sharpened into clear green hues, and I instinctively scanned the row of trees and dusty buildings across the street before glancing ahead of me to see Worthy on point. Then I looked over my shoulder to find Ian, Reilly, and Cancer stepping out from the wall they'd flung themselves against at the sudden intrusion.

"Anyone get spotted?" I transmitted.

No response, and I listened for the sounds of men shouting in the building beside me to determine if we'd have to transition to an emergency assault.

Instead I heard only the distant barking of more dogs and the snarl of an engine down a side street perhaps a block away.

"We're clear," I concluded, keying my radio mic. "Let's go."

Worthy continued moving ahead of me, and I trailed him by a few meters as our file resumed. Once I'd turned the next corner in pursuit of my pointman, I could distinguish the silhouette of a dome and minaret obstructing the skyline to my front.

As religious institutions, mosques were typically off-limits in all but the most damnably provable exceptions to the rule. Even then, we faced a heavily guarded and culturally sensitive objective where the omnipresent risk of civilian casualties was catapulted to its maximum—so much as a single wayward step could shut down our program at once and in full, no matter how lofty our intentions or surgical our use of force.

"*Eyes-on breach point,*" Worthy transmitted in a Southern drawl.

A moment later I could see it too, a short row of stairs ahead that ended at the back door of the mosque. Everything after that point occurred exactly as it had in our rehearsals: Worthy fanned out to the left of the entrance, assuming security down the mosque's outer wall as I knelt beside him to aim in the direction we'd come from to establish an intersecting field of fire in an L-shape.

Cancer and Reilly did the same to the right of the stairs, and each sub-element took turns stripping shawls off and tearing at the Velcro seams of our thawbs to ditch the local attire in scattered heaps outside the building.

I yanked my HK416 buttstock to the fully extended position as Ian moved up the steps to apply his explosive breaching charge against the door. As a result of that responsibility, he would be the last man inside the building; for all his accolades as an intelligence operative, Ian was outmatched in varying degrees by every other teammate's marksmanship skills, and he did his finest tactical work from a supporting role whenever possible.

I keyed the mic for my command frequency.

"Khanjar Two, we're at the breach point, what's your status?"

A man with a thick Arabic accent replied, "*Khanjar Two is standing by to move to the target.*"

"Cut power, cut power, cut power."

A pause before he replied, "*One moment...okay, he says it is done. The grid is down.*"

"We're going in; begin movement for pickup."

"*Khanjar Two is moving.*"

Ian transmitted, "*Breach is set.*"

Glancing sideways to confirm that Ian was crouched between Reilly and

Cancer on the far side of the door, I thumbed the transmit switch for my team net and ordered, "Stand by for initiation: five, four, three—"

But that was as far as I got in my countdown when someone inside the building chose the worst possible moment to fling the door open. Seeing a flex linear charge neatly adhered beside the hinges, he shouted in alarm.

Ian clacked off his breach at once, the strip of explosives shearing the door from the frame in one direction and turning the guard into a smoldering mass of flesh and bone. The guard's body bounced off the far wall before spilling down the stairs amid the receding cloud of flame that sent smoke and dust billowing out onto the street below.

Reilly was on his feet before the echo had faded, moving through the breach point with Cancer behind him. I was next, drilling two rounds into the charred remains of the fallen guard whose rifle had been corkscrewed by the sling around his neck and came to rest across his throat. Vaulting the body, I landed on the steps and moved toward the open doorway with Worthy at my back.

2

___

Charlottesville, Virginia, USA

I pushed the shopping cart across the slick vinyl floor, pausing for my wife to deposit a tub of yogurt.

"All right," Laila said, ticking off the item on her phone, "almost done, and we'll need to pick up wine on our way out."

Amid the full knowledge that "almost done" meant another fifteen to twenty minutes of driving the cart through a 12,000-square-foot grocery store, I offered what would likely be my only other contribution to our excursion.

Smiling triumphantly, I said, "We don't need wine. I picked up a few bottles for you yesterday."

"Elise drinks rosé."

"Elise?"

"Oh, I thought I told you. The Pattersons are coming over for dinner tonight."

"Right," I muttered. "The Pattersons."

My daughter gave me a conciliatory pat on the arm. Her gesture served as both confirmation that her mother had in fact told me and a measure of sympathy that my night would consist of bland conversation with Mr.

Patterson, a corporate drone with all the charisma and self-confidence of a houseplant.

Laila's eyes narrowed suddenly, her gaze dropping to her phone.

"Shoot. I forgot to grab the tempeh."

A few months ago I had no idea what that word even meant.

But our grocery trips had gotten considerably more involved since my daughter made the abrupt decision to become a vegan, a notion that she'd gotten from God knew where and vigorously defended with a host of justifications ranging from animal welfare to personal health to the environment. At first Laila and I thought it was just a phase, surely to be forgotten the next time we passed by a Chick-fil-A drive-through.

But Langley hadn't wavered, and so our routine shopping lists now included such items as tofu and fermented soybean patties, also known as tempeh.

I offered, "I'll grab it, just tell me where—"

"No," Laila shot back, composing herself before smoothing over her response. "No, thank you. I'll be right back. Take Langley to get some cereal, would you? Next aisle over, she knows what kind."

Then my wife was gone, making her way through the leagues of shoppers who flocked to Wegmans like as many moths to a flame.

I looked down at my daughter. "I could've handled it, you know."

Langley gave a mournful shake of her head. "You never would have found it, Dad. Come on, let's get cereal."

She led the way, and I dutifully pushed the cart after her.

For anyone wanting to learn what being a professional warrior *wasn't* like, then most Hollywood war movies would be a great place to start. Even minor accuracies in such films tended to be the exception rather than the rule, and the Iraq War surge-era blockbuster *The Hurt Locker* was no exception.

And while it was tactically ludicrous, the movie achieved what I'd long considered the pinnacle of authentic cinematic insight into the life of a combat vet: the scene where the hero's sense of alienation from his own domestic existence, the appalling meaninglessness and despair of the return home, was thrown into stark relief in 90 glorious seconds of screentime.

The setting was, of course, a grocery store.

It was a genius decision by the screenwriter, for all the reasons I was encountering now.

Nowhere was I of so little use to my family than here, a shopping mall-sized emporium of food, where the disparity between a poverty-ridden combat zone and excessive American consumption reached its dizzying peak. Every instinct that made me good in a gunfight was not only useless here but actively counterproductive—there was little need for hypervigilance and continual threat assessment amid waves of bovine shoppers swiping through recipes and shopping lists on their phone. And seeing as I couldn't cook to save my life, I had no idea what combinations of food to buy or in what quantities, and was utterly clueless as to where to locate items in the store even if I did.

The result was my current predicament, relegated to cart-driver who could only follow precise instructions for retrieving select items. Even then, I very often failed to complete my assignments without my wife or daughter providing some form of corrective intervention.

But upon entering the cereal aisle, my spirits lifted.

"All right, kiddo," I said, letting the shopping cart come to a full stop, "it's just you and me now. What'll it be? Frosted Flakes? Lucky Charms? Wait, I've got it."

Snatching a box off the shelf, I turned to face my daughter triumphantly.

"Cinnamon Toast Crunch. Breakfast of champions. You used to love this stuff."

Langley was unimpressed.

"When I was little, maybe. It has way too much sugar."

I raised an eyebrow, giving the box a shake for emphasis. "Says your mom, maybe."

"Says me, Dad."

"You're eight years old: the time to eat this crap is now, while you've still got the metabolism of a spring jackrabbit. Take it from a guy who misses those days."

She took the cereal from me, returned it to the shelf.

"I don't like the energy crashes while I'm at school. Or jiu-jitsu."

The jiu-jitsu classes were another thing—neither my wife nor I ever took karate, so we were surprised when our daughter innocently asked to attend a free trial class. That was months ago, and she'd been committed to the sport ever since. Langley Rivers was a paradox: a girl equally concerned with her ability to take down grown men as she was protecting animals.

I watched her stroll down the aisle and select her preferred box before depositing it in the cart. "Plant-based, grain free, nine grams of protein per serving. You should try it."

"I did, once. Haven't been able to un-taste it since."

"I'm going to win you over one day. You know you can be vegan *and* drink bourbon, right?"

"You can?" I asked, feeling my phone buzz in my pocket. "Hold on a sec."

I withdrew the phone, saw the word *UNLISTED*, and looked up to see my wife returning with a block of tempeh in hand.

"It's work," I said, "I've got to take this."

Laila gave an accommodating nod, as if to indicate that the fate of our grocery expedition didn't exactly hang in the balance of my personal participation or lack thereof.

Walking away from my family to avoid any risk of chance eavesdropping, I answered the call.

"David."

A woman responded, "David, this is Mayfly."

"Who?"

"Meiling Chen."

The name got my undivided attention. Callsigns like Mayfly were typically reserved for radio communications, and hearing one over the phone had caught me off guard. It shouldn't have, however, because career CIA officers had a way of inserting their callsign in lieu of an actual name at every possible opportunity. And as far as my employment went at that particular institution, this woman was the top of the food chain.

"What can I do for you?" I asked.

"I'd like to meet."

The feeling was mutual; while this woman had run Stateside support for my team on one previous operation—actually, I thought, make that *half* an operation, owing to a sudden promotion after her predecessor Duchess's death—she'd been conspicuously absent from our debrief upon return.

"Okay," I said. "When?"

"You're with your family. I want to respect that."

My senses went to full alert, and I discreetly scanned the passing shoppers with a renewed sense of threat detection. No overt surveillance, which was to be expected from America's foreign intelligence service.

Chen continued, "It'll be quick. Meet me in produce."

"Produce?" I asked.

"Where they sell the fruits and vegetables."

"I know what produce is. I mean you're here, right now, in Wegmans?"

Chen laughed softly. "You didn't think all these meetings had to occur in a parking garage, did you?"

3

Reilly had a feeling tonight's operation was going to be a shitshow.

The scene at the breach point had thus far confirmed his suspicions, with Ian turning an emerging guard into a crispy critter by virtue of his door charge. Now Reilly proceeded as the first man leading his team through a doorway that was, according to the source sketch of the building interior, a dedicated women's entrance.

He cleared the dissipating smoke of the flex linear charge, nostrils thick with the smell of explosive residue and roasted flesh, and found the HK417 in his hands suddenly drift upward and sideways as if of its own accord. His point of aim instinctively spun toward a flash of movement that his brain was only now beginning to consciously process.

Reilly fired twice at the shadow that appeared on a stairwell landing, having just enough time to see that one or both rounds had struck the now-recoiling armed man at the end of his infrared laser. Then he swept his point of aim downward and continued toward the doorway. The chuffing sounds of suppressed gunfire assured him that his teammates were in the process of neutralizing the threat in full, and Reilly slowed to a walk to allow them to close the gap before pivoting left through the next threshold.

He button-hooked toward an empty corner, then reversed his aim and drifted toward a bookshelf-lined wall before proceeding down the long room serving as a library. Reilly heard his teammates spilling into the room behind him, their footsteps audible between muffled shouts in Arabic coming from further inside the building. The fight wasn't over yet, he thought while moving toward the next open doorway, certain that he'd once again be the first man through.

Bursting into a mosque carried with it a certain feeling of taboo, not that this building served as a place of worship in anything more than a limited daytime capacity. They wouldn't be entering into the main prayer hall anyway, instead penetrating further into the administrative area.

Reilly reached the far corner and turned, closing with the next doorway as he registered the silhouettes of two teammates moving along the far wall. No need to slow down this time, he realized; they'd be right on his ass by the time he flowed into the next room, and so the medic picked up his walking pace in an effort to gain as much ground as possible before the element of surprise faded entirely. He chose not to button-hook this time, instead sidestepping the threshold and making a beeline for the next corner.

But he'd scarcely made it two steps when his night vision turned to an eye-searingly bright shade of white, the result of someone flipping on the overhead lights—which, he considered, should have been impossible given an Agency rep was supposed to have his source cut the fucking power grid by now.

There were no good options at a time like this, when the playing field of visibility suddenly swung in the opponents' favor.

So Reilly did the best he could under the circumstances, continuing in his direction of movement to clear the "fatal funnel" of the doorway behind him, a magnet for enemy bullets in every sense of the words, so his team-mates could enter. He used his non-firing palm to thrust his night vision device upward, and by the time he was blinking to clear his now-limited field of vision, a barrage of unsuppressed gunfire rang out.

The echo of the automatic bursts was loud enough to conceal the loca-tion of the source, though the hissing pops of plaster showering out from the wall ahead made him confident that he was the intended target.

Reilly made the unorthodox decision to stop and lower to a crouch, wheeling sideways to sweep his rifle over the plastic foldout tables and chairs signifying a dining hall. His intended point of aim was the rough location of a doorway on the floor plan, and by the time he saw it, he identified a shooter just inside the room, merrily blasting away from the hip without any particular consideration for accuracy.

It was an oversight he paid for with his life as Reilly delivered three subsonic 7.62mm rounds to center mass, the only shots he had time to fire before the enemy fighter got lit up like a Christmas tree by the combined efforts of David, Cancer, Worthy, and Ian shooting in unison. And with that handled, Reilly flipped his night vision up on its mount to transition to a white light clearance.

It was all he had time to do before a teammate grabbed the handle of his armored plate carrier from behind, giving a tug with the words, "Come up."

Rising to continue the clearance amid a burning desire to reload, Reilly saw that two assaulters were closing with the far doorway. His tenure as first in the door had come to an end, at least for now: once the dance of close-quarters battle had begun inside a building, the flow continued however it had to until the objective was secure.

He rushed to catch up with the lead element of his team, only briefly glimpsing the new number one man racing toward the doorway.

But after years of training and combat operations around the world, Reilly knew the other four men by the smell of their flatulence, much less the briefest glimpse of their figures. Any enemy fighters ahead wouldn't remain standing for long—Worthy had just taken the lead.

Worthy advanced without the benefit of night vision, left thumb poised on the pressure switch for his rifle-mounted taclight in preparation for crossing into the shadows beyond the doorway.

With three enemies confirmed dead, he knew at least two fighters were at large in the building—maybe more, if the CIA's information was incorrect. Which it very possibly was, Worthy thought, considering the power grid was supposed to have been cut off by now.

He saw Reilly and David advancing on the far wall, the former dipping his barrel to concede that Worthy had right-of-way into the corridor that supposedly lay beyond the dining hall. Worthy flowed through the door, sweeping his HK416 across the space beyond and seeing that the floor plan the CIA had provided was indeed accurate so far. He slipped toward an L-shaped intersection in the hall ahead before being gut-punched by an over-whelming urge not to round that corner.

That feeling coincided with the sound of a metallic pop beyond the bend. Worthy stopped near the edge, holding up his left hand in a fist and then pumping it in a downward motion over his shoulder before kneeling.

He felt the knees of the man behind him pressing against his back, then heard a shuffle of canvas followed by a quiet snicking noise over his head before Cancer hurled a fragmentation grenade around the corner and down the next stretch of hallway.

At the same moment, a man shouted *"Kes ommak—"* before his voice was drowned out by the deafening blast of a belt-fed machinegun opening fire. The salvo ripped through the hallway intersection and slammed into the wall to Worthy's right, the grenade blast drowning out everything else. He winced against the blast of smoke and plaster dust that blew outward in a horizontal mushroom cloud, waiting for the visibility to clear and the shrapnel to settle.

He momentarily wondered which had come first, his instinct to stop or the distant sound of a belt-fed machinegun's manual safety rotating to the fire position.

Worthy couldn't be sure, and at this point it didn't matter; he pivoted on his knee and activated his taclight to take aim in the hallway beyond. The fog of the grenade blast lifted to reveal a prone fighter blown in half behind the remains of his PK machinegun, and the partially obscured legs of his more distant comrade limping away. There were precious few situations where shooting below the pelvis was justified, and this was one of them.

It took Worthy a half-dozen rounds to score a definitive hit, blowing out the retreating opponent's calf and causing him to fall below the still-rising cloud of debris for a trio of kill shots that removed him from the fight once and for all. Satisfied that Cancer stood behind him, Worthy executed a tactical reload that ended with the full expectation that his teammates would come flowing around his side to proceed down the hall. And when that didn't happen, he realized that he was the only one who could see the hallway was clear from his kneeling vantage point.

So he rose to a crouch and proceeded forward, cueing his team to follow as he swept his HK416 below the smoke and dust just overhead. Years as a competitive shooter had honed his reflexive marksmanship to a razor's edge—the combat maxim was to move no faster than you could accurately engage targets, and to that end Worthy could move faster than anyone on his team.

He slipped past the two fallen opponents and chose to bypass a pair of closed doors, opting instead to continue movement toward the final L-shaped intersection ahead.

Beyond that corner was their final destination, and ideally they would encounter no further opposition. Four men now lay dead, though any value to knowing the total number of guards was far outweighed by the simple fact that every member of the early warning network—to say nothing of random Yemeni gunslingers of various affiliations awakening from their khat hangover—would be descending on the mosque any minute now.

Not until he neared the last turn in the hall did he register a thumping sound: a fist on wood, occurring in bursts with pauses in between. Worthy knelt and transitioned his HK416 to a left-handed shooting position, then waited to hear the thumps again before lowering himself to the prone and angling his weapon around the corner while maintaining the maximum amount of cover and concealment.

There was an unexpected fifth fighter, knocking on a closed door before furiously testing the handle. Then he glanced sideways to find himself looking directly into the business end of Worthy's suppressor.

The pointman fired two precisely aimed shots, then three more in rapid succession. His target fell dead, and Worthy remained in place as his team-mates spilled into the last stretch of hallway, one of them giving the fallen guard another double tap for good measure.

Worthy pushed himself upright and, upon seeing that Ian had rear security covered, directed his attention to the locked door that David, Reilly, and Cancer were now stacked to breach. After positioning himself on the opposite side of the entrance, Worthy called out in a loud voice that was equal parts forceful and angry.

"Name?"

A man proudly replied with a Yemeni accent, his voice muffled by the door, "I am Faisal Haidar."

"Are you alone?" Worthy shouted back.

"Yes."

"How many guards in the building?"

"Five."

"Unlock the door—*do not open it*. Turn around, take five steps, and put your hands up. You don't, and you're dead."

He heard the clack of a deadbolt, waited a beat, and then gave a nod.

David turned the handle and threw the door open, and Worthy flowed inside and raised his HK416.

He cut right, clearing his first corner before sweeping his aim in the opposite direction to identify a lone, obese figure in a traditional white thawb that covered his body from ankles to wrists. He was facing away from Worthy, both arms raised over his head.

By the time Worthy scanned past the man, David and Cancer were already inside with no shots fired. With the immediate clearance complete, he advanced on the surrendering captive to search him for weapons.

The man looked over his shoulder, revealing a craggy, weather-worn face and a cheek bulging with a comically large wad of khat, and then spoke in an irritated tone.

"What took you people so long?"

4

I strolled through the Wegmans produce section, trying to determine which of several unaccompanied women was Meiling Chen.

She'd seen my picture but I hadn't seen hers, and while I could reasonably infer an Asian heritage by virtue of her last name, only one female matched that description. A slight woman with Asian features was wafting through the stands of fruits and vegetables with a canvas shopping bag, attired in a work-from-home outfit that was business casual at best: khaki slacks and a cotton blouse with the sleeves rolled. Everything about her broadcast a soccer mom rather than a CIA officer charged with running a highly compartmentalized targeted killing program, and yet she was the only one to lock eyes with me, flash a familiar smile, and approach.

The back of my neck burned with embarrassment. What had I been expecting, a trench coat and sunglasses?

"Meiling," she said, offering her outstretched hand.

"Always nice to put a face to the voice on the command net. David."

We shook hands in the manner of casual acquaintances, after which I hastily added, "I don't have much time."

Chen smiled.

"I've got three kids under the age of ten," she offered, "the youngest still in diapers. Lack of time is a familiar concept, and this won't take long."

"Great. Thanks."

She began, "I wanted your agreement before proceeding with the formal portion of your next assignment, and it's always nice to get away from the office. This seemed a better solution for both of us than summoning you to Langley to discuss."

Stuffing my hands in my pockets, I rocked back on my heels and admitted, "At the risk of underestimating my contribution to my daughter's cereal selection, I'm inclined to agree. You have our next target?"

"I do."

"Well," I continued, "after the intelligence windfall we brought back from Serbia, it better be someone in the stratosphere of Erik Weisz's network."

Her face betrayed the slightest flinch at my mention of the name, and I unapologetically waited for a response. If my team had spent just over two years following the trail of a major terrorist facilitator while armed with little more than reckless determination and a pseudonym, then the least Chen could do in return was to give me an idea of how important this new target was.

After a moment of silence, her expression relaxed.

"The intel you recovered brought a lot of threads to pursue, and we've had our people running them down all over the world. Your target isn't in Weisz's inner circle, but we have indications that he knows who is. That's why we need him alive."

I felt my jaw settle. "You know how much more dangerous it is for my team to capture someone alive than to kill them, right? You'd better, because if we do this thing—"

"It's less dangerous," she interrupted, "when the source is a willing defector."

Recoiling at the notion, I asked, "Then why do you need my team at all? You can have a rookie case officer hold his hand on the way to the airport."

Chen grinned slightly, as if I'd just exposed my ignorance.

"Unfortunately, he is under guard that serves to prevent him from leaving as much as to provide protection. It's going to be a fight to reach him."

Now it was my turn to grin. "A fight, we can handle. What's the location?"

"Aden."

I nodded. "Cool. I've never been to Yemen."

"And you won't be there long. Charter flight followed by a night raid, and then it's an in-and-out to action the objective and retrieve the target. Return to base by sunrise, and hand him off to our interrogators."

"Follow-on targets?"

"None planned, at least not in Yemen, which isn't to say there might be a stand-down period for us to confirm that. But there are two conditions that I'll need your agreement on before we make this official."

"Hit me."

"First, his death needs to be faked, and convincingly so. I'll need 'kill' confirmation photos, as it were, that are authentic enough at the outset for our fabrication people to doctor up for later distribution."

I considered that request, an odd one given our usual charter of facilitating *actual* kill confirmation photos, often at great danger to ourselves. This variation was unprecedented, though certainly not impossible—hell, I thought, Ian might even have a bit of fun with the challenge.

"We can do that," I said. "No problem."

Then, when she didn't immediately reply and looked instead lost in thought, I tried to jog her memory with a single question.

"What's the second condition?"

5

Haidar was bleeding like a stuck pig.

"Take much more," he complained, "you really will kill me. How much do you need?"

Ian shook his head. "If you want to survive retirement, we need enough to make it convincing."

His reply was spoken with as much patience as he could manage while standing before an old, highly irate Yemeni. Ian manipulated a leather hole punch tool to make circular incisions around the unbuttoned midline of the man's thawb, simulating the effects of a cluster of bullet impacts.

Reilly was off to the right, managing the flow of blood from an 18-gauge needle in the crevice of Haidar's left elbow to a grounded transfusion bag that was filling with the assistance of a latex tourniquet and a sponge ball in his hand that was, at present, going unused.

"Keep pumping," Reilly said, a frustrated medic dealing with a surly patient.

With a dramatic groan, Haidar continued squeezing the ball to force blood flow down to the line.

Ian returned the leather hole punch to his drop pouch and recovered a waxy sheet of paper with fleshy, Hollywood-grade moulage adhesives that looked for all the world like bullet wounds. Peeling the stickers off one at a time, the intelligence operative applied them to the mat of gray hair on Haidar's chest and robust belly, one for each puncture in his full-length garment. The moulage process was virtually identical to what it would be for simulated casualties at the Special Operations Combat Medic Course, with one exception: all the blood had to be real. If Erik Weisz's previous actions had been any indication of his resources, there could well be some degree of forensic analysis performed here, and indicators of various chemicals and natural products used to create simulated blood were a no-go.

David transmitted, "*Doc, we've got a lot of movement out here, starting to pop heads and no sign of our pickup. What's your ETA?*"

"Five minutes," Reilly answered.

"*Make it three*," the team leader replied, "*because we need your guns in the fight.*"

"Copy."

Upon clearing the room that Haidar had unlocked for them, the now-absent trio of team members had secured the door, then breached it from the outside with the use of a hooligan tool to leave evidence of a forced entry before unceremoniously firing a few "misses" into the far wall. Then David had proceeded along with Cancer and Worthy to secure the pickup site on the street outside the mosque. Any unease that Ian felt about being left more or less alone with a supposedly defecting source whose motivations were dubious at best was quelled by two facts. First, Reilly was sufficiently large to knock Haidar's head clean off his shoulders should the need arise, and second, the fact that their exfil platform had yet to arrive represented a far greater concern.

Ian applied a final moulage adhesive to Haidar's chest, then selected a particularly grisly section that looked like a 5.56mm exit wound and slapped it on the back of the Yemeni's right hand.

He was prepared to explain the seeming disparity—when an enemy was unarmed or out of ammo, they commonly held up their hands as if trying to block bullet impacts by sheer force of will, and thus took a round through their palm before it sailed into their torso—but if Haidar had any confusion about the last-minute addition, he gave no indication. Instead he resignedly chewed his khat like a piece of livestock processing hay.

Ian re-buttoned the man's thawb and said, "Done."

By then Reilly had snatched the sponge ball from Haidar, removed the latex tourniquet, and stashed both items before tying off the tubing of his transfusion bag. He was now in the process of removing the catheter, and once complete, Ian instructed, "Lie down on your side."

Haidar did so while making it abundantly clear through huffs and sighs that this was a most unwelcome inconvenience, and once he was on the ground, Reilly applied a generous quantity of blood beside him.

Then he grabbed Haidar and rolled him onto his back atop the spreading pool of crimson, leaving Ian to kneel and adjust the holes in the thawb's fabric that were largely aligned with the moulage wounds below. When he was finished, he stepped out of the way so Reilly could paint various blood splatters across Haidar's shirtfront.

As Reilly worked, Ian scattered a group of shell casings just inside the door and in a fan extending toward the nearest two corners—all of them had been previously fired by the three 5.56mm team weapons carried onto the objective. Then he procured his camera and prepared to document the death of Faisal Haidar.

By the time Reilly moved clear of the body, the Yemeni man looked for all the world to be as dead as could be with one notable exception.

"Are we done yet?" he asked, looking up at Ian.

"Put your head down, close your eyes. Flip your right hand, palm down..." Ian surveyed the ensuing scene, then added, "Mouth open, tilt your head to the left."

Ian was satisfied with the result—no doubt the Agency's finest photo alterations specialists could generate convincing photos regardless of any moulage intervention on Ian's part, but the real issue here was making the crime scene match the base photographs. Beyond that...well, he thought as he photographed Haidar from several angles, he couldn't imagine what additions would be required beyond a slight pallor adjustment to the ruddy color of the man's face.

The only question that remained was whether his team's snatch operation would be worth the effort that had thus far transpired, to say nothing of the upcoming exfil.

There were a finite number of groups vying for power in Yemen, but the fractal nature of conflict in such a shattered country resulted in factions within factions. That diversity necessitated an analysis of Haidar that went far beyond his affiliation with al-Islah, a Sunni Islamist coalition with deep ties to the Muslim Brotherhood, and into tribal oppositions to Iranian support of the far more dominant Houthi movement.

And while any number of Western governments would brand this man a terrorist and leave it at that, Ian knew that the chaos pervading Yemen at every level made strange bedfellows. Amid a landscape of extremism and proxy influence, none of Haidar's individual delineations amounted to much. He had access and placement to divine the inner workings of larger militant dealings, but so did hundreds of others. He was dissatisfied with his party's progress, a condition that plagued everyone of moderate to high intelligence regardless of which side they served, and he was financially motivated to better his circumstances after a long and spartan existence in a failed nation.

The combination of these factors made Haidar a compelling prospect for source intelligence, as did the fact that he had nothing to lose. His wife had taken their children and fled with her brother a year ago, leaving Haidar ample time to question exactly how much longer he intended to pursue an arguably hopeless path toward Yemeni reform along Islamic lines. When the Agency had identified him in a tertiary network analysis following the exploitation of digital media captured four thousand miles away in Serbia, establishing clandestine contact via a well-placed CIA case officer was a foregone conclusion.

Exactly what Haidar had told that case officer remained a mystery to Ian's team, though the scope of the initial conversation must have been deemed of paramount importance. The CIA immediately set up an operation not just to bring the man to safety but to erase any suspicion of Western involvement in his disappearance, which would conclude with an eventual resettlement under an alias in Jordan, one of the Agency's many such deals in what amounted to an international form of witness protection.

Ian snapped a final picture, hearing a rustle as Reilly secured his medical equipment and withdrew a final item from his pack.

David's voice came over the team net once more.

"Doc, Angel, pack him up NOW and get your asses out here."

"We're coming out," Ian replied to save Reilly the trouble. Then he released his transmit switch and continued, "Haidar, stay where you are. We're going to move you."

The Yemeni's eyes fluttered open and he asked, "Move me where?"

By the time he looked over to see the rectangle of black, double-stitched waterproof vinyl material lying next to him and began to object, it was too late: Ian and Reilly grabbed him by the shoulders and ankles, struggling to lift the heavy, blood-dripping man upward and sideways before lowering him into the open body bag.

Cancer had just completed his third reload of the evening's festivities when Ian's voice crackled over his earpiece.

"We're coming out now."

Damn well better be, Cancer thought, rising from behind the short wall lining the mosque roof to sweep his accurized HK417 across the street that, by now, was supposed to be an active pickup location.

But no cavalry had yet come, leaving himself, David, and Worthy to defend the mosque by engaging targets across an urban sprawl that would have been difficult to cover with all five shooters on his team, much less the three that remained gainfully employed in picking up the slack.

The first enemies to fall were those brazen and stupid enough to come running down the street in full view of the American shooters. Easy kills, for the most part, but Darwinian principles ultimately prevailed, and the subsequent attackers had been wise enough to flit between windows and alleys, relocating in between automatic bursts and holding the line and probing the team's minimal perimeter defenses as they flooded in to reinforce the counterattack.

Cancer saw a small figure race out of an alley to look at the target building—child, unarmed—and he fired a single subsonic round into the building ten feet left of the bystander, a warning shot that had its intended effect of scaring the kid back from the direction he'd come.

Then a white light appeared from a second-story window, shining down on the street before drifting toward the mosque. Cancer aimed at the source, finding an old woman directing a handheld spotlight under the misguided assumption that because she didn't have a weapon, no one would take her out. He proved her wrong with two shots that caused her to fall from sight, a perfectly legal kill under rules of engagement that permitted the death of enemy spotters as much as armed combatants.

Not that Cancer was much of a stickler for rules.

The ROE could be twisted six ways from Sunday, one of which manifested when Cancer's next shot against a rifle-wielding man attempting to cross the street missed and sent the fighter scurrying toward the door from which he'd emerged. Well that was no retreating enemy, Cancer mused as he took aim, but a bad guy clearly maneuvering toward a more advantageous firing position. The attempted retreat lasted exactly three steps before a 7.62mm round to the spine sent him flopping to the ground, and Cancer was about to deliver a follow-up shot when the man's body was crushed beneath the eight enormous tires of a Patria armored vehicle that swerved to run him over.

"Trucks are here," Cancer announced over his team frequency, the only words he could manage before a barrage of heavy machinegun fire erupted from the Patria's turret and those behind it in the newly arrived convoy, all running blackout as they screeched to a halt beside the mosque.

David transmitted, "*Consolidate at the breach point and prepare for exfil.*"

Cancer abandoned his fighting position and moved for the stairwell, unable to stop himself from glancing sidelong at the changing tides of the fight below.

In general, formal Arab militaries had an effectiveness record that was spotty at best and catastrophically bad at worst. Most of the historical and academic authorities Cancer had read on the subject—and he'd read a lot —tended to attribute this to a rigid cultural hierarchy where officers maintained total control while the noncommissioned officer corps was deprived of the autonomy required by the fluidity of warfare. Cancer's firsthand experience had affirmed that theory many times over. Officers were by definition a minority of any fighting force, and an army in which they held the only decision-making authority was almost unquestionably doomed to failure.

But the armed forces of the United Arab Emirates, and in particular the special operations units under their Presidential Guard, were a stark exception to the regional norm.

Within seconds of the Emirati convoy's arrival, Cancer's services as a rooftop marksman were no longer required. There was now a quartet of heavily armored vehicles securing the street below, a Patria 8x8 at the front and rear along with two mine-resistant ambush-protected trucks of the variety that US forces had used in Iraq and Afghanistan, and from the looks of it, all four Emirati turret gunners knew exactly what they were doing.

By the time he converged on the stairwell, he'd witnessed remarkably disciplined bursts of well-aimed gunfire that discouraged any meaningful resistance against this incursion into an enemy stronghold within Aden's urban sprawl. And by the time he descended the steps two at a time to reach the landing, Cancer had completely forgiven the tardiness of his Emirati counterparts. Sure, they were late, but the team had survived and the vehicle crews had more than made up for a lack of punctuality by way of accurate and overwhelming firepower. A fair tradeoff, he considered as he carefully stepped over the enemy fighter that Reilly had dropped upon entering the mosque, careful not to slip in the blood as he made his way down the final stretch of stairs.

By the time he reached the ground level, he saw David and Worthy just inside the mosque's back door—or more properly, what was left of it. Shockingly, however, there was no sign of the remaining two team members until Reilly rounded the corner with both hands gripping one side of a bulging body bag.

Ian was managing the other end, struggling to shuffle forward at Reilly's pace as a result of the considerable disparity in strength. Rotating his slung weapon toward his back, Cancer darted to them and grabbed an extra handle to manage some of the weight.

He heard David transmit, *"Copy, I've got eyes-on,"* and saw the team leader shining his infrared laser outside the doorway. Within seconds, there was a flurry of movement outside as dismounted Emirati commandos secured the immediate area.

Then he called out to them, "Exfil to the MaxxPro."

David and Worthy slipped outside, followed by the trio of men carrying Haidar as they negotiated their way through the door frame. Once they'd made it down the stairs and into the semicircle of Emirati soldiers covering down on the immediate area, David grabbed the handle of the body bag opposite Cancer. Together the four men turned left to follow Worthy toward the convoy, which was still firing in periodic bursts as threats emerged from the windows overlooking the target area.

They made their way past the Patria point vehicle, its tires slick with gore from running over the fallen combatant Cancer had shot, as well as a second armored vehicle that he recognized as a BAE Caiman.

But their destination was the third truck, an International MaxxPro, an enormous tank of a truck with a V-shaped hull to deflect the blasts of road-side bombs away from the passenger and crew compartments. By the time the four men and their cargo rounded the back and entered a wave of diesel fumes amid the loudly idling engine, Worthy stood beside the lowered ramp bearing stairs that led into the cabin. Cancer and David released their hold on the bag, leaving Reilly and Ian to fight their way into the vehicle single-file.

Worthy boarded next, then Cancer—by the time he darted up the stairs and into the red-lit cabin, the body bag had been deposited between the twin rows of inward-facing drop seats. Cancer had just enough time to slide into one before David boarded and hit the switch to raise the ramp.

"We're good," Cancer shouted toward the drivers. "*Yalla, yalla.*"

The truck didn't move immediately, presumably owing to the fact that the Emirati operators were still making their way back into the other vehicles. By the time David dropped into the seat beside Cancer, however, the MaxxPro lurched forward and slowly gained speed, and the convoy was underway.

Cancer swept his gaze across his teammates and, upon confirming that Reilly was sufficiently unemployed, indicating no one had sustained an injury, he leaned back in his seat and released an exasperated sigh.

So far, so good, Cancer mused—they'd made it to Haidar without dying, then created a crime scene and carried him out in a body bag for the benefit of any observers whose reports would eventually reach the ears of Erik Weisz, wherever in the world he was. Now, they were on their way back to the Emirati base in Aden.

Plenty could still go wrong, with IEDs a chief concern despite the fact that their drivers would be taking an alternate route back to base. Hell, Cancer thought, if they strayed from this largely government-controlled region, they risked encountering mine-resistant ambush-protected vehicles of equal abilities to the one they rode in now being freely operated by the Houthis and Al Qaeda. And he didn't even want to consider a confrontation with them at present.

With his night vision raised, Cancer looked at David seated beside him, the team leader's features visible in the red glow of the cabin lights. He looked troubled, pensive, as if he'd seen something that was weighing heavily on him.

Cancer clapped his shoulder and asked, "Hey man, you all right?"

David met his eyes, then looked to the body bag and back again without saying a word.

"Yeah," Cancer said in response to the unasked question. "Yeah, we should."

6

"What's the second condition?" I asked.

Chen went silent, moving out of the way for a mom to push her shopping cart past with a toddler riding at the helm like it was his own personal Roman chariot.

Once the woman and her child were out of earshot, Chen met my eyes and delivered her response.

"Simple," she said. "Neither you nor your men attempt to procure information from him."

I almost laughed. "Why would we?"

It was practically a rhetorical question—sure, my team managed some minor intelligence work once in a while, all of which was more a result of our placement at the pointy end of the national defense spear and Ian's job specialty than any mission assignment per se. We were pipe hitters first and foremost, and Chen telling us not to question a turncoat source was akin to warning a tenured professor not to eat crayons.

"Exactly," Chen said by way of explanation. "Then it's a nonissue."

Frowning, I replied, "Well now I'm curious."

She gave a helpless tilt of her head, indicating that the particulars were too boring to warrant mentioning.

"There are very specific information requirements as they pertain to sources and their handlers. Anything a source conveys must be documented, and in often staggering detail. Even if you wanted to spend hours writing up a report—which I don't imagine you do—no one on your team is a qualified case officer. That brings a legal conflict into play if the source changes his story at any point. So the short answer is that either you don't question him, or I send a non-tactical case officer as a straphanger for your snatch op. Would you prefer that?"

I bristled at the implication.

"Absolutely not."

"So it's agreed," she concluded. "Your men go in alone, and you and the source enjoy a silent ride back."

I wondered if there was something she wasn't telling me, if there was more to her admonition not to conduct questioning than something as blasé as legal considerations.

But I decided not to push my luck; my team had our next op, and it was going to be a quick turn. Easy day for the shooters, and unquestionably a win for my wife and my teammates' girlfriends who all too often waited days or weeks for our return, which sometimes came with inexplicable injuries ranging from bullet wounds to, in my case upon returning from Serbia four months ago, a broken leg on the mend.

"Done," I agreed.

Chen started to extend her hand, then suddenly reversed the motion. "Did you tell your wife we were meeting?"

I glanced at her left hand, which bore a gold band supporting a not-insubstantial diamond.

Nodding to the ring, I asked, "Did you tell your husband?"

She grinned. "My *wife?* No, I didn't."

"Right," I said. "Mine thinks I'm on a work call."

"You are," Chen replied, hoisting a green mesh bag from her basket and holding it out to me with her parting words. "Take my word for it: a woman can never have too many avocados in the kitchen."

7

As the MaxxPro engine roared and sent the heavy vehicle forward and away from the mosque, my thoughts immediately turned to Meiling Chen.

I considered her admonition not to question our captive, and wondered whether she was being truthful about the legal considerations of us attempting to procure information. The entire exchange at Wegmans had seemed banal at the time, and I'd scarcely given the matter a second thought.

Now, speeding through the streets of Aden with a willingly snatched captive, Chen's motives were cast into sudden suspicion, from her soliciting me in my hometown all the way to handing me the fucking avocados—and she was right, God help me. Laila had accepted the addition to her grocery list as if it were the most normal thing in the world, seeming almost appreciative that I'd taken it upon myself to get them. I wondered if Chen's consideration of not including a case officer on the op was a legal one, or intended to protect her career—after all, she could write off the loss of a few expendable contractors. A full-fledged CIA officer was another matter, and given how much friction we'd encountered trying to get in and out of the target building, to say nothing of a risky journey back to the Emirati base, there were better than passing odds that the only non-tactical straphanger would be the one to get shot in the face.

There was no denying an undercurrent of weirdness to the meeting with Chen, and yet I found myself questioning whether anything Haidar said would be valid in the least: he'd willingly condoned the deaths of his entire security detail, men who had protected him and at one point, his family as well, and done so as a convenience in covering his own tracks. Would anything he told us prove true?

The mental debate quickly became a matter of how little I trusted the source versus how little I trusted Chen, and ultimately the determining factor came down to neither participant in this unfolding affair.

Instead I thought of a piece of advice imparted by Chen's predecessor, Duchess, before her death in a home invasion had seemed a remote possibility much less an imminent danger.

First rule of working in the CIA: don't trust the management. Second rule: don't trust the labor. The only person we can rely on in the end is ourselves...

I looked over at Cancer in the dim red light of the MaxxPro cabin, then to the body bag, then back again.

"Yeah," Cancer said without hesitation. "Yeah, we should."

Kneeling down, I unzipped the body bag and pulled the seams apart.

"Talk," I said, using a tone normally reserved for holding a gun to someone's head.

Haidar pushed himself to a sitting position, squinting at me in confusion.

"*Madha?*"

"Drop the Arabic. I want to know everything you told your handler, and everything you're going to tell him on arrival. Go."

"I am not supposed to say—"

Cancer grabbed the man's hair and jerked his head back.

"And we're not supposed to ask," Cancer cut him off. "But none of that matters, because this conversation never happened. We just saved your ass, and a whole lot could go wrong on the way before we make it back to base. If you want to arrive in one piece, you better start dishing some information."

Haidar looked around to the other team members seated on either side, as if trying to determine whether this was some kind of entrapment.

Ian gave him an affirming nod. "You're off the record. Go."

With a flustered sigh, Haidar began, "A very important man is in Yemen. Right now, today."

"Good," I said, nodding eagerly. We'd been assigned the mission to recover Faisal Haidar after nearly being killed in the effort to recover sensitive materials in the Balkans, and the fact that military operators hadn't been tapped for the job meant that he had knowledge of Project Longwing's greatest pet project: pursuing Erik Weisz, the name whispered in the wake of geopolitically impossible alliances resulting in fantastically ambitious terrorist strikes.

My team had desperately hoped this source had knowledge of a key player in Weisz's network, and the sooner we extracted that name and got to work finding him, the better.

I continued, "What's his name?"

Haidar blinked quickly, swallowed, and whispered two words.

Leaning in, I tapped my ear and said, "I'm hard of hearing—too many close-range gunshots, so don't make me add one more inside the truck. Speak up."

"Fulvio Pagano," he replied, only slightly louder this time.

I frowned, leaned back, and looked from Ian to Cancer for any sign of recognition. Nothing.

Then I asked, "Who the fuck is that?"

"Fulvio Pagano," Haidar repeated, as if saying it a third time would clear up any misunderstanding.

But then he glanced about fearfully, his gaze settling on me before he went on.

"The man who goes by the name of Erik Weisz."

8

Reilly walked beside Faisal Haidar, escorting the Yemeni man through an early morning sunrise in near-lockstep with Cancer on the opposite side.

Cancer asked, "You're sure about this?"

"Yes," Haidar said impatiently. "I am sure."

They walked across a layer of packed sand, navigating a channel of wire-lined fabric Hesco barriers filled with dirt and erected as impromptu protective walls, approaching a plywood building with a key-coded entry lock. Visually, the setting was ubiquitous with any number of former US military outposts in Afghanistan to the point of déjà vu.

But nowhere in Afghanistan bore the seawater air of Yemen's southern coast, a scent that made Reilly homesick for his childhood beaches in California.

And the sign on the door before him proclaiming AUTHORIZED PERSONNEL ONLY was translated into Arabic as well, a final reminder of where they were: a sliver of the Emirati military base in Aden designated for use by US intelligence.

As they closed the final distance with the building, Cancer said, "Tell me again."

Haidar groaned, unenthused by the prospect of relaying his information once more; he knew as well as they did that he'd be doing little else in the coming hours, albeit for the CIA rather than the ground team that had extracted him from the mosque.

But he recited his knowledge nonetheless.

"He is in Al Hatarish, north of the capital. This may change, but yesterday he was there. I do not know which building. But it is not a large town, and he is protected by the Houthis. If you look for unusual security, you will find Fulvio Pagano."

Cancer replied, "Good. And remember, we didn't ask you shit and you didn't say shit."

"Declan made me swear I would not speak to you. Of course I will not tell him."

They came to a stop before the door, and Reilly punched in the door code from memory before opening it for Haidar to enter.

He did so, coming to a stop along with Cancer and Reilly to square off with a group of men who'd fallen silent at the sound of their entry.

Reilly could identify each of the four at a glance.

The two Neanderthals who could have been mirror images of himself and Cancer were just that, former special operators turned CIA contractors albeit with the purpose of serving as a protective detail. The chubby gray-haired man in khakis and wire-rimmed eyeglasses was an interrogator. Under other circumstances, he would have appeared as a kindly grandfather, but he likely had decades of experience shaking down terrorist suspects, deciphering truthful intent from deception before a word was spoken, and forgetting more about human psychology than most would ever know. He could probably manage a waterboarding session with as much skill as Reilly could insert an IV catheter under night vision, in both cases the result of long and steady practice.

And the fourth one, the kid—well, that was a case officer, looking like a geeky graduate student with a thermos in one hand and a notepad in the other. He'd probably completed operations officer training a year or two ago and was in the right place at the right time to catch a trophy-sized marlin—or a trophy-sized but extremely convincing liar—in the form of Haidar as a source.

There was a brief exchange between Haidar and the kid, who nodded toward Reilly and Cancer with the words, "Thanks, fellas, we'll take it from here."

Haidar willingly accompanied the procession into the hall without so much as a rearward glance at the men who had captured him, although the youngest in the group was halted when Cancer gently put a hand on his shoulder and asked, "Hey man, could you hang back a second?"

"Yeah," the man said.

"You the case officer?"

He gave a nod, a charming smile. "Sure am. Name's Declan. I'm the one who recruited Haidar."

Cancer nodded, waiting for the main group's footfalls to proceed out of earshot.

When that transpired without a further word being spoken, the case officer looked uneasy.

"So...what can I do for you, brother?"

"You're not my brother," Cancer shot back. "The three cats loading mags right now after shwacking a bunch of bad guys on the objective, they're my brothers."

Reilly grabbed his sleeve and whispered, "Let's go."

But Cancer was on a roll, swatting Reilly's hand away and continuing, "This big bastard who almost got smoked when the lights in the target building went on mid-clearance because you *fucked up* the power grid shutdown, he's my brother."

Then the sniper advanced a menacing step, jabbing a finger in the kid's face.

"But you?" he asked. "You're the guy who was sitting here drinking coffee while we were on target, then tried to leave the room just now like nothing happened."

The case officer sputtered, "My source said he flipped the switch—"

"And if one of my boys got shot out there," Cancer went on, unslinging his assault pack to rip out a rolled mass of material before slamming it into the man's chest and knocking him back on his heels in the process, "then you'd be needing this right now."

The case officer struggled to cradle the slick vinyl in his arms while burdened by his notepad and coffee thermos, looking down in a panicked effort to determine what it was. Upon realizing what had just been shoved at him, he released it and stepped back.

Haidar's blood-smeared body bag slapped against the plywood floor, partially unrolling of its own accord.

Reilly forcefully grabbed Cancer by the arm, stopping him from advancing further as the case officer fled the room.

But Cancer wasn't finished, calling after him, "Lucky thing we're better at shooting people than you are at running them as sources or you'd be leaving Yemen feet-first."

His last words were overshadowed by Reilly announcing loudly, "Thanks for all the help, bro. Bang-up job, hope we work together again real soon."

Then he lowered his voice and hissed, "Dude, easy. Jesus. We'll chub him later."

By then Cancer had deflated completely, shrugging free of Reilly's grasp and tilting his head in both directions to pop his neck. He released a pleasant sigh, then casually plucked a pack of cigarettes from his pocket and slid one between his lips.

"All right. *Now* we can go."

They exited the building the way they'd come, Cancer leading the way between the Hesco barriers as he flicked his cigarette to life with a lighter. The moment this was complete he came to a sudden stop at the sight of David approaching with rapid steps.

The team leader's eyes were shielded by sunglasses against the morning light, and he was still wearing his sweat-soaked combat shirt as he waved a finger between them.

"You're both fired," he said abruptly. "Hand them over."

Reilly blurted, "I lost mine."

"No, you didn't. Let's go."

Reilly unleashed a dramatic sigh and then, in defeat, pulled his shirt collar aside with one hand while reaching for his neck with the other.

Since 9/11, the thriving global economy of mercenary service had been enriched by countless former US special operators with no desire of a peacetime existence in the homeland they'd fought for. It was a legal gray area into which the United Arab Emirates happily entered, granting military contractors an inflated rank in their armed forces for the duration of their employment. Such work generally involved the receipt of target packets on key Yemeni individuals that the UAE designated as terrorists, after which said individuals were often eliminated by gun or bomb blast. Kind of like what Reilly did for a living on behalf of the Agency, he mused, but in exchange for a far bigger paycheck.

But Reilly had desperately hoped to keep a souvenir of the mission, one that he reluctantly removed from around his neck: a chain bearing a metal dog tag with his name and blood type engraved in English on one side and Arabic on the other.

Before handing it over, he asked, "You really think they'll notice if—"

"There's only five of us," David cut him off, snatching the chain. "They'll notice."

Cancer, by contrast, handed in his dog tag like it was a nagging inconvenience, unceremoniously ending his brief tenure of service as an Emirati soldier. Then he took a drag of his cigarette and used the exhale as an opportunity to ask, "What now?"

David pocketed the chains.

"I've got to turn these in to the Emirati commander." Then, with his brow wrinkling, he went quiet before continuing.

"Head back to the tent—Ian needs to tell us what the hell is going on."

9

Ian was trying to focus on his laptop when Reilly and Cancer barged into the team's allocated space on camp, a long, dome-topped Alaskan military tent divided into a sleeping area and planning bay. The interior smelled of gun oil, sweat, and urine, that last stench courtesy of an adjacent latrine trailer that attracted every fly within fifty miles.

"Pointman of the year," Cancer called out, "what's good?"

Worthy looked up from his cot where he was seated with one boot on either side of an open ammo can, shucking bullets into the magazines deposited by team members with more pressing responsibilities. "It's all good, brother. Try the Bud NA."

Reilly descended on the row of coolers at the back of the tent, concealed from outside view by virtue of some carefully draped ponchos.

"No time for that, I want the good shit. Ian, how about a Horse?"

"Not now."

"You sure? It'll put some hair on your chest—"

"I said not now!" Ian barked, pulling his laptop closer to him atop a ramshackle plywood desk.

He heard Reilly make a tsk-tsk noise and disapprovingly mutter, "Touchy, touchy..." before the sound of a cooler opening, a guffaw of

Cancer's laughter, banter between the three men interspersed with metallic hisses of cans being cracked open.

And in that moment, trying to sort his final thoughts before David returned and demanded them in full, Ian regretted his proficiency at picking locks.

The Emiratis had provided the team an open invite to their dining facility, as well as limitless access to their depot of ice, bottled water, and field rations—a bountiful offering, though nowhere near as bountiful as the contents of a mysterious refrigerated cargo container behind their officer quarters.

David had identified the container during a liaison meeting with the Emirati commander and accidentally-on-purpose reported its location to Cancer, who in the interests of plausible deniability ordered the remaining three members to embark on an unattributable nighttime raid to see what the container held. There certainly existed padlocks so specialized that only a master locksmith could crack them, but none of those had yet found their way into Yemen, and Ian made short work of the surreptitious entry using a pick and a tension wrench from his survival kit.

Then, with Worthy posted as a lookout, Ian and Reilly made their entry with empty duffel bags slung across their backs.

They'd found far more than they could carry, or want to carry, for that matter. The mission was only a success to the extent it went undetected for the duration of the team's stay on the Emirati base, and so Ian had directed a modest harvest from the rear of the ample storage shelves before replacing everything as they'd found it.

The end result was being loudly consumed by Worthy, Reilly, and Cancer now: cheese-filled pastries, basbousa cakes, dumplings slathered in date sauce, and a mind-bending variety of baklava. All of this was washed down with similarly pilfered beverages that ranged from Arabic Coke products to non-alcoholic Budweiser to an Austrian energy drink labeled *POWER HORSE.*

All of that was fine when there was no brainwork to be done, but less so on the tail end of a hasty and unexpected deep dive into the identity of a man Ian hadn't known existed just a few hours ago and, he'd soon found, whose past raised more questions than answers.

The tent door banged open and slammed shut, and Ian looked up to see David striding in.

"Horse me," he said, dropping onto his cot and holding out his hand while staring at Ian. "Haidar's either a liar looking for an all-expenses-paid trip out of Yemen, or the best-informed source we've ever heard of. Which is it?"

Cancer slapped an energy drink into David's open palm, and the team leader cracked it open and took a sip without his gaze leaving Ian's.

Ian swallowed and shifted in his foldout chair to face his team, then shrugged.

"Could be either."

A majority of the four remaining team members groaned in unison.

Only Worthy was immune, waving his baklava in a twirling motion as he drawled, "Yeah, yeah, we get it. You're an intel guy, not a psychic, expectation management and all that. So which is it?"

Again, Ian shrugged.

But this time he said with some conviction, "I think Haidar is probably telling the truth."

Cancer had stripped off his boots, and now peeled off a sock that he tossed in the air without warning.

"I'm throwing the bullshit flag," he declared, pulling off the opposite sock. "We've never had so much as a whisper about Weisz's true identity in the umpteen missions we've run with Longwing, and this guy claims to not only have his identity but to know for a fact that he's in Yemen right now. Why should we trust him?"

Ian frowned.

"It's not because of what he claims, it's because of the name he gave us."

"Pagani?" David asked.

"Pagano," Ian corrected him, "Fulvio Pagano. Only records of significance I could find date back a few decades, but I think I've found our guy."

He consulted his laptop. "It starts with the Red Brigade, a Marxist-Leninist group that tried to turn Italy into a revolutionary state and break free of NATO. They did bombings, assassinations, bank robberies, kidnapped an American general. Basically raised hell throughout the seventies and eighties."

Reilly looked up from a box of dessert items in his lap. "You're telling us Fulvio Pagano is a geriatric?"

"No. Vitale and Ravenna Pagano were high-ranking members of the Red Brigade, both arrested in 1986 after which they spontaneously confessed and then reportedly died in custody, which you can take to mean they were tortured to death to give up the names of others in their organization. Fulvio was their son. He was nine."

"Oh," Reilly said, carefully selecting a piece of baklava. "Gotcha."

Ian explained, "There's some childhood foster records for him, but it's mostly a dead end until 1996, when his name starts showing up in connection to investigations into the 'Ndrangheta, an organized crime syndicate. They've been around since the 1700s, left the Cosa Nostra in the dust, and are now considered one of the most powerful mafias in the world. Operations on five continents, big business with the cartels, you name it."

Worthy nodded approvingly. "So he's a crime boss."

"It's hard to say. I haven't had time to scrub all the reports and the organization is pretty impenetrable anyway, but his name appears with increasing frequency until 2004. Last reports are that he died in a car bomb in some kind of power grab by another 'Ndrangheta faction. Police informants confirmed his death, he hasn't been heard from since, and the file was closed."

"That fucker," Cancer spat, "so he's still alive."

"Maybe," Ian allowed. "It's a pretty compelling background for someone to develop an extreme dislike for Western governments writ large. He would've been involved in the smuggling racket, had connections between illicit networks, gun running, take your pick. Perhaps even became an apex predator of organized crime and decided to drop off the net because his operations were more effective when conducted with less fanfare in the underground. Or, given what we know about Weisz, the fact that Pagano vanished a year after the invasion of Iraq could indicate he decided to counterbalance what seemed at the time to be a Western takeover in the Middle East."

He let that sink in for a moment, then added, "Or maybe the identity of Fulvio Pagano is just another degree of separation for whoever this guy really is. Either way, based on how quickly the Agency wanted Haidar to be delivered to interrogators, I think he's telling the truth. Weisz is in Yemen right now, and very likely still in Al Hatarish."

David drew a long breath.

"Well not to ask the obvious, Ian, but...why in God's name would he come here?"

Ian surveyed the group. "Who's got a guess?"

No one spoke.

It wasn't that there was a dearth of plausible answers to the question; there weren't any answers *at all*, no matter how illogical.

Weisz surely had protection from any number of extremist groups, the benefit of financial and material support. But if you wanted to die in an imaginative number of ways ranging from tribal misunderstanding to factional competition to a random airstrike or drone attack, it was hard to choose a better location than Yemen, where one or all of the above could take place as easily as not on any given day.

That wasn't to say that the country, if you could call it that while keeping a straight face, wasn't a terrorist playground. The Iranians were supporting the Houthis, who maintained control of roughly a third of the country and a majority of the population, against an opposition consisting of Yemeni government forces backed by Saudi Arabia, UAE, and America, among others, all while AQAP plotted international attacks in their continued attempt to become the single most dangerous franchise of Al Qaeda. It was a bloody civil-slash-proxy war with a side order of pestilence and famine on a biblical scale, playing out amid a never-ending supply of high-end missiles and drones whose use was punctuated by brief ceasefires when everyone involved ran out of ammo.

And while all that added up to Yemen's immense potential for a man like Erik Weisz, there was simply no business here that he couldn't just as easily conduct using a key emissary equipped with a suitcase or five of cash.

Ian shook his head wearily. "I don't know, either. It doesn't make any sense."

"Which," Worthy added, "neatly sums up everything about Weisz's operations. They never make any sense right up until they do, and there's usually a catastrophic attack at the end of his logic."

But Cancer was undaunted, hoisting his Power Horse can and all the carcinogens contained within it toward his teammates.

"Let's not sell ourselves short. Credit luck or being in the right place at the right time, but we've been squeezing Weisz dry. Thwarted two attacks and severed his access to a Russian-based weapons mega-broker."

Worthy added, "While capturing a gold mine of intel in the process—hat tip to David for that last one."

"Don't mention it," the team leader said.

Reilly swallowed a dumpling near-whole, pointing out in the process, "Then why wouldn't Chen give us some heads-up?"

For this, too, Cancer had an answer.

"Remember the unofficial Son Tay Raider patch?"

"Yeah," Worthy replied, "a mushroom. 'Kept in the dark, fed only horse shit.' Funny how history has a way of repeating itself."

Then Cancer said, "It doesn't matter. If Weisz really is in Yemen, then we're going in after him, and we'll get that tasking when David checks in."

Reilly chewed thoughtfully.

"I agree. Mayfly probably wanted us focused on the source extraction, and not worrying about greasing Weisz until its approval was a done deal."

"Unless..." Ian began, letting the question hang.

"Unless what?" Reilly asked.

David supplied, "There *is* no follow-on mission."

The medic continued pilfering his dessert box, selecting his next bite as he commented, "She wouldn't have to notify us in advance. We always deploy with a full loadout in case there's a change of plans, and she knows that better than anyone. No reason to risk compromising the info about Weisz when there was a better than passing chance of us getting rolled up during last night's snatch operation."

Ian waited patiently for them to go silent, at which point both men met his eyes to see that their considerations weren't the point he was referring to.

"Oh shit," Reilly mumbled.

David looked pale.

"You think the mission has already been handed off to JSOC."

Ian nodded slowly.

But Cancer objected, "I can give you three reasons why that's not the case, and they all revolve around SEAL Team Six operations here: 2014 hostage rescue attempt, and the raids on Yakla and Al Hathla. Executed hostages, civilian casualties, and an American operator killed in action. Yemen's no playground, and after all the political embarrassment, if the administration needs dirty work done—especially for a ghost like Weisz, whose death won't exactly be cheered by the public because they have no fucking idea who he is—they're going to send a deniable force to hedge their bets. That means us, period, end of story."

"Especially," Worthy added, "after we spearheaded identifying that piece of shit and then followed his tracks all across the globe. If someone's going in after him, it better be our team."

Ian flexed his back, crossing his hands behind his head.

"I can't argue that Yemen is particularly resistant to one-night unilateral operations, or that it makes sense to use an expendable crew if things go sideways. But I can't see Chen not at least alluding to the possibility of a follow-on operation, and the fact that she forbade us from interrogating Haidar is the nail in the coffin. When David checks in, she's going to put us on standby if we're lucky or send us home if we're not. Either way, I think there's a troop or more of Tier One guys gearing up to hit Weisz instead of us."

Cancer leaned over to slap David on the shoulder. "Well, get it over with, fucker."

David took a final sip of Power Horse, then set his can down and rose to approach Ian's workspace.

He came to a stop beside the satellite radio, lifted the mic without sitting down, and transmitted.

"Raptor Nine One, Suicide Actual."

Meiling Chen responded, "*Suicide Actual, Raptor Nine One, go ahead.*"

After clearing his throat, David continued, "Haidar has been handed off, and photographs depicting his untimely demise are on the way. We're refitting now and will be ready for another pump if required, how copy?"

"*Good copy,*" Chen responded. "*Be advised, no mission tasking at this time. Stand by for particulars of your return flight, anticipated within 48 to 72 hours.*"

David met Ian's eyes, shaking his head as if to say *you were right*, and then he concluded, "Understood. Suicide Actual, out."

The silence in the tent was broken only by a helicopter thundering overhead until Reilly chimed in with his best impersonation of Chen's voice.

"Be advised, continue processing oxygen into carbon dioxide in your shithole camp until I tell you otherwise."

Cancer stood and walked toward the radio, recovering his pack and, for the first time in the history of Project Longwing, offering a cigarette to David without being asked.

His hand trembled slightly as he concluded with an air of grave finality, "JSOC has already been tapped. This is it, boys: all we can do now is wait for news that Weisz has been killed or captured."

10

Meiling Chen hung up the phone.

"That's it," she announced to her staff, scanning a panel of digital clocks displaying various time zones around the world and locating Arabian Standard Time. It was just after eight in the morning, which placed her in an unenviable position: 23 hours after ordering David's team to stand by in Aden, she was going to have to reverse her order in the strongest possible terms.

Chen glanced across the tiered seating levels descending to her front, all of them fully staffed by intelligence and support professionals ranging from a former Ground Branch officer manning the operations desk to an Agency lawyer on the opposite side of the room.

Summoning her most authoritative voice, she called out, "David's team just received their final authorization to go back in."

A stunned silence followed, but only for the briefest of moments. Wes Jamieson was the first to snap, and when the burly operations officer broke, it was with an offended if not outraged voice.

"Ma'am, if we do that it's going to—"

"Did I say authorization?" she cut him off. "Perhaps a better word would be that they just received their final *order*."

Her response silenced the former Marine, though even amid her momentary victory she wondered how true her words had been. Because Chen could have resisted, could have dug in her heels—to what avail, she couldn't be sure—but instead she'd ended the call with a polite yes, sir, and hung up the phone without a second thought.

Chen addressed him again before she could second-guess herself.

"Are all elements ready?"

Jamieson spoke almost through gritted teeth, his objection now tangible in tone if not words.

"Yes, ma'am," he began. "The Seahawk will be ready to launch within ten minutes. Infil and support aircraft are currently static for maintenance and crew rest, and will be on-line by 2100 hours local."

Without waiting for any additional dissent to accrue, Chen lifted the satellite radio hand mic and transmitted, "Suicide Actual, Raptor Nine One."

"*Raptor Nine One,*" a man responded almost immediately, "*this is Angel. Suicide Actual stepped out, I'll relay your traffic.*"

"Stepped out to where, exactly?"

A pause.

"*He's in the latrine.*"

"Then get him," she responded impatiently. "I'll add that this is time-sensitive in the extreme."

"*Stand by.*"

She questioned herself again; the last thing she needed now was any further delay for launching this operation past the point of no return, particularly when the entire Project Longwing staff was questioning her leadership.

Chen looked at her staff, whose resistance was apparent by their collective silence as much as the sporadic glances toward her workstation, positioned at the highest tier in the rear of the room, with a God's-eye view of the oversized display monitors on the far wall.

At present those monitors were broadcasting a mix of muted Arabic news channels, along with satellite imagery of the operational area. Notably absent were real-time tracking capabilities on their target, whose very presence in Yemen, much less his day-to-day movements, were instead informed by a patchwork of intelligence assets and a miraculously assembled handful of cell phone numbers maintained by security personnel responsible for ensuring safe travel during his visit.

How long that visit would last was the biggest unknown about this entire operation, although the Agency knew just enough about the man to be sure he wouldn't remain in Yemen for long.

The clock was ticking down toward an imminent departure, and particularly after the disastrous setback that had turned Chen's entire staff against her, she was left to grapple with the sheer absurdity of her official order being delayed by the fact that David Rivers was on the can.

Finally, mercifully, his voice emitted from the speakerbox.

"*Raptor Nine One, Suicide Actual. Go ahead.*"

He sounded about as pissed as Jamieson had, the men's tones almost eerily similar.

Chen keyed her mic and replied, "You need to have all men and equipment at the helipad in ninety minutes. I'm relocating your team offshore, to Carrier Strike Group 8 in the Gulf of Aden."

"*Good copy,*" he said, now sounding like a jubilant little kid. "*Advise on operational loadout required.*"

"More details forthcoming once you make it to the ship, but plan for an open-ended insertion and linkup with host nation assets to facilitate a kinetic operation in the vicinity of Al Hatarish. Your team is going back in tonight."

"*Target?*"

It was difficult to gauge from his tone whether or not he already knew; a man as practiced at lying as David Rivers wasn't going to tip his hand one way or the other.

She'd forbidden him from questioning Faisal Haidar not out of any pretense that he'd obey but rather to delay the inevitable. If the Emirati convoy was ambushed, David's team represented five men who'd prevailed against certain death far too many times to be killed in one fell swoop. Haidar might die, perhaps all of the Emiratis and some of the team, but one or more of David's men would make it out of the fray—and if they were tortured into revealing their source's information, it would scare Project Longwing's highest-value enemy into hiding.

Chen swallowed hard, then replied, "Target Number One—you're going after Erik Weisz."

11

Cancer leaned against the rail, gazing westward as the sun's fiery orb continued its descent over dark, shimmering water and, somewhere beyond the horizon, the shores of Africa.

Aden's smothering, stagnant heat had been replaced by warm gusts of sea air, sand and plywood shacks by the staggering vistas of open water around him. After hours of rapid-fire information dumps, contingency planning, and route memorization, this was a moment for peace and centering—and, given the particulars of the mission ahead, very likely the last moment of peace he'd have until either Weisz or his team had won.

He snickered to himself, considering that such dramatic thoughts were occurring from the deck of the world's shittiest cruise ship.

A majority of the 5,000-plus people aboard worked below the highly restricted flight deck and rarely saw the sun. And unlike a cruise ship, the aircraft carrier was surrounded by the warships of a destroyer squadron, logistics and supply vessels, and one guided-missile cruiser, to say nothing of the likelihood that a nuclear-powered attack submarine or two were cruising beneath the waves.

The only downside of this layover aboard the USS *Harry S. Truman* was no smoking allowed, a regulation that even Cancer was keen to respect while standing atop a 4.5-acre flight deck coasting some fifty feet over the Gulf of Aden.

Instead he popped a pair of nicotine tablets into his mouth, settling them into place beside his gums. The tabs were meant for slow release, having been designed to wean quitters off cigarettes rather than bridge the gap between smokes, but they were sufficient to hold him over until a more civilized form of nicotine consumption availed itself.

This was an ass-backwards way to infil, he thought, with the team redeploying south from Yemen's coast to an aircraft carrier in the Gulf, then back again to penetrate deep into enemy territory far north of their previous location in Aden.

But boarding an infil bird in full view of the Emiratis before flying over a major population center wasn't exactly the gold standard for a covert operation; it was far better to launch unseen from the open water before undertaking a multi-leg infiltration route over desolate areas of desert, at least if survival beyond their opening minutes on the ground was a remote concern.

So that was how they'd ended up here, and it was the first major decision by Meiling Chen that Cancer actually agreed with.

Reilly gave voice to that concern a moment later, slapping the rail to Cancer's left in a sudden outburst.

"Man, she should have sent us in last night—Weisz isn't going to remain in one place for long. Why hold us back if JSOC wasn't tapped for the hit?"

Ian replied from Cancer's opposite side, raising his voice to be heard over the wind.

"The delay was deliberate. Some threat, some political ramifications. No way this was just negligence on her part."

Cancer didn't reply, though he disagreed in full—Chen had told them that a flight home was imminent, which was unacceptable even by spook standards. He wouldn't have minded her withholding the exact details, even their target's identity, but the fact that she'd chosen to outright lie to them was a level of deception not even her predecessor in Project Longwing would have stooped to.

This was like the military all over again. Hurry up and wait, then get far too much information at the last second before being shot out of a cannon into enemy territory.

Except this time, it wasn't the result of some late-breaking intelligence. Chen had the fucking information, she'd just decided not to advise the people who were in a position to do something about it. Cancer had no experience at the decision-making altitudes of such operations, having been destined by choice and aptitude to spend his career in the trenches of the tactical realm. Before, he simply didn't trust Meiling Chen any more than he would anyone outside his team.

Now, he actively doubted her ability to do her job in a way that would contribute in the slightest to his men's survival on the ground.

Worthy, as ever, remained the pragmatist. Whatever his take on the current circumstances, he voiced no complaint and instead called out, "Heads up, boys—here he comes."

The four men turned in unison, the view behind them obscured by rows of parked aircraft ranging from fighter jets to E-2 Hawkeyes, the far less glamorous twin turboprop planes that upheld seven-meter-wide radar domes over their fuselages, to Seahawk helicopters outfitted for everything from anti-submarine warfare to search-and-rescue in the event a sailor or an entire aircraft went into the drink.

But the aircraft that Cancer fixated on now was fuglier—more fucking ugly—than anything aboard the *Nimitz*-class carrier, even the Hawkeyes.

The MV-22 Osprey looked like the lovechild of a drunken one-night stand between a Chinook helicopter and the last small cargo plane remaining at the bar during closing time, demurely running out the clock with a Schlitz in hand.

And while the resulting aircraft wouldn't win any beauty pageants, the rotating tiltrotors at the end of its stubby wings accomplished its stated purpose: combining the range and speed of a similarly-sized turboprop with the ability to take off and land vertically as a helicopter would. The Osprey had the capabilities of both parents, with the looks of neither.

The Marine pilots were beginning their preflight checks, having ended a meeting with the ground force commander who was approaching the team now.

David was laughing for no apparent reason, his eyes crinkling with a glimmer of insanity. Cancer knew the look well; it wasn't unique to David, but a reaction demonstrated by combat troops the world over and likely since the beginning of human history. It wasn't confidence, and it certainly wasn't delight; instead, it conveyed the blue-collar resignation of a grunt being sent into a slaughterhouse at the orders of someone who got paid more to survey the effort from afar.

He suddenly became aware of his teammate's eyes upon him, and the expression vanished. In one fell swoop, David Rivers was poised, in control, effecting the facade that he had to as team leader. It was a terrible charade, surely visible to the rest of the men as well, yet they all remained silent as David came to a stop and spoke.

"We've got some time before takeoff, but they want us to load up now and clear the deck for the Hawkeye and F/A-18s to launch."

Cancer tried not to laugh at that. The Hawkeye was all well and good to serve as airborne early warning, which was of particular relevance when enemy drones and long-range missiles swarmed like as many songbirds over contested regions of Yemen.

But the fighter jets would do little more than loiter offshore to provide close air support in the event the infil bird went down and required the launch of search-and-rescue. Once the team's boots hit the sand and their Osprey took to the night skies, they'd be on their own.

David continued, "We'll do our final mission brief and radio checks on the Osprey. And look, I know you guys are suspicious of Chen. But let's not forget she relayed Haidar's info back to us when she specified Al Hatarish. As far as I'm concerned, that's a point in her favor. We've been after Weisz for years, all spilled blood in the process—"

Reilly blurted, "No, we haven't."

"What?"

"I got blown up, Worthy and Ian have both been shot. But you and Cancer have come out pretty unscathed from the whole thing."

"*Unscathed?*" David asked. "I fell off a cliff in China and broke my fucking leg in Serbia."

The medic gave an unsympathetic shrug. "Still not blood, though."

David thought for a moment before his expression brightened. "Colombia—I took that bullet shrapnel in my shoulder, remember?"

"Oh yeah. Forgot about that. Guess Cancer's the only one who's come out clean."

Cancer shot back, "Hey asshole, I got shot too."

The other four men all looked at him in confusion. With a frustrated grunt, Cancer explained, "In the Philippines, remember?"

No one seemed to know what he was talking about; finally David's face flashed recognition and he waved his hand dismissively.

"That was a ricochet, doesn't count." Before Cancer could object, the team leader continued, "Point is, we've finally got a chance to get Weisz. We're in the finals now, and whatever happens, win or lose, the season is going to be over soon. Everyone feel good about this?"

Worthy shook his head vigorously.

"Abso*lutely* not," Reilly declared.

Ian merely tilted his head, shooting David a stern look.

David looked at Cancer and asked, "How about you?"

Being chosen to go after the king of bad guys in the form of Erik Weisz should have been a victorious moment.

Instead, the plan they'd been issued was so tactically ludicrous, so devoid of any reasonable degree of risk mitigation or supporting intel that Cancer wondered if they'd even make it to their linkup.

Finally he said, "Good thing we're used to playing it fast and loose. I don't know how this will go down, but it ain't gonna be by the books. Frankly, I'd consider it a miracle if any of us make it out of Yemen."

"Good," David replied cheerily, "so we're all in agreement: the plan is fucked. Let's roll the dice one more time."

He held up a fist, and each team member tapped it with their knuckles in succession as they threaded their way toward the Osprey, each step bringing them closer to the badlands of Yemen, closer to Weisz.

12

The aircraft cabin shimmered with a dim green glow, the result of a few overhead dome lights illuminating my teammates on the drop seats on either side of the cargo area. I looked right to see the rear crew chief, barely visible against the closed ramp, then heard the dull roar of an identical MV-22 Osprey lifting off from the carrier's flight deck.

As the sound faded, I lowered my night vision and fixed my gaze on the parked fighter jets visible beyond the porthole window opposite my seat.

That lead Osprey was a decoy ship, destined to lead the way into Yemen before breaking off on an alternate flight path at a higher altitude, where it would make several "false insertions" by touching down at a series of desert landing zones far from our actual operation.

Meanwhile, our bird would make a nap-of-the-earth flight between villages, returning the way it had come after we'd been dropped off.

And while I was certainly grateful for the presence of a second MV-22 that night, it was about the only layer of insurance, and a frail one at that, standing between us infiltrating uncompromised and being pursued immediately after stepping off the bird. Every fighting group in Yemen—and there were quite a few—employed dedicated observers to detect intrusions. Early-warning networks aside, all it took was one stray nomad, sheepherder, or child to spot a group of Americans and send up the alarm, a fact that had all too much historical precedent.

The elite men of SEAL Team Six had faced a series of disasters and early compromises while operating here, all while using impeccable protocol and far more troops and aerial support than we would. And they'd been conducting one-night operations that were either unilateral or accompanied by contingents of Emirati commandos, who were themselves seasoned special operators.

By contrast, we faced a mission of unknown duration with a slipshod local militia. In a place like Yemen, host nation forces presented their own set of challenges, particularly when money rather than ideology was the determining factor—they could plan on betraying us from the outset, or change their minds at the arrival of a better offer. And even if they intended on playing ball, there was a very real possibility that they would at some point take offense at some real or perceived disrespect and turn on us completely. Green Berets, the subject-matter experts of working alongside local forces, politely referred to that particular contingency as a "catastrophic loss of rapport," and it would be the death knell for our mission against Weisz.

My seat trembled as the Osprey's engines spooled to full power, and the view out the porthole window suddenly shifted.

I watched the raised wings of tightly parked aircraft fall out of sight as the Osprey made a vertical ascent. There was a glimpse of gulf waters, then total darkness beyond, before I felt my body sliding sideways with horizontal acceleration. The proprotors hammered loudly against the air, and a sudden drop made my stomach lurch as the bird cleared the flight deck and entered the open sky.

Then we were away, gaining speed over the waves and making a northward turn toward Yemen's shores.

Once I was reasonably certain that we weren't going to plummet into the waves—a very real concern for anyone who didn't routinely conduct operations from maritime vessels, a population that included everyone on my team—I scanned my men.

The main disparity from our previous mission was the choice of weapons. For a close-range, short-duration op like the snatch we'd just done at the mosque, it was usually best to err on the side of familiarity with our usual loadout of Heckler & Koch rifles.

But this was a more or less open-ended infiltration of enemy badlands, and the ability to reload with locally procured ammunition was a top priority. We'd adjusted our loadout accordingly from the stockpile of gear that we knew well enough by now to deploy with the not-unlikely event of a change in mission; Worthy, Ian, and I thus carried suppressed Galil ACE 32 rifles chambered with the same 7.62x39mm rounds as countless Soviet weapons in circulation worldwide. Only Reilly and Cancer had stuck with their babies in the interests of long-range marksmanship, the former with his accurized HK417 and the latter with an M110 sniper rifle.

And the infiltration rituals, I saw now, had already begun. Worthy stared at the screen of his encrypted phone, reviewing map imagery of the route he'd be leading on the way to our linkup point. Ian busied himself by swiping through a tablet, and while I couldn't see the screen, I knew he was going over the intelligence of tribal affiliations in our area of operations, information that he'd normally have days or weeks to pore over but in this case had received just hours ago. A shitshow all around, I thought.

And Reilly, in true Reilly fashion, leaned his head back and was either trying or had already succeeded in going to sleep.

Cancer chose that moment to lean over, knocking his shoulder into mine and quoting, "'Once more unto the breach.'"

I turned off my night vision to conserve the batteries, rotating it upward on its mount and replying in a voice that was low enough only for him to hear.

"You think she's *trying* to get us killed?"

"Sure seems that way," Cancer said, then added, "And the Old Testament David Rivers I met all the way back in our mercenary days wouldn't have minded a bit."

I sighed.

"Before a wife and a kid, sure. Why not? Today's a different story."

"Apparently Chen didn't get the memo. Don't sweat it too much. Maybe Laila can get a free American flag out of the deal."

"Maybe," I mused. "You've always had a way of finding the silver lining, haven't you?"

"What can I say, I'm an optimist at heart. You're worried about the locals we have to meet up with."

"Sure am. You?"

"One step at a time. I'm more concerned about making it to the linkup in the first place without getting hit."

"What do you figure our odds of that are?"

"Zero."

Well, shit. There was no such thing as a human crystal ball when it came to combat operations, but Cancer was about as close as I would find in this lifetime.

He continued, "By the time we get to the linkup point—*if* we get to the linkup point—our local assets will be the least of our concerns."

"Why's that?"

"Because we're going to need them to get the hell out of there. Otherwise whoever we mix it up with on the way in will find us and finish us off. The devil you know and all that. Besides, if the linkup goes bad, I'll make them pay for it."

"No, you won't," I said with all the dead seriousness I could summon to my voice. If our contacts betrayed us, the entire team was done for, perhaps with the exception of Cancer in his sniper overwatch position. "You'll write us off and start your evasion."

Cancer grunted. "Yeah? And how far do you think I'll make it on my own?"

"Farther than anyone else could manage. That's your problem to worry about, not mine. I'll be in Valhalla already, remember?"

"You've got a point. Guess it's worth a shot. Wouldn't want my last mission to involve an infil on the ugliest bird ever created."

I couldn't argue with him there, though the MV-22 did have its advantages. The bird could carry thirty-plus troops provided they were seated on the floor, not quite as much as the MH-47 Chinook we'd previously ridden into battle, but admirable given the Osprey could fly a thousand miles—almost three times the combat radius of a Chinook—before requiring an aerial refuel.

Our infiltration route would take but a fraction of that, and despite the nap-of-the-earth flight detracting from optimum efficiency, the bird would make it back to the carrier with well over half its fuel supply remaining.

"If we pull this off..." I said absentmindedly, letting the thought fade and beginning a new statement instead. "It doesn't get any bigger than Weisz."

"Nope. We've been chasing his network since the beginning, and now we've got a chance to decapitate it."

"So it's definitely worth the risk."

"Not *this* much risk," he corrected me, "but we're not the ones giving orders here. They said to go, so we're going. Just take things one minute at a time once we get in, and we'll see what shakes out."

The stress was already building within me, a knot of tension forming deep in my chest. A very real burden came with being in charge of these men, and it weighed heavily on me, a responsibility that I managed with varying degrees of proficiency. Cancer would advise me as well as he could but would ultimately back my decisions whether he agreed with them or not. Sometimes we saw eye-to-eye, but occasionally my instinct overrode any and all objections to the contrary. So far I'd managed to keep everyone alive, though the margins were so narrow in previous Project Longwing operations that I had to credit luck more than any particular skill on my part.

That much would all be well and good if each mission represented a clean slate; instead, my men and I had endured immense injury and trauma since the beginning of Project Longwing, and those physical and psychological wounds had been accumulating. At this point we all had scar tissue over scar tissue. And while I didn't acknowledge that to anyone but Reilly for fear of eroding their confidence in me, the truth was that none of us spoke of such things because all we could rely on was each other, and demonstrating weakness, however justified, would bring to our collective consciousness a chink in the armor that had kept us all alive so far.

I wiped the palm of my shooting glove across my face and said with exasperation, "If we make it back from this, I may have to take up smoking."

"If we make it back," Cancer responded coolly, "I may have to quit."

13

The Marine crew chief turned away from the open ramp and called out their final time hack.

"Thirty seconds!"

Worthy echoed the command and heard his teammates do the same, then he adjusted his position to balance on the edge of his seat, bracing his feet against the metal floor in preparation to stand when instructed. With his night vision down, ruck straps adjusted over his shoulders, and Galil rifle held barrel-down between his legs, there remained only two things to do: unclip and stow his retention lanyard, which he did presently, and then wait.

The crew chief steadied himself with one hand on the fuselage interior and then lowered himself to kneel at the edge of the ramp, leaning forward to peer down over the edge with a nylon tether and a radio cord trailing behind his back. Worthy's team had completed their final round of radio checks, and there was no point looking back at them now—nor did he attempt to scan past the ramp to determine what surroundings lay beyond.

Instead, the crew chief remained his sole point of focus.

Night vision relied on enhancing ambient light, and on low-illumination infils like this, the near-blackout conditions could be a literal killer. Men had died in training and combat from running down a Chinook ramp or leaping off the bench of a Little Bird when a gust of turbulence thumped the bird in a manner almost identical to touchdown, and Worthy had no desire to share that fate much less lead his team into freefall fifty feet over the desert.

As to what that desert contained at the moment, it was anyone's guess.

Analyzing the color-coded maps of territorial control in Yemen was like trying to decipher a toddler's attempt at finger painting in real time: a sloppy mess of conflicting and ever-changing hues that blended into one another to create total chaos.

Houthi Islamists controlled the western third of the country to include the Red Sea coastline and most of the country's population, as well as the former capital city of Sana'a. That was a fascinating level of progress given that, one, they'd only been in existence for a few decades, and two, their slogan of *God is the Greatest, Death to America, Death to Israel, Curse on the Jews, Victory to Islam* was more or less the beginning and end of any coherent foreign policy aims.

The internationally recognized Government of Yemen had fled to the temporary capital of Aden, roughly a hundred miles from the front lines of Houthi territory and, paradoxically, within a large swath of southern coastline primarily owned by the Southern Transitional Council, a separatist movement demanding its own country be carved from Yemen's landmass. While the Emiratis supported the secessionists, the government denounced them and maintained tenuous control or at least influence over a majority of central and northeast Yemen. That swath of land included key oil fields and pipelines, at least for now—it was inconceivable that the Houthis wouldn't make a ploy to capture those resources at some point, ceasefire or no ceasefire.

But the fun didn't stop there. Scattered patches of hinterlands were owned by Al-Qaeda in the Arabian Peninsula, or AQAP, which remained dedicated to international attacks while spawning a Yemen affiliate known as Ansar al-Sharia, whose stated purpose was fighting the Houthis and government forces for territory. That was to say nothing of Haidar's former organization, Al-Islah, a fractured tribal coalition vying for political and military control with the backing of the Muslim Brotherhood.

For Worthy's team, the problem wasn't so much any one particular group, but the fact that they were about to be inserted into the central highlands of the Shabwah Governate, exploiting a rugged no-man's land that was contested between three groups. If they were attacked, the offending shooters could be government loyalists of the Yemeni National Resistance, Houthi fighters, Southern Secessionists, or a spinoff faction of any of them, all of which could easily assume they were attacking their rivals. And that was before Worthy considered inadvertently falling victim to an airstrike at the hands of the Saudis or the Emiratis, both of whom attacked various factions depending on which was considered the greatest threat at that moment.

All told, Yemen was a rare country in which the term "shitshow" didn't do justice to the reality on the ground, and Worthy's team was about to run headlong into the fray in the hopes that their so-called local assets remained true to their professed motivation—which was, of course, money.

Worthy felt the Osprey flare for landing, airspeed slowing dramatically as a pelting wave of sand whipped through the cabin. There was a jarring thump that Worthy could only assume was the landing gear making landfall, and his confirmation came a split second later when the crew chief stood, stepped out of the way, and swung his arm sideways toward the ramp. The Marine had barely completed the motion when Worthy was on his feet and jogging across the sloped metal until his boots hit the desert.

And then he ran like hell.

His course took him in a straight uphill line across sand and rock, legs moving as fast as he could while remaining upright with the weight of his ruck, scanning for threats to his front with the knowledge that his teammates would cover the flanks and rear. The highlands appeared as a world of green shadows around him, mottled ridges of desolate, arid hills, as he increased the distance from the Osprey that was already, from the sound of it, spooling for takeoff.

Ordinarily ground troops would fan into a kneeling semicircle and pull security until their infiltration platform had departed, but given the lengthy historical precedent of unanticipated Yemeni fighters compromising the best-laid plans—to say nothing of the fact his team was now on the ground with no air support or possibility of exfil—Worthy had instead advocated for the bird to land at a reverse azimuth to the first leg of their dismounted movement route, and then he would run in a straight line until he got his bearings. David had readily agreed to this arrangement. If the rotorwash of the Osprey rising vertically skyward was sufficient to bowl over one or more men in their ranks, then so be it; they'd catch up, because the formation wouldn't be stopping anytime soon.

As he moved, Worthy heard the hammering chop of the MV-22's tiltrotors rise in volume until it reached a crescendo, a torrent of wind blasting him from behind before finally dissipating as the Osprey lifted skyward and began its return flight to the carrier.

"*Bird is away,*" David transmitted. "*LZ ice.*"

That latter part of the message was for Worthy's benefit, indicating that the landing zone had thus far proven to be free from enemy presence. The alternative was the "cherry" call, and if that were the case, Worthy would have heard enemy gunfire by now; if any bad guys had advance notice of the team's arrival, they likely would have waited until the Osprey had departed before opening fire, but not much longer than that.

A few moments later the team leader continued, "*Racegun, slow it down. Everyone else, make a diamond.*"

Only then did he slow to a walk, grateful to end his run with the heavy rucksack that slowed his every effort. They knew little about Weisz's location other than he was currently being tracked in the vicinity of Al Hatarish, an unremarkable town on the northern fringes of the capital city of Sana'a. But Chen had warned that the terrorist leader's movements within Houthi territory would be fluid, and without specifics of where or how they could conduct a kill or capture mission, the team had packed a burdensome amount of equipment that included grenades and demolition supplies.

Worthy performed a security scan to the front before turning around to survey his teammates in a staggered file behind him, gradually spreading out into a triangular formation with the exception of Cancer, who remained at the centerline to pull rear security. One massive figure trailed behind everyone else, running to catch up, and Worthy knew at a glance that Reilly had eaten shit in the scramble from the landing site.

The disadvantage to a diamond formation was that it took longer to cover ground than moving in single file. But it provided far better security, and David's judgment call made perfect sense given there were no aerial platforms to provide advance notice of enemy presence. Speed was of the essence now, but it wouldn't do them much good if they trundled ducks-in-a-row into a hasty ambush.

Worthy directed his gaze forward, identifying no threats before finally checking the azimuth on his wrist-mounted GPS, finding that he'd veered twenty degrees left and adjusting course accordingly.

Then he continued on his current heading, threading his way up an incline of loose rock and hard-packed sand as he fought toward the high ground and the first checkpoint of their eleven-kilometer route.

14

"Here they come," Cancer transmitted. "Three dismounts, two hundred and fifty meters to our six."

His first indication of enemy presence hadn't been anything so crude as a white light or even an infrared laser slicing the darkness; instead, he'd detected little more than dark shadows of movement during one of his continual rearward checks as the last man in the formation. If they'd been wearing better camouflage, he might not have seen them at all. They appeared to be moving with their heads down, following the trail of footprints with periodic forward scans.

He paused to observe the ease with which the human silhouettes navigated the terrain, then added, "They're rolling blackout, following our tracks. Looks like they haven't spotted us yet. Advise we take them before the riverbed."

The timing of this development couldn't have been much worse.

Roughly half of the team's ground route remained before they arrived at their linkup site, where a poorly-vetted partisan force of questionable intent may or may not arrive at all, much less at the appointed time. And if they did show up, they could either comply with the plan or kill the Americans for the cash that was promised up front in exchange for their full cooperation.

Enemy contact would chip away at the three hours remaining to move another six kilometers, and while they'd tried to build as much flex time into their plan as possible, both sunset and sunrise were harsh mistresses that had little regard for tactical realities. Provided the team could deal with the current threat and make it to their linkup, they still needed time to set up security and sniper overwatch in order to have any degree of risk mitigation against the very real possibility of betrayal.

Added to this host of factors was the regrettable terrain before them.

Yemen's central highlands were a rolling plateau whose fringes the team navigated now; if they went much further, the terrain would drop into the endless expanses of sand that comprised most of the country. And while the team had no intentions of exposing themselves in such a manner, they'd been steadily descending toward a dried-out riverbed comprising 75 meters of total exposure in the worst linear danger area of their entire route. The likelihood of enemy spotters or maneuver elements on the far side was immense, leaving David with two choices: either try to race across and set up a reverse ambush to take down the pursuers when they crossed into the open, risking the team's annihilation in the process, or do as Cancer recommended and deal with the threat before advancing into further danger.

But the decision was David's alone, and Cancer held his breath as the team leader transmitted his response.

"*Racegun, pick up the pace for twenty meters up the high ground, then buttonhook right and take us around the ridge, below the military crest, to set up an ambush on our backtrail. We better haul ass.*"

That was an understatement, Cancer thought. The maneuver would require them to deliberately close the distance with opponents who were moving with just as much ease as the team was at present, indicating the benefit of night vision devices originally provided by the Saudis, Emiratis, Iranians, or even Americans, depending on which side the pursuers currently fought for and/or who they'd killed to obtain the optics. But whether due to the team's superior camouflage or their far superior night vision, they hadn't yet been spotted; David had made the right call in pressing for an audacious response before the terrain limited their options, and now all that remained was to execute the feat as quickly as possible.

From Cancer's perspective, the outcome of David's order was immediate.

The formation surged forward in a near-jog to keep up with Worthy, who made a 90-degree right turn and charged up the adjacent slope.

Each team member reached the point of his route departure before following suit, and Cancer committed the point to memory. It represented the final threshold of deception, and if any pursuers made it far enough to see the sudden change in boot print direction, they'd immediately know they were in the crosshairs. It was up to the team to eliminate them before that occurred, and by the time Cancer pivoted at the designated spot, the formation had collapsed into a file on their way uphill to double back on their tracks.

He followed them as the last man, not seeking to determine their final ambush location but his own.

As the only sniper in their ranks, he was less concerned with intersecting fields of fire than he was with positioning himself somewhere that he could observe the entire enemy force and thus pick off anyone who successfully fled the kill zone. While a larger reinforcing element was probably already on its way, so much as a single survivor with a radio could relay a pinpoint location for the team, a virtual death sentence when weighed against the pursuers simply vanishing until a search party located their bodies. By then, with any luck, the team would have already reached their linkup and be on their way to relative safety.

Cancer's solution came in the form of a craggy overlook jutting out from the ridge, a vantage point that would provide a clear line of sight into the low ground and enable him to watch the enemy approach head-on. In other circumstances it would have been a perfect location for a machinegun to lay down a spray of bullets across the long axis of the overall target, but Cancer's M110 precision rifle would have to suffice and, with a maximum effective range of 800 meters for point targets, should do so quite nicely.

"I'm setting up here on the ledge," he transmitted.

David had no cause to question the sniper's judgment nor any time to do so, and he replied over the net, *"Happy hunting."*

The team continued their reverse semicircle as Cancer scrambled onto the outcropping, unslung his enormous rucksack, and flipped down his rifle's bipod legs before settling into a prone position. He adjusted his body until the trio of pursuers became visible through his night vision, still little more than mottled figures against the desert backdrop, albeit far more distinguishable as they closed the distance.

Then he rotated his night vision upward, settling his right eye behind his scope.

In the span of seconds, his view had shifted from crystal green hues to total blackness to a photo negative effect where every heat signature was illuminated in an ethereal white glow. Jagged flat rocks stood out, for example, as they radiated warmth absorbed during daylight hours, and even they were hard to distinguish compared to the radioactive blaze of a human silhouette pumping heat into night air that was twenty degrees colder.

Cancer watched three of those silhouettes now, and he analyzed the murky peripheries of their shapes before transmitting to his team.

"I'm in position. They're moving online, looks like rifles only—can't make out any rockets. Definitely have night vision, eyes on the ground looking for tracks, no situational awareness. Take your time setting up a kill zone, this'll be shooting fish in a barrel."

"*Copy*," David replied, audibly fighting for breath, "*another minute and we'll be set.*"

Cancer kept his sights trained on the three men, not bothering to visually confirm his team's location. After all, he didn't need to; the four men were flanking along the military crest, an area just below the high ground where they could move without silhouetting themselves against the open sky and becoming clearly delineated targets in the process.

And as he waited for them to set up an ambush, his main thought was that he could spare them the trouble by eliminating all three targets right now. And if they so much as glanced uphill toward his teammates, he would.

But the possibility of them getting a radio call out was just one reason he didn't open fire.

Cancer certainly had the skills to eliminate the approaching threat, but the vast experience gained in acquiring those skills had taught him that the most well-aimed bullets sometimes resulted in a flesh wound that sent the enemy scrambling for cover, and occasionally missed altogether. Paradoxically, even a blind pop shot fired by a frantic and untrained opponent could, against all conceivable odds, result in a chance kill shot a few hundred meters away. The more scrapes a gunfighter had been in, the less he was willing to leave to chance, and Cancer had seen many scrapes in his day. With this much riding on making their linkup free from pursuit, it was worth the wait to catch the trio of men below in a five-way crossfire.

The most pressing question at present was *why* they were being followed. In the best-case scenario it was just a group protecting its territory, and the discovery of five sets of boot prints was a reason to go hunting. Because if the pursuers had been sent to kill the Americans, it meant someone had tipped off the enemy and a greater threat remained.

As for *who* was following them, Cancer thought, it didn't really matter.

Houthi fighters would be inclined to honor the *Death to America* portion of their credo no matter the circumstances, and while government loyalists or Southern secessionists may well be inclined to permit the team to go along their way if identities were established, there was no way to do so amid a covert nighttime infiltration—and that was to say nothing of the fact that one or more of the men below could provide or sell information related to the presence of five armed men in the hinterlands of contested territory. All Cancer knew was that the inbound tracker element wasn't affiliated with the team's designated partner force, which was a certainty by virtue of the Agency's coordinations.

So Cancer and his team had to close the loop at once and in full, and that meant dropping every pursuer near-simultaneously. It was a harsh reality, but so was war. Combat didn't concern itself with the sanctity of human life, only tactical advantage, and in that latter regard the team held the upper hand over the men navigating the ravine.

The takedown should have been exceedingly simple, and it was—right up until David transmitted again.

"*Cancer, change of plans. Those three guys are dragging a maneuver element, trailing by two hundred meters. Looks like five more...six...seven that we can see.*"

Well, Cancer thought, wasn't that a motherfucker. They'd just gone from a numerically superior force to being outnumbered behind enemy lines, and the only question that remained was how to react.

"All right," he replied without breaking his focus on the first three men, "confirm you can take the three trackers and I'll transition to the main group—"

"*Negative*," David cut him off. "*We can't move any further, and we're going to lose sight of those three by the time everyone else enters our kill zone. You'll have to take the lead group down while we engage the other seven.*"

Then, after the briefest hesitation and with a trace of humor, he added, "*Make that eight.*"

"All right," Cancer replied, already beginning to shift his body in anticipation of sweeping his M110 much further right than he'd initially planned. Had he anticipated this possibility, he'd have selected a better position from which to direct his fire at closer targets. The single upside, if it qualified as such, was that he'd only have to aim as far as the sudden right turn in his team's boot prints—by the time the trio of pursuers discovered that, the jig was up.

Once he'd resettled into a new firing position, he performed a hasty analysis and keyed his radio mic.

"Be advised, we've got a minute or less before I have to drop these cats."

David said, "*I figured, and by then the maneuver element will barely be entering the kill zone. We'll need you to transition immediately and start putting rounds down.*"

"Got it. Do me a solid and direct your fire from left to right. Flush them toward me."

"*Wouldn't have it any other way.*"

Cancer ignored the subsequent radio chatter of the team leader providing guidance to Worthy, Reilly, and Ian; instead, he kept his sights trained on the farthest of the three men below, watching the group proceed within 150 meters of his suppressor.

At this range, he couldn't miss.

And when the trio came to an abrupt halt, the central man's gaze spotting the change in trail well ahead of time, Cancer pulled the trigger.

Ian was shocked to hear Cancer's next transmission.

"*All three trackers down,*" the sniper declared without trying to conceal the triumph in his voice. "*Let's rock and roll.*"

From his location at the center of the ambush line, Ian hadn't heard the slightest indication that a trio of men had just dropped dead in the ravine to his right; then again, between the whistling breeze and his team's overall predicament, he wasn't in much of a position to question the update.

The staggered formation of eight men was drifting into the kill zone, and it became apparent that they witnessed the sudden fall of their three-man tracking element when a shout arose and they raised their weapons.

Other than that minor wrinkle, everything started according to plan.

David was the first to activate his infrared laser, which glinted off the rearmost man. That was immediately followed by three more shadowy beams whose glowing dots shuddered and jolted as their respective weapons opened fire, crisscrossing across the now-bolting enemy fighters.

By engaging the trailing men first, they'd hoped to drive the formation up the ravine and into the sights of Cancer's thermal optic. But the sudden initiation instead caused the enemy to scatter like cockroaches, in every direction at once.

Three of them fell dead in the opening salvo, while only one ran in the intended direction of movement. A pair of fighters darted back the way they'd come, vanishing from view in a display of speed that was nothing short of unbelievable.

As for the remaining two, they seemed to disappear into thin air. After registering the lone visible runner collapse without a corresponding laser illuminating his body, Ian realized first that Cancer had taken the kill shot, and second, that the two bogeys had flung themselves against the slope directly below the ambush line, effectively removing themselves from view.

"*Doc in pursuit,*" Reilly transmitted, the first radio message since the main engagement began. He was going after the runners, which left the remaining four team members to sort out their options.

David asked, "*Cancer, you see anything?*"

"*Negative, I'm relocating now.*"

Ian rose to a knee, then to a standing position, angling his barrel downward in an attempt to establish visual contact with the pair of enemies at large. He didn't have to scan for long before spotting one of them, though it took him a moment to process the sight.

Whoever he was, the man wasn't hunkering down or even searching for cover; instead, he was climbing the hill as fast as he could, one hand wielding his rifle and the other grasping for support against the slope.

It was a heroic but exceedingly misguided effort. The terrain was too steep for him to crane his neck in order to see uphill, much less engage his attackers, and Ian's laser appeared as if of its own accord and drifted into alignment by the time the intelligence operative realized the second opponent was similarly climbing to the right, now lit by two beams as Worthy and David took aim.

There was one last volley of suppressed shots from the remaining ambush line, and Ian's target bounced slightly with bullet impacts before falling flat against the slope and convulsing in the throes of death.

Ian transitioned his aim right, ready to back up his teammates only to find the second fighter's body careening downhill amid the loud clacking of his rifle striking the rocks, dark smears of blood marking his path.

Switching off his laser, Ian pivoted and ran, moving in pursuit of Reilly's receding figure as the medic rounded the crest and then cut right along the high ground.

Reilly fought his way uphill before finally planting his boots atop the crest.

He'd abandoned his rucksack at the ambush line's left flank, where his HK417 would theoretically be put to good use as he fired at any survivors fleeing up the ravine. No one had planned on two of them running in the *opposite* direction, yet that was exactly what occurred.

And if Reilly wasn't able to obtain a sufficient vantage point in time to eliminate them before they disappeared altogether, then the team was about to have a colossal problem on their hands. A mysterious set of tracks was worthy of investigation by a squad-sized element, sure. But the reported elimination of a majority of that squad would indicate a rival faction trying to seize the contested territory once and for all, and a single radio call would serve as an APB for every bad guy within 20 miles to converge as fast as possible with guns blazing.

This thought hung heavy on his mind as he clambered uphill, no longer concerned with silhouetting himself against the stars. He'd gladly assume that risk for the sake of safeguarding his team's infiltration, however temporarily, and by the time he crested the ridge, sweating and wheezing with the sudden bout of exertion at 2,500 meters above sea level, Reilly feared it would be too late to turn the tides in his favor.

An S-shaped curve of the ravine was barely visible below; the low ground was devoid of movement, indicating he'd missed his opportunity.

But then he saw a fighter race into view, followed by another by the time Reilly brought his HK417 to his shoulder and thumbed a pressure switch.

The infrared laser beamed between the rocky slopes, quavering wildly and just as visible to the enemy as it was to him. Neither opponent so much as broke stride, and Reilly tucked his elbows downward and pressed the buttstock into his shoulder before compensating for an unstable standing position the only way he could. Sending subsonic round after subsonic round at the fleeing men, he discharged the contents of his magazine as fast as his right index finger would allow.

The outcome was hard to determine at first, with bullet impacts whiffing sand in a wide orbit around the racing pair.

But whether due to distraction or actually being hit, the lead man wiped out on the ground. In that moment, Reilly thought, but would never divulge to his teammates, that the fall was due to a misplaced step rather than any particular marksmanship abilities on his part. Whatever the case, the second fighter tripped over his comrade, a human domino going momentarily airborne in one dramatic fall.

Reilly leveraged the sudden chaotic delay to tighten up his aim, then drilled bullets back and forth between the two figures until his weapon was empty.

He conducted an emergency reload, letting his empty magazine freefall to the ground as he slammed a fresh one into position. There was no movement among the collapsed figures, both either dead or doing a convincing job of faking it. Reilly sent a controlled pair into each man to be sure and then, out of instinct, began a sweep for further threats before thinking better of it and scrambling off the crest before some unseen sniper could dial him in from afar.

A clatter of loose rock caused him to whirl around, and he saw Ian making his way uphill.

Panting, Reilly transmitted, "Got them both, have eyes-on Angel."

"*Nice shooting,*" David unenthusiastically replied. "*Now get your asses back here, now—we need to hustle if we're going to make this linkup.*"

15

I kept my rifle in one hand, using the other as an additional point of contact as I proceeded alone toward the base of the hill.

Cancer transmitted abruptly.

"I've got visual on multiple headlights, three hundred meters and closing fast."

Assuming the inbound vehicles belonged to our intended partners, they were arriving seventeen minutes ahead of schedule. Super.

My cautious descent turned into a downhill scramble, trying not to trip on the way to my destination behind a cluster of boulders. I'd broken my right tibia in Serbia, had only recently gained full functionality, and had no intentions of repeating the experience.

As ground force commander, it fell upon me to expose myself first and establish bonafides. If all went well I'd summon the rest of my team, currently positioned in the shadows as part of a three-part security plan.

Worthy was closest, tasked with providing immediate support in the event the linkup went bad and I was either killed or, more preferably, came sprinting toward him.

In the event of the latter, and provided we survived long enough, Worthy and I would bound back under the protective fire of Reilly and Ian, both stationed further uphill with our rucks in a medium-range vantage point overlooking the linkup area.

But Cancer held the most unusual role of all.

Sure, he was serving in his usual capacity as sniper, perched on a slab of high ground of his own selection. Because he was most likely to find himself as the last living team member, however, he carried a beefed-up survival kit in addition to the majority of our cash beyond the initial payment to our Yemeni assets. Both were somewhat hollow assurances that he'd have so much as a slim chance of escape, but they were better than nothing.

If I transmitted the code word "avalanche," everyone would open fire; by contrast, "hellfire" meant that myself and the closest three team members were fucked, and Cancer was to begin evasion at once. Whether or not he complied was ultimately up to him, as under those circumstances I'd have precious little opportunity for reproach. But by my math, one teammate with a snowball's chance in hell of living until the next sunset was better than zero, and I'd insisted on the contingency plan regardless.

Finally I reached the low ground, arriving without incident and taking cover behind the cluster of rockfall just as the glow of headlights spilled across the dirt road to my front.

"In position," I transmitted, wondering if the vehicles would stop at all and, if so, whether their occupants would execute a seamless linkup or try to take us out in an act we'd referred to as pulling a Steve Miller Band— take the money and run.

Reilly gave voice to that possibility a moment later, singing quietly over the net.

"*Five young contractors,*" he began, "*with nothing better to do-oo...*"

"You're not helping," I shot back.

A moment later, Cancer scolded, "*Doc, keep your fat ass quiet. Suicide, looks like two pickups leading a cargo truck. They've got an extra Hilux bringing up the rear, but other than that it's looking good.*"

I could hear the vehicles now over the wind, a low growl of engines amid the crunch of rocks beneath tires.

Then Cancer said, "*They're coming to a stop now...yep, right at the linkup point.*"

The engine noise cut out, replaced by car doors opening. These people were at the right place at more or less the right time, and all that remained was to see if they performed the right action—though at this point, I'd have settled for two out of three.

"*Four guys getting out,*" the sniper announced, "*all armed... make that five. One's going around the front and...there it is. Lead vehicle just popped the hood.*"

One of the men shouted something in Arabic that made my blood run cold.

His statement was followed by raucous laughter from multiple men. It was now or never, I decided.

Keying my mic, I whispered, "I'm giving the signal. Stand by."

With that I procured a red lens headlight from my pocket and held it over the boulder to my front, flashing the beam three times before dropping my hand behind cover.

Cancer waited a beat. "*Nothing. These guys are hanging out, smoking. I can't even tell if they saw it.*"

Ian confirmed, "*They didn't.*"

"Roger," I said, "stand by."

I repeated the signal as the men continued to hold a loud conversation, and Cancer repeated, "*Nothing.*"

Then Worthy transmitted, "*Clock's ticking, Suicide. Shit or get off the pot.*"

Easy for him to say. I reluctantly rose to a crouch before standing to expose myself.

Two Nissan pickups were parked in front of a cargo truck, with a Toyota Hilux stationary in the rear. The men had dismounted and were arrayed in a loose cluster around a tall central figure who appeared to be holding an informal court.

I held my rifle barrel-down with my firing hand on the pistol grip, buttstock pinned to my side, prepared to assume a shooting position without appearing as a sudden threat. By activating the taclight to project a disc of radiant white across the ground beside me, I notified the men of my presence.

To my surprise, they didn't even seem to notice. The central figure continued his animated monologue, wild gestures marked by the burning ember of his lit cigarette.

The scene was unlike anything I'd encountered during my time working with host nation forces; I certainly wasn't expecting Rambo lookalikes, but these men had zero regard for their own security. Were they trying to lure me into a trap?

When I approached within ten meters without drawing so much as a wayward glance, I cleared my throat loudly and announced, "Gentlemen."

This garnered a *wait a minute* gesture from the speaker, who concluded his monologue with a high-pitched flourish that drew a round of delighted laughter from his armed counterparts.

Only then did he direct his full attention to me, raising his cigarette quizzically and asking with a Yemeni accent, "Where are your men?"

I ignored the question and, reasonably certain that I wasn't going to get shot, asked, "Do you know the way to Shabwah?"

"Why in the fuck would I—"

His question was interrupted by one of his people chattering quickly in Arabic, after which the central man gave a heavy sigh and responded in a dull monotone.

"Yes, yes, I know the way to Shabwah. But the road is blocked by construction."

Well that was one way to establish bonafides, I thought, though he'd at least provided the correct response.

I closed the remaining distance, finally identifying the man from his broad nose and sunken eyes.

Naji Baterfi was a hired gun of an Agency contact, but just barely.

The only meaningful records on the guy were established by an American Special Forces team close to a decade ago, when he was stood up as a ratline contact on call to facilitate covert operations. Baterfi had earned his stripes as a Southern Secessionist, battling his government over control of Yemen's coast before realizing the effort was futile, turning his motivations to purely financial matters, or both. After that he'd become a hired gun leading a militia band for profit, a career shift that had taken him far north of his beachside home along the Gulf of Aden.

But that was well before a significant portion of Yemen had fallen to the Houthis, and since then, as far as we knew, Baterfi had been in the wind with zero oversight whatsoever. His willingness to work with the Americans could have remained steadfast or, more likely, he could have changed allegiances anywhere from one to five times in the interim.

Whatever the case, my team and I were about to find out firsthand.

Coming to a stop before him, I asked, "Are there any threats in the area?"

"This is Yemen," Baterfi quipped. "If there was a threat, you would be getting shot. Now hurry, we have much ground to cover."

I keyed my mic and whispered, "We're good. Security, bring it in."

This caused Worthy to rise and appear from the darkness, followed by Reilly and Ian descending from the high ground with their rucksacks along with mine and our pointman's.

When the Yemenis glanced in their direction without the slightest change in body language affecting their nonexistent security posture, I continued, "Cancer, let's go."

"*Moving*," the sniper replied.

As the rest of my team converged on the trucks, I extended my hand and said, "I'm Suicide."

"Baterfi," he replied, completing the handshake. "And as long as you have my money, you may count on my help."

"I do, and thank you. We took out some guys who picked up our trail on the way here—who were they?"

"Who?" he asked incredulously. "Did any survive?"

"No."

"Then it does not matter *who* they are, but *what*. In this case, dead. Not my men, and if I do not care who you killed, why should you?"

I almost chuckled at the comment, thinking to myself that when a few hundred thousand civilians had fled the country and millions more were internally displaced and starving to death, Baterfi had no reason to concern himself with the identity of a handful of armed men who'd found themselves in the wrong place at the wrong time. That more or less closed the topic for further discussion.

Once the rest of my team arrived, we loaded the trucks quickly. Ian and I joined Baterfi in the second pickup, and the remaining three men climbed aboard the cargo truck.

Then the convoy roared to life, pursuing the lead Nissan pickup north toward Sirwah.

16

Worthy cursed himself for his own complacency, but he was beginning to actually feel safe around Baterfi's men. Any perception of safety was, of course, the absolute *last* thing that should have been on his mind right now.

But there it was regardless, a gut instinct that stood in stark contrast to feeling like shit was about to hit the fan. The sensation was both nauseating and exhilarating, and had saturated his entire body for the duration of the mission up until a few minutes ago.

They'd been traveling for close to an hour now, riding in the covered bed of a Mitsubishi Canter box truck over roads that ranged from potholed dirt to potholed pavement, with predictable levels of discomfort. But it sure beat walking, and the cargo area was big enough to hold himself, Cancer, and Reilly, along with their rucksacks and two of Baterfi's fighters, one of whom procured a wad of khat and stuffed it into his cheek before offering an open produce bag filled with leaves toward Worthy, who politely shook his head.

"Trying to cut back," he offered.

The fighter shrugged and put the bag away, and Worthy checked his Android phone, which displayed a map of western Yemen.

Watching his GPS icon drift across the screen, he transmitted, "Coming up on Manin Al Ashraf, should be heading four kilometers due north before turning west toward Sirwah."

The travel arrangements required him to act as a sort of reverse point-man, sending location updates to David and Ian as they busied themselves with establishing rapport and siphoning intel from Baterfi.

"*Got it*," David replied from the second truck, "*good contact*."

The second part of the message was to indicate that the team leader could still see the Mitsubishi behind him—an unfortunate alternative would be if Baterfi's people suddenly split up the team by sending the vehicles in separate directions. If that occurred, they'd have to react swiftly and violently.

But Worthy didn't suspect that would be the case, not because they couldn't easily kill him and his teammates, but because the two fighters they had been engaging in periodic attempts at conversation didn't seem to give a flying fuck about anything. There was no burning ideology behind their responses in broken English; more likely, they were here out of a financial motivation that would work in the team's favor provided they remained the highest bidders.

He put his phone away and rose from his seated position atop his rucksack, stepping on it and bracing his hands against the side.

The bed was surrounded by flimsy sheets of metal like any other third-world box truck, and while the walls were solid, the strips of bars near the ceiling resembled a horse trailer. It was a useful feature for transporting livestock, which the team more or less was at present, but more importantly it allowed them to rise and survey the outside world, which had yet to come to life in the early morning hours.

Worthy did so now, seeking a glimpse of Manin Al Ashraf only to find that it couldn't be missed. Agricultural fields, stone fences, and low buildings extended as far as his night vision could range, the landscape vivid under an endless sky just starting to brighten with the approach of sunrise.

A flash of light caught his eye, and he focused on a blazing fireball that rocketed skyward in the distance.

"Net call," he transmitted, "massive explosion eight hundred—"

His final words were obscured by the deep, booming concussion rocketing across the landscape, and he continued, "Eight hundred meters northeast."

The other men in the truck scrambled upright to catch a glimpse of the blast, which had now receded into a greasy plume of smoke.

Cancer asked, "What the fuck was that?"

The Yemeni who'd offered his khat a minute earlier grunted with disapproval.

"Airstrike."

"An *airstrike?*" Cancer exclaimed. "What about the ceasefire?"

"Saudis do not care."

Worthy was taken aback by the man's ambivalence, though, to be fair, getting killed by an American-made bomb would be a more twisted degree of irony for the team than any Yemenis on the ground.

The man quickly assured them, "No worry, no worry. Saudis no bomb roads."

The other Yemeni man chuckled in agreement, nodding enthusiastically before suddenly growing somber and providing a final insight into the matter.

"Unless," he said, "they miss."

17

Cancer dismounted the box truck with his rucksack and weapon, climbing down into sunlight that had gone from nonexistent to blinding in the span of an hour. He shook his head in disbelief as he marveled at his surroundings. The convoy was parked in a sandy courtyard lined by ancient stone walls and weathered buildings in varying states of disrepair.

Turning in place, he saw colossal stone pillars and minarets with faint traces of engravings that remained despite centuries of wind and weather. It was as if he'd climbed out of the truck and onto the site of an Indiana Jones film shoot, and that wasn't far from the truth.

Cancer was at his core a history buff, and he'd looked up Sirwah to find that it had been a fortified oasis city and economic powerhouse, though that time had come and gone somewhere around two thousand years ago. The modern-day infrastructure consisted of a grocery store, hospital, mosque, and a defunct government office intended to support the few thousand impoverished Yemenis who called Sirwah home.

The only indicators of the city's former glory were historical ruins like the one Baterfi's men now occupied. This site would have seemed immeasurably old if its exact age wasn't a certainty—this particular temple to the moon god Almaqah dated back to 700 B.C.

Cancer knew this because archaeologists had documented the site exhaustively right up until the Houthis started taking over the countryside. Now, the temple that had survived millennia of warfare beginning with swords and spears was outlasting the current conflict, one whose weapons of choice were 500-pound bombs and long-range missiles.

The site was a testament to the human condition, the sacred and the profane, creation and destruction, and Cancer didn't register his complete and total lack of situational awareness until he heard Worthy call out.

"Hey man, you coming?"

Cancer snapped out of his awestruck stupor, seeing that Baterfi was leading his team inside the temple's central building, an imposing and once-sacred sentinel that outlasted the ravages of time.

He hastened to follow them, turning his analytical focus from historical to tactical. The walls and minarets were well fortified to resist ground attack, though the location was too remote for anyone to bother trying to seize it. It was a wise choice for a man like Baterfi to occupy, representing a free fortress of sorts that the militia leader could claim without firing a shot.

Cancer's first order of business was to walk the grounds, starting with elevated vantage points and working his way down, and evaluate the security posture or lack thereof. If Baterfi's actions at linkup were any indication, there was much work to be done.

That suspicion was confirmed as Cancer caught sight of a man beside the doorway his teammates were slipping through.

The guard, if you could call him that, was seated against the wall with a cheek full of khat, worn Kalashnikov resting in his lap, lips spread in a grin of stained and missing teeth as he watched the Americans pass. He was attired in a worn-out kameez, a traditional loose-fitting shirt that had once been white but was now a dusty hue of the desert itself, with a scarf of camouflaged material draped over his head to shield his eyes from the sun.

Cancer stopped beside him, dropping to a knee and asking, "English?"

"*Na'am*," the guard eagerly replied, his grin widening as he held up an index finger. "Amrika, number one!"

Looking toward the doorway, Cancer called out, "I need a translator."

Then he held his left palm open to show he meant no harm and delicately removed the scarf from the guard's head, examining it closely to find it had been cut at the edges to sever it from a larger swath of fabric.

David appeared in the doorway, sounding pissed. "Can this wait?"

"No," Cancer replied, not taking his gaze off the material. "It can't."

Baterfi arrived a moment later and asked, "Problem?"

Cancer rose, the weight of his ruck eliciting loud pops from both knees as he held the cloth out.

"Ask him where he got this."

"I do not have to," Baterfi said nonchalantly. "Sabahi's militia captured an Emirati spy in Al Jawf. They split up his gear and traded some of it with my men."

"How recently?"

"Yesterday. Why?"

"Yeah," David intoned, now furious at the delay, "why?"

Cancer returned the scarf to the guard and put a hand on David's shoulder, walking the team leader a few steps away. Before he could speak, David whispered in a low growl, "Whatever this is about, we'll handle it later. We've got Weisz to worry about."

"More than you know," Cancer agreed. "The rag that guard is using as a scarf is cut from a sniper cloak."

"And military equipment more or less grows on trees in Yemen—"

"You're gonna want to listen to your elder here, young pup. I'm not talking about a regular ghillie suit. Everything about that fabric down to the camouflage ink is designed to reduce heat signature and radar cross section. You have unlimited funding and want to reach out and touch someone when they're looking for you with infrared and thermal optics, that's what you wear. It's high-dollar, cutting-edge shit, and I don't know where it came from, but it wasn't off an Emirati."

The team leader considered that, now appearing sufficiently chastised. "Worst-case scenario?"

"Erik Weisz got wind of our plan and sent some god-tier mercs out to find us."

David looked up sharply, then turned to face Baterfi. "Where is this Emirati now?"

The militia leader shrugged.

"He is a guest of Sabahi's men. They have him at their *funduq*. The Emiratis will either pay a ransom or... you know."

Baterfi made an odd clicking sound through the side of his mouth, drawing a thumb across his throat.

Well that settled it, Cancer thought—Baterfi had just used the word *funduq*, meaning hotel, to describe the facility where the man was being held. It was fitting slang for private prisons in Yemen, which were as abundant as any actual paid lodging. The main players—Houthis, government, secessionists, pick your cliché—all had their own prisons scattered across their various strongholds, but so too had every pickup team of militiamen laid claim to a structure or two in which they could stuff their captives. Prisoners were currency, often captured with the express intent of trading for equipment or weapons, leveraging in negotiations, or, when one's opposition could afford it, simply selling for ransom.

David declared, "I want to talk to this guy. Have them bring him out here."

"I can order them to do nothing," Baterfi shot back with equal conviction. "But if you were to pay the ransom, they could deliver him in, say, two hours."

Cancer's eyes narrowed. "How much?"

Baterfi rocked back on his heels, eyes drifting skyward as he undoubtedly calculated his finder's fee and added it to some real or imagined lump sum.

"Ten thousand," he said with conviction.

Cancer whispered, "Ian can fudge the books. Happens every mission."

"Make it seven," David said, "and don't tell them who wants the guy. This is coming from you, not us, *hal tafhamu*?"

Baterfi performed a graceful bow, as if before royalty.

Then, rising with a smile, he withdrew a cell phone from his pocket.

18

Ian stood back from the second-story window, keeping himself hidden as he watched the Hyundai sedan roll into the courtyard with a sand cloud trailing in its wake.

The car slowed before wheeling back the way it had come, braking to a halt with its taillights facing Naji Baterfi and a semicircle of his men, all armed to the teeth. A driver and passenger quickly exited, the latter embracing Baterfi before accepting a satchel that the militia leader unslung from his shoulder. It held seven thousand USD in non-sequential bills from the team's funds, minus whatever fee had been subtracted in the interim. Then, after a brief conversation, the driver opened the trunk.

A man was curled inside, bound at the wrists and ankles and braced in the fetal position in anticipation of a beating. Instead, he was greeted by one of the men removing a burlap sack from his head to allow Baterfi to snap a picture of his face using a digital camera. Then the hood was replaced and the captive was hoisted out of the trunk and into a standing position to begin the next phase of his journey—one that would, inevitably, end in an untimely demise at the hands of Ian's team.

But not until they found out what they needed to know.

Ian stepped away from the window as Baterfi's men marched the captive into the building, where his teammates would take over and deliver him to the interrogation room.

Which was a lofty term for the space Ian had prepared.

In contrast to the dusty, doorless interior spaces of the temple building where his team would reside until receiving further guidance on Erik Weisz's whereabouts, a single room had a modern door fitted to it. The only contents upon their arrival had been sand-covered sheets of reinforced plastic, leading Ian to believe that archaeologists had once used it for cataloging and storing artifacts found on site.

He peered inside the room now, making a final appraisal of his team's additions: a heavy wooden chair relocated from the first floor, along with a foldout chair facing it from a distance of two meters. The scene was eerie, lit by a trio of headlamps arranged in a triangle and inadvertently resulting in the appearance of some kind of spiritual ceremony, though what was about to transpire was very far from it.

Then came the sound of heavy bootsteps shuffling up the stairway, preceded by a leaping set of footfalls from someone moving ahead of the main group. David appeared in the hallway wearing his full kit with rifle, advancing quickly toward Ian and holding out an item in his right hand.

Ian accepted the digital camera, checking the display to see his captive's face and almost laughing at the sight.

The man certainly wasn't Emirati, though he could see why his capturers had applied the label—racism and xenophobia were just as alive and well in the Middle East as they were anywhere else in the world, to an incomprehensibly high degree. Sharing a language or national border carried less weight here than the affiliations of tribe and sect, so it was no surprise that the Sabahi's militia had presumed an outsider to originate from the UAE, whether by birth or the constant employ of foreign fighters inside Yemen.

Ian guessed that his new captive was Latino, very possibly from Colombia. By virtue of combating Communist expansion and the War on Drugs, the country received a fantastic amount of military training and equipment from the United States. Young Colombian men were transformed into super soldiers for the second largest army on the continent, sent to battle internal threats in often horrific combat, and then received a laughably insubstantial pension. It was a recipe for producing mercenaries on an industrial scale, and the output had frequently embarrassing results—most recently, perhaps, was the Haitian presidential assassination by veterans of the Colombian military, some of whom had received US training in their home country *and* America.

If Erik Weisz wanted to find highly skilled trigger-pullers for hire, he'd have to look no further than Colombia to find them. But that raised the obvious question: why bother? This was, after all, the Middle East. Even if Weisz had advance knowledge of Project Longwing's ground team arrival in Yemen, there was no need to send in the top international talent to ferret them out. An endless succession of local tribes, militias, and part-time soldiers would gladly take up the task for the paltriest sums imaginable.

He handed the camera back to David as three more men emerged from the stairwell—two of Baterfi's men hauled the restrained prisoner by the arms as he blindly shuffled his feet forward. Ian had only seconds to assess the captive as he was swept into the interrogation room with the burlap sack over his head.

The man wasn't much taller than Ian, but probably fifteen or twenty pounds heavier. Most of that weight was consolidated in his upper body, his muscular shoulders and biceps stretching his sweat-soaked tan shirt. No tattoos that Ian could see, and he wore Crye Precision desert multicam pants. The boots were Salomons, broken-in but otherwise in excellent condition. No belt or watch to evaluate—those had probably been stolen within minutes of his capture—which left Ian little to go on other than the man had impeccable taste in fatigues and combat footwear.

Ian followed the group inside, stepping back to observe Baterfi's men lower the prisoner into the wooden chair. David used flex cuffs to affix his bound wrists to the seatback, then knelt to apply two more cuffs, binding each of the man's ankles to a chair leg—a wise precaution, as a man with full use of his legs and the proper motivation could do serious damage.

David looked at Ian, who gave a nod of approval.

Baterfi's men departed immediately, leaving David to close the door and take up a position behind the captive.

Ian's last act before commencing the interrogation was to confirm the orientation of the holster on his hip that bore the satisfying weight of his

Glock 19, a last-ditch protective measure should the prisoner manage to break free and overcome the security afforded by David and his Galil rifle. With that complete, he advanced two steps and gently pulled the burlap sack from the man's head, casting it aside and speaking in a cordial tone.

"*Buenos dias, parcero,*" Ian began. "*Cómo te llamas?*"

A look flashed across the man's face at the sight of Ian—or, more precisely, at the fact that he was white. Was it relief? Surprise? Ian couldn't say for sure, nor could he begin to extrapolate much meaning even if he'd been able to pin the emotion. There was no shortage of mercenaries available to all sides for the right price, though the balance of probability discounted Iranian involvement by virtue of their phobia against American spies.

Ian dropped into the open chair across from the captive, crossing one leg over the other and folding his hands in his lap. When no response came, he continued, "I'll settle for your rank or service number. You know your rights under Article 5 of the Geneva Convention. You're obligated to provide all three and nothing else, so pick one."

The man blinked, surveyed the room with a particular emphasis on the lone exit, and then looked at the floor without speaking.

Ian responded by assuming a firmer tone, dropping any pretenses of camaraderie.

"I have no doubt you've had some training in how to resist interrogation, but I can assure you that I've had far more. So here's the deal: I'm not going to do any good cop, bad cop work on you. There's only one game we're going to play right now, and it's called reality. You're not an active-duty servicemember, and even if you were, Yemen's short on oversight at the moment. I can do whatever the hell I want with you, and I will. You've seen my face and you know there's a bullet waiting for you at the end of this. So don't make me resort to torture. We can sort this out like gentlemen, now can't we?"

His use of the word *torture* caused the man to meet his eyes at last. After a brief pause, he asked, "You're American, aren't you?"

The man spoke with a neutral accent, which Ian thought was an interesting wrinkle. "You're very perceptive."

"JSOC?"

Ian delivered a bland smile. "I think you're misunderstanding the information flow here."

"All right," he said, clearing his throat. "I think it's clear we're playing for the same side, so I'll come clean. Here's the truth: I'm a Canadian servicemember. Master Warrant Officer Daniel Munoz."

"Unit?"

"JTF 2."

"*En français*," Ian tested him.

"*Deuxième Force opérationnelle interarmées, FOI 2.*"

"Motto?"

"*Facta non verba*," he replied proudly. "Deeds, not words."

Ian closed his eyes and gave a nod, then said, "Tell me about your mission."

"We were detached to a coalition task force, assigned to emplace equipment."

"What kind?"

"A hub station, under the Harvest Shine program. Are you familiar?"

"I am," Ian said, opening his eyes and blinking his vision into focus. "Whose communications were you monitoring?"

Munoz frowned. "The main event."

"Why?"

A pause, and then a swallow. "I'm going to choose my words carefully, okay?"

When Ian nodded, Munoz continued, "The Houthis have won the civil war. The world has been expecting them to do what Hezbollah did, but the Houthis...there are indications that they're trying to turn the temporary ceasefire into a permanent government, to solidify control and bring in the tribes they're fighting to the south and east. That means a push for the oil fields, and once they have that wealth...we all saw how things went for ISIS."

"I understand."

Munoz seized on the apparent agreement, speaking more quickly as he went on.

"Neither of our governments wanted the Houthis to win, or Assad to continue, or Putin to invade. But we all have to deal with the reality that things we didn't want to happen have happened. Now it's a matter of damage control and charting a way ahead, and the Houthis have made some quiet overtures to the West that they're willing to make a deal. My team's mission was to emplace equipment that would allow intel services to confirm or deny whether their intent is genuine, or a means of extending the ceasefire to push for another offensive—"

Ian began laughing then, a slow chuckle that rose in pitch and intensity until it became an almost hysterical bout.

Munoz went silent, suddenly wary, and Ian tried to compose himself amid a surging wave of subtle fear that was building into an ever-mounting terror inside him.

The layers of this man's cover story were falling away like as many petals from an onion, and try as he might to let the facade unfold in the manner of a typical interrogation, Ian decided to dispense with the fore-play. His team's survival depended on it, and even then he may well have been too late to influence what was seeming like an increasingly inevitable outcome.

He held up a hand to keep his captive silent, flinching with the unpleasant reality that now faced him. David's eyes were wide as he stood behind Munoz, raising both hands in a *what the hell* gesture. Ian ignored him, knowing that all would soon be explained—but not by him.

Ian gave a long, slow exhale, then tilted his head back to examine the ceiling before meeting Munoz's eyes once more.

"Listen," Ian said, "I know exactly why you're here, and who sent you. I know your real objective and how you ended up in our hands. And I know," he concluded, "that I'm the only hope you've got left. So now you need to come clean *for real*."

"I am…" Munoz stammered. "I'm telling you everything. What else do you want to know?"

"You can start with your unit. I already know who you are, I know what this is, but I need you to tell me."

Munoz remained steadfast. "I've told you the truth, and I've done it on faith that you're not some merc out here bushwacking for money. And until you confirm otherwise, I've got nothing left to say."

Ian drew a shallow breath, feeling his composure falter with each passing moment. He forced himself to focus, almost murmuring the final words he could manage before losing control.

"Munoz...whatever your name is...I'm telling you, man, this is checkmate. If I have to ask again, you're not going to have a choice."

"My story stands, and if you reach out to my government, they'll confirm—"

He went silent as Ian leapt from his seat, drew his sidearm, and advanced with three rapid steps to press his Glock barrel into the man's right eye.

"You're going to say two words," Ian shouted, "and only two words, in response to my next question. If they don't match what I know *exactly*, I'm going to blow your fucking head off. What unit do you belong to?"

The man hesitated, but just barely. He knew that his interrogator was reaching a feverish level of desperation and would, in fact, kill him, perhaps better than Ian himself did. And in that split second, Ian silently prayed that he was wrong. If he wasn't, then his entire team was just as fucked as the man before him.

Then Munoz responded, confirming his worst suspicions.

"Project Longwing."

My heart dropped to my stomach and a gut-wrenching wave of nausea overcame me in the span of one second.

Ian removed his pistol from the man's eye, turning to pace the room with his Glock in hand. I'd known the man longer than anyone else on our team and had never seen him so distressed, an unfortunate reality that bore grave implications for the fate of our mission.

"Hey," I snapped, "put the gun away."

He did so, succeeding on the second attempt with a trembling hand.

Then I spun to face the prisoner, jabbing a finger in his face and speaking with unbridled fury.

"And you, asshole, talk fast. What's your real name?"

"Dan Munoz," he said quietly, gaze darting over my tactical vest and weapon, his first clear-cut indication as to the identity of his latest captors. Then his eyes met mine. "That part wasn't a lie."

I took a step back, lowering my hand. "But you're American, and so is your team."

"That's right."

"Listen to me carefully, Munoz, because this is how we're going to establish bonafides. One person sent your team into Yemen—you're going to tell me that individual's callsign, and I'll tell you their name. Then we cut the shit. There's no time to keep secrets from each other. Ready?"

"Mayfly."

"Chen. Meiling Chen."

He gave a solemn nod.

I was only then beginning to fully grasp Ian's despair, which was more than warranted under the circumstances.

My heart was beating faster now, and I lowered myself into Ian's seat, situating my rifle across my thighs before saying, "How many teams in Project Longwing?"

"Just mine. We were the pilot team—at least, I thought we were."

"How long have you been together?"

"We were assembled three months ago. All of us were SpecOps crossing over to contractor status. We'd just completed our training cycle when she sent us here. This was our first mission for the Agency."

The sheer fuckery of this was overwhelming. After all the blood my men had shed in pursuit of Weisz, after one of his attacks had very nearly killed my wife and daughter, and after I'd almost had my ticket punched in Serbia, Chen had sent in a cherry team to serve as the executioner. I had no doubt Munoz's people were all-star special operators in the military; they'd have to be, if assembled to serve Project Longwing in a tactical capacity. And sure, they'd been captured outright.

But targeting Weisz was my team's right, not theirs. I'd never forgive Chen for this, and vowed to myself in that moment that if and when I had the chance to get my pound of flesh for this transgression, I was going to take it.

Filing the thought away for future reference, I said, "Tell me about your team. What's your task organization?"

Munoz stared at the floor between us, looking lost in thought.

"Five guys total. I filled the sniper billet. The other slots were for team leader, intel specialist, medic, and JTAC."

I looked over my shoulder at Ian, who was standing in the corner, arms crossed, staring at the floor as he listened.

"Of course," I said. "You guys have a slot for a JTAC."

"One slot, yeah. But we've actually got two," Munoz said. "I've got the basic qualification from my time in the Marines, but our main guy, Kendrick, was a Combat Controller."

So Chen had doubled the playing field of operational teams, and was smart about it: my team had no one qualified to direct aerial fires in a professional capacity, and that deficit had forced us to take an active-duty Air Force service member with us into Libya.

But a highly compartmentalized targeted killing program was only as good as its ability to operate without outside support becoming aware of its existence. Whoever had decided on the task organization for a second ground team—probably Chen herself—had reviewed our operational history and corrected the oversight.

I felt the back of my neck burning.

"What was your infil?"

Munoz's lip quivered.

"Osprey, off the USS *Harry S. Truman*."

Probably the same fucking bird and flight crew that we used. Since the pilots had made no mention of that fact during my commander brief, I imagined they thought the first team was happily pursuing their classified mission.

"When?" I asked.

"Two nights ago."

"Target?"

No hesitation.

"Fulvio Pagano, goes by Erik Weisz."

"Fantastic," I snapped. "What happened?"

"It was our partner force...the Khab Militia...I was in sniper overwatch for the linkup, and they rolled my guys right away. I saw them get taken alive. My team leader, Griffin, transmitted the order for me to begin evasion because it was too late for me to make a difference..."

"I get it," I said, sparing him the effort of relaying further specifics. My team, after all, had the same plan. "What then?"

"I made it two klicks along my evasion corridor, then got trapped. Whoever rolled me, they held me through the next day and night, then transported me here."

My mind was racing now. "This part is important, so get it right—did you communicate with Chen in any way after your team got captured?"

He shook his head.

"I was evading nonstop right up until I got caught. No time to set up satellite comms, and they stripped my gear at the point of capture."

Pausing to take a breath, I glanced back at Ian. "Why aren't those four guys being paraded in front of every news camera in Yemen right now?"

"No idea," he said. "There's a half dozen reasons the Houthis might choose to keep this secret, and none of them matter right now. But if they haven't spun this for a PR victory in the past 36 hours, it's unlikely they will."

Then I turned back to face Munoz. "Well I hope you're ready for more bad news, because I've got a lot of it. Your men aren't the first Longwing ground team. We are. At least," I caught myself, "I hope we are. And I'm the team leader. We've been tracking Weisz all over the globe, and the last place we thought we'd find him was here. We came to Yemen for a one-night source recovery and found out our main target was here after the fact."

I let that sink in for a moment, then added, "Chen kept that information from us, then put us in a holding pattern while your team went in. When your mission went tits-up, she ran the exact same play—Osprey infil from the carrier—using a different partner force. That means not only does she not give a shit about your people, but she doesn't give a shit about mine either."

Munoz's jaw tensed, and he spoke through gritted teeth.

"That doesn't surprise me."

Ian abruptly asked, "Why not?"

Our captive gave a slight shake of his head. "Griffin, my team leader, has some friends at the Agency, so he asked around about her. Apparently she's got a reputation for getting people killed. We were told to be careful."

Then he observed my blank expression and went on, "You guys didn't know?"

"She took over Project Longwing just before your team was assembled. Her predecessor got killed—"

"In the States?"

"Yeah, in the States, and we can only presume as a result of Weisz. This is our first mission with her running the show, and as you can see she's been doing a bang-up job so far."

Munoz's eyes suddenly filled with tears, taking on a glassy appearance that reflected the light of the headlamps.

"You've got to help my guys," he gasped. "If I was kept alive, then so were they...they're being held somewhere, and you've got to...I've got to..."

Seeing that words were coming hard for him now, I interrupted, "Oh, I know they're being held alive. No shortage of prisons in Yemen, I'm told. The militias here aren't in the business of missing a payout, and they're not going to stop at taking whatever cash your guys had on them. They'll try for a ransom as well, and Project Longwing is unattributable so we all know how that will work out. But I've still got a prerogative to get Weisz."

"My guys," Munoz pleaded. "Listen, man. We've got to get them. I'll help you get Weisz, but we have to *get those guys* back."

I sucked my teeth for a moment, considering both his request and the somewhat unimaginable extent to which it would conflict with our primary mission in Yemen.

"Let me talk to my people, because we've got to unfuck this somehow." Then, thinking aloud, I added, "You're under my command from this point forward. I'm going to lock you in here with some food and water, and our medic will look you over in a bit. Until then you're going to eat, hydrate, and pull your shit together because we're going to need you. Don't go action hero on me. You'd be an idiot to try and escape, because—"

Munoz cut me off with firm determination.

"I'll sit my ass wherever you tell me, and do whatever you need when the time comes. I'm good in a gunfight; all my guys are. You can count on me. But I'm begging you, think of what you'd do if it was your team that got rolled up and not mine."

"I already have," I said, "and I'd be trying to make the same bargain. Believe me, I'm no more thrilled about four Americans rotting in a Yemeni prison than you are. Just give me some space to talk to my guys."

He said nothing, but his eyes were locked on mine, haunted and vulnerable. This was like looking in a mirror, I thought, because I felt exactly the same way.

Then, in lieu of any better way to wrap up the dialogue, I jerked a thumb over my shoulder.

"That's Ian, our intel guy. And I'm David."

With a helpless sigh, I concluded, "Welcome to the team."

19

"Now I know what you're thinking," Reilly said with a kindhearted chuckle, "of course I'm a natural soldier. Look at the size of me, right?"

Then, without waiting for a response, he said, "Wrong."

He gazed out at the sun-drenched landscape beyond his guard position, an elevated minaret lookout post that provided shade by way of merciful overhead cover. Window cutouts surrounded him on all sides but he focused his attention to the south, where the closest thing to a main road bisected Sirwah with a single dirt offshoot threading its way toward the current hideout.

Something about the panoramic desert vistas had him in an introspective mood, feeling wistful as he reflected on the past few years of his life. Sure, on one hand the view represented a 360-degree ring of dangers, the entire lethal horizon packed to the brim with people who would gladly kill him and his team or worse.

On the other hand, though, there was a certain beauty to the savage desolation of mottled slopes rising up from the sand to meet the cloudless azure sky, an ancient land that he surveyed from an ancient vantage point.

Reilly glanced over to his Yemeni partner for the current guard shift, then looked back out and confided, "The truth is, Pehzan, I got into this business to be a medic. To help people."

He groaned quietly. "And you want to know what I've gotten out of it? A whole lot of issues from spilling gallons of enemy blood all over the world. So much so that I wonder who I'd be, what I'd actually be capable of, if I'd led a normal life. If I wasn't weighed down by all the carnage I've seen, and inflicted." After a pause, he added, "The question becomes soul crushing when I think about it, so I try not to."

He sucked down a mouthful of warm water from the flexible hose clipped to his tactical vest.

"And the worst part is I'm not the only one; if I was, I could deal with that. The others don't confide in each other, but they all talk to me because I'm their medic. All of them are hurting as bad as me, and they're hurting more and more with each mission. So I don't just bear my own pain, I bear all of theirs. It's not like I'm a young single guy anymore. Now I'm with Olivia—my girlfriend—and we've been talking about settling down. I mean, *really* settling down. Starting a family, leaving all this chaos behind. Instead of me going off to war every few months and not knowing if I'll make it back."

He hesitated then, considering another sip of water and deciding to forge on instead. "The truth is—and I haven't told this to anyone—when I found out who our target was, I didn't get excited because of a chance to stop terrorism. I got excited because if we get him, if we actually *get him*, then this whole thing might finally be over."

A ragged sigh followed him speaking this truth out loud; it felt good to give voice to the thoughts in his head, despite and perhaps because of the precarious circumstances in which he currently found himself.

"And the hardest part for me isn't the risk that I'll die. Every time one of our guys gets hit, and I'm running over to help, my worst fear is that they're either dead already, or that my skills won't be enough to save them. It's medic guilt, man, and I carry that with me all the time. So on the outside, sure, I look like a professional." He tapped his sternum with a finger. "But in here?"

Reilly gave a quiet, disingenuous laugh. "In here, I'm fucking terrified, Pehzan. Just a scared kid trying to keep everyone alive—"

"*Net call,*" David suddenly transmitted over his earpiece, "*I need everyone in our team room, now.*"

Reilly keyed his mic and responded, "Who's staying on security?"

"*Leave it to Baterfi's men,*" the team leader said.

Reilly looked behind him, where his guard partner was blissfully sleeping in a foldout chair, his head angled back against a minaret wall. The medic's attempts at conversing in English and broken Arabic had resulted in obtaining Pehzan's name—at least, Reilly assumed the word was his name—before the man closed his eyes and went nonverbal beyond a few sputtering snores.

Frowning, Reilly keyed his mic and said warily, "Hey man, fair warning, my host nation counterpart has been passed out and drooling on himself for the past hour, and—"

"*Forget the security,*" David insisted. "*We don't sort some shit out in the next ten minutes, security's not going to matter.*"

Well that sounded ominous, Reilly thought as he hastily conducted a final scan, though stranger things had happened in the course of Project Longwing missions. He hoped the team leader was being melodramatic but suspected that wasn't the case based on previous experience. David was impulsive and at times reckless, but not overly prone to letting emotion get in the way of objective judgment.

Whatever the captive had said in interrogation, it was of dire importance. And under the circumstances, that meant Erik Weisz was likely aware of their presence in Yemen and a full-scale blowout from Baterfi's hideout was now in the works.

Reilly adjusted his HK417 across his back on its sling and placed a hand on Pehzan's shoulder.

"I have to run. You've got this, brother. Stay strong."

No response from the man. Reilly moved to the ladder before descending it quickly, navigating the hallways of the ruins to enter his team's chosen operations center: a creepy alcove amid an already creepy pagan temple, currently distinguished by the withering stares of three teammates watching him enter.

Worthy and Cancer were seated side by side in foldout chairs, while Ian stood before them like a teacher who'd been interrupted in the middle of reprimanding a pair of problem students.

"Where's David?" Reilly blurted.

"He's talking to Baterfi," Ian said. "Have a seat."

Reilly grabbed a chair and dragged it next to Worthy, sitting down as he ventured, "Apparently I'm the last one to know, so whatever this is, tell me."

Ian crossed his arms.

"The prisoner we just brought in isn't an Emirati. He's an American, Daniel Munoz, and he's part of a second Longwing team."

The medic's eyes went wide. "A second team? What was their mission?"

"Weisz."

Reilly threw up his hands. "If they're here, then why are we here? How did she expect two teams to go unnoticed in Yemen?"

"For one thing," Ian pointed out, "we're in a country that's roughly the size of Texas. And she didn't plan on sending both teams after Weisz. We were her backup plan. She chose the other team to go in, not us."

Cancer added with disdain, "This was their first Longwing op."

Reilly needed a second to process that, and responded more loudly than he'd intended to.

"After everything we've done, she used a *brand-new* fucking team to go after Weisz?"

Ian hastened to clarify, "They infiltrated while we were still in Aden. Their partner force was bad, took four of them prisoner at linkup. Munoz was the sniper, so he made a short evasion before getting rolled up by another militia. All Chen knows is that the entire team went dark on comms, so as far as she's concerned they're all in prison or dead. And with that knowledge, she chose to send us the following night. Same mission, different partner force."

Cancer interjected, "Which explains why she had us stand down in Aden."

"Along with," Worthy explained, "the zero-notice retasking. We were the only other deniable asset on call."

Reilly glanced from one team member to the next. "So if I'm understanding this correctly, in addition to Weisz hiding out somewhere in Yemen, we've got four CIA contractors stuffed in a private prison somewhere—"

"Correct." Ian nodded.

"—and Chen doesn't give a shit if those guys, or our team, live or die."

"That's about the long and the short of it, yes."

"Well, we've got to—"

But before he could finish the thought, David swept into the room and ended the exchange in five words directed at Ian.

"You get everyone caught up?"

"Basically," he agreed, "yeah."

David gave a curt nod and turned to face the seated team members.

Before he could speak, Reilly blurted, "What did Chen have to say for herself?"

The team leader appeared startled by the question.

"*Say* for herself?" David asked, incredulous. "She didn't *say* anything, because I haven't told her we have Munoz and I don't plan to. As much as I'd like to call her out on this mess, she'd just give us a blanket order to ignore the rest of his team at the risk of being disbanded when we get back. It's a hell of a lot easier for me to just lie to her in the first place. I can promise you she's not going to do anything that will actually help us develop this situation."

Cancer leaned forward and warily asked, "Develop this situation how, exactly?"

David hesitated, letting his gaze drift across the assembled team members before he spoke again.

"I just talked to Baterfi, who's got a source that will likely be able to pinpoint the missing team's location. But the guy won't meet us here, so that information would come at a cost in terms of money and risk in going to see him in the first place. We can't trust Baterfi's men to do it for us; one, they won't be able to validate the information even if they made the trip, and two, they probably wouldn't make the trip at all. My guess is they'd bleed us dry for cash by producing false tips that require more investigation."

Seeing that no one debated him on that last point, he continued, "And Munoz, understandably, wants us to go after his guys."

Cancer exploded.

"That's bullshit and you know it."

"And now that I know where you stand," David said, turning his attention to the others, "who agrees with him?"

Ian raised his hand.

"Anyone neutral?"

No response.

"Opposition?"

Worthy and Reilly lifted their arms, Reilly with a particular emphasis.

David gave a frustrated grunt. "A fifty-fifty split. Perfect. Reilly and Worthy, you're up first. Sell me on why we should go after the other team."

Worthy pointed a finger at the medic, giving him clearance to speak his mind first.

But Reilly had trouble finding words that adequately voiced his emotions, and he stammered before mustering a coherent reply.

"I'm...I'm not even sure why we're *talking* about this. Another team was hung out to dry and, as far as Chen is concerned, so were we. She sent us into the exact same slaughterhouse, and it's a miracle we're not dead or in prison right alongside them. But since we're not, we've got an obligation to do everything in our power to save them. Longwing is unattributable—no one's going to bail those guys out, and they're going to be tortured until whoever's holding them realizes they're not worth the food bill, if they're getting food at all. That means four Americans dead, four contractors *just like us*. And if we don't do anything to get them back, then we might as well hang up our spurs because we don't deserve to call ourselves warriors."

Ian looked down at the words, and Cancer gave an audible, mocking snort.

Reilly swung his gaze to the sniper. "If those guys were active-duty military, we wouldn't have to worry about them because JSOC would be sending in the intergalactic ninja death squad right about now. But the Agency doesn't give a shit about its covert operators, which means there's just us. And I don't want to go into battle with anyone who thinks we don't have a duty to do our part, for better or worse."

Cancer opened his mouth to reply, though David beat him to it. Sensing that things were about to get out of hand, the team leader spoke firmly.

"Understood. Worthy, you have anything to add?"

Worthy didn't appear to have any opinion in the matter whatsoever; instead, his drawled response was issued quietly, without fanfare, and in a thoughtful tone that made Reilly wish he'd been more in control of the emotions surging through him right now.

"I met an old World War II vet once," Worthy said, "a guy from my hometown, back when I was a kid. He was with a search-and-rescue team, tasked with recovering downed pilots behind enemy lines. Showed me his unit patch: angel wings around planet Earth, and the globe had a cross at the top and an inverted cross at the bottom. Their motto was, 'We'll go to heaven or hell to find you.'"

He paused a beat. "I'd say that's a lot more noble than another dead terrorist, no matter how high ranking. That's all I have to say about this."

A moment of silence followed, shattered by David's next order.

"Cancer and Ian, you're up. Sell me on why we should write off the other team."

Cancer's anger had been mounting for a myriad of reasons, with the discovery of a second Longwing ground team now least among them.

He'd fully expected Reilly to cry over the perceived injustice of the situation and gladly volunteer to run into certain death in a misguided attempt to do right by his own childish ideals.

But Worthy casting his vote in the same camp felt like a betrayal; previously, Cancer had regarded the pointman as an ally when pragmatism needed to prevail. He knew he should let Ian take the lead in presenting a reasonable counterargument, but shot off at the mouth before he could stop himself.

"For starters," Cancer began, "we volunteered for this, and so did they. The entire point of Project Longwing is to be deniable, and that means the shooters are expendable. Anyone who has a problem with that shouldn't have taken the paycheck in the first place, so let's not delude ourselves with any moral indignation just because someone finally paid the price. We've got a job here that requires our full attention and resources, and if we start deviating from that it's going to be us dead or in prison instead of those other four fuckers."

Ian quickly intervened, "Don't get me wrong, Reilly, I don't like this any more than you do." The intelligence operative hesitated. "But consider what the mission actually is: Erik Weisz. Two barely foiled plots, and the one he pulled off killed five thousand civilians. What's his next one going to achieve? This isn't about the four guys rotting in a Yemini prison, as horrible as that is. It's about the civilians we're supposed to be protecting. If a ground team gets sacrificed to that effort—ours or Munoz's, it doesn't matter—but Weisz gets taken off the battlefield, it will have been worth it."

"Facts," Cancer insisted, then added, "and let's talk about the miraculous survivor. If Munoz evaded, it means he didn't fire a shot. Now I don't care what order came over comms when you guys were at linkup, I was going to drop as many people as I could and go down in flames."

Worthy spoke softly. "That doesn't mean Munoz made the wrong decision."

"Maybe not by your standards," Cancer shot back. "But by mine? I have no intention of sending our team into harm's way to rescue his guys when he ran off with his tail between his legs."

David intervened, "We're already in harm's way, and that's not about to change with Chen running the ship. Forget about what Munoz did or didn't do, and start thinking about the way ahead."

Ian spoke next, shifting his weight uneasily from one foot to the other.

"There's only one way. We take out Weisz while we still have a chance. Munoz is just another shooter until that job is done, and once it is we can get him home."

"And what about those other four Americans getting the shit beat out of them right now?" Reilly demanded.

"If there was a way to save them, I'd be all for it. But if we try to do that, we kill ourselves in the process. It's that simple. Now that's all good in theory if Weisz's head wasn't on the chopping block, but it is. We miss him now, we take our eye off the ball for one second, when's the next time he sticks his neck out? I hate to tell you this, but he's already aware a team got captured trying to get him, and that's going to inform his risk matrix going forward. We spent two years trying to find him, and if we miss our shot now it's going to be another two or more before he surfaces. Maybe never. How many civilians are going to die because we didn't take him out?"

Cancer gave a slow clap as Ian concluded his speech, then added, "Everyone in Yemen is trying to kill us except for Baterfi, and he could change his mind at any moment. That means our concern isn't Munoz's team, it's *our* team."

"Noted," David said. "Anything else?"

"Yeah," Cancer said, "but you and I need to discuss it in private."

The team leader tapped his watch.

"Tick tock, motherfucker. Chen is going to hit us with Weisz's current location any minute now. We're all big boys here—if you've got something to say, say it now."

Cancer raised his eyebrows, giving David one last chance to go back on his words. When that didn't happen in the next half second, he continued.

"Fine. You're the team leader, and in the end this is up to you. But you better get your shit together if you want to have a team left to follow you after that little stunt you pulled in Serbia."

"What stunt—"

"Going rogue to recover intel, and sending the rest of us in the fire to get you back. *That* little stunt."

David looked taken aback, almost stammering as he responded, "It was risky, yeah, but if I hadn't done that we wouldn't have made it to Yemen in the first place."

"And a repeat performance," Cancer shot back, "is going to make damn sure that we don't get out. You better make your decision carefully, and not let any bleeding heart bullshit get in the way of putting your men first."

I felt my confidence melting away as I met Cancer's glare. His final comments represented outright insubordination if we'd been having the conversation in private much less in front of the team, but I'd given him the clearance to speak freely, and holy shit had he leapt at the opportunity.

Everyone was waiting for my response, and I glanced out the window beside me to gather my thoughts.

On one hand, I felt almost betrayed by Cancer's visceral denouncement of my leadership abilities; on the other, he'd merely stated what everyone else had been thinking ever since I'd more or less gone rogue on our mission in Serbia. My actions had severely tested their confidence in me, and added to that was the current divisiveness on which course of action was acceptable, if not necessary. Whatever I decided would alienate half my team.

And while such judgment calls were part and parcel of being ground force commander—a job that was certainly no popularity contest—I faced the additional challenge of being torn myself. I could no more advocate for a single-minded pursuit of Weisz than I could cast aside that critical mission to do what I knew in my heart was right by trying to rescue a previously unknown sister team.

My teammates, at least, had taken a side in the debate. I was supposed to be the most clear-minded of all of them, and yet still felt completely and utterly undecided.

With my gaze fixed on the landscape beyond the ruins, I asked, "What's the intel value of those four guys being interrogated?"

"Negligible," Ian replied, "if I'm being perfectly honest. They don't know about us, so there's no risk of a compromise there. Worst-case scenario, they'll divulge their target along with the fact that the Agency gave them a facility and guns and sent them off to kill. None of that is exactly a state secret. Those guys don't have nuclear launch codes any more than we do."

I watched him closely, then forced myself to look away. A very palpable darkness was growing within Ian, either from being shot in Belgrade, or being this close to Weisz, or both.

Minutes earlier, I'd watched him melt down while interrogating Munoz without knowing why, knew that it wasn't an act, and had to restrain myself from tackling him when he shoved a pistol in the man's face. The second Munoz admitted he was a member of Project Longwing, Ian's unraveling made perfect sense—he was an intelligence operative, and understood the implications better than any of us.

We were all feeling the pressure that had been building for God knew how many missions of pursuing Erik Weisz, and now that he was almost within our grasp, we faced the worst curveball imaginable: a second ground team.

It was an impossible dilemma.

My team was divided in two, and death could await at the fulfillment of either side's recommendation. I believed in both arguments, yet believed in neither of them. Abandoning a sister team to the enemy was every bit the sin that allowing countless civilian deaths would be. I could choose to expend resources and run a mission off the grid on behalf of Munoz's team, or I could do what Chen told me to do and go after Erik Weisz alone. The only option denied to me was to make no choice at all, and I checked my watch before issuing a response.

"You win."

"Who?" Ian asked, glancing toward Reilly. "Me, or—"

"Both of you. All of you. Everyone's going to get what they want. Worthy and Reilly, you're going to take Munoz, a few militia guys, and some cash to meet with Baterfi's source and find out where the other team is being held. Ian, Cancer, you stay here and start planning the hit against Weisz once the latest intel comes in. And since he's the primary mission, I stay here too."

Cancer wasn't satisfied with that, and quickly objected, "If you split our team, you condemn both efforts to failure. What if Reilly, Worthy, and Munoz don't come back? The rest of us won't have the manpower to take down Weisz, not even close."

Worthy added, "And if we find where the POWs are held, we'll need everyone *plus* the militia to even consider a rescue."

I bowed my head, acknowledging all sides of the argument—no one was wrong, and no one was right. In the end, I was trying to thread an exceedingly dangerous needle the only way I could.

Looking up, I responded, "This isn't about me trying to pacify everyone. It's as unforgivable to let Weisz escape as it is to hang another team out to dry. The entire situation is fucked, and we're right in the middle of it. We could all die in a botched prison break as much as we could trying to kill or capture our main target. But that doesn't mean we shouldn't try to accomplish both."

Then, as if synchronized by divine provenance, everyone looked from me to Cancer.

I could tell Cancer wanted to object further, could see it in his face, but he must have known well enough from my own expression or tone or both that I would indulge no further debate.

He asked instead, "Is that final, boss?"

"Yeah," I replied, giving him a final nod. "It most definitely is."

20

Worthy rode in the passenger seat as the Toyota Camry cruised northwest on Jihanah Road, a two-lane highway that represented the most civilized infrastructure he'd seen since infiltrating the previous night. Midday traffic was substantial, a very good thing for the purposes of three Americans remaining uncompromised in a civilian vehicle.

He glanced at the phone in his hand and said, "Two kilometers to left turn."

The driver, Ghazi, had a high school level of education and spoke passable English, which made him a gem among Baterfi's ragtag force. Regrettably, however, the young Yemeni had just enough confidence with his second language to be dangerous.

"I am hearing you, cowboy." He altered his native accent to mockery as he continued, "Two kee-la-meetas, lay-uft teeurn."

Reilly spoke from the backseat, sounding impressed.

"Was that your impression of Racegun?"

"Pretty good," Munoz commented. "Hey Ghazi, call him a peckerwood. Southerners love that."

The driver looked over and immediately parroted, "You are *pecker*wood. Pecker. Wood."

Worthy felt a slight quiver in his right eyelid.

He glanced over his shoulder at Worthy and Munoz in the backseat. Both wore the same conspiratorial smile along with casual Western attire and jackets with shawls, carefully curated to merge with the area's civilian populace while providing storage and concealment for ammunition and grenades. They looked as ridiculous as he did, however, with the checkered shemagh scarfs perched atop their heads and wrapped loosely around their necks to hide Caucasian faces.

"Doc," he said, "Bulldog, don't make me stop this car. You're not going to like it if I do."

They typically referenced one another by callsign in the presence of host nation fighters, and Munoz had been forced to produce a moniker that met the team's demanding standards—nothing flattering unless specifically authorized by David, something simple and, if at all possible, self-effacing.

To that end, Munoz's normal callsign of Shadow had been struck down immediately; he'd reluctantly settled on Bulldog, a testament to his squat and immensely stocky frame, and this entry had been permitted in the annals of team lore.

And while Reilly continued smiling, Munoz looked sufficiently chagrined as he offered as much of an apology as a special operations veteran was capable of.

"Hey," he said with a shrug, "my family are Cubans from Puerto Rico. They call us Jews of the Caribbean."

Worthy turned back around, placing the driver under his smoldering gaze for a moment before looking back at the road with the declaration, "And I don't sound like that."

Ghazi echoed, "I dawnt sawn like day-att."

Reilly gave a delighted titter of laughter and noted, "Getting better. Keep practicing, Ghazi."

Directing his attention to the phone once more, Worthy provided his next update.

"Five hundred meters until our left turn."

He looked up to scan the ground ahead and almost immediately fixated on a sight in the distance that made his blood run cold.

Just off a side road was a civilian gas station, or at least one that *used* to belong to civilians; at present it was ringed by armed men, one of whom was refueling a pickup bearing what appeared to be a 73-millimeter recoil-less rifle, a pure vehicle vaporizer if ever he'd seen one.

And horrific as the sight was, it paled in comparison to what lay beyond.

The dusty clearing behind the station held a few scattered sheds, but it was first and foremost a parking lot for mine-resistant ambush-protected vehicles, or MRAPs, not unlike those used by Emirati special forces in extracting the team from their snatch mission in Aden. Some of them were the exact same models, a BAE Caiman and an International MaxxPro among them, along with a pair of Oshkosh M-ATVs.

"That's not good," Munoz quipped from the backseat.

"They could be inoperative," Worthy managed. "Maybe they're just relics of the old government, kept on display to project power."

Ghazi hissed, "This is why I do not come here. And I am confident *that* one works."

Worthy followed the man's gaze to the road ahead, where a second MaxxPro sped toward them in the opposite lane.

He scanned it closely, assessing first the full skirt of cage armor designed to trigger rocket-propelled grenades on contact, and then the turret, spray-painted with Arabic graffiti and hosting the unmistakable profile of an M2 .50 caliber machinegun. Along with the truck and every other MRAP in the depot he'd just spotted, the weapon was produced and sold exclusively by the United States.

The MaxxPro roared past with Yemen's red, white, and black flag flapping from a pole on the rear edge, leaving Worthy to check his phone and comment, "Next left."

"Gladly," Ghazi said, spiriting the sedan off the main road. There were no exit signs, overpasses, or stoplights, just tire marks guiding the way across sand and onto the side streets of Bayt al Hadrami.

The journey had taken them close to two hours west of Baterfi's temple and into a town that would have been unremarkable were it not a suburb of Sana'a, Yemen's largest city and capital. If they went much further north, they'd be within a stone's throw of Houthi headquarters and all the security that entailed—enough, Worthy thought, to make the MRAP depot he'd just spotted look like an afterthought. That tragic geographic proximity was enough to make him rethink his vote to pursue intelligence on the captured Americans, and yet the source refused to hold the meeting anywhere else.

But the sheer number of civilians worked in their favor. Sana'a had a population of 2.5 million, and the surrounding urban areas were teeming with people and vehicle traffic. In a very real sense, they were safer now than they had been while trekking across the highlands on their way to meet Baterfi.

At least until anyone took a closer look at the vehicle's occupants.

"Just under a kilometer until our next left," Worthy said. "Speak up if you see anything that looks off."

Ghazi's local knowledge was about all they could rely on for warning signs. The dirt road to either side of their vehicle was lined with civilians making their way to or from the market, a mix of ages that included children kicking soccer balls.

So far, so good, Worthy thought, trading his encrypted smartphone with its navigation app for a locally procured device that he dialed now.

The call connected on the first ring and he heard the greeting, "*Salun hilaqa.*"

The words meant "barbershop," having been selected as a convenient means of both getting rid of anyone who'd dialed a wrong number and assuring Worthy that the conversation could proceed normally. Any other greeting meant that David was answering with a gun to his head, an unfortunate contingency plan for the possibility that Baterfi's hideout was seized.

"We're a minute out," Worthy said, "will update once the meeting is complete. If you don't hear from me within an hour, you better start working on a story about how me and Doc went missing and you guys didn't."

"Already have," David replied without hesitation. "Sasquatch attack. I saw the whole thing—fucking horrific."

"Solid. Wish me luck."

"Don't die."

Worthy ended the call and pocketed the cell phone that represented his only means of communication with the remaining teammates: they were too far to speak over the team net, and satellite radio link was out because, well, the Agency would hear it, too. Any hope of liberating American POWs would evaporate the moment Chen found out that Worthy's team knew about them in the first place, after which she'd institute failsafe measures to prevent exactly the type of illicit shit they were trying to pull off right now. David had lied to his team's CIA superior many times in the past, and in every event his deceptions were successful only because their handler thought everything was going according to plan.

As he continued to provide directions to Ghazi, the view out his windows shifted from a tight cluster of buildings to open desert, the town giving way to wide spacing between properties and the plants of a few small agricultural fields sprouting up between low mud walls.

The lack of visible civilians now was both a blessing and a curse. If the source intended on an uneventful meeting, he'd essentially removed almost all risk of the Americans being spotted. If this was a trap, however, almost all of the early indicators—an absence of children in plain view, for example—were removed from possible detection.

"There it is," Worthy said, pointing as their destination revealed itself ahead: a row of three long, low buildings arranged parallel to one another. Worthy knew the configuration well, having grown up near a similar facility in southern Georgia. It was a poultry farm, each shed designed to hold thousands of chickens until they were large enough to slaughter.

"Bulldog," he said.

Munoz responded, "Yeah?"

"I know it's your boys we're looking for, but I won't have emotion getting in the way of this transaction. I want you to listen, pull security, and keep your mouth shut. Got it?"

"Yeah," he said. "I got it."

Ghazi pulled off the road and onto a drive that led to the three buildings, and Worthy continued, "Don't screw this up—it's a miracle we got this little excursion approved in the first place."

"I figured. What was the split?"

He considered whether to answer that, and then he said, "Fifty-fifty."

No response.

"But," Worthy added, "those in favor are here right now, so if this goes south we both went in with our eyes open."

It was the last thing he had time to say. A man stepped out from behind the rightmost building, waving them toward him. Ghazi complied, pulling between the buildings and coming to a stop when the man's wave turned to a closed fist.

He wore a tattered blazer with the sleeves rolled up halfway, a blue handkerchief tied into a headband, and had no visible weapons as he approached the passenger door.

Worthy rolled down his window and heard the first orders of the meeting.

"Turn off the engine. Leave your weapons in the car."

Ghazi keyed the ignition off without so much as waiting for an American to confirm the request—an inauspicious start to things. Worthy said, "Your boss took a risk to meet here, and we need to make sure he stays safe. For his own security, and ours—"

"Leave the weapons," the man repeated. "Or go now."

There were no circumstances under which Worthy would've enthusiastically left his rifle behind, but doing so minutes after spotting a Houthi armored vehicle depot should have undoubtedly represented an outright refusal.

He considered the WWII search-and-rescue motto—*we'll go to heaven or hell to find you*—that he'd so nonchalantly offered to his team earlier that morning. Now he had to decide whether to live up to those words even if doing so meant dying for them.

"All right," he said, turning his head toward the backseat. "Weapons stay here."

There was no need to specify that the order applied to their rifles only —Galil and HK417 for Worthy and Reilly, respectively, and a battered but serviceable suppressed AK-47 provided by the militia for Munoz. No one was going to voluntarily surrender the sidearms and grenades concealed on their person, and provided they didn't get frisked, those tools would represent their only hope of self-defense.

Worthy exited the vehicle along with his comrades and Ghazi, the driver looking about apprehensively as if trying to ferret out the location of any surrounding gunmen. Worthy didn't bother; they were there, to be sure, but tucked out of view unless the need arose or a trap was sprung.

Instead, he led the group in pursuit of the scrawny Yemeni who headed toward an adjacent building, coming to a stop before the door and pounding on it three times. He waited a beat before a fourth strike, then repeated the sequence once again.

The door swung open, revealing a dim interior with sunlight streaming through a row of windows near the ceiling.

Worthy followed the man inside, taking a half-step through the doorway with his adrenaline firing—he might have sufficient time to give the "landslide" order that would send the rest of his team scrambling back to the car before he was killed. Then, upon seeing the half-dozen armed men arranged in a semicircle before him, he realized that however honed, his shooting abilities wouldn't be sufficient to save them if this was a trap.

21

"They follow the intel," Gossweiler said. "They don't have to like it, they just have to do it."

Meiling Chen faced the man from the seat at her OPCEN desk. He'd positioned the nearest chair so close that she could smell his aftershave, and then he'd leaned in to reduce the distance even further.

Senator Thomas Gossweiler looked surprisingly youthful for a man in his seventies, though his features presently formed a stony foundation of willpower culminating in a fixed stare of his ghostly blue eyes. It was all Chen could do not to squirm in her seat; her entire staff had turned against her after Gossweiler more or less commanded her to send in David's men on the heels of losing an entire ground team. Whatever was about to transpire here, Chen would have to deal with it long after the senator returned to his duties in Washington.

"Sir," she managed, nodding toward the greater OPCEN area where her staff was arrayed, "my recommendation is that we continue to monitor our target's movements to obtain a time and place more conducive for a kinetic strike."

Gossweiler was unmoved. "Weisz could disappear at any moment, and I've been working with this ground team longer than you have. They're big boys. They'll figure it out. That's what we're paying them for."

The timing of his short-notice visit couldn't have been much worse, coming as it did on the tail end of an intelligence curveball that risked throwing their entire mission into jeopardy.

Then again, there wasn't a good time for such visits at all.

US senators couldn't simply show up at an Agency operations center, much less throw their proverbial weight around to influence decision-making.

The Chairman of the US Senate Select Committee on Intelligence, however, could do just that, and in spectacular fashion—particularly, she thought with disdain, when he was one of five politicians besides the president who were fully briefed on the executive order authorizing para-military targeted killing operations. It was common knowledge at the CIA that the more compartmentalized a program was, the more severe the limited oversight for it became; and in that regard, things didn't come much more compartmentalized than Project Longwing.

Chen offered, "Senator, we have no remaining tactical elements left to commit to this effort. Griffin's team is dead, captured, or some combination of the two, and just because that hasn't been exposed on Al Jazeera yet doesn't mean it won't be—which, I think you'll agree, drastically reduces the level of risk we can knowingly assume with Rivers and his men. And even if this doesn't hit the media, I'll remind you, Senator, that if we lose Rivers's team now, Weisz will unquestionably make it out of Yemen."

"And I'll remind you," Gossweiler coolly replied, "that it was your decision, not mine, to send in a newly assembled ground team instead of the one that's been running every mission to date. I have my doubts as to whether we'd be in this predicament if you'd followed my strongest recommendation. And if I've been heavy-handed since then, Meiling, I can assure you it's because I'm trying to fix the mess you've created."

The words stung her like a whip, and she could offer no defense—not because she didn't have one, but because doing so would expose how perilous her authority here truly was. An outside assessment may well conclude that the team with more covert, not military experience be sent in as the primary assault element against Weisz.

But apart from Griffin's men having the kind of impeccable military records that the first Project Longwing team could only dream of, Chen knew what Gossweiler didn't: that David Rivers *couldn't be trusted*. He'd abandoned his men to pursue intelligence in Serbia and very nearly gotten his entire team killed in the effort to recover him, and then he'd outright lied to her about why he was late to set off for the Croatian border afterward. Chen didn't know what he'd been lying to cover, but she knew with great certainty that it wasn't the flat tire he'd claimed. Her operations officer had prepared her for the disparity, passing her a handwritten note with advice that had doubtless stemmed from his longer working experience in Project Longwing.

IF THE GROUND TEAM THROWS YOU A CURVEBALL, <u>ROLL WITH IT</u>.

Before she could marshal a response, Gossweiler went on, "And let's not forget the sheer number and leadership potential of terrorist talent wiped off the map by Rivers and his men without drone strikes or collateral damage. They represent exactly the type of unattributable, surgical direct action that I envisioned when this program was in its early phases, and they've done their jobs without a single media leak or tell-all memoir to show for it."

Then he leaned even closer to her, his face darkening as he concluded, "I suggested *and approved* the formation of a second Project Longwing team specifically because of how many times we nearly lost the first. We didn't inform one team about the other for precisely this scenario. No one expected this to run forever without casualties, and I'm not going to tuck tail and run just because we got a little blood on our hands. I don't expect you to, either."

Chen's interactions with Senator Gossweiler had been limited prior to this, and provided no grounding as to whether he was always this ruthless. Maybe, she considered, his motivations were tempered by the fact that Weisz had orchestrated the kidnapping of his daughter. If it had been one of Chen's kids, her judgment would have been clouded to the point of oblivion. In the end, however, she concluded that Gossweiler's daughter wasn't the driving force behind his total resolution.

Instead, it was Erik Weisz.

And what choice did she have? His withering gaze made it clear enough that to resist would have been to get fired and replaced by someone else, and very possibly someone worse for the job than herself.

Then he removed all doubt.

"We're burning daylight, Meiling. One of us is going to make that call. And if I have to do it, the last order you gave to Rivers will be the last order you ever give."

She lifted her hand mic and transmitted, "Suicide Actual, this is Raptor Nine One."

David replied at once.

"*Raptor Nine One, this is Suicide Actual. Go ahead.*"

She delivered her message with crisp authority out of Gossweiler's presence far more than any sense of conviction.

"Be advised, we've lost fidelity on Weisz's current location. A late-breaking intel hit doesn't help with that, but it does provide his location as of approximately 0545 local time tomorrow morning, and again sometime between zero seven hundred and zero eight hundred the following day."

"*Copy,*" he said, "*send it.*"

Chen responded with a grid coordinate that she read off her computer monitor. He repeated the numbers back to her and she confirmed, and in the time it took for him or Ian to plot the location, David asked, "*Why the 24-hour delay between those two time windows?*"

"Based on the location," she said breezily, "we assess that Weisz will be taken to meet with senior leadership at an unspecified location to the northeast—a one-way mountain road, I'm afraid, and quite inaccessible. That means you need to have eyes-on that known location by zero five hundred tomorrow, positively identify his vehicle, and orchestrate a kill or capture mission somewhere along the only road he has available to make his return trip."

Now there was a pause, and a considerable one at that. If there was any possibility David had typed in the wrong grid, it was removed by his hesitation now.

At last he transmitted, "*I'm hoping we got this wrong, but the grid you provided is in Zughaynah.*"

"Correct," Chen supplied.

"*Which is in the biggest swath of Al Qaeda-owned ground in Yemen.*"

"That is my understanding, yes. I said from the beginning that as far as the intelligence available to us is concerned, his travel itinerary is fluid."

"*Yeah,*" David shot back, now unable to control himself, "*fluid within Houthi areas. But AQAP-controlled territory may as well be its own separate country—Baterfi has no freedom of movement to get in, much less operate there.*"

What could she say to that? Not much, particularly considering Senator Gossweiler was hovering over her.

She sided with brevity and responded, "Your job is to generate solutions. Generate them."

"*Let's think about this,*" David said, almost stammering now. "*The last hit on Weisz was in the vicinity of Al Hatarish, which is firmly in Houthi control. Al Qaeda's strongholds are all landlocked, so he's got no way out of Yemen unless he crosses into Houthi or government-held territory. Since there's exactly one road that crosses the lines into Zughaynah, our odds of success go up exponentially if we hit him either before he makes it into Al Qaeda's backyard or after he leaves it.*"

Ground teams, Chen thought, usually assumed their Agency headquarters to be an omnipotent deity with access to any and all possible information that could mitigate their tactical risk; such was very rarely the case, and never less so than now.

She presented the unfortunate reality with the most compassion she could manage under the circumstances.

"I do not have his route information, and even if I did, there's no vehicle description to go off. He's not leaving a digital signature, and our best information is coming from peripheral communications intercepts among the local groups anticipating his arrival. At present that consists solely of the time and location I specified, which means you must proceed in the manner I described: positively identify his vehicle in the morning, then use that vector to capture him when he returns the following day."

Another pause, this one almost as long as the first.

Then David responded with a single word, his tone more suited for the words "fuck you" than what he actually said.

"*Stand by,*" he concluded, and then the radio link went silent.

22

Cancer used a hand to intercept the mic on its way to my mouth, halting my imminent and emotional transmission with harshly spoken words.

"If her operations staff had a viable solution, we'd be hearing it by now. They probably advised her against having us pursue Weisz into Al Qaeda-ville, and she's ordering it anyway. That means we're gonna have to turn chicken shit into chicken salad, so focus."

"Concur," Ian said, spinning the laptop back toward him to analyze the terrain.

"Stand by," I transmitted, throwing the mic down and lifting my local cell phone to summon Baterfi with a text.

The three of us were seated at the shabby table we'd turned into a planning desk in a second-story room of the temple, and I tried to collect my thoughts amid the reality that the very sound of Chen's voice now caused a pang of revulsion in my stomach.

I had no issues being lied to for the sake of compartmentalizing intelligence; as far as the Agency was concerned, our operations involved an extremely high risk of capture. Munoz's team had already found that out the hard way.

But I couldn't overlook the fact that Chen made the same gamble with the lives of my men immediately afterward. Taken in conjunction with

Munoz's insight into her character—namely, that she had a reputation for getting people killed—I imagined that Chen had somehow painted her career into a corner by way of blood, and thus had no further incentive to mitigate risk.

Her goal, as ours, was to kill or capture Erik Weisz. The difference was a matter of consequences: for her, failure would mean a resignation letter. For us, failure consisted of a supremely horrific death in Yemen, and I'd gladly buffer my team against that fate using all my hard-earned skills in lying to authority figures.

Besides, I thought, my return transmissions had left quite a lot unsaid: that we knew about the other team and had recovered Munoz, and that perhaps she'd like to consider having us look into the small matter of four captured Americans.

I cut my gaze toward Cancer, who was busy chewing his left thumbnail, a mannerism I'd never seen before. Not good.

Ian spoke quickly, his eyes focused on the laptop screen.

"The route is close to six hours, and since we can't drive in, we'd have to leave here within the next hour, do a vehicle drop-off on the outskirts of Houthi territory around nightfall, then walk through the hills until sunrise to set up an observation point on the high ground. Even then we'd only have a chance of making it into position by the following morning, and assuming all that worked out, three of our guys are off chasing intel, which puts them out of the running to make the trip at all."

I offered, "We can't do the hit tomorrow morning anyway. All we need is to get eyes-on Weisz's vehicle for positive identification. Cancer and I can do that by ourselves while the rest of the team moves into position for a kill or capture mission the following day."

"Assuming," Cancer said, leaning forward and placing a closed fist on the table, "that we don't get compromised. But even if I could range a sniper shot from the nearest high ground—which I can't—we'd never make it out, much less have a chance of capturing him alive. Then we have to consider how we're going to get the rest of our team in. Pulling off a hit in Al Qaeda's backyard is going to require all of us plus Munoz, and since we don't have birds, we're sure as shit going to need a vehicle exfil."

Ian asked, "Then how are we supposed to conduct the actual mission—"

He went silent as Baterfi appeared in record time, his eyes darting with reptilian alertness that could only be a result of the wad of khat in his cheek.

"Yes?" Baterfi asked.

I turned to face him.

"You said you can take us anywhere but AQAP territory."

"Almost anywhere, yes."

Ian turned the laptop to face him, then pointed to Zughaynah as I continued, "Who can do better? How can we get a vehicle big enough for six, seven guys across Houthi lines and into Al Qaeda ground, then back again?"

Baterfi leaned down to analyze the laptop, nose wrinkling at the sight.

"Without dying?" he asked.

Ian blinked, assuming the question was rhetorical.

When Baterfi's eyes instead ticked to mine without a response, I snapped, "Yes, fucker! Preferably without dying."

A grin crept across the militia leader's face, the expression looking ghoulish against his bulging cheek—a sure indication that whatever he was about to say would cost us money, and a lot of it. Then he cocked his head to the side and thoughtfully quipped, "There is only one way."

23

Reilly saw Worthy halt just inside the doorway of the chicken shed.

It was an exceedingly rare moment of hesitation for the man, and Reilly almost reversed course while drawing his concealed Glock. But then Worthy proceeded inside, slowing his pace to a gradual crawl and swinging his gaze from left to right to indicate the spread of possible opponents within.

Then Reilly saw them too; he entered the building's shadows to make out a loose array of six men with automatic weapons. They were standing casually, none taking aim, nor did they need to; if they'd intended to capture the three Americans alive, he suspected, they would have waited before revealing their presence.

Instead the skirmish line was intended to defend their master, a man reported to be far older than anyone now visible.

The Yemeni who led them inside explained, "These men will watch your car until you return. Come, come."

He walked toward a far corner, an apparent dead end that Worthy nonetheless followed him to.

As far as spycraft went, an abandoned poultry facility wasn't the most glamorous of source meeting locations.

It did, however, appear to be an effective one.

Reilly could tell by the thick dust in the air that this site hadn't seen human presence in weeks or months. Under other circumstances it could have easily served as an emergency safehouse; of all the places in Yemen that were unlikely to be occupied during the current crisis, a food production plant had to be at the top of the list.

He glanced over his shoulder to see Munoz entering, followed by Ghazi, and by the time he looked forward, their guide was kneeling to fling open a hatch in the floor.

The man lowered himself inside and disappeared, followed in short order by Worthy, who surely intended to use him as a human shield if a trap lay below. By the time Reilly closed the distance, he saw a flimsy metal staircase descending to a basement chamber.

He maintained a decent interval from Worthy, prepared to draw his pistol at the slightest disturbance and hearing the stairs groan under his weight as he descended into a room with no exits. The space was lit by propane lanterns that illuminated four gunmen at the far corners, each armed with a rifle and situated as bodyguards to protect two central figures.

The first was seated, and Reilly ascertained at a glance that this was their source.

His appearance matched everything Baterfi had said: he was immeasurably old, leathery face creased with a lifetime spent in a poverty-ridden desert, and his expression seemed to indicate he'd weathered every storm of the past seven or eight decades in Yemen, and would likewise come out of the current civil war unscathed. Whenever this guy dropped dead, Reilly intuitively sensed, it would be the result of natural causes.

Omar Moftah's survival was due in large part to the profession he'd forced amid endless political instability. In a shattered nation where allegiances and armed groups came and went like shifting sand, he'd wisely made a name for himself in buying and selling information, and maintaining connections everywhere to keep himself informed of developments that could result in a payday.

And his next payday had just arrived in the form of three Americans.

Reilly was more caught off guard by his assistant, a woman in a loose-fitting silk thawb dress with her face concealed by an embroidered shawl wrapped around her head and shoulders. Judging by her eyes, she was in her twenties at most.

Worthy came to a stop before Moftah, standing a respectful distance away as Reilly took up a position to the pointman's left. Munoz stood on the opposite side, leaving Ghazi to approach and mutter a greeting in Arabic.

Then Worthy began, "*As-salamu alaykum*. Thank you for meeting with us."

"*Al Arabia*," the woman said quietly.

Ghazi translated the English portion of Worthy's introduction, though it was impossible to tell if Moftah understood; he said nothing, eyes cold and dispassionate.

Despite the lack of spoken word, Ghazi nonetheless translated the man's response.

"The money."

Reilly slowly reached inside his jacket pocket to remove four stacks of bills and passed them to the young woman, who began counting them in silence.

Finally she muttered a word in Arabic, after which the old man spoke at last. His voice was raspy but clear, coming in short bursts to allow Ghazi time to convert the message to English.

"You come seeking the foreigners...there are four. None have yet spoken...nor have they needed to. All have been beaten," Ghazi translated, quickly adding, "but not badly. The Houthi high command are seeking customers."

A pause, and then Moftah cleared his throat loudly before continuing.

"Whoever will pay the most...but if the price is not to their liking —*madha?*"

Moftah repeated himself, and Ghazi went on, "If the price is no good, they will begin to question the men for information, in order that they may sell that information. The Houthis will not begin questioning the men until they cannot sell them...they will not, because their interrogators question until the prisoners are dead."

Munoz visibly stiffened at this last sentence, though he said nothing— no small level of restraint, Reilly considered. He wondered if he'd be so disciplined if Worthy, David, Ian, and Cancer were in Houthi custody and he was the lone representative begging a sister team to facilitate their return.

Worthy asked, "How long until the questioning begins?"

Once Ghazi translated, Moftah nodded and replied, "Those seeking to buy the prisoners have five days to provide their offers."

"And how much do the Houthis want in exchange for all four men?"

Reilly held his breath without realizing it. In the best of circumstances, they could simply buy the men's freedom as they had with Munoz. Providing funds to a fanatical group was reprehensible, sure, but if his own government had inadvertently sent seven billion dollars' worth of military hardware into the open arms of the Taliban, then his team could surely live with a far lesser transgression to save a sister team.

But he already knew that wouldn't be the case; however much they could divert from their operational funds, Erik Weisz would provide far more.

"Six million US," came the translated response, and once Moftah spoke again, Ghazi said, "Any less than this, and the information becomes more valuable."

And that sealed it, Reilly thought as he released his breath. They couldn't begin to beg, borrow, or steal a fraction of that amount, much less afford to pay it outright.

Worthy asked, "Where are they being held?"

No translation required for this next bit.

"Sana'a," Moftah replied.

That was yet another unfortunate development, Reilly thought.

The capital city was an ironclad stronghold for the Houthis, and while the team could certainly slip in amidst the population, any tactical action would occur while surrounded by thousands of die-hard fighters and local supporters.

Omar Moftah produced a folded piece of paper and held it out to Worthy, who accepted the offering and opened it.

Reilly stepped closer to see a map of Sana'a, annotated in Arabic and marked with a single red dot. He momentarily wondered why Moftah would give them this information—it seemed obvious enough that the three Americans were present off the books, and that the US wouldn't be paying up to save the prisoners. Or maybe Moftah simply thought Reilly's team was an advance element for a future hostage rescue, and a bigger payday awaited him further down the line.

Ghazi continued translating, "Most political captives are sent to Sana'a Central Prison. But when the Houthis want to hide inmates from Western intelligence, they send them here, to *Funduq 'Aswad*—the Black Hotel. There, the prisoners vanish. Only Houthi guards and interrogators are allowed in. Iron gates, guard towers, dozens of sentries. I cannot tell you more than this, because to linger outside is to be arrested."

The revelation of a Houthi black site explained why the captured Americans weren't being paraded down the streets of Sana'a as evidence of a military conquest. The Houthis already owned a third of Yemen and had precious little need for more propaganda; to them, the prospect of revenue and/or intelligence was where the real value was.

The fact that the black site was within the capital city, however, was nothing short of a sucker punch from the universe. If this man's information was accurate, the four Americans were being held a scant 15 or 20 minutes up the road, yet by virtue of Houthi presence, they may as well have been on the moon.

And even if Reilly's team was united in taking on the suicidal risk such a rescue would require, it didn't help that the enemy response would likely include the MRAPs at the depot they'd spotted on the way in.

Worthy must have been thinking the same thing, because he asked, "We passed a motor pool for armored vehicles on the way here. Can you tell me anything about it? Where did they come from? Do the trucks work?"

As Ghazi relayed the inquiry, Moftah's female assistant checked her watch again and spoke quietly in Arabic.

"This will be the final question," Ghazi said, and once Moftah rattled off a particularly impatient response, he continued, "America sells these trucks to UAE, to Saudi Arabia. Both countries give them to the militias they support. Some are captured, some are abandoned, some are sold to the Houthis in *alsuwq alsawda*—not the arms bazaar, but the, the..."

"Black market," Worthy said. "I get it."

The woman spoke next, and Ghazi translated, "This concludes the meeting. For his security, we are to remain here until he is gone. They have people watching on the outside. Ten minutes, and then we may leave."

Worthy gave a deferential nod. "We understand, and will wait according to the instructions. Thank you for meeting with us."

It was a courteous attempt to set the stage for a future meeting, though Reilly suspected that wouldn't happen. Moftah seemed particularly irritated as he struggled to his feet without assistance, then shuffled past the Americans and toward the stairs without so much as a sidelong glance in their direction.

His female assistant followed for a moment, then approached Reilly and leaned in to whisper in perfect English.

"Omar could have received far more money for betraying you—he is helping because he hates the Houthis down to his bones. The man who brought you here may not show the same level of discretion, and now he knows how much you are worth. So too will his friends, because the militiamen have long tongues. Be careful who you trust in this place, you understand?"

Reilly nodded and she stepped back, ordering the remaining gunmen to follow with a flick of her wrist and moving toward the stairs in pursuit of Omar Moftah. Soon the entire strange procession vanished from view.

Ghazi broke the silence with a chortling laugh as he approached Reilly and delivered a swift elbow to the medic's ribs.

"That woman was fine, no? Very fine. Tell me, what did she say to you?"

24

Cancer watched Baterfi closely, considering the militia leader's proposed solution to getting a vehicle into and out of Al Qaeda territory. It was, he thought, a somewhat elegant loophole in the otherwise rabid security posture among the competing groups within Yemen.

David seemed convinced from the outset.

"Yeah," the team leader mused aloud, "that just might work."

Baterfi was quick to amend his statement, however.

"I must warn you: there is only one road to this area, and vehicles must pass through a checkpoint to be searched."

Cancer replied, "Using the way you described, our guys can withstand a search on the way in. The real question is, does Al Qaeda search vehicles on their way out?"

Baterfi recoiled. "Why would they?"

Then, and only then, did Cancer snatch the laptop while giving David a nod of agreement.

The team leader said, "We need a car and a driver to drop off two of us near Adh Dhimrah, leaving as soon as possible."

Cancer remained peripherally aware of the unfolding dialogue, making sure that David was checking all the right boxes. Beyond that, however, he was scanning the route that Eric Weisz would be traveling between Zughaynah and the hinterlands of an Al Qaeda mountain stronghold they couldn't possibly hope to penetrate in the short time available.

"This is not a problem," Baterfi replied. "You may leave now, if you wish."

David continued, "The rest of the team needs to move as soon as they return, and I want you to travel with them. Along with additional security vehicles in case they run into trouble on the way."

"Again, not a problem. But for the truck that will take you to Al Qaeda's territory, to Zughaynah, it will be very expensive. Not just for the danger, but also because of—"

"We can pay," David cut him off. "Find out how much and my men will take care of it, within reason."

Cancer was busy scanning the route, looking for a suitable ambush point and finding a dearth of good options in terrain that ranged from open desert to dried-out riverbeds before gradually rising toward mountain plains to the east. Meiling Chen seemed blissfully unaware of the fact that no one knew what vehicle Weisz would be moving in, or what his security would consist of.

But to Cancer, it was obvious that Al Qaeda would view Weisz as a VIP financier, and in their ideological fervor, they would be far more protective of their organizational funding than their own lives.

That meant the presence of one or more trucks filled with gun-toting and trigger-happy extremists, and such odds were insurmountable without an array of rockets and launchers that had simply been too heavy for the team to carry into Yemen in addition to the gear required for an open-ended mission. Nor were locally procured rocket launchers an acceptable solution—in taking out a moving convoy, they couldn't rely on the split-second functionality of any weapon that had been floating around the desert for years.

The only solution, he thought as he located a single spot on the road that might solve all his team's problems, was to approach this the same way that resistance fighters had from Afghanistan to Syria, inflicting carnage upon numerically superior and better equipped forces.

To pull this off, Cancer's team would have to become the insurgents.

"There's one more thing," Cancer said abruptly, silencing a conversation between David and Baterfi that he'd drowned out in its entirety.

Both men looked at him, and Cancer fixed his gaze on the militia leader before continuing with grave emphasis in his voice.

"We're going to need building supplies. Wood planks, two-by-fours if you can get them, plus hammers and nails."

"Of course."

"And explosives," Cancer continued. "Lots and lots of explosives. Is that going to be a problem?"

Baterfi laughed.

"Have you forgotten where you are, my friend? The biggest arms bazaar in Yemen is an hour away. I can get you anti-aircraft guns, if you have the money."

Ian looked suddenly uncomfortable, and for good reason—the intelligence operative would be the only one left to receive the delivery. With half the team plus Munoz gallivanting around Bayt al Hadrami in search of intel and the other half about to depart toward Al Qaeda's biggest stronghold in the region, the poor bastard was about to be the lone American remaining at Baterfi's hideout.

But Ian composed himself and said to Baterfi, "Find out the price per kilo and maximum quantity for every type of demolition you can access within the next four hours, and I'll tell you what we need."

"I will make some calls," the militia leader responded. Without further request for clarification, he left the room.

David looked over and said, "You've got it?"

"Yeah," Cancer responded, knowing full well the team leader was inquiring about a viable ambush position, and that if any reasonable alternatives existed, he'd have been consulted at some point in the process. "I've got it. Ian, you've got sixty seconds to tell me and David what we need to know before going in."

Ian pressed the heels of both palms against his eyes as he replied.

"The area is bordered by Houthis to the west, and the UAE-backed Southern Transitional Council on every other side. The fact that it's been unassailable by both groups speaks to its geographic inaccessibility, as well as the skill of its fighters."

"How skilled?" Cancer asked warily.

Ian set his hands on the table.

"I'll put it to you like this—the opposition has an endless supply of people and foreign resources, so they don't have to be good. But no one's supporting AQAP except themselves, and to hold ground against God and everyone means they're highly trained and supremely motivated. You can expect a mix of local tribesmen and foreign fighters in their ranks."

David asked, "What does Weisz want with them?"

"Well," Ian mused, "AQAP has managed to pull off the USS *Cole* bombing, the Khobar Massacre, assorted kidnappings and domestic attacks, and captured the city of Mukalla and its central bank to the tune of 120 million dollars. Their number one goal right now is orchestrating international attacks, and it's a safe bet that Weisz is trying to help them any way he can. What surprises me is that he's playing them and the Houthis, even though both sides are fighting each other and—"

"Fine," Cancer cut him off, "we can worry about the rest later. David, you better update our judge, jury, and executioner at the Agency—we've got to get moving."

25

"Take a right up here," Worthy said, "straight for half a kilometer, and then we're two turns out from the highway."

"Okay," Ghazi confirmed, steering the Toyota around the bend to reveal Bayt al Hadrami, which looked largely as it had on the way in: plenty of civilians, children included, normal traffic flow, and no bloodthirsty Houthi fighters prowling the crowd.

Reilly commented from the backseat, "Looks good."

"Yeah," Munoz agreed, "it does."

Gone was the joking banter that had characterized the westward route to reach their source meeting; it would resume, Worthy presumed, once they reached the main thoroughfare of Jihanah Road.

Or perhaps not, given the MRAPs they'd seen on the way in and soon would again.

He produced his local cell phone, preparing to update the rest of his team in Sirwah that they were on their way back. They were probably counting the minutes since Worthy's last status report, waiting with baited breath to find out how well or ill-fated the unauthorized side mission had turned out.

Until a few moments ago, the outcome was a mystery even to the men in the car with him right now.

As they waited for Moftah to depart the poultry farm, Worthy had mapped out a range of possibilities in the event they emerged above ground only to discover their vehicle—and two team weapons—missing and gone for good. Stealing a car wouldn't be a problem, but making a two-hour return trip before anyone noticed and reported the theft and/or carjacking would be problematic to say the least.

But they'd made it out of the chicken shed to discover their rusty Toyota Camry parked as it had been, all rifles accounted for, and Worthy had spotted an SUV peeling away at the sight of them: the final spotters, ensuring that no one tried to steal their car or its contents. Omar Moftah had promised a secure transaction, and he'd delivered.

At least, Worthy thought, if his information was true at all.

Assuming that was the case, the map now folded in Worthy's pocket served as a damning confirmation of the team's inability to influence the status of their four imprisoned counterparts; if there was any scenario where rescue was impossible, it was a heavily defended prison within the Houthi stronghold of Sana'a.

Still, he felt infinitely better now that they were in motion and blending in with civilian traffic. They'd successfully retrieved the designated intelligence and could worry about its validity, much less what to do with it, once safely back at Baterfi's hideout.

Brushing the thought aside, Worthy dialed and brought the cheap local phone to his ear.

He got concerned in a hurry when three rings elapsed without an answer, but the call finally connected, and a man spoke.

"*Salun hilaqa.*"

After allowing himself a relieved breath, Worthy replied, "Source meeting complete, we're en route back to base now. Four minutes from the highway."

The man transitioned to English then, which served as Worthy's first indication that he wasn't speaking to David, but Ian.

"How was the meet?"

The list of obligations that would prevent David from personally handling communications for a split team element in harm's way was

exceedingly short—an urgent consultation with Baterfi or taking a piss—
and Worthy hoped it was the latter as he sent his traffic.

"Moftah gave us the spot and what he knew of the defenses, and said
we've got five days before the prisoners are tortured to death. The only
question is whether he was lying."

"Well, was he?"

Ian would analyze the finer points of the new information in due time,
but for now, the intelligence operative was seeking the base instinct of the
man who'd stood eyeball-to-eyeball with a source that he would never
meet. To that end, Worthy responded with near-total conviction.

"No," he said. "No, I don't think he was."

"I'm prepared to copy. Relay everything he told you, starting with the
location."

He was in the process of retrieving the map when Ghazi emitted an
audible gasp. Worthy glanced up to see a Y-intersection seventy meters
ahead where a Hilux pickup was screeching to a halt to partially block the
road. A standing fighter in the back was casually orienting a pintle-
mounted MG 3 machinegun at the incoming traffic that was now braking to
avoid a chain reaction of rear-end collisions.

Reilly called out from the backseat, "We're boxed in."

Worthy spun to see a sedan halting behind them, stopping just short of
their rear bumper as a car to its rear did the same.

He whipped his head forward to find that four now-stationary vehicles
stood between his team and the armed pickup. A pair of men in fatigues
and head wraps leapt out of the latter and approached the nearest driver
while brandishing Kalashnikovs; they were unquestionably Houthi fighters, which left Worthy to search for indications that his split team was
compromised and that this was a deliberate attempt to stop their vehicle.

But the civilians on either side of the street continued strolling as if this
was the most normal thing in the world, making no effort to depart the area
or even alter course. Of course, he thought; if this was a targeted interdic-
tion, the Houthis would be dedicating armored vehicles, not a run-of-the-
mill pickup with a single belt-fed weapon.

The sight before him was just a routine shakedown for bribes of money, khat, and cigarettes that probably occurred a dozen times each day across the hundreds of towns and villages under Houthi control. This was a case of being at the wrong place at the wrong time, and perhaps fatally so: there was no way to reverse out of the situation, and no side streets where they could attempt a detour.

"Stand by," he said to Ian, "we've got a checkpoint."

Then he looked to his left and asked, "Can you bribe them?"

Ghazi was visibly pale.

"We are dead."

"It's going to be kinetic," Worthy said into the phone. "Need you guys to launch on support for emergency pickup—"

Ian cut him off.

"Negative, negative, no team support. I can send one of Baterfi's drivers for a vehicle swap once you make it past, but that's it."

"Do it," Worthy replied, ending the call and considering the only two options left to him.

Ideally he could dismount with Reilly and Munoz, then conduct a circuitous walking route through the town and link up with their driver after he'd passed the checkpoint alone.

But Ghazi had just heard the asking price for captured Americans straight from Moftah himself, and would probably eagerly arrange their capture when he reached the Houthi fighters ahead. The only way to motivate him otherwise was to keep an armed team member in the car with him, and besides, Worthy thought, no way would his team medic make it through the side streets of Bayt al Hadrami unnoticed.

He turned to face the backseat and issued his orders.

"We're on our own. Doc, you're staying in the car. Munoz, you and I are going to dismount and work our way through the crowd on foot. Once compromise is imminent for us or the vehicle, we drop the Houthis and get back in so we can haul ass back home."

"Got it," Munoz said eagerly, pulling his shemagh scarf over his mouth.

Reilly, however, was considerably more upset about the proposed arrangement.

"Why do I have to stay in the car?"

Worthy's anger flared then, and he felt his pulse surge as he stated the obvious.

"Because you're a foot taller than any man on the sidewalk, and we need someone to shoot Ghazi if he doesn't follow instructions."

"Oh." Reilly slumped down in his seat with the sudden acceptance that the average male in their current surroundings was five-foot-three. "Yeah, I guess that makes sense."

Before he turned back around, Worthy's gaze lingered on Munoz.

"I don't know how good your shooting is, but it's not better than mine. Trail a few meters back and follow my lead."

"Done."

Worthy turned back around and donned the sling of his suppressed Galil, its collapsible buttstock already at its shortest position in anticipation of Worthy firing from inside the vehicle. Once on foot, the only means of concealing their rifles, albeit temporarily, came in the form of long shawls draped over their shoulders, and Worthy hurriedly arranged his over the weapon as best he could.

He inserted his radio earpieces beneath the cloth swaddled over his scalp while conducting a final assessment of the scene before him—the two Houthis were speaking to the lead civilian driver, their weapons now hanging on slings. They were clearly strangers to a sudden threat to their otherwise unquestionable dominion over the populace here. The machine gunner in the back of the pickup was far more vigilant, however, watching the shakedown closely but paying no mind to the cars at the end of the row.

"Go," Worthy said, opening the passenger door and stepping out nonchalantly.

He eased his door shut and Ghazi rolled the Toyota forward, indicating that the lead car had cleared the checkpoint. With only three more vehicles to go before the Houthis discovered a giant white man in the Camry's back-seat, Worthy would have to accelerate his approach.

Munoz fell in behind him as Worthy crossed the street between vehicles, then slipped into the flow of pedestrians moving north between shops. Along with the blasts of car horns throughout the town he heard scattered conversations in Arabic, and fully expected someone to shriek in alarm at the sight of two men proceeding along the street with barely hidden weapons; but whether or not anyone noticed remained a mystery he didn't care to pursue.

Instead, he ensured the Houthis weren't fixated on him as he drifted to the left, closer to the storefronts, knowing he had to get visibility around the blind corner of the Y-intersection ahead and hoping he'd somehow have time to do so before the men at the checkpoint became alerted to the danger bearing down on them.

Whatever was around that corner instinctively concerned Worthy to an abnormal degree, though he didn't realize why for another second—the machine gunner atop the pickup was fixated exclusively on the nearest vehicle at the checkpoint, giving not so much as a curious periodic glance to the side street.

"There's more bad guys around the corner to the left," he transmitted. "Doc, once this goes down, I need you to get a field of fire down that street and hold it while me and Bulldog load up. We'll egress to the north."

"*Copy*," Reilly answered.

Worthy left unsaid the obvious problem: the number and armament of the yet-unseen "bad guys" would cast a very definitive vote on if and how the egress itself would occur. But the die had been cast, and now all that remained was a fluid unfolding of events that would end with the deaths of one side or the other.

The next vehicle accelerated clear of the checkpoint, leaving two more between Ghazi's Toyota and the armed fighters now twenty meters ahead. Worthy quickly mapped out the engagement in his head before glancing back at Munoz, confirming he was a couple meters back and one to the right—that much was all well and good, though his performance in the upcoming engagement represented a grave concern.

Fighting men developed a certain chemistry with one another after going into battle, and at this point in their working relationship Worthy could intuit Reilly's responses in a gunfight almost before they occurred.

By contrast, Munoz was an unknown quantity; certainly he had enough military experience to hold his own, and was no coward. But negotiating an enemy checkpoint before they'd so much as shared a training range together was a horrendous circumstance to test both assumptions.

Worthy fixated on the machine gunner in the back of the truck. The man was definitely locked and loaded, a belt of linked 7.62mm rounds stretching from the weapon's feed tray to a massive ammo can welded onto the rotating mount. He'd be the first to go, if all went according to plan; the dangers of a few men with rifles on street level were considerable, but nothing compared to a general-purpose machinegun with an elevated vantage point. The gunner could kill all four of them in a split second while turning their exfil vehicle into a smoking hulk, and do so well within the limits of a single protracted burst.

As if sensing that someone was watching him, the gunner diverted his gaze from the nearest car to the civilian foot traffic. Worthy was still ten meters distant, much farther than he'd hoped to be when he initiated the firefight, and he continued walking in the hopes of closing his range before the gunner locked eyes with him, a momentary expression of confusion crossing his face.

Worthy slipped his Galil from beneath the shawl, bringing it to a firing position at his shoulder as the gunner strove to return the favor, swinging the MG 3's enormous barrel sideways.

He'd barely initiated the effort, however, when Worthy opened fire; Yemen was short on professionally trained gunslingers with finely honed reflexes, and the gunner had surely never seen anyone take aim as quickly as the white man shooting at him now. And, Worthy noted with pleasure after seeing his first three subsonic rounds result in as many hits to the upper chest, he never would again.

The gunner dropped out of sight, his spasming body creating an enormous racket in the pickup bed.

One of the dismounted Houthis looked toward the truck, now a convenient distraction that allowed Worthy to open fire on his partner, who was turning to scan the civilians beside him.

Worthy shot two rounds, both impacting around the man's sternum, before transitioning left to the remaining opponent—his backside erupted with a quartet of bloody pockmarks from Munoz's suppressed AK-47, causing him to go rigid as Worthy switched back to his previous target to finish the fight.

Bizarrely, there was no reaction whatsoever from the civilians around them; this felt like a slow-motion dream where he and Munoz were engaged in combat amongst a civilian population wholly unaware that a gunfight was occurring at all.

Worthy's barrel found the man he'd shot twice; he was now slumped halfway against the car, gripping his AK-47 but unable to raise it as the pointman fired three more rounds. The dying fighter jolted, firing a single bullet that blew his own left foot apart before falling in a heap.

That first unsuppressed gunshot may as well have been an atomic bomb; the crowd fled in all directions amid a cacophony of shrieks and screams, sprinting in a widening orbit away from the sound.

Worthy broke into a run, making for the corner ahead to secure the westward-running leg of the Y-intersection amid the sounds of an engine revving and the repetitive crunch of metal on metal—Ghazi ramming the remaining civilian vehicles at Reilly's order, he was sure, in order to force their cars clear of the checkpoint for what would hopefully be a hasty exfil.

Worthy slowed as he approached the corner of the building ahead, preparing to use it for cover as he took aim down the street. Given that the crowd was evaporating, he could safely assume anyone not running away was an enemy combatant. As he knelt and pivoted around the corner, however, he saw that no shortage of figures met that criteria.

A scant block away was a Hilux pickup with a cab-mounted machinegun. It must have been a near-identical checkpoint, likewise stopping northbound traffic before the highway; and while Worthy couldn't make out how many dismounted fighters were present through the fleeing civilians, he rose to a standing position to get a clear angle on the only one who mattered right now.

In the time it took him to rise, his target panicked and opened fire, not at him but at the mass of pedestrians suddenly converging on the second checkpoint.

The machinegun roared to life with a sickening blast of automatic fire that shredded into the crowd, dropping a cluster of civilians in one momentous burst—the only shots the gunner would fire, as it turned out, because Worthy drilled him with subsonic rounds until he went sprawling sideways and out of the pickup bed.

Worthy faced a scene of total chaos: a group of civilians dead and wounded, the surviving pedestrians forming a panicked wall between him and whatever Houthi fighters were hidden beyond. Judging by the sound of scattered popshots, they were indiscriminately firing at imagined threats and continuing to kill innocent people in the process.

The pointman's reaction occurred without any conscious thought on his part, which was just as well, because if Worthy had time to think about it, the window of opportunity would have come and gone.

He scrambled away from the corner, rounding the initial pickup and clambering into the bed and over the body inside. It was a suicidal degree of exposure to incoming gunfire that he could overcome only by his next action: seizing the pistol grip of the MG 3 machinegun and wheeling the weapon clockwise on its pintle.

By some miracle, he wasn't shot in the time required to align the blade front sight with the second pickup. Worthy could make out four Houthis from his elevated vantage point, one of them in the process of putting the machinegun back into operation.

Worthy leaned his shoulder into the MG 3 buttstock while thumbing the cross-bolt safety to place the weapon in firing mode. Within a split second, his right index finger had settled across the trigger, which he pulled back with satisfying ease.

He braced for the recoil—the MG 3 was a NATO-caliber derivative of the WWII machinegun affectionately termed "Hitler's buzzsaw," a nod to the unholy chatter it made while dispensing bullets at the rate of 20 rounds *per second*. With that rate of fire, the enormous risk Worthy was undertaking would pay off when he vaporized the four Houthis and their truck until the ammo can went empty or he decided to call it quits.

But his trigger squeeze caused the bolt to slam forward without firing a round.

Worthy performed immediate remedial action with blinding speed, wrenching the charging handle rearward before slamming it forward to reset the bolt and attempting another trigger squeeze with identical results: a sharp metal *thud* that caused the weapon to momentarily tremble in his grip before going still.

The next step would have been to repeat the process and, instead of pulling the trigger a third time, open the feed tray cover before properly seating the belted ammunition into position. At this point, the procedure was a theoretical abstraction, because the enemy fighters had taken note of his position as indicated by the slew of weapons now shifting toward him, including the other machinegun.

Worthy released his grip and vaulted backward, his calves clipping the edge of the pickup bed and flinging him horizontal on his airborne descent before he fell clear of the truck. He had no idea how close the incoming gunfire came to shredding him apart from the bottom up, only that it wasn't entirely inaccurate. He had, it seemed, succeeded in preventing at least some additional civilian casualties, albeit only by presenting himself as a far more pressing target.

His impact with the street sent a crippling shudder of pain from his tail-bone to the base of his neck. Worthy wondered if he'd just become para-lyzed, finding he didn't only when the sight of Ghazi's Toyota Camry barreling toward his face presented sufficiently urgent motivation to test his mobility by rolling out of the way with six inches to spare.

Reilly braced himself as the Camry swerved right to avoid hitting Worthy. The medic winced in anticipation of feeling the tires thump over a human skull, but Ghazi's sudden evasive maneuver seemed to have the desired effect of avoiding the fallen American.

And while that was no small victory, Reilly had never seen an engage-ment go from textbook perfect to total disaster in such a brief flitter of time. One moment his teammates were drilling the fighters at the checkpoint without consequence, and the next there were incoming bursts of machinegun fire and Worthy was catapulting backward like Neo in *The Matrix*, falling almost directly into the Camry's path.

In between those events was the deliberate ramming of a civilian vehicle whose driver seemed frozen in terror; he'd sped off after a few strikes against his rear bumper, and now Reilly had to get into the fight.

He was sitting cross-legged on the Camry's backseat, having already rolled down the window and wrapped his left palm over the door frame, thumb serving as the notch of an impromptu shooting rest that supported the upper receiver of his HK417. It was the most stable firing position that a man of his size could manage inside the vehicle's cramped confines, and he was ready to lay down withering supporting fire to cover the exfil of his dismounted teammates—provided Ghazi could actually get him into position.

Instead the Camry soared clear past the side street as Ghazi overshot the Y-intersection entirely, and Reilly's view out the window was suddenly blocked by a sandy wall.

"Back up," he shouted, "fifteen feet."

Ghazi then reversed the Camry too far—the pickup truck was now directly in front of him, and to his left he saw Munoz helping Worthy off the ground a safe distance away. And while the pointman's head was intact, a pleasant surprise given that Reilly half expected it to be pancaked by the Camry, he was able to move only with assistance. It would take them time to round the sedan's passenger side, much less get in, which wouldn't do them any good if Reilly couldn't provide some fire support in the interim.

He yelled, "Forward, you fucker! Ten feet."

Ghazi exclaimed, "I do not know feet—"

"Three *meters*," Reilly shouted, "so I can see past the truck."

Ghazi's next driving maneuver finally succeeded in achieving Reilly's intended placement, though the sight took a moment for him to comprehend.

Civilians lay in a bloody mess down the block to his left, and anyone still standing was now parting like the Red Sea to either side of the road— great for Reilly's visibility down the street, but a mixed blessing when he saw *why* they were scrambling out of the way.

A Hilux pickup was speeding toward them, a mobile battering ram whose standing gunner explained the bursts of incoming machinegun fire Reilly had heard. The medic took aim and resisted the urge to fire reflexively, instead pumping three careful shots, at least one of which bowled over the man in the pickup bed.

Then he lowered his sights and accelerated his rate of fire, drilling a half dozen subsonic rounds at the driver in a feverish attempt to compensate for the wild diversion in bullet trajectories when they passed through auto glass. His only indication of a hit came when the pickup swerved slightly toward the passenger side, its engine noise quieting far too late to have much effect on its momentum. It crashed into the original checkpoint truck with enough force to send the front quarter panel skidding sideways into the Camry's rear bumper, lurching the car forward.

But he heard the door behind him being flung open, followed by a pained grunt from the backseat as the vehicle rocked with the weight of a new, clumsy occupant.

Reilly had no visibility to make additional shots, his view of the second pickup blocked entirely by the first. Placing his weapon on safe, he cradled it in his left elbow while using his right hand to retrieve a fragmentation grenade, then pulled the pin and kept the spoon compressed until he heard the passenger door slam and Munoz shout, "Go!"

Ghazi floored the gas pedal too quickly for the Toyota Camry to put down effective power, resulting in a slushy movement that took a moment to transition to forward acceleration. Once the sedan began to cover ground, Reilly gently hucked his grenade downward, aiming for a low angle that would bounce the projectile beneath the first pickup.

Then he resumed his two-handed grip on the HK417, leaning out the window to take aim at the checkpoint intersection, now receding as the Camry sped away. A pair of Houthi fighters darted into view, raising their rifles in an effort to open fire that was doomed from the start. Reilly shot at them anyway, though his marksmanship from the moving vehicle was far less effective than the grenade that detonated with its intended effect.

The pickup deflected the blast, which channeled the ensuing energy—and more importantly, shrapnel—in all directions at the height of a standing man's Achilles tendon. Both men were momentarily eclipsed by a low cloud of black smoke that they fell into, deaf and crippled for life, before the road curved and all Reilly could see were Bayt al Hadrami's buildings flashing by without a civilian in sight.

He ducked inside the vehicle and reloaded, seeing that Munoz was now riding shotgun.

Worthy was in the backseat, fumbling for his phone as he addressed Ghazi.

"Take the second right, then the next left. Go east on the highway—

we're going to have to get some distance, then ditch this vehicle and move on foot to an emergency linkup."

The first response didn't come from Ghazi, who appeared to have lost the power of speech; instead, Munoz spun around from the passenger seat.

"Man," he gasped, eyes darting across Reilly and Worthy to check them for injuries, "that felt *cathartic*."

26

Ian shielded his eyes from the sun to observe the Hyundai SUV as it entered the temple courtyard. The vehicle's black paint was covered in a layer of sand that turned it a dusky shade of brown, and he waved at the driver to come to a stop at his side.

He questioned the wisdom of that decision when the passenger door opened before the vehicle had come to a full stop, leaving Ian to wonder if he was about to get punched in the face by one or more of his own teammates.

But rather than leaping from the SUV and approaching at a run, Worthy instead exited with a pained slowness before limping toward Ian, a process that was drawn out enough to allow Reilly and Munoz to exit and fall in behind him. Only Munoz seemed to bear an expression of relative calm; the other two men looked angry in the extreme, and Reilly in particular had murder in his eyes.

For Ian, this represented the icing on a particularly bitter cake.

He was watching two team members plus Munoz return from an unsanctioned intelligence collection effort while two more embarked on a sanctioned but extremely ill-advised surveillance effort in a bad area nested within already prohibitive enemy lines.

Ian was the only connective tissue between two simultaneous split team operations; the hours and days ahead would be perilous even if everything went according to plan, and that was almost never the case. In his mind, it wasn't a question of whether something would go wrong, but how many things would and in what succession, and if his team could successfully react and adapt when the time came.

Because the time would indeed come, and probably sooner than later.

He gave a nod to Worthy and asked, "What happened to you?"

"Fell out of a truck," Worthy shot back angrily, coming to a stop. "And it didn't help that we had to hunker down in some backroad shithole for two hours hoping that Baterfi's guy would be able to find us."

Reilly eagerly added, "Yeah, so how about that support he asked for, asshole?"

Ian stared at them, unblinking.

"You guys done?"

Worthy shrugged. "I think so, yeah."

"Good," Ian said, "because I'm in charge of you guys, effective immediately. Worthy, you're second-in-command."

He extended a hand toward the Volkswagen Transporter van parked behind him. "Everyone's gear is already loaded. We're moving out. Baterfi will ride with us." He raised his eyebrows to convey the obvious: that as long as the militia leader was with them, his cell phones were in team possession until a call was needed, meaning he wasn't setting up a sabotage. Then Ian continued, "We've got two vehicles full of militiamen as our escort."

Munoz asked, "Where's David and Cancer?"

"They already left. Moving to set up a surveillance site in the AQAP-controlled region to our south. Weisz is going to be passing through early tomorrow morning, and once he does, the rest of us have less than 24 hours to be in position to hit him on his way back out."

Reilly marched toward the panel van, looking in the back as he called over his shoulder, "Why didn't you mention this when we were waiting for our driver?"

"Because if you guys got rolled," Ian said with a steady voice, "the last thing we needed is for anyone to know that a couple of our guys are tiptoeing into the badlands after dark. Load up, I'll explain everything once we get on the road."

"On the road?" Reilly asked, spinning around and jerking a thumb toward the van's contents, which, in addition to their rucksacks, included lumber and a trio of yellow palm oil containers that were, to any veteran of the Afghanistan and Iraq Wars, immediately identifiable as storage for ammonium nitrate powder. "How in the hell are we supposed to get all this plus ourselves into Al Qaeda territory on that kind of timeline?"

Ian glanced upward, noting a wispy cloudbank infringing on an otherwise azure sky.

Then he looked back to the medic and responded, "Believe me when I tell you, we're going to do it the only way we can."

27

The sun had descended to the horizon by the time Worthy finally climbed down from the Volkswagen van—a process that was, after a jarring four-hour ride south from Baterfi's hideout, murder on his aching back.

He was the last one out, setting foot on solid ground as Ian and Baterfi beelined to a waiting Yemeni extending his hand in greeting.

The rest of them stayed back, forming a loose trio and mindful to keep their rifles pointed down as they awaited guidance. Worthy noted that Baterfi's security men from the two escort vehicles were doing the same, but no one seemed to pay them any mind and Munoz gave a low, appreciative whistle.

"Did we die in a car crash on the way here? Because this must be heaven."

Worthy took in his surroundings, finding the sight before them jarring —compared to the war-torn wasteland they'd encountered so far, this was practically the Garden of Eden.

Hilltops of rock and sand surrounded him in all directions, but the vast swaths of low ground were packed with lush greenery, a sea of healthy plants ranging from low shrubs to trees reaching up to twice his standing height. Fields were subdivided by pristine stretches of barbed wire and dotted with stone towers where armed men stood watch over the fiefdom.

The guard posts, Worthy knew, weren't there to protect the crop from the military and militia forces that freely ravaged the rural, village, and city populations across Yemen; no one would dream of disrupting the operation here or at the countless identical facilities across the country, all of which were universally held sacrosanct by all parties involved in the ongoing conflict.

Instead, the only real danger to the crop here was from petty thieves.

Reilly's reaction was considerably less profound.

"So that's khat, huh?"

"Yeah," Worthy muttered. "That's khat."

He assessed their more immediate surroundings—an array of vehicles parked in the clearing between fields, the nearest being an Iveco box truck with its rolling door open to expose a cavernous interior.

Ian turned from his ongoing meeting with Baterfi and the other Yemeni man, pointing to the Iveco and giving a thumbs up.

Worthy turned back to Reilly and Munoz and said, "All right, that's our ride. I want you guys to complete a full vehicle inspection—gas, oil, tires, fluid, and leaks—and then we can start the modifications."

Both men moved out, neither looking particularly thrilled with their assignment. By all appearances, the Iveco box truck was a rust bucket no better than a vast majority of the vehicles rattling around Yemen, and the entire team now depended on its functionality for everything, including their own survival.

As they departed, Worthy approached Ian's meeting-in-progress, trying to conceal the pained limp in his step as he processed the scene around him. Pre-mission preparations had always included a lengthy brief delivered by Ian on the target nation's social, political, economic, religious, and military status. But receiving that information in the team's Stateside isolation facility was one thing.

Seeing it firsthand was quite another.

In terms of food, Yemen's problem wasn't simply a dearth of agriculturally viable land, although that had certainly gone downhill as a result of climate factors both natural and manmade; instead, it was the fact that virtually any arable regions were used to grow khat.

This problem was compounded exponentially by what Worthy saw in the distance: a pair of enormous water tank trucks parked end-to-end, apparently having recently returned from topping off at a distribution point. Men were clustered around both, using generators and hoses to fill a seemingly endless supply of yellow jugs that would be carried by hand to water an exceedingly thirsty crop.

There were only a handful of countries worldwide with a greater degree of water scarcity, and Yemen's solution had been to drain sources like the Sana'a basin at wildly unsustainable rates to provide for their khat supply. Nine out of every ten gallons of extracted freshwater was dedicated to agriculture, and close to half of that was reserved for khat alone. As rich landowners dug deeper to access an ever-reducing water table in order to fuel khat production, shallow village wells ran dry. And Yemen was forced to import drinking water in addition to food, heaping another two crises on top of the overarching political disaster.

Worthy continued approaching Ian as spikes of pain punctuated the dull ache in his back. As he stiffly walked, he considered that khat's great tragedy was that the entire population could quit without any withdrawal symptoms. It wasn't physically addictive in the slightest, in stark contrast to legal substances like tobacco and alcohol, much less Schedule I drugs like heroin, cocaine, and amphetamines. Khat was completely legal in several East African countries that had never seen anything close to epidemic use.

But the plant's potential for psychological dependence, however mild, elevated it to the status of sacred substance in nations where desolation and famine were the norm. In moral terms, the team's financial support of khat smugglers was as distasteful as paying cocaine traffickers to transport them across Colombia.

In tactical terms, however, the farm's distribution vehicles represented their one and only ticket to easily cross territory held by government, Houthi, and Al Qaeda forces. Each of the three battled the others to the death, but none were willing to infringe on the free trade in khat.

Worthy closed the remaining distance with Ian, who abruptly ended his conversation to provide an introduction.

"This is Sufyan Pamir, he runs the plantation."

Pamir extended his hand and Worthy shook it, assuming the man to be of roughly the same age, though long sun exposure made him look much older. He was attired in a headscarf and a blazer worn unbuttoned atop his thawb, and an ornamental belt and curved jambiya dagger were strapped across his chest. The dagger's sheath was covered in gems, conveying the immense wealth that his profession had imparted upon him.

"*Ahlan wa sahlan,*" Pamir said.

Worthy returned the greeting with the words, "*Ahlan bik.*"

Ian continued, "Pamir can get us in and out, but we have to buy the truck, plus the load of khat in its entirety."

Worthy frowned—Ian should have known the first topic that needed to be addressed.

He nodded respectfully so as not to undermine Ian's status as commander, then said, "All right. But we need a blowout plan."

Baterfi cocked his head in apparent confusion, unsure how to translate that request.

Ian supplied, "If the farm gets attacked, how can we get out?"

Nodding, Baterfi relayed the inquiry in Arabic. After Pamir pointed to a dirt road between crops and replied, he provided the English version.

"No one will attack a khat farm." Baterfi nodded toward the trail. "But this path leads to the farthest southern field, and there is a gate to the back road. From here, you may reach Owen Al-Down."

Worthy nodded in approval. "And we need at least one vehicle, big enough for all of us, plus a driver ready to move at a moment's notice."

Pamir threw up his hands at the translation, gesturing with palms turned skyward as Baterfi spoke.

"You own the truck now, and may do with it as you wish."

"Driver? *Sayiq?*"

Pamir's response seemed inordinately long for the question, and Baterfi translated.

"The driver is Raed, and his services come with the truck. In addition, I will provide one man with a single rifle—his name is Tariq. This is all we are permitted by Al Qaeda in the event of hijackers on the way to their territory."

"Excellent," Ian intervened, "I will need them waiting with the truck until we leave. Now we can discuss the transport."

As Baterfi spoke, Pamir's lips spread into a wide smile, teeth stained brown from chewing his own product.

Never mind that the entire country was starving and within a few decades of entirely depleting its supply of drinking water with no solution in sight—Pamir would transport the American team with the same dedication that he tended to his crops, and for the same reason.

Cash.

Ian continued, "When's your next scheduled delivery?"

Baterfi relayed the response and, from the sound of it, added his own commentary by way of explanation.

"There is no schedule. Khat leaves are only good so long as they are fresh: two days, maybe three. When a truck arrives with the harvest, it will sell the product anywhere it goes. Any buyers with access to the truck, you see, can split up the purchase and greatly profit from selling in smaller amounts."

The declaration shouldn't have surprised either American; the rules of wholesale versus retail pricing applied worldwide. Ian had said that the average Yemeni spent somewhere between one quarter to half their income on khat, and nothing that Worthy had seen seemed to contradict that statement.

But Pamir's smile faded before he spoke solemnly and Baterfi translated, "One small problem. Al Qaeda has a rule, even for khat smugglers: no one moves at night."

Worthy asked, "He can take us in the morning, then?"

"*Fi alsabah?*" Baterfi asked.

Pamir nodded. "*Na'am, la mushkila.*"

With that, Baterfi said, "Yes, morning. Morning no problem."

But by then Pamir was speaking once more, and the translation was considerably less optimistic.

"He says this is good, very good. Because if Al Qaeda catches anyone moving about at night..."

Pamir paused his speech to raise both hands, followed by discreetly pantomiming the action of firing a rifle on fully automatic.

Worthy nodded his understanding, and found his thoughts turning immediately to the fate of David and Cancer.

28

"Hurry up," Cancer transmitted over my earpiece. *"If we can't see the village from that high ground, we're fucked."*

I had mixed emotions at that moment in time, the least of which was that I was fatigued to the point of lightheadedness after a full night of pointman duties across terrain that was, to put it politely, rugged. On one hand, I *had* been hurrying, moving about as fast as my legs could go up the steep slope while still maintaining some shred of situational awareness, and the sniper's admonition seemed a pointless barb.

On the other hand, Cancer had many unenviable qualities but tended to use the term "we're fucked" only when it applied in the extreme.

In that latter case, I had to agree. There was no Plan B when it came to getting eyes-on the supposed presence of Erik Weisz; in two years of continual operations, we'd never had so much as a chance to accomplish what we stood to now. If we didn't get into position before the hard time stated by Chen, we couldn't see him—and if we couldn't see him, we couldn't plan the strike that could prevent years or decades of terrorist attacks.

The sum total of these realizations caused me to access some hidden surge of strength, and I picked up speed to an extent unimaginable at any point over the past eight and a half hours of our infiltration.

I ran uphill with no further regard to the possibility of land mines or IEDs; though to be fair, the view through my night vision was so glaringly bright that I probably would have spotted either without much effort.

What we battled now wasn't sunrise—still just over an hour distant—but BMNT, a military acronym for "begin morning nautical twilight," which was an elaborate term for that moment of early morning when it was just bright enough to actually see shit with the naked eye. Because while traipsing over the hills with night vision was all well and good, any advantage afforded by our technology and tactics went out the door the moment anyone with a set of binoculars could spot two white assholes in camouflage running around.

That moment was fast approaching, and while we'd covered a remarkable amount of ground without enemy contact, the possibility of that happening had slowed our effort to the brink of failure. The elevated terrain across the northern swath of Al Qaeda territory was dotted with bunkers carved out of the hillsides, each new vista requiring a complete halt, followed by an extensive scan with thermal optics, before we determined that no human presence was returning the favor.

Such counter-surveillance was time-consuming in the extreme, and the arrival of daylight would be complicated by the risk of overhead observation; to the best of our knowledge, AQAP didn't have any drones.

But as a courtesy bestowed by Iran, the Houthis had *lots* of drones of both the reconnaissance and attack varieties, the latter of which had been employed not just against their enemies in Yemen but in cross-border aerial warfare against oil facilities and civilian airports in Saudi Arabia and the UAE. It was a safe bet that by the time we heard a faint buzzing in the sky we'd already be compromised, and left to hope that the offending unmanned aerial vehicle was equipped with cameras rather than a warhead with 18 kilograms of explosives and ball bearings.

Added to this was the fact that Cancer and I were operating alone with no options for reinforcement or even exfil, and moving on foot through the hills and into Al Qaeda country was suicidal to say the least.

Therein, however, was the genius of our current plan, if we could call it a plan at all.

AQAP had a lengthy track record of being assaulted by Tier One forces to know that US shooters arrived by aircraft before completing a lengthy walk toward their objective. They had no reason to suspect that two dick-heads were making the journey far from any conceivable landing zone—Cancer and I had dismounted a vehicle in the backroads of Adh Dhimrah, just outside Al Qaeda jurisdiction—simply because any military unit capable of accomplishing the feat was far too sane to actually contemplate doing so.

Finally I made it up to the high ground, an achievement that came and went in seconds as I scrambled down the opposite side to avoid silhouetting myself against the early morning sky for any longer than absolutely required. Only after I'd made it a few meters downhill while scanning for immediate threats did I finally peer toward the horizon.

Dropping to a knee under the weight of my ruck, I took uneven breaths as I whispered, "Thank God."

Then I transmitted to Cancer, "We made it."

The ground before me descended to a saddle of low ground traversed by an arid riverbed and a paved road that ran parallel to it; between the two, a semicircle of low buildings was interlaced with dirt paths, the village of Zughaynah in all its modest glory.

Cancer must have been following close behind, because he jogged past me only seconds later, following a diagonal path to my left as I rose to follow him. Choosing a surveillance site was a skill he'd be far better at than I would, and at this point I was so physically and mentally exhausted that I'd have gladly followed him to a resting spot atop broken glass.

The saddle of ground he picked appeared only slightly better than that, sand interspersed with loose rock that formed jagged angles that would soon support our collective bodyweight.

He stripped his rucksack and I followed suit, lowering it gently to the ground before lying down to his right with just enough clearance for him to operate his sniper rifle, now abandoned on its bipod. He extracted a sheet of material from his pack and whipped it open before casting it over our new position.

I grabbed one end and secured it over my rucksack, then lay still for Cancer to do the same on the opposite side before crawling beneath the camouflage netting from behind. Once he was in position, we both hurried to make our final arrangements while we still had some semblance of darkness remaining—him by assuming a shooting position and testing his sector of fire by pivoting the sniper rifle left and right, and me by setting up my spotter scope.

After digging its tripod legs into the loose sand as deep and level as I could, I raised my night vision and put my eye to the optic, its laser rangefinder providing both a distance and grid reference to the target. It took a few attempts before I dialed in the exact location Chen provided, a flat patch of desert four hundred meters past the nearest building.

"3,200 meters," I said quietly.

"All right," Cancer replied. "Make sure you dig that tripod in."

But I'd already busied myself with panning my spotter scope left, aligning it with the nearest identifiable landmark in the form of an L-shaped structure from which I could make hasty adjustments as the situation unfolded. I reduced its magnification setting before taking my eye away from the scope, lowering my night vision, and scanning for movement in the village.

It was utterly still.

"Well," I said quietly, now almost bleary-eyed at the end of my adrenal reserves, "that sucked."

Cancer said nothing, which left my mind to register more immediate discomfort.

We would, unless compromised, have all day to subtly improve our fighting position by removing the rocks now digging into our bellies, and perhaps even employing the inflatable shooting mats we'd packed. For now, the camouflage netting would provide at least some degree of concealment.

It also, regrettably, had all the thermal efficiency of a wool blanket, retaining not only heat but the smell of our breath and Cancer's omnipresent cologne of cigarette smoke.

We remained quiet, still catching our breath as we sipped from the water hoses extending from our rucksacks. The ambient light soon rendered my night vision useless, and I removed my head mount before noticing that Cancer had already done so. For a moment I considered setting up my satellite antenna for a radio check and then decided against it

—there was nothing Chen or the rest of my team could do to help us now, and my attention was better spent observing the village as the sky brightened with the approach of dawn.

The silence remained for long minutes as we recovered our strength, and only then did my thoughts turn to whether Cancer would give me the cold shoulder all day. We'd certainly had our scrapes in the past, but the relationship between any ground force commander and his senior advisor was like a marriage—you had to patch things up eventually, because in both cases the phrase "until death do us part" held equal sway. Since we were now holed up well within Al Qaeda ground, the sentiment may well be put to the literal test.

I saw movement outside the village and tucked my face behind the spotter scope.

"Dogs," Cancer muttered. "Forget it."

By then I'd sighted the offending group, a pack of hounds loping from the buildings into the open desert.

"It's just dogs," I confirmed.

Everything went quiet again, though the silence between us had a noticeable tension until Cancer spoke.

"Nicotine?"

Was this a peace offering, I wondered, or just common courtesy?

Taking another sip of water, I replied, "I think I've already got a contact high from your kit. But yeah."

He deposited a white tab in my hand and I stuffed it between my gums and cheek, grateful that tobacco cessation products served equally well in the opposite capacity. After an all-night foot movement across steep terrain, I wanted nothing more than to drink some water and pass out, but with the alleged arrival of Erik Weisz fast approaching, I'd stay awake however I could.

Then, without preamble, Cancer said, "Winds are light and variable. I bet you I could elevate my point of aim and take the shot from here. If I miss, no one's going to notice a subsonic bullet in all the commotion."

I almost laughed, unsure if he was joking or actually considering the possibility.

"Hard no."

"What's the matter," he asked, "you don't trust my marksmanship?"

"Your accuracy is the least of my concerns. But you'd be lucky to lob a round that far with a Barrett, much less the M110. And you said it yourself —Weisz isn't dumb enough to stand around in the open. Besides, even if you miraculously tagged him we'd never make it out."

Cancer snickered. "I'd need all my fingers and toes *and yours* to count the number of times we shouldn't have been able to make it out and did anyway."

The statement was oddly off-brand for the sniper, who'd thus far been the voice of cold, hard logic whether I wanted to hear it or not.

I replied, "Making suicidal tactical plans is my area of expertise, not yours. And didn't you just bash my decision making in front of the team?"

"You said I could speak freely."

"Which you did, thank you very much. But that doesn't mean you should become a hypocrite, unless..."

I paused, feeling the tingle of the nicotine tab in my cheek along with a subsequent increase in alertness. Suddenly, I pieced together the animus behind the sniper's otherwise contradictory statements.

"Wait a minute," I said, glancing over with a rueful grin. "I think I know what this is about."

"It's 'about' accomplishing our mission, something that rescuing that other team has nothing to do with—"

"The case of beer," I interrupted, the words hanging heavy between us.

He remained silent, causing me to hold my breath—things were already awkward between us, and I may well have just exacerbated that tension to the breaking point.

When he replied, it was with a dismissive tone.

"Don't be an asshole."

And that did it.

I'd just hit an emotional touchpoint, and whenever that occurred with a member of my team, there was only one option for the remainder of the conversation—to push harder.

"It's my nature," I pursued. "But be honest, Cancer. Honest with me, honest with yourself. Everyone else has made a primary kill and gotten the case of beer award at the end of a mission."

"I haven't been keeping track," he said, the tension clear in his voice.

"Sure you have," I responded, "And you can't tell me there's not a part of you that chafes at being the one, the *only* one, who hasn't put one of our targets in the dirt."

"Who are you, Sigmund-fucking-Freud?"

"Right now I am, yeah. Even Ian got a kill…"

I let the sentence trail off, considering what had been bothering me.

Then I continued, "And while we're on the subject, I'm worried about him. Remember when he wasn't gangster at all? We used to make fun of Ian. Now he's the darkest guy here—present company excluded, of course."

"He's still a distant second to me," Cancer said defensively. "But yeah, I don't think he got into the intelligence game thinking this would be his career. You should be worried about Worthy and Reilly along with him, though, because we're all getting darker."

"Because we're so close to Weisz?"

"Partly. Mainly, though, it's because everyone's asking themselves whether this was worth it."

I pulled my eye from the spotter scope to look at him. "What's that supposed to mean? We have a chance to cut off the head of the snake, complete our real mission, to serve our country—"

"In exchange for what, exactly?" Cancer hadn't broken his focus through his sniper scope, and I continued my surveillance as he continued, "Think about it. Chen is lying to us, and ever since Munoz sang like a bird, everyone's seen the evidence of how easily men like us are left to twist in the wind by the same country they're serving."

"That's the job," I said.

"Hey man, you don't have to convince me. But consider who we're working for. Chen, Gossweiler, all those fucks who are more than willing to brainstorm counterterrorism. You think any of them are willing to grab a gun and head into the sandbox? They're not. Sure, they've got grand ideas all day, but if they had to face the choice of doing it themselves or it not getting done, it wouldn't get done. They rely on dumb volunteers like us who are willing to throw our lives away. Every military industrial complex since the beginning of time runs on the illusion that there's some glory in this shit, because if the system stopped perpetuating that, they'd have no volunteers to fight their wars for them."

I considered his words before pointing out the obvious flaw in his logic. "Then why are you here?"

Cancer gave a raspy laugh.

"You think I'd be doing this if I could make it on my own without combat? I've got news for you: I wouldn't. Now don't get me wrong, I thrive on this shit and so do you. But we're the only ones. The other three aren't junkies like us. They'd all have a total meltdown if their faith in the system collapses. That faith has been corroding from the cost we've paid, and it's corroded even further now that they've actually seen another team hung out to dry."

"Wow, Cancer. I never took you for much of a philosopher, but—"

"Shut up."

"—at this point you're a regular Socrates—"

"No," he whispered harshly, "I mean *shut up*. You hear that?"

I went quiet, hearing only the constant ringing in my ears; a fun fact about permanent and irreversible hearing loss universal to combat vets was that real silence would forever remain a distant memory. It occurred to me then that he'd detected a UAV overhead, and I momentarily considered that my degree of faith or lack thereof in the capabilities of the Houthis' finest drone pilots would be the determining factor in whether to run or stay put if the thing dive-bombed us with an explosive payload.

But after a moment, even I could make out what Cancer was talking about.

"Guess that explains how Chen had an exact grid for us and nothing else."

"She knew," he argued, "she just didn't tell us. No way the Agency didn't intercept some kind of communications about something this big, I promise you that. What I wouldn't give for a SAM right now."

"Well we didn't pack one, and even if we'd bought one off the black market, would you trust a locally procured SAM?"

He gave a frustrated grunt before admitting, "No. Not for this."

"Me neither," I said. "We're going to have to do this ourselves."

A surface-to-air missile would have had its benefits, however; the sound of rotor blades had reached us just before the appearance of a black dot in the sky to our right, the speck growing in size until I could make out the aircraft profile of an Mi-17, a Russian-designed transport helicopter painted with desert camouflage. That made it the most significant military hardware we'd seen that wasn't either paid for or directly supplied by the United States, although it was unlikely that the Yemeni Air Force's Soviet benefactors had anticipated a significant portion of that particular military branch defecting to the Houthis.

The result was catastrophic, beginning with Su-22 fighters attacking the presidential compound in Aden complete with a MiG-29 flying combat air support. Saudi Arabia had subsequently targeted any exposed Houthi aircraft they could find, which ensured that most were destroyed or concealed in relatively short order. And while there had been multiple sightings of Houthi-operated helicopters, to the best of our knowledge none had yet traipsed across Al Qaeda lines. Given AQAP's abundance of surface-to-air missiles, such a flight would mean certain death; unless, of course, the two groups were united in some strategic alignment.

Such cooperation between enemies against a greater foe—namely, Western powers—had been Weisz's calling card, leaving no doubt that Chen's information about his sudden arrival in Zughaynah wasn't wrong.

As the helicopter drew near, Cancer announced, "Vehicles inbound."

I looked left to register a three-truck convoy proceeding west toward the preordained grid. The first and last vehicles were security, two Ford Ranger pickups with belt-fed machineguns and truck beds loaded with armed fighters.

The central truck, however, was a white SUV caked with sand, probably originating from the mountain highlands where dirt trails were the only means of reaching the most senior AQAP leaders hidden in remote villages.

I said, "Looks like the SUV is our huckleberry."

"Mitsubishi Pajero," Cancer clarified. "And yeah, I'd say so."

Lights began flickering on in the windows of Zughaynah as civilians investigated the sound of rotor blades approaching; like us a scant minute or two earlier, they'd probably had no idea that an aircraft was going to touch down a few hundred meters from their homes.

The convoy crested the westernmost fringes of the village, then cut south into the desert, driving away from us before braking to a halt as armed men leapt from the pickups to form a half-circle of security around the vehicles.

By then the helicopter was dropping toward them in a choppy and irregular descent that didn't project any discernible skill on the part of the pilots beyond keeping the bird in flight. I should've known from the stated linkup time just before sunrise that this would occur: the aircrew was unqualified or incapable of flying under night vision, and so the transfer had been arranged just after first light.

I took to my spotter scope then, tracking from its orientation with the nearest building into the open desert until I'd centered the SUV in its field of view. Lifting my eyes from the optic, I watched the helicopter flaring toward its final landing point fifty meters south of the vehicles; and once that touchdown point was known, I returned my gaze to the spotter scope and delicately braced my fingertips against its surface for hasty realignment and magnification.

It wasn't hard to locate the aircraft as its wheels touched down, though no sooner had it appeared than it flittered out of sight again. The pilots had bounced the landing, and I scanned left until I reacquired the bird, my view soon blocked by the Al Qaeda fighters jogging toward its tail.

The rear ramp lowered within seconds, and I increased my scope's magnification to take in the sight.

I could make out two figures emerging from the aircraft with duffel bags, though they were only momentarily visible before merging with the group clustered beneath the tail boom. The collective mass then marched toward the trucks, and I struggled to discern which two had just departed the idling Mi-17. Panning my spotter scope to follow the group movement, I could make out a flash of silver hair well above the average Yemeni height —my first clear glimpse of Erik Weisz. The sight filled me with a gut-churning sensation of elation.

Project Longwing's ultimate target disappeared a fraction of a second later, my line of sight abruptly blocked by the SUV that he vanished inside.

I zoomed out my optic, seeing the men leap into their original trucks as the convoy wheeled northward, moving toward us on their way to the main road. The helicopter's engine roared to full power but I kept my focus on the vehicles, which reached the paved stretch and, as Chen promised, cut east toward the mountains before accelerating to a breakneck pace that carried them out of view.

By then the Mi-17 was rising in a lazy upward trajectory, its nose dipping before it too made a counterclockwise turn, accelerating directly toward Cancer and me.

"Hold the net," Cancer said with no small sense of urgency.

Together we grasped the camouflage netting over our heads, holding it in place in anticipation of the inevitable.

The helicopter careened toward us, soaring above the hillside slope in a lazy left-hand turn that brought it ever closer to our recon position until the cockpit flashed past at eye level.

I actually caught a glimpse of the pilots' white helmets and mirrored visors before the bird angled broadside. It flashed a mottled tan and brown fuselage lined with porthole windows before whipping out of view on its way back west, toward Houthi territory.

Then the rotorwash hit us, forcing me to close my eyes amid a churning wave of hot air and sand that whipped across our position. I struggled to maintain my grip on the camouflage netting as it billowed upward. If we hadn't been holding it in place, the entire mass of fabric would've gone flying skyward like a hot air balloon, broadcasting our position to God and everyone below.

The spotter scope flew backward and cracked across the bridge of my nose, causing me to flinch; worse still, the impact dislodged the nicotine lozenge and sent it into my throat, causing me to choke—if Cancer had to administer the Heimlich maneuver to save my life, I'd never hear the end of it. I coughed hard to free the tablet before spitting it on the ground, Cancer's laughter audible amid the chop of the receding aircraft.

As the wind subsided I readjusted the netting over us, freeing both hands to erect my spotter scope once more and scan the village for any indications that we'd been spotted. A daylight retreat in full view of Zughaynah would be fatal, to be sure, but if that was our only choice, we'd better get moving as soon as possible.

I saw no indications that would be necessary, however, watching as a few of the building lights extinguished without further ado.

"You're bleeding," Cancer said with no small amount of amusement. "I told you to dig that tripod in."

After touching the bridge of my nose, I saw that the fingertips of my shooting glove were now glazed with fresh blood.

Ignoring Cancer's comment, I asked, "You think the pilots saw us?"

"They should have—we could've hit them with a rock. But I think they were too busy trying not to fly into the mountain. Hell of a way to die, for them and us."

I nodded, then said, "Weisz got into the SUV."

"Yeah," Cancer replied, "he did. Doesn't mean he'll be returning in it, though—they might switch him to a decoy. We'll have to take out the whole convoy."

"Agreed. It's not the best situation to be in, but..."

At that moment, the magnitude of what had just transpired began to sink in. I felt a lightheaded wave of euphoria, then continued, "...we just... we just *saw* him, Cancer."

"Yeah," he agreed, sounding incredulous. Then his voice hardened. "You feel that? The bloodlust coursing through your veins?"

"Yep. Sure do."

"We're at the one-yard line now, David. And tomorrow, we're going to take it to the finish whether any of us make it out or not."

There was no pessimism in his voice; quite the opposite, in fact. Ten minutes earlier he'd been pontificating on the meaninglessness of this entire enterprise, but now that we'd actually laid eyes on Weisz, all debate was gone. A very Pavlovian response had kicked in, for him and for me, and I sensed our collective energies constricting to a laserlike focus of completing the mission at all costs. And in that moment it dawned on me that people like Cancer and me volunteered for combat service not because of any illusion of glory, but rather because we were hardwired to do so, for better or worse.

After a final scan of the village, I rolled to my side and reached into my kit for the next device I'd need in the operation against Erik Weisz: my satellite radio antenna.

29

Reilly sat atop his ruck beside Worthy and Munoz, both men cradling their weapons as the sun rose over the khat farm.

Ian knelt in the middle, palming a radio set to speaker mode and continually checking the display, probably making sure he had a clear satellite signal. Which he should, Reilly thought, considering that the antenna assembly hadn't moved from its position near his feet, nor had its view of the sky been obstructed in any way for the past half hour they'd been sitting there.

And yet, no transmission came from David or Cancer, who may or may not have made it through the hills in time to establish overwatch for the supposed arrival of Erik Weisz.

And as they awaited a transmission, the silence hung heavy between the men.

The air of suspense contradicted the otherwise tranquil nature of their surroundings, morning sunlight glistening across fields of khat, the first shift of boys and young men already beginning the day's harvest.

Worthy said without prompting, "They made it. No way Cancer would've let them fall behind."

"Yeah," Munoz agreed, checking his watch. "Probably not with much time to spare, so we've got to give them a chance to set up comms."

Neither man acknowledged the possibility that they had been killed, and Reilly thought that omission was just as well. They'd made all possible preparations for the next leg of their journey, if there was to be one at all. The only thing they could do was monitor the net in the hopes that a transmission would arrive.

Reilly spat into the dirt and noted, "Breakfast was good."

"No," Ian shot back, "it wasn't. And if you're shitting yourself in the truck, it's going to be a really long ride to Zughaynah *and* we're going to need a new medic. Because I'll never work with you again."

The statement took Reilly aback. He was considering how to respond when, as if in approval of Ian's reprimand, David's tinny voice emitted from the radio speaker.

"Angel, this is Suicide Actual."

Reilly felt a knot form in his stomach—was it nerves, he wondered, or breakfast?

Because while Yemen was starving, the khat business was booming and the men on the farm suffered no shortage of food.

His team had enjoyed a meal consisting of all-they-could-eat gruel, a salty wheat dough floating in greasy chicken broth. The dish had been served with a side of, well, slightly different gruel, a buttery bread mash with mushy banana and dates. His teammates had viewed the offerings as a recipe for projectile diarrhea, but Reilly feasted as if it were his last meal on Earth; which, depending on the contents of David's transmission, it may well be.

Ian transmitted back, "This is Angel, standing by to receive."

"Copy, Angel," David replied, *"break. Raptor Nine One, Suicide Actual."*

Chen responded at once.

"This is Raptor Nine One, Mayfly speaking. I read you loud and clear."

Now that all three parties were speaking on the same encrypted satellite frequency, David launched into his update.

"Observation report follows: at zero-five-four-zero local, one-by Mi-17 helicopter approached target grid from eastern heading, break.

"Prior to touchdown, three vehicles traveled down the unnamed paved road and established landing zone security: two-by Ford Ranger technical trucks driving lead and trail, one-by Mitsubishi Pajero SUV, appeared unarmored, break.

"*Approximately twelve personnel with small arms. Once the helo touched town, two—I say again, two—individuals departed the aircraft with duffel bags, one with silver hair consistent with Erik Weisz. Both men entered the SUV. Convoy departed to the east along the paved route, helicopter egressed to the west, break.*"

There was a lengthier pause this time, and then the team leader concluded, "*Mayfly, I assess positive identification, advise you track Weisz's movements and facilitate a strike once he's departed AQAP territory.*"

That was wishful thinking, Reilly thought, though he felt immeasurably grateful that someone involved in the op had at least a minimum regard for the survivability of a kill or capture mission against Weisz. That person certainly wasn't Meiling Chen, though David had done his part in advising her well, however futile the effort.

"*Suicide Actual,*" Chen transmitted, "*Raptor Nine One concurs with your assessment of PID and all available intel confirms the same. However, no assets are available to facilitate your request. Proceed as per your original plan, over.*"

Another pause before David went on, during which time the knot in Reilly's stomach tightened. It must have been nerves, he concluded; breakfast had been nothing short of delicious.

"*Copy, break. Angel, I verify the primary course of action as per our previous plan. You are 'go' for launch at this time, how copy?*"

Ian responded, "Good copy. We're moving now, will send a comms shot once we get into position."

And that sealed it—Worthy and Munoz rose and shouldered their rucksacks, moving out to the truck as Ian concluded the exchange and began breaking down his communications equipment.

Reilly stood with a sense of dread, crediting the main source of his unease to the unfortunate realities of what their movement would require.

He turned to face the Iveco, its cargo area currently empty save the team's modifications: a three-sided box covering built out of lumber they'd brought from Baterfi's hideout, creating an impromptu false-floor assembly over the load of explosives. The remaining space had enough room to conceal four men and their equipment but not much more.

And the structural integrity of that meager hiding place had better hold, he thought, because Pamir's men were about to cover it with the load currently arrayed in the dirt to his right: countless bales of khat representing a street value of roughly one hundred thousand dollars, about fifty times the annual income of an average Yemeni. The team had to pay that cost from their ever-dwindling operational fund, along with the price of the truck that most likely wouldn't be emerging from Al Qaeda territory unscathed.

To make matters worse, the team couldn't risk rigging a satellite antenna anywhere on the Iveco truck. That inconvenient fact meant that if they were discovered and killed, David and Cancer's first and only indication would be when their transmissions went unanswered into eternity. The only protection Reilly and his three counterparts had against the prospect of imminent death was Pamir's assurance that the khat loads were never removed from the truck as part of the checkpoint search procedures.

That assurance, however, was only as good as Pamir's willingness to deliver on his promise to transport them across enemy lines, to say nothing of the possibility that some new and ambitious Al Qaeda supervisor decided to spot check the vehicle by extracting the load. If that happened, it would be like a terrorist Christmas: four Americans who couldn't move, much less defend themselves, instantly doubling the number of incarcerated Project Longwing in Yemen—provided, of course, they weren't simply executed on sight.

Seeing Reilly's hesitation, Ian put a hand on his shoulder and asked, "You ready?"

"No," the medic replied.

"Me neither," Ian said in a chipper tone, then his voice darkened considerably. "Now get in."

Time to be a good little soldier, Reilly thought with disdain.

Against his better instincts, he lifted his rucksack and moved to join Worthy and Munoz as they clambered beneath the wood platform.

30

Ian shifted uncomfortably, feeling like this ride was never going to end.

He was lying on his back in total darkness, sandwiched between Worthy and Munoz, as the Iveco's shoddy suspension relayed every crack and pothole in the road directly to his spinal column. Ian's head was cocked uncomfortably against a palm oil container; he'd need a trip to the chiropractor once this was over, at least if his pillow didn't somehow detonate and incinerate him along with the truck and all its occupants.

There were squeaky groans from the wooden framework supporting the weight of khat bales overhead, and by now he was rethinking the feasibility of this plan—it would be supremely ironic, he reasoned, if the driver and his armed passenger reached their destination and unloaded the khat only to discover the four elite paramilitary operators had been crushed under the bales of a flowering plant.

And even if the bracing held, they still had to go undiscovered by any number of parties that could choose to search the truck. In addition to being at the mercy of government and Al Qaeda forces, the team faced a very real threat of common hijackers. While such thefts were rare, even Pamir admitted they did occur from time to time, and Ian had enough combat experience to never dismiss the possibility of fate's most absurd interventions.

The sole positive factor in their ride so far, if he could count it as positive at all, was that Reilly hadn't literally crapped his pants—yet—though the alternative may have been worse.

"Good *God*," Munoz gasped at the latest in a successive wave of rotten flatulence.

Ian said, "If you don't knock it off, the Al Qaeda checkpoint is going to smell you coming."

"I'm trying," Reilly protested. "I'm nervous."

Worthy said angrily, "We're all nervous, you fat shit. But you're the only one who ate that slop they gave us, aren't you?"

"Yeah," the medic admitted, sounding defeated.

Then, mustering some semblance of dignity, he offered, "But you guys don't know what it's like to have a hyperactive metabolism. Maintaining muscle mass means taking your calories where you can get them."

No one bothered replying to that, and for good reason—if their response was in any way similar to Ian's, the other team members were busy pulling their shirt collars over their noses for a comparatively merciful reprieve of their own body odor.

In a perverse way, Reilly's gastrointestinal distress served as a welcome distraction. Without the benefit of a clear GPS signal, they were riding blind in every way; Ian's efforts to track their progress were limited to a time-distance analysis that presumed the driver was adhering to the agreed-upon route.

And if that were the case, they should be arriving at the AQAP border any minute now.

The drive from the khat farm didn't take long; they'd been traveling for just over an hour now, though the distance spanned a veritable eon in terms of risk. They'd already moved from an area of Houthi control into a region administered by government forces of the UAE-backed Southern Transitional Council, which was as reliable of a transition as they'd get in the current ceasefire.

But the departure from government-held ground was another matter entirely.

Al Qaeda in the Arabian Peninsula honored no ceasefires between the military or the Houthis; they hated both sides equally, were likewise reviled by each, and maintained a tenacious grip on hinterland territories that were, by virtue of terrain defensibility, virtually uncontested. Added to that status quo were repeated Saudi and Emirati bombing runs, along with select US drone strikes and ground raids to attack key leadership, which had congealed to make the surviving AQAP strongholds almost impervious to penetration by anyone with the slightest intention of making it back out alive.

JSOC had accomplished the feat only with the full gamut of combat air support, and even they had taken their licks. For a small team of covert operators expected to work autonomously, a harrowing ride in a khat truck wasn't just the best possible chance of a successful insertion, it was the only one.

They'd already cleared the final government checkpoint in Lawdar—at least Ian assumed they had, judging by the sounds of Arabic banter and someone accessing the cargo area to extract a bale of khat by way of greasing the route for a return trip.

That put them somewhere along a five-kilometer stretch of no-man's land that would end in Bi'r al Mashayikh, the first village secured by Al Qaeda. Provided they made it in at all, the driver would proceed another five kilometers to Zughaynah, where, if David's report was accurate, Erik Weisz had set foot earlier that morning.

Ian pulled his shirt down, testing the air with a shallow breath before committing to a full inhale.

No sooner had he completed the action, however, than Reilly's bowels purged another pocket of gas, this time so loudly it was probably audible to the driver.

"God*dammit!*" Worthy hissed.

Munoz groaned before managing in a pained voice, "My...my eyes are watering."

Reilly, too, sounded like he was crying as he pleaded.

"I'm sorry, guys. This is no picnic for me, either. If I could hold it in without exploding in a cloud of entrails, believe me, I would—"

"Knock it off," Ian said, his senses leaping to full vigilance. He'd thought he detected the truck slowing down, though it continued to cruise before the sensation repeated; the driver was definitely braking now, and if Ian's location tracking had been close to accurate, that could only mean one thing.

The truck came to a stop, the engine going silent amid shouts of Arabic that were far more stern than those he'd heard at the government check-point. The anger inherent in the commands was so intense that Ian feared the driver and his passenger were about to be executed.

But the responses from both came in the form of a merry greeting, followed by the vehicle rocking slightly as both exited.

A moment later the truck's rolling door rattled open, and Ian felt another rocking sensation as a bale of khat was extracted from the back. He sensed that one or more of the guards was climbing on the tailgate to inspect the load, almost all of which they'd have to remove from the truck before spotting the wooden supports that concealed the American fighters.

An exceedingly tense few seconds elapsed before the truck bed shifted and the rear door was rolled back into place and secured. There were more murmurs of Arabic, now in a conversational tone, then a burst of laughter.

Ian was suddenly grateful for Yemen's unhinged psychological dependence on khat. AQAP's fervent ideology meant there was no buying their way into the region they were attempting to enter, and the necessity for a vehicle exfil precluded Ian's split team from simply walking in as David and Cancer had.

And yet, in the most fiercely defended pocket of land in a war-torn country, members of the most fanatical terrorist group on earth were none-theless programmed to allow the free passage of a truck carrying their stim-ulant of choice, and ensure that their comrades further up the road did as well. Unless the team was discovered in the coming seconds, they were going to pay dearly for that oversight.

Ian heard the truck doors slam and the engine fire to life; the transmission made a grinding sound, and then the vehicle began rolling forward in a moment that was so anticlimactic Worthy couldn't believe it had actually occurred as perceived.

"Was that it?" the pointman asked.

"Yeah," Ian said, "that was it."

He felt a sense of giddiness that fell somewhere between elation and debilitating fear. He let the emotion course through him without trying to suppress it—a fool's errand, given the intensity—and it finally gave way to an almost malicious glee. Ian had felt rage welling up within him ever since this mission had begun, and at this point he was far more concerned with Erik Weisz's fate than his own. They were closer right now than they'd ever been, the culmination of years of struggle and loss coming to a head for a single attack that was less than 24 hours distant from this moment in time.

Ian laughed aloud, unable to stop himself; then, he spoke the last words that any of the four men would utter before the vehicle made its next stop on the khat delivery route.

"We're in the lion's den now."

31

Cancer was roused from his slumber by a hard shake of his shoulder, followed by the last voice he wanted to hear right now.

"Wake up," David said, "we've got a vehicle inbound."

The words pulled Cancer fully out of his dream, a semi-lucid recollection of a night in his younger years that had ended in a Bangkok hotel room with two stunning local women and a bottle of SangSom—combat dreams were always the best dreams, though regrettably those most likely to be interrupted.

He grunted as he rolled onto his stomach beneath the camouflage netting, elbowing David's radio out of the way to assume a grip on his sniper rifle.

The temperature had plummeted since he'd gone to sleep, and the terrain ahead was blanketed in an orange glow with the approach of sunset.

He directed his gaze to the paved road, correctly assuming from David's lack of further details that he'd easily be able to locate the offending vehicle with the naked eye. Once he had, he sighted it through his scope, adjusting his aim until he'd acquired a magnified view.

Vehicles had been coming and going from Zughaynah all day, none of which had presented the slightest indication of anything other than normal civilian activity save one: an Iveco cargo truck that stopped to make a morning khat delivery before rattling on down the road, deeper into Al Qaeda territory, with the rest of the team safely concealed in its cargo hold.

Whether or not they had remained uncompromised up until now was still a mystery.

There had been no radio transmissions up to the start of his nap. That much was to be expected, given Ian couldn't hazard the exposure required for satellite communications until closer to nightfall, when the local curfew restricted every civilian to remain indoors.

In the meantime there wasn't much to do besides rotating sleep shifts, though that may well change in violently short order depending on what the vehicle drifting into Cancer's crosshairs did in the coming moments.

It was a Hilux pickup, a common sight in third-world countries all over the globe, but this one bore a black jihadi flag, which was to Al Qaeda what a flashing light bar was to police cars in the States.

There was no one in the bed, though judging by the truck's speed he could safely assume the quad cab was loaded to capacity with armed men who had somewhere to be. Cancer intuited the explanation behind the vehicle's sudden appearance within a few seconds of sighting it, though he reserved judgment until the vehicle swerved off the main road and made its way to a building near the center of town.

Once it came to a stop, three men in black uniforms armed with rifles leapt out, moving toward the building entrance with an air of incontestable authority before disappearing inside.

Cancer abandoned his sniper rifle, shifting his position until he lay on his back once more, his view consumed by the camouflage netting draped overhead.

Folding his hands atop his chest, he said, "If they were coming after us, they would've sent more than one truck. Anything over comms yet?"

"Just radio checks from Mayfly," David responded, sounding incensed. "So what the hell is going on in that building?"

Cancer closed his eyes. "Shariah court. They like to close cases within a day. Judge made a ruling so he could be home by supper, and those Al Qaeda shitheads are down there administering justice by cutting off some poor bastard's hands, or head, or both. Wake me up when you hear from our guys."

Then he sighed contentedly, trying to coax his mind into resuming the dream that had been so brutally interrupted.

He was just starting to drift off when a voice spoke, so quiet as to be almost unintelligible.

"*Suicide Actual, Angel.*"

It was Ian.

"Hey," David said, shaking Cancer's shoulder again, "I heard from our guys."

Groaning, Cancer rolled back onto his stomach and leaned his head toward the radio between them. It was set to speaker mode out of a reasonable degree of caution that after their scramble to reach an observation point ahead of Weisz's arrival, whoever was on guard might nod off despite the assistance of nicotine.

David transmitted back, "Angel, Suicide Actual. How are you guys holding up?"

Ian replied, "*We're in position in Hadiqat Al-Zaytoun. Drivers are camped out for curfew, and we're waiting for darkness before making a foot movement to the ambush point.*"

"You'll be staying with the driver, right?"

"*Hundred percent. The only thing I trust him to do without a gun to his head is chew khat. Any updates?*"

"Negative," David assured him, "all quiet here. We'll break down here in an hour and a half and start walking. We'll be arriving from the north, should reach the ambush point by oh-two hundred, and will link up with the other three guys over the team net."

"*Good copy, I'll check in for final approval before they step off.*"

David looked over with an incredulous expression, shaking his head in utter disbelief.

"Is this thing really going according to plan?"

"For now," Cancer said. "Give it until morning, though. Once we kick off that ambush, there's going to be some curveballs."

He considered leaving it at that, but then decided to give the team leader something to chew on.

"And the exfil is going to be a wild ride," he said with a smile, "if we make it that far."

32

Worthy trudged northeast across the dry remnants of the riverbed, briefly pausing to perform a 360-degree scan.

The sky was clear, the stars and a sliver of moon providing sufficient ambient light for his night vision to deliver a crystal panorama of the terrain around him: scrub brush dotting the riverbed's edges, the ground rising up into undulating ridges on three sides. No movement save the occasional flitter of bats overhead, and Worthy triggered his watch display to illuminate the dial before proceeding. 0137.

Shit.

He looked down to confirm the boot prints marring the sand to his front, aligned himself to his original direction of movement, and continued his march. There was perhaps only one rule of combat that applied universally across all militaries and operating environments—never go anywhere alone—and he was breaking it now.

Worthy heard a transmission over his earpiece.

"Racegun, you good?"

It was Munoz, which served as a positive indication that Reilly was gainfully employed with his primary task for the evening.

"Fucking peachy," Worthy replied. "How's it coming along?"

"Making progress. Still no word from Suicide and Cancer."

"All right," he said, a perfunctory conclusion to the brief communication that reflected his mood: bitter, tired, and above all, in pain.

This was as professionally embarrassing a situation as Worthy had ever been in, and he'd had some zingers in his day. The route itself was a four-seam meatball right down the middle of the plate, and the team's ground movement should have been a relative home run despite the 32 kilos of each man's jerry can of ammonium nitrate fertilizer: 6.85 kilometers across largely flat ground that, as best as they could tell, was free from enemy observation.

Sure, he thought, they weren't just behind enemy lines, but behind *the most deadly* lines as they existed within a larger framework of *already bad* lines.

The ambush point resided well between the lowland villages at the outskirts of the territory and the highland enclaves where Al Qaeda's most high-value individuals resided. Absent the passage of a key convoy, the desert out here wasn't worthy of defending for seven klicks in either direction, and thus there was no need for enemy spotters to be lying in wait.

Worthy had planned to lead the way for the entire movement, and instead found a stiff back slowing his pace to the extent that Reilly had to take point on his behalf, the first time he'd ever had to cede his duty to another team member due to injury with the exception of the one time he'd been shot. Eventually he fell so far back that Munoz had to carry his explosive-filled rucksack for him, at which point Worthy had used his authority as leader of the three-man element to issue the only change of plan: the other two were to proceed at the quickest possible pace to the ambush point, where emplacing explosives would require the lion's share of remaining darkness, and concealing individual shooters the rest.

There was no disputing the necessity, and after a halfhearted attempt to object, Reilly swiftly moved out with Munoz in tow.

It couldn't have come at a worse time: while closing the final distance and with their ultimate target practically within their grasp. Worthy was in disbelief that he'd been the one to slow the effort when they were *this close*, and now he had a deep sense of shame to heap on top of all the issues he'd accrued in the service of Project Longwing. He'd honestly believed he was the only one suffering until finally divulging his concerns to Reilly after a

Stateside training mission. It had been a pivotal exchange; in addition to the knowledge that he was far from alone, the medic had provided him the first of many capsules that had been easing his psychological pain ever since.

Worthy continued walking alone, hoping to at least arrive before David and Cancer made their way down from the high ground; as things stood, however, he would very likely be the last one to make it.

His first sight of the ambush point came in the form of a sudden aberration in the shadows around the road to his far left, a barely perceptible infrared flashlight beam that extinguished a moment later—a good sign, he thought, because Reilly wouldn't risk using such a device until he was tackling the finer points of setting up an ignition system.

"I've got you in sight," Worthy transmitted. "Three hundred meters out."

Munoz answered, *"Cool, just keep an eye out for the dogleg and follow it straight in."*

He spotted it within a few steps—the tracks before him made a 90-degree turn to follow a narrow tributary notch heading due north, and Worthy followed suit with the assurance that he'd soon be stationary. There was only so much Percocet he could take while retaining his ability to fight, and what he needed now more than anything was to rest his back.

Within a few steps of the detour, he heard a new transmission, this one from David.

"Racegun, Suicide."

"Go ahead," Worthy replied, trying to quicken his pace out of an engrained competitive instinct to beat the team leader into position.

"I can see the ambush point, on my way in. Cancer's staying high to scout out a sniper position. Any updates?"

"Yeah, be advised, Doc and Bulldog are already there. I'm a few hundred meters out, approaching from the south. Try not to shoot me."

"Do I want to know why you're late?" David asked.

"Definitely not."

"Race you there."

That fucker, Worthy thought. He wouldn't have made the challenge if he wasn't already in the lead.

But his irritation turned to relief as he identified the ambush point ahead.

The dried-out tributary he followed now created a sharp divot beneath the paved road, with a resulting gap afforded by a low bridge braced by supporting beams. At present that gap was filled by a crouching Reilly, who was in the process of finalizing his explosive charges beneath the structure. No digging was required, a plus considering any security elements screening the route would easily identify a significant ground disturbance ahead of the convoy's arrival.

As for where the individual shooters would be positioned and concealed in the surrounding terrain, Worthy would have to sort that out when he arrived—along with the recently arrived figure who waved triumphantly from atop the bridge.

David scrambled down into the tributary bed, jogging toward him at a clip that, were he to attempt it right now, would've left Worthy on the ground and writhing in pain.

He came to a stop, flexing his back as the team leader slowed before him.

"All right, man," David whispered. "Come clean—why are you walking like an 80-year-old man?"

"Back spasm. Had to reverse-Superman out of the pickup."

"Right. Okay."

It was then that Worthy noticed a dark smear across the team leader's upper lip, looking black under his night vision.

"Why's your nose bleeding?"

David shrugged helplessly. "Helicopter blasted a spotter scope into my face."

"Of course. Ready to set up the ambush line?"

"Yeah," David replied. "Let's do that."

The two men walked together then, closing the final distance with the bridge.

33

Adrenaline flooded my body at the sound of Cancer's transmission.

"Stand by, incoming from the east."

I picked up the olive drab box from its resting place in front of me, grasping it in both hands.

The blasting machine was roughly the size of a Big Mac, with twin wires snaking out of ports in the front. There were two button switches at the rear of the box, and I depressed the left one with my thumb and held it, watching closely until a tiny green light flickered on beneath the words *READY TO FIRE*.

My right thumb trembled off the right side of the device, perhaps an inch away from the remaining button that would, when depressed, send an electrical impulse through the cords and result in the near-instantaneous detonation of three blasting caps embedded in as many containers of ammonium nitrate and aluminum powder rigged beneath the bridge to my left.

I held my breath; above all else, I was ready to get this damn thing over with.

Operating in enemy territory was one thing. Lying in wait in broad daylight a stone's throw north of the highest-speed road in this swath of Al Qaeda territory was quite another.

We'd already encountered civilian traffic as the sun rose beyond the mountains. All of it had been spotted well ahead of time by Cancer, who was perched on an adjacent hillside in his usual capacity as team sniper.

But by virtue of his position or limited lines of sight or both, he could identify inbound vehicles long before he could distinguish what they were. So far there had been one truck loaded with chicken crates, a young boy shakily piloting a motorcycle while a woman in a burka—presumably his mother—straddled the seat behind him and held onto his waist, and a rust-colored pickup of 1980s construction. None of those specifics, however, had been known to us until we'd waited out a nerve-racking interlude between Cancer's "stand by" announcements and his later descriptions.

Those collective seconds consisted of emotionally gutting suspense that stretched my patience to the breaking point, partially and perhaps especially because there was nothing any of us could do to defuse the tension—not even move.

That particular restriction applied doubly so to myself: I was in a shallow prone fighting position dug out of the earth and covered by camo net and sand, neither of which I could risk disturbing. And since I'd be the one initiating the ambush by detonating the explosives, I was closest to the low bridge they'd been generously applied beneath. Demolitions of any meaningful quantity didn't warrant inclusion on our packing list, but we'd come prepared to use locally procured explosives by bringing with us the far lighter components of electric blasting caps and firing wire, the latter of which we carried in sixty-meter lengths.

And as a result of the nonlinear wrinkles in terrain required to conceal the wire, I was currently positioned a scant thirty meters from the kill zone.

Reilly and Munoz were arrayed along the hillside to my right, all of us watching the bridge from an oblique angle to catch sight of Weisz's convoy as it slipped past, heading away from us on its return trip to Zughaynah.

And somewhere on the hillside to our front was Cancer.

Now that we were all in position, our proximity to Erik Weisz took on an almost surreal, detached quality; it felt like I was going to wake up at any second to find this entire thing had just been a fantasy.

No such luck, I thought as Cancer transmitted again a moment later.

"*Negative*," the sniper informed us. "*Just a motorcycle.*"

I lifted my left thumb off the charge switch, watching the green light on my blasting machine extinguish before carefully setting down the device with a shaky breath.

Lowering my head, I gazed through the gap between earth and camouflage netting, listening to the motorcycle approach for interminable seconds before it and its rider appeared, crossing over the bridge and puttering down the road.

Once it had vanished from view, Cancer proclaimed, "*No inbound traffic at this time—we're clear.*"

Ordinarily, being positioned at an ambush involved total silence; however, the fact that we hadn't been apprehended was proof positive that no one had any idea we were here, least of all the hordes of Al Qaeda fighters who would have long since made their displeasure at our presence well known.

And since everyone on the team must have been feeling the same physical and emotional fatigue I was, I decided to pay tribute to that fact.

"Every time you say 'stand by,'" I replied to Cancer, "it shaves ten minutes off my life. This whole wait has been bouncing between sheer terror and wanting to pass out."

"*You won't be tired for long,*" he assured me. "*Once Weisz shows up, I guarantee that sleep will be the furthest thing from your mind.*"

Worthy then transmitted, "*Maybe we should have brought some khat with us.*"

"Great idea," I shot back, "let's see how we do on drugs in the middle of a combat mission."

An awkward silence ensued, leading me to wonder if I was the only one who hadn't been chewing khat.

But no, I decided, we played things fast and loose as a team but not *that* fast and loose.

"What?" I asked.

"*Suicide,*" Reilly responded with a tone so dead-serious that I thought he was about to come out of the closet, "*I'm on 200 milligrams of psilocybin right now.*"

I waited for some follow-up, and when no one spoke, I keyed my mic again and asked the obvious question.

"What the fuck is psilocybin?"

He clarified, "*Magic mushrooms, Golden Teacher strain. I grow them myself. Just a sub-hallucinogenic amount, taken every third day. It's called microdosing.*"

For a moment I couldn't tell if he was messing with me; then, when the ensuing silence assured me he wasn't, I gave a breathless gasp and asked, "Why?"

"*Because,*" he said unapologetically, "*the first half dozen PTSD therapies didn't help, and I was tired of drinking myself to death.*"

This was a strange time to admit to drug use, I thought, especially when the entire team was listening—and, presumably, waiting to see how I'd react to the revelation.

I said, "You're supposed to be setting the example of health for our guys."

"*He is,*" Ian interrupted. "*Doc told me about it, and I'm doing it too. One hundred and fifty milligrams is my sweet spot. Now I'm sleeping like a baby for the first time in years—or at least I was, until we got to Yemen.*"

Both men must have registered that I was momentarily speechless, because Ian added by way of explanation, "*Killing bad guys is only half of our mission. The other half is getting right and staying right, so we can go back to do it all over again.*"

Before I could respond, Worthy transmitted, "*I get by with just a hundred milligrams. Got me off the anti-depression meds I never told anyone about except for Reilly.*"

"Christ," I said, "Cancer, I suppose you're doing shrooms too, aren't you?"

"*No way,*" the sniper responded flatly.

"Finally," I said, "someone's sober besides me."

My momentary relief was shattered when Cancer went on, "*I mean, sure, I tried Doc's capsules. Made me way too relaxed. That's why I switched to micro-dosing LSD. Ten micrograms every three days sets me straight—good, clean focus.*"

Swallowing, I said, "This can't be good for you guys."

"*Sure,*" Ian responded, "*if you want to believe the same government that's been promoting a failed War on Drugs for a half-century with junk science and scare tactics.*"

Then Reilly weighed in, "*My drinking is down to a few beers on the week-end. How 'healthy' is the half-gallon of bourbon you're inhaling every night when we're Stateside?*"

I bristled defensively. "Eight shots, tops. Occasionally ten, maybe twelve. I mean, aren't all those drugs addictive—"

The medic cut me off.

"*Psychedelics are anti-addictive, because you build tolerance way too fast. Do me a favor and look up the research coming out of Johns Hopkins, Yale, or Stanford when we get back. There's a reason that psilocybin is on the FDA fast track as a breakthrough cure for PTSD and depression.*"

My temper flared.

"Cancer is doing acid. He's lucky he hasn't jumped off a building yet."

Ian interjected, "*LSD affects the same serotonin receptors in the same way. Difference is, there is way too much stigma attached from the sixties for most scientists to attempt getting their research approved by the government, especially when there's an open door to psilocybin studies right now.*"

I was speechless, an exceedingly rare condition that left me questioning everything I thought I knew about the four men I'd been serving with.

Reilly offered, "*Enjoy your booze, though—you're basically using a government-approved drug that destroys your health.*"

I became suddenly aware that it wasn't just my men on the team net right now, but Munoz as well.

"Bulldog," I said, "tell me you're not doing this bullshit too."

There was a pause before he replied, "*Never heard of it, to be honest.*"

Then, a moment later, he added, "*I might have to give it a go.*"

I sagged into the ground, trying to process what was happening and first having to discount the possibility that it was all one elaborate practical joke. The military and, indeed, any fighting profession in which I'd been a part of whether mercenary or Agency had been drinking cultures almost in the extreme; alcohol represented bonding, decompression, and self-medication wrapped in one convenient package, and anyone who didn't partake was often regarded with suspicion unless there was an AA membership attached to their refusal.

Psychedelic drugs, by contrast, were for tree-hugging hippies who stood against everything the warrior caste represented. A merger of the two worlds seemed almost ludicrous to me, and yet apparently it was already occurring amongst the men I trusted most—and if it worked for them, I wondered how many active-duty service members were suffering under random drug tests that my team, as government contractors, were exempt from.

More troubling still, I thought, was that I'd been deliberately excluded from this information, probably as a result of the anticipated judgment I'd wield in response. And, to be fair, my initial reaction was not exactly one of open acceptance.

"All right then," I declared. "Fuck it. If we manage to make it back to the khat farm, I'll try it for myself. Who's going to give me some?"

I expected to be welcomed into their subculture with open arms; instead, no one spoke.

Ian broke the silence. "*I didn't bring any extra.*"

Reilly said helplessly, "*I'll make you some capsules from my latest batch when we get back. Don't know how long this mission will last.*"

Then Cancer added his two cents.

"*Suicide, I know you better than you know yourself. You're going to like LSD a lot more. And no, you can't have any of mine—I need to stay sharp.*"

The next transmission came by way of a Southern drawl.

"*Maybe you could try the khat,*" Worthy said, "*and see where that gets you.*"

Well wasn't this a bitch, I thought, though before my mind could proceed further, Cancer transmitted again.

"*Stand by.*"

I picked up the blasting machine once more, wondering what clarification Cancer would provide next—another chicken truck, perhaps, or another motorbike toting some dipshit to see relatives in Zughaynah. My mood had been sliding steadily downhill for the better part of an hour, and if this mission had taught me anything, it was that above all else in Yemen, things got worse before they got worse.

"*Positive ID,*" Cancer transmitted abruptly.

My body fired to full alert, left thumb pressing the switch as I waited for the green light to blink on.

The light remained unlit by the time he continued, "*PID three trucks from the landing zone, Ford Rangers in lead and trail, white Mitsubishi Pajero in the middle, ten-meter vehicle spacing, twenty seconds out. Angel's moving for pickup, no eastbound traffic, ambush line is hot."*

Keeping my left thumb down, I used my right hand to key the radio switch for a final transmission.

"Copy, all elements stand by for initiation."

By now I had a serious problem—the damned capacitor within the device I held hadn't yet produced the 450 volts required to send a sufficient charge down the line and into the electric blasting caps, and I was running out of time.

I waited another second before releasing the charge switch, then pressed and held it again.

The approaching engines were audible by then, and I faced a moment of blinding fear that this was it; after two years of paramilitary deployments following a trail of breadcrumbs toward a mysterious terrorist leader who was finally in our sights, the attack was about to fail because the piece of plastic shit in my hands had chosen that exact moment to encounter a glitch.

Then the first Ford Ranger rattled into view, appearing from beyond the hillside and sweeping across the bridge. Weisz's SUV was next, and I forced my gaze to the miniscule light bulb before me that, a split second later, finally blinked before displaying a steady green glow.

It was almost too late—almost, but not quite, with the Mitsubishi's front bumper already clearing the lead edge of the bridge as I thumbed the *FIRE* switch with my right hand and held it down, feverishly hoping that after the charging malfunction, the initiation system would work as advertised.

A thunderclap of noise and light erupted from the bridge, causing my heart to leap with an almost delirious sense of joy. The explosives had detonated all right, and perhaps even a split second too soon.

The blast caught Weisz's SUV beneath the engine block, sending the entire vehicle airborne by its force. Its roof pirouetted through the sunlight north of the bridge, flying toward me in a maelstrom of utter devastation before beginning its downward arc.

The SUV impacted on its driver's side quarter panel, sparking a great cloud of sand and rock before the truck's momentum carried it even further. To my horror, the vehicle entered a barrel roll that sent the mass of twisted metal and shattered glass careening side-over-side toward the base of the hill, on a direct collision course with my concealed position.

I had no time to react, much less spring upright and dart away in time to survive the inevitable. In killing Weisz, I'd just killed myself.

This was an absurd turn of fate, I thought. And that was the last thing to cross my mind before I closed my eyes and, overcoming an otherwise immobilizing wave of panic, curled into the fetal position.

David was dead, Reilly thought, killed not by Weisz's vehicle but by the very hand of God. What other force could explain the almost pinpoint precision with which the SUV had gone airborne with the blast, then landed at such an angle to send it in a catastrophic corkscrewing roll directly toward the team leader?

No random act of physics, this, though Reilly forced his mind to the more immediate task at hand—there were still two truckloads of Al Qaeda fighters to contend with, and if he didn't get his HK417 in the fight, any or all of the surviving team members may well join David in Valhalla.

But regardless of the painstakingly delineated target priorities for everyone present, he faced an almost immediate crisis in deciding where to direct his fire.

Reilly was supposed to put his elevated position and the superior range of his 7.62mm weapon to good use in engaging the lead vehicle, currently speeding away toward Cancer's sniper position, but the departure of Weisz's SUV from the road changed everything.

Its pinwheeling course across the earth had churned up a trail of rising sand that would soon block Worthy and Munoz's view as effectively as a smoke grenade, and now that David was entombed beneath the truck, both shooters were effectively removed from the fight.

That left Reilly to engage the trail vehicle before its occupants opened fire on the remaining ambush line, and to that end he took aim toward the ravine to see that the final truck in the convoy was swerving to avoid the mushroom cloud of smoke and sand billowing upward from the shattered bridge.

The driver's impressive reaction time did nothing to save him or his vehicle from plunging into the short ravine just south of the blast, where the pickup's front bumper descended sharply before impacting with a force that sent the fighters in the open back scattering like rag dolls. Some crashed into the cab before ricocheting into the bed, while others were flung free of the truck entirely, their airborne progress marked by frantic flailing limbs that would soon be shattered.

Reilly sent his first shots into the cab, knowing that anyone with a seat-belt presented the most immediate threat and finding that assumption validated when both passenger side doors flung open. Two men attempted to exit at the same time, unknowingly stepping directly into his sights and paying for it by absorbing bullets that either were or soon would be fatal.

The momentary victory erased any remaining tactical benefit of the element of surprise, however, and the rest of the fighters wisely decided to scramble out of the driver's side of the truck, where their movements were concealed by the wrecked vehicle. Reilly's next indication of how many had survived the crash with their ability to fight intact came by way of muzzle flashes over the bed and beyond the tailgate, and he was opening fire by the time the hails of automatic gunfire became audible over the still-receding echo of the initial explosion.

He tagged the man by the tailgate, his proof arriving in the form of a downed fighter spilling out from just behind the rear bumper. Then he directed his aim above the truck bed before sweeping shots left and right, trying to keep any enemy heads down long enough for Worthy and Munoz to see what they could.

Reilly's first indication that one or both men were back in the mix came when a flurry of bullet impacts thudded into the side of the pickup. His next step was to break his focus from the optic, shifting sideways to gain an instant of situational awareness as he re-oriented down the road. The Mitsubishi SUV had finally come to a complete stop, resting on its roof, the dust finally receding enough for the remainder of the ambush line to engage the trail vehicle.

The medic reloaded while cutting his eyes to the paved road where the lead Ford Ranger continued to speed without impediment. Cancer had thus far failed to kill the driver, and if it proceeded much farther it would clear the kill zone entirely.

Cancer fired a fifth round through the windshield of the lead pickup. The exact point of impact was impossible to determine amid the glare of sun on glass, but by now his hopes of immobilizing the vehicle by killing its driver had come and gone within seconds of the explosive blast at the bridge.

The vehicle continued speeding forward, apparently uncontested; the fighters in the back should have been falling dead with the assistance of Reilly's precision fire, but that simply hadn't occurred. Now it fell upon Cancer alone to stop the truck before it disappeared beyond the hillside crest below.

There were two very good reasons to stop it: first, Weisz might be in the vehicle, having switched places in the convoy to survive a pinpoint ambush like the one currently unfolding. Even if he wasn't, and the lead truck made it out, its passengers would be able to call for reinforcements sooner, and those precious minutes could be the difference between the team having to shoot their way out through six men or six dozen.

Cancer abandoned his efforts to shoot the driver; the road was straight and the vehicle operator was probably ducked behind the dash now, steering off faith alone while flooring the accelerator.

The sniper directed his aim to the engine block instead, ripping rounds in a ploy that was hopeful at best. The proper tool for the job he attempted now at this range would be a .50 BMG or 300 Win Mag rifle, neither of which he'd packed in lieu of a more general purpose weapon fitting their anticipated mission profile, and at this point, he'd have to put down as many bullets as possible to hit a critical mechanical component.

To that end he fired as quickly as he could while maintaining any reasonable degree of accuracy, nearing the end of his magazine before streams of black smoke shot out of the ever-increasing number of holes in the truck hood.

The vehicle sputtered to a gradual halt, its momentum carrying it forward as he transitioned his aim to the fighters in the bed—they wouldn't be concentrated for long before leaping out and scattering in all directions, effectively removing the odds of eliminating all survivors. He managed a single shot at the mass of men before his bolt locked to the rear.

Cancer performed what may well have been the fastest emergency reload of his career, dropping his empty magazine while grabbing a fresh one from the row lined up beside his weapon.

He'd barely sent his bolt forward before dialing in the still-rolling truck once more, seeing first that it wouldn't come to a complete stop until it cleared his field of view, and second that the situation had pivoted in the best possible way.

The armed fighters were dropping like flies as they attempted to leap out—Reilly had finally gotten his HK417 into the fight. Cancer added his precision fire into the mix, landing as many shots as he could while he still had the chance.

Worthy fired his final two rounds, both impacting the motionless figure of the last man he could identify in the kill zone. Then he conducted a scan for further opponents from his prone fighting position, sweeping his aim left and right beneath the canopy of camouflage netting stretched overhead.

The supporting fire from himself and Munoz had been severely delayed by the dust cloud erupting in the wake of the SUV rolling across the desert like a tumbleweed before coming safely to rest atop David's fighting position. Once visibility cleared, however, Worthy had gone to work.

The first priority was the fighters making their last stand behind the crashed trail vehicle. Most of them had been dispatched in relatively short order before he and Munoz turned their attention to those flung free from the blast. Their bodies were scattered in and around the ravine, four shapes in varying states of consciousness and movement with grotesque injuries both external and, without a doubt, internal as well.

Worthy had engaged each of them in turn, and done so well within the limits of his second magazine of the ambush, by the time he turned his attention to the SUV. It was resting on its roof, the upturned chassis horrifically mauled by the blast, one wheel roasting in an ongoing swath of flame. No movement of anyone trying to exit, he saw, and if anyone did survive the vehicle's execution of a thirty-meter cannonballing roll, they'd be the easiest targets of his career.

A standard ambush would call for close to a minute of silence before determining that all enemies had succumbed to withering fire and risking an assault on foot; Worthy gave it five seconds before reloading his weapon, and in that span of time, Reilly transmitted.

"Lead truck has stopped, think we got them all."

"Keep it dialed in," Cancer replied, *"I'm relocating to get eyes-on."*

Well that was just perfect, Worthy thought. If Reilly had the only line of sight on the now-stationary first vehicle in the convoy, and David was dead, then the maneuver element was down to two men.

The only question that remained was whether to hold in place until Reilly could increase that number to three; more of an academic consideration than anything else, he mused, because they didn't have the manpower to secure the objective or even the time to do so amid the overwhelming risk that an intrepid member of Al Qaeda's middle management had radioed out an SOS at some point in the melee. Their exfil would have to occur the moment Ian arrived in the khat truck, and if they didn't have positive identification of Erik Weisz by then, they'd never get it.

The next thought to flash through his mind was that responsibility for the next phase of the operation was on him alone—there was no one left to give the order.

"Assault," he transmitted, "assault, assault."

He slithered forward, clearing the camouflage netting, then stood and raised his Galil, feeling the headrush that inevitably followed rapid movement after hours of remaining stationary. The immediate throb of pain rippling up his spine was another matter altogether, and he forced the thought from his mind to confirm Munoz had likewise left his concealment behind before proceeding down the hill toward the SUV.

Perhaps the only positive turn of fate was the vehicle's resting place.

They'd anticipated it flipping forward or sideways in the blast, placing its final location within a few meters of the ravine if not inside it. The fact that the explosion launched it in an airborne barrel roll before it had rocketed side-over-side directly toward the ambush line meant that he and Munoz didn't have much ground to cover before clearing the wreck and extracting any intelligence of value, which would hopefully include a photograph of one very dead Erik Weisz.

That minor convenience was in no way worth the loss of their team leader, but at the moment he'd take any tactical advantage he could get.

Worthy was halfway to the Mitsubishi SUV with Munoz to his right flank when the impossible occurred, and not for the first time in the twenty seconds since they'd attacked Weisz's convoy. A sudden flash of movement caused him to take aim, and he very nearly opened fire before realizing what he was looking at.

David Rivers was rising from the dead.

I pushed myself to my feet, instantly mummified by a blanket of camouflage netting that I cast aside with one hand, holding my weapon with the other.

Then I looked down, half expecting to see my own corpse on the ground and a light in the sky that my spirit would, against my best efforts, begin floating toward.

But despite the overwhelming indications that I was dead, there was an equal amount of evidence to the contrary. To the best of my knowledge, near-death experiences didn't typically involve accounts of anyone's head ringing like it was being bashed side to side in a cathedral bell, nor the sting of sand in their eyes, nor a deep, unwavering anger rising up from the depths of their gut to a breaking point of sheer, blinding rage.

If this was the ultimate liberation of death, I thought, it sure wasn't as peaceful as it was cracked up to be.

The patch of ground I'd been lying atop all morning was just that, an empty patch of ground. I saw the handheld blasting machine, which had been cast aside somewhere in my roll to the fetal position and now rested upside down with the wires askew.

And that device was a tiny representation of the grander sight before me: the driver's side of the Mitsubishi Pajero, which was curiously inverted and rising less than three meters from where I now stood, with Worthy and Munoz advancing to either side.

At this point I should have transitioned back to my duties as ground force commander, taking charge and supervising the site exploitation after assuring my teammates that I was, in fact, alive.

Instead I pushed my rifle back on my sling, drawing my sidearm and advancing toward the vehicle while shouting four words at my counterparts.

"Out of my way!"

Worthy had knelt to aim at the vehicle's occupants, and without breaking his line of sight, he called back, "I'm changing your callsign to Zombie—"

"Fuck off," I yelled back, silencing him as I dropped to the ground to wave my pistol across the SUV interior. The doors would never open again, I could see at a glance, having been partially compressed during the vehicle's roll, but that same momentum had blown out all but a fraction of the side windows. At this point I'd slither inside like a goddamn tunnel rat if I had to.

The driver and front passenger may as well have been one person— neither had been wearing seatbelts, and appeared to have pinballed into one another and the SUV cabin until they were little more than a jellified mass of tangled limbs. No danger there, I thought.

A far more compelling sight awaited me in the back, however.

The man facing me was just beginning to wake, finding himself in a position that was, in equal parts literal and metaphorical, awkward.

He found himself hanging upside down, held in place by the seatbelt that had saved his life only to be looking into the face of an American with murder in his eyes and a pistol in his hand.

This was no Arab but a Caucasian man—a personal assistant, probably, with an intimate knowledge of the terrorist inner workings we'd been so desperately trying to ferret out.

Planting my Glock barrel against the center of his forehead, I waited for his panicked eyes to meet my own before smiling.

"Good morning," I said, pulling the trigger to send a 9mm jacketed hollow point into his skull.

The outcome was predictably catastrophic, a pelting wave of blood and bone fragments, cerebrospinal fluid and brain matter fanning out from the exit wound to spray the vehicle interior. It wasn't the best move as far as collecting intelligence was concerned, but I'd be damned if it didn't make me feel immeasurably better.

I stood and walked around the back of the SUV to approach the passenger side, with Worthy scrambling to advance ahead; he knew better than to try and stop me, but he'd damned well make sure I didn't die from my own stupidity. The man had gotten his start as a bodyguard, and he'd remain one until the end.

It was at that point I realized I hadn't heard a single radio transmission since the ambush began; the result, I observed now, of my radio earpieces having become dislodged somewhere between initiating the explosives and my rebirth as a sand-covered instrument of American vengeance.

I didn't bother coming up on comms, continuing my approach until I reached the rear passenger side window—or, more properly, what was left of it, currently a few fragments of glass that remained at the doorframe's edges.

Then I knelt with my pistol in hand, finding what I'd been waiting for.

A seat-belted figure was hanging inverted, this one bearing the gray hair and etched face matching our best descriptions and photo renderings of Erik Weisz.

"Just the man I wanted to see," I said.

There was no response from the man, his features slack and eyes shut as the inner contents formerly contained by his assistant's skull oozed down one side of his face.

He may have been playing possum, and I didn't know or care—if the man seated next to him had survived the crash, I reasoned that Weisz had too, and he wouldn't meet so merciful a fate if I had anything to say on the matter.

I holstered my sidearm and drew my Winkler knife in its place, using the blade to saw his seatbelt apart at the juncture of his hip.

The speed with which his body crashed into the SUV roof assured me that he was either dead already or fully unconscious, and I used both hands to pull him out of the wreck.

With that complete, I knelt beside the body and took in my surroundings: Worthy beside me, now facing outward to pull security; Reilly darting down the hillside toward us; and finally, Munoz to my right, dragging an enormous black duffel bag free of the rear window.

Before bothering to insert my radio earpieces, I performed an action that was of no tactical value but nonetheless of immeasurable importance.

Removing a shooting glove, I pressed an index and middle finger into Weisz's neck below the corner of his jaw.

And then, after a three-second hold that assured me I wasn't imagining the pulse, I smiled for the second time that morning.

"Go right," Ian shouted, "right, *right!*"

The driver, Raed, had been maneuvering as fast as the Iveco Eurocargo was capable of maintaining its grip on the road. Its traction had been severely tested as they rounded the bend around the hillside, and was about to be further strained as a result of the obstacle in their path.

The Ford Ranger hadn't exactly appeared out of nowhere; judging by the sheer quantity of bullet holes perforating its windshield and hood, it had been stationary for some time.

But Ian hadn't seen the damn thing until Raed began whipping around the hillside, spotting the pickup a moment before the driver by virtue of his position in the passenger seat.

Raed responded with admirable reaction time as a result of the stimulant leaves he'd been chewing like a man possessed, veering off the road and into the open desert. Ian managed one sidelong glance at the lead Al Qaeda vehicle as it whipped past in a narrowly avoided blur of blood-spattered metal, and then the khat truck turned into a bouncing rollercoaster of groaning chassis across the undulating sand and rock.

But the driver had cranked the wheel a little too quickly, and Ian felt the vehicle tilting perilously to the right before settling once more—if they flipped this thing now, it would be the end of the exfil attempt. Then he cried out, "Slow down—left, easy, easy!"

Another overcorrection almost tipped the vehicle to the opposite side, the truck an unstable and exceedingly front-heavy desert missile without the benefit of cargo weighing it down.

The load of khat had been jettisoned in a ditch outside Hadiqat Al-Zaytoun, freeing space for the team to board but reducing the vehicle's off-road capability to what it was now: a white-knuckle scream ride that could end at any moment, and in the worst possible way. It was at that moment Ian suddenly remembered the man in the back—Tariq, accustomed to riding literal and metaphorical shotgun as the only authorized security against street hijackings.

Now the scrawny Yemeni was probably shitting his pants in the cargo area, stripped of his weapon and even cell phone—both had been confiscated by Ian, along with the driver's, before the intelligence operative had searched their persons as well as the vehicle for any other methods of communication and finding none. The entire operational security protocol had been met with outrage right up until Ian offered a hundred-dollar bill for each man, presented as a generous cash bonus for the inconvenience, at which point both men had eagerly offered up their belongings.

Finally the khat truck slammed down on all four tires, and Raed guided it back onto the road and toward the ravine bridge. Ian got his first chance to see the outcome of his team's ambush, and if his pulse wasn't hammering at such a rapid clip, he would've thought he was dreaming.

Everything appeared to be going according to plan; sure, the lead Al Qaeda vehicle had proceeded a good bit farther than anticipated, and there was now an inverted SUV that had somehow managed to clear the demolished bridge by a substantial margin, but he could make out the trail security vehicle crashed in the ravine as it should have been.

Other than those minor details, he saw David, Worthy, and Munoz securing the pickup site while using whatever cover they could find, sweeping their barrels in search of emerging threats. But it was the sight of Reilly that brought Ian the greatest cause to question his current reality.

The medic was approaching the linkup site at a jog, his pace slowed by the weight of a tall, silver-haired man draped across his shoulders in a fireman's carry.

Ian had studied the available photographs of Fulvio Pagano ever since the identity became synonymous with his better-known pseudonym, Erik

Weisz, and the face had lingered in his thoughts for days. The visual images, however, were just a footnote to the idea of a man who'd been lurking in the shadows of an international terrorist syndicate for years. Now, against all odds, Weisz was unconscious and being toted toward the khat truck with all the ceremony of a sack of potatoes.

Most incredibly of all, the fact that he was being carried out meant he was alive, and that opened up a whole new world of possibilities for Ian to collect intelligence.

At least, he thought, if they managed to make it out of Al Qaeda territory.

"Flip a U-turn," he ordered, "*slowly*—and stop this shitbox."

Raed was all too eager to comply, muttering to himself in a stream of Arabic that could have been a prayer, or profanity, or both.

The view through the windshield transitioned to the hillside they'd just cleared, and with it the sight of Cancer making his way down from the high ground. Ian had flung open his door before the truck had come to a complete halt, and he very nearly leaped out before remembering a critical step in his checklist.

"Kill the engine."

The driver cut the ignition and, at the sight of Ian's open palm, extracted the key and handed it over.

Ian clasped it tightly in his hand, thinking it would have been more than a little professionally embarrassing if the driver he was supposed to control had decided to speed off while his team was loading.

Then Ian stepped into the desert, carefully managing the two weapons slung over his shoulder—his Galil, and Tariq's AK-47—as he ran to open the tailgate before the first occupant boarded.

Or, to put it more properly, the first two.

Reilly came to a stop with the complaint, "This cat is heavier than he looks," before un-shouldering his load and rolling it into the back.

Erik Weisz's limp body hit the cargo area, his head covered in gore that would have represented a fatal injury unless it had come from someone else. Ian couldn't fathom the explanation and didn't bother asking, instead taking up a security position off the rear bumper as David and Munoz arrived, the latter with a tremendously large duffel bag.

Without a word, they climbed into the covered bed after Reilly had negotiated it.

Worthy was next, moving with a pained shuffle before stopping at Ian's
side and speaking.

"Good to see you, brother."

Ian handed him the truck key, which the pointman snatched before
moving out to the passenger seat.

There were two very good reasons for him to occupy that spot on the
way out, the first being his unparalleled capacity for close-quarters shooting, whether inside or outside of a vehicle.

And second, any response by the men in the back of the truck would
require hasty mobility, and the pointman's movements were severely
restricted by virtue of his injured back.

Ian heard a final set of running footfalls, looking over his shoulder to
see Cancer approaching at a jog and calling out to him.

"A little warning about that AQ truck would've been nice."

"Yeah?" Cancer asked, then added, "Fuck yourself," as he came to a stop
and carefully handed his sniper rifle to Munoz in the back as the truck
engine fired to life. Then Cancer vanished inside the cargo area, leaving
Ian to rise and climb inside before securing the tailgate as David
transmitted.

"Go, we're good."

"*Moving*," Worthy responded over the team frequency as the truck
pulled forward, threading its way back onto the road as Ian took in the sight
of the cargo area.

Tariq was in the back, seated on the wooden false-floor frame as
instructed, one hand pressed against the cab. He was also, Ian noted, practically green with nausea, both his lap and the two-by-fours he sat atop
greased with vomit, saliva, and ejected khat leaves.

Reilly had finished flex-cuffing Erik Weisz's wrists and ankles, abandoning the unconscious terrorist figurehead to take up a position at the
rear of the vehicle, where Munoz and Cancer were already stationed for a
hasty exit should their gunfire be required at some point during the
remaining drive.

All three men remained all-business, flowing through their exfil procedures with clockwork precision; but at the moment, their collective poise served to highlight a single glaring disparity.

David Rivers looked like he'd just awoken from a particularly compelling dream, his eyes glazed with a faraway look that conveyed extreme disinterest in the situation now facing his team. Before Ian could consider why that might be, Worthy transmitted.

"*Hang on, guys, we're going off-road for a sec.*"

The cargo area shook as the truck rumbled into the desert, bypassing the downed lead vehicle a hell of a lot more carefully than it had the first time. Ian steadied himself until he felt pavement beneath the tires once more.

Once the ride smoothed out, he asked David the first thing he wanted to know.

"Where's the man he was traveling with? The personal assistant?"

The team leader shrugged without looking his way, as if this was an unimportant detail.

"Died in the crash," he said.

Munoz turned one hand into a finger pistol, placing the tip of his middle finger against his forehead and dropping his cocked thumb.

David corrected himself.

"He died immediately after the crash."

Ian managed to hide his immediate sense of crushing regret, knowing that it wouldn't do him any good to express disapproval. There was nothing anyone could do to reverse the execution, and judging by appearances, David wouldn't have gone back on his actions even if he could.

But there was still one action Ian could take in his capacity as an intelligence operative, and it didn't require Erik Weisz to be conscious.

He shifted toward the restrained captive, reaching beside him to pull the captured duffel bag closer. Its weight was far greater than could be explained by the contents of luggage and toiletries, and Ian held out hope that whatever was inside was worth the effort required to haul it from the ambush site. After locating the zipper, he yanked it down a few inches to peer inside, then he stopped himself for a moment, mindful to conceal the contents from Tariq sitting beside the cab.

David asked, "What is it?"

Ian tipped the opening to face him. "Intel."

The sight seemed to shake the team leader from his stupor; he blinked rapidly before his eyes went wide, as if trying to clear his vision.

It was a fitting reaction. Inside the bag was a barely contained avalanche of stacks of hundred-dollar bills strapped together with bands labeled *$10,000*. Some quick mental math told Ian that he was now in possession of a cool million, maybe even one-point-five.

That amount of cash opened up considerable opportunities for what services they could buy in Yemen; it also, regrettably, increased the odds against them tenfold.

The obvious first step was to not show that money to anyone outside the team, but there was far too much of it to conceal even if they had multiple empty rucks to dedicate to the task, which they didn't. That meant their newfound fortune had to stay in the duffel, which presented the problem that their only viable excuse for carrying it back from the raid was that it contained intelligence materials, which had almost as much financial value as far as the Houthis were concerned.

In partner force operations, a good rule of thumb was to not trust anyone, and Ian's team lived by that ethos whenever possible. But the reward for betraying them had never been higher, and the intelligence operative had no intentions of making that known to the Yemeni fighters who had, thus far, been willing accomplices.

He pulled the zipper shut, first abandoning the bag and then, after reconsidering, shifting it into position to use as a seat. The rest of the team had since assumed cross-legged positions on the floor of the cargo area, settling in for the short and hopefully uneventful ride past Zughaynah and back into Southern Transitional Council lines.

No sooner had that thought occurred to him, however, than he heard Worthy's next transmission from the cab.

"*Stand by.*"

The entire team awkwardly transitioned to kneeling positions in unison, expecting the worst and getting confirmation of the same as the pointman continued his message.

"*We've got an Al Qaeda convoy coming in hot from the west—looks like four vehicles, make that five. Heavy weapons on the lead, middle, and trail trucks, fighters in the back with small arms, and a couple of sedans in between. Estimate fifteen, one-five, bad guys."*

That brief report was about all the team needed to know; details became superfluous once you were outnumbered by a certain degree, Ian mused. They wouldn't be able to take down such a force, not that it would stop them from trying, nor was the rickety khat truck capable of outrunning even the most lethargic of vehicle pursuits—although such an attempt was probably better than the alternative.

He felt the truck slow as Worthy went on.

"They're flagging us down. Wait for my call."

Worthy ended his transmission, turning his attention to Raed in the driver's seat.

"You give them the story we rehearsed. Nothing more, nothing less. Don't get fancy."

Raed grunted.

"You forget that I live here. I know how to deal with these men."

The words contained enough confidence, but Raed's uncertain tone gave Worthy reason to question the sanity of his team's remaining plan. It was a miracle they made it this far, and now the fate of everyone in the truck—with Erik Weisz least among them—hinged on a few Arabic sentences that would hopefully be taken at face value.

And whatever the outcome, Worthy was about to find out firsthand.

The khat truck slowed in tandem with the convoy approaching in the opposite lane, led by a Hilux pickup whose driver was still waving at them to stop.

He did so with the apparent knowledge that his gunner, a teenage boy, wouldn't relinquish his dual grip on the KPV heavy machinegun mounted over the cab. The devastating weapon was aligned with the khat truck's windshield, which now contained a grim and intensely forbidding scene: behind the lead pickup were two nearly identical vehicles down to the KPVs, armed fighters in the back, and black jihadi flags that gave the appearance of desert pirate ships.

A pair of unmarked sedans was interspersed among the trio, an innocuous enough sight until he considered what was inside them. If the cannon fodder rode in unprotected pickup beds, Worthy could safely assume both cars contained the more elite fighters who were held in reserve until the situation warranted some advanced maneuver on foot.

Worthy was struck by the sheer zealotry that the inbound convoy represented—it was easy enough to dehumanize the lot as madmen bound by a shared psychopathy, but the genetic markers were no more unevenly distributed in Yemen than anywhere else on earth. America had no shortage of fanatics despite being one of the more prosperous nations; but if he were to strip away the economic opportunities, ready food supply, and history of remaining untouched by various meddling colonial powers and their chosen military interventions, his native population could just as easily produce legions of willing suppliants for any number of extremist organizations.

And despite the fact that it may be his last consciously felt emotion in this lifetime, he thought, the desperate men now bearing down on his team engendered a fleeting moment of pity.

Worthy ensured his shemagh was situated over the bridge of his nose, speaking his final guidance as Raed rolled down his window.

"Remember, it was an airstrike. And you could still hear the drones circling—don't forget that part."

"I know, I know," Raed said impatiently, and before Worthy could consider any further words, it was too late—the lead Al Qaeda pickup and the khat truck came to a complete stop with their drivers in perfect alignment.

Worthy made a desperate bid to appear nonchalant amid the gut-wrenching possibility that his scarf could fall at any moment. The Al Qaeda driver shouted a string of Arabic—the trail pickup now blocked the lane to their front, its gunner leveling a KPV at the engine block.

If Raed panicked and deviated from the script, Worthy would have precious little time to put his Galil into play, and no way to shoot his way past the convoy; it was all or nothing, the fate of his team coming down to the composure and acting ability of a pudgy and khat-fueled Yemeni.

To his credit, however, Raed responded with casual aplomb, going on to speak quickly and with surprising conviction to deliver what Worthy hoped was their agreed-upon fictional narrative. The man had draped one arm out the open window, gesticulating with both hands in dramatic Arab fashion, his tone conveying both fear at the nonexistent airstrike and a familiar camaraderie that indicated the Al Qaeda devotees in the truck opposite were a final and virtuous line of defense in a world gone mad.

As Worthy waited to gauge the enemy response to this information, he was struck by the absurd parallels between both sides in the current engagement. The men of the Al Qaeda convoy would accept without question whatever determination was made by the lead driver, and do so in a hierarchical order no less rigid than that of his own team. Hell, he thought, there were five Americans in the back right now who would either stay put or leap out into imminent death depending on whether or not Worthy spoke a single word over their radio frequency.

As if to emphasize this similarity, the passenger in the Al Qaeda truck was practically a mirror image of Worthy: similar height, build, and attire, down to a shemagh pulled up over the bridge of his nose.

Worthy detected the man scrutinizing him then, and he deflected the effort by leaning forward to look up beyond the windshield, scanning for visible aircraft before repeating the display out his passenger window.

He wondered if he was being too dramatic and, to avoid suspicion, halted the search only to discover that his alter ego in the other truck was now doing the same thing.

Then the whole exchange was simply *over*, Raed barking a farewell in Arabic with a wave of his hand before accelerating the khat truck forward and focusing his attention on the road.

The Al Qaeda convoy likewise lurched into motion on their eastward course, the trail vehicle clearing the lane as the enemy vehicles continued at a far slower rate of progress. Worthy watched his sideview mirror until he could make out the receding vehicles, now spreading out into a looser formation, presumably out of a preponderance of caution that at any moment, one or more Hellfire missiles would come screaming out of the sky.

He reversed his gaze to fixate on Raed, now driving merrily along as if nothing had occurred.

"They believed you?" Worthy asked.

"Obviously." Raed sounded offended that the pointman had so much as a moment of doubt. "I spent two years at Sana'a University. I was in the acting club."

"No shit? What happened?"

"Khat paid better, my friend."

Was this guy being serious, Worthy wondered, or making a joke?

David transmitted, "*Hey Racegun, how about an update—we shooting people or what?*"

"Not yet," Worthy replied. "Apparently I'm sitting next to the Yemeni Daniel Day-Lewis. Al Qaeda convoy moved out, and we're making a run for the checkpoint."

Cancer noted that an immediate sense of relief washed over the cargo area —he'd been seated next to Reilly at the rear passenger-side corner, prepared to leap out and engage far targets while David and Munoz handled the lead vehicle in the Al Qaeda convoy.

Upon hearing Worthy's transmission, the other three men visibly relaxed. Cancer looked behind him, where Ian stood watch over the motionless figure of Erik Weisz as well as Pukie, which the sniper had not-so-affectionately termed the still-nauseated Yemeni khat guard. Ian, too, looked immensely comforted by the news, flashing an exasperated but nervous smile that Cancer didn't return.

Instead, he looked back to the other men before speaking his mind.

"Don't start slapping each other's asses just yet," he began ominously, "because we got a long way to go before the locker room. All we did was buy ourselves a few extra minutes, and we better be long gone from AQ jurisdiction before any of those fucks make it to the ambush site."

No one responded, either in affirmation or dissent—Cancer's proclamations invited neither—and he was pleased to see an air of discomfort take hold among the other men. Discomfort was welcome right now, as were the acceptable alternatives of fear, anger, and/or bloodlust.

Complacency, however, was one indulgence he couldn't abide either now or until the team returned to America, if they did at all.

Cancer was especially delighted to note the chagrined appearance of one David Rivers, the only man who realized how perilous the current gambit truly was.

In truth, the airstrike excuse would only serve to delay any detailed examination of the ambush site. After all, any Al Qaeda devotees worth their salt would be reluctant to race into the crosshairs of an unmanned aerial vehicle orbiting overhead, searching for follow-on targets to expend any remaining munitions before returning to base.

But the fact remained that the Al Qaeda convoy would soon be depositing a few expendable and unarmed men to approach the kill zone on foot under the not-misperceived notion that Western rules of engagement prohibited the deliberate engagement of possible civilians. The first men to reach the devastation surrounding the bridge wouldn't have to be master detectives to conclude a gunfight had taken place, and once *that* particular word got out, the khat truck that Cancer's team rode in now would become the subject of a territory-wide search; survivable under some circumstances, but not when only one road spanned the gap to government territory.

His team's only hope was to clear the lone remaining Al Qaeda checkpoint before that occurred, and in the coming minutes they'd know the outcome one way or another.

Worthy transmitted, *"Al Qaeda checkpoint ahead, and...wait one."*

The air of urgency returned to the team, David and Munoz taking a knee beside their rucks with weapons ready, and Reilly tensing for imminent enemy contact as Cancer patted his shoulder by way of confirming that he, too, was ready to rock and roll. These were the moments that warriors lived for, the adrenaline-soaked anticipation in the final seconds before a life-or-death confrontation presented itself with a fury that demanded the utmost levels of combat-honed instinct to survive.

Then the transmission continued.

"Yep, there it is—they're waving us through."

The complacency that Cancer had struggled to keep at bay returned almost in full, with Reilly pumping his fist in celebration as the truck rattled onward.

David and Munoz likewise relaxed, resuming their seated positions atop their rucks and grinning like idiots.

"*We're clear,*" Worthy continued. "*Entering no-man's land, 9.4 kilometers to government lines.*"

"Well," Ian said after David had confirmed the transmission, "that was anticlimactic."

Cancer had a pre-programmed response, and he glowered at the intelligence operative as he delivered it.

"*If* we make it back to the khat farm, I want this truck refueled first thing. Munoz, you'll be driving it for the blowout plan—"

Munoz interjected, "This truck is burned."

"Which is why," Cancer continued, "we use it as a magnet to draw out pursuers. Worthy and Reilly in the back to shoot it out with anyone who follows us. Van is in the lead with me driving, David riding shotgun, Ian in the back to interrogate Weisz. And Baterfi stays with us so we have control over his security men—if we get hit at the khat farm, I want them fighting a delaying maneuver before they run, and then we ditch them altogether. Because if word about Weisz's bounty gets out, the odds of them selling us out are greater than the odds of them helping us."

"Concur," David said. "What's the route?"

Reilly answered, "Back road out of the farm to Owen Al-Down and access to the N6, and from there we can travel any way but north until we're free from pursuit. We've got three bed-down sites plotted in each cardinal direction."

Cancer nodded. "Good. So you and Worthy shoot it out until I can maneuver the van to eliminate whoever follows us out. Then we abandon this truck, consolidate in the van, and we're off the grid. So that's the blowout plan, if we make it back to the khat farm in the first place— because if it's not Al Qaeda that gets us pinched, it could be those government fuckers at the next stop."

There was a moment of silence before Reilly commented.

"So what if...ah, never mind."

"What?" David asked.

"I'm just thinking," the medic continued, "what if...I mean, if the government checkpoint demands a search—"

Cancer interjected, "We kill 'em. All of them. What's the problem?"

"Yeah, I get that. But just supposing there's too many, and we're not going to make it out..."

His words trailed off, though Cancer knew well enough what the conclusion of the thought would entail. Judging by the faces of David and Munoz, both men were thinking the same thing.

Cancer felt a flush of heat across his face as Reilly went on.

"In that event, if worse comes to worst...who gets to kill Erik Weisz?"

The cargo area filled with overlapping voices as each man blurted out the case in his favor. Cancer remained silent for a few seconds, trying to maintain control of his actions and finding himself wanting.

"He's mine," the sniper shouted, the volume and tone of his voice a verbal gunshot that silenced the rest of the team.

His intensity evoked a palpable tension, and Cancer glared down at each man in turn as if hoping to face some dissent that he could crush by sheer force of will if not his fists.

Everyone's face assumed a grim and very sober expression—or almost everyone.

To Cancer's surprise, it was Munoz whose face blossomed into a smile.

Then the man abruptly sat up, placing a hand on his hip and making a formal announcement with an exaggeratedly pompous British accent.

"I come," Munoz began, "to claim the right...of prima nocta."

"Yeah," Cancer agreed, nodding slowly. "This guy gets it—it's my noble *fucking* right."

That seemed to somewhat defuse the tension between the men, which was extinguished altogether when Reilly shrugged and muttered, "Don't mess with the old guy on the team, I guess. Whatever."

Cancer scanned the men for any indication that his words were not those of God Almighty, and a sudden instinct in his gut caused him to fixate on David Rivers, who was trying to keep his face neutral but was unable to suppress a gleam of mischief in his eyes.

But the look came and went in a flash, after which the team leader's shoulders sagged and he said with casual ease, "Sure." Then, parroting Reilly's sentiment, he concluded, "Whatever."

The sniper felt an inkling of suspicion then, though the feeling was interrupted when Worthy's voice came over the radio.

"Government checkpoint in sight. Let's see if they buy our story."

Once again, the team tensed for an imminent gunfight, though not, Cancer saw, with the same vigor as they had when initially stopped by the Al Qaeda convoy. One near-miss got everyone's attention, a second was less interesting, and by the time the third came and went, they'd all be convinced of their immortality until the first enemy gunshot brought everyone back to their senses.

And that moment may have been fast approaching, Cancer thought as he felt the khat truck slow to a halt. He heard a murmur of Arabic beside the cab, interrupted by the frantic voice of his driver calling out a panicked and ongoing response.

Cancer knew well enough what the driver was supposed to be announcing, the entire script part and parcel of a carefully orchestrated deception plan: Al Qaeda was massing for a frontal assault of the government lines, mobilizing dozens of vehicles carrying hundreds of fighters. The khat truck had sped past the final terrorist checkpoint to outrun the attack, which would surely be arriving any minute.

To be fair, there was at least a kernel of possibility to the fabrication, because who knew if those crazy Al Qaeda bastards would in their eternal brutality decide to pursue the offending khat truck into certain annihilation. Whether or not they did, the story should have been sufficient to put the government soldiers on the defensive, concerned with meeting the incoming threat rather than wasting time by searching a vehicle that had crossed back and forth countless times in the past.

And if they didn't, he thought with relish, he'd have ample opportunity to put his weapon to good use once more, along with every other American in the truck. Because any debatable sovereignty of Yemen's Southern Transitional Council came a distant third after both the survival of his team and the successful exfiltration of one Erik Weisz, not just the highest-value target his team had taken down to date, but the most significant in a very long and exceedingly complex matrix of known terrorists.

The truck suddenly pulled forward, requiring Cancer to steady himself against Reilly to keep from falling—it was his only indication of how the exchange had gone until Worthy transmitted a moment later.

"*Looks like they bought it. They told us to get out of here, and everyone at the checkpoint is gearing up for a fight.*"

Cancer found his gaze drifting to Erik Weisz, still unconscious on the truck floor, as Worthy continued, "*I wouldn't spike a football just yet, but...well, boys, I think we just made it out.*"

34

"*Raptor Nine One, this is Suicide Actual.*"

Chen heard a collective and very audible gasp of relief among the staff, and she reached for the hand mic as if it represented her salvation; at this point, it very nearly did.

Since the team's last transmission—the call had come from Cancer, notifying her that the team's target was inbound—tension in the OPCEN had risen to a very palpable breaking point, a single unstated question hanging heavy in the relative silence.

Had they just lost their only remaining ground team?

She keyed the mic and said, "Suicide Actual, Raptor Nine One. Send it."

"*Be advised,*" David said, "*we just made it back to the khat farm. All personnel and equipment accounted for. No injuries. And we have Weisz in custody.*"

Chen felt an abrupt wave of lightheadedness.

That final line seemed almost too good to be true. While the stated mission for this incursion was a classic k/c, kill or capture, the fact that it had to occur well within Al Qaeda lines made the "c" part of the equation an almost theoretical consideration more than anything else.

She replied, "Has he said anything yet?"

"*Negative,*" David answered, suddenly sounding immeasurably fatigued. "*He was knocked out during the ambush. Hasn't woken up yet, and he may be brain dead or close to it.*"

Chen was undaunted. "The medical staff aboard the carrier will make that determination. If he regains consciousness in the meantime, I want Angel to conduct the most thorough questioning he's capable of and keep me posted in real time. Did you recover any intelligence from his vehicle?"

"*Except for his phone and pocket litter, no. His vehicle rolled over in the blast, and whatever else he had was trapped inside.*"

Chen's response wasn't over the radio net, but rather to her staff.

"They leave tonight," she announced. "Jamieson?"

The operations officer was already holding one arm skyward, hand clenched in a victorious thumbs-up.

She transmitted, "Copy all. Your orders are to remain in position until nightfall before beginning movement. Exfil will occur at LZ Lima at 0045 with all personnel including your package."

"*Same platform?*"

"Correct. One Osprey touching down while a diversion flight conducts false insertions to the east."

"*We'll be there,*" David proclaimed, "*and if there's nothing else, I need to assess security and check on Sleeping Beauty.*"

"Nothing else from me. Outstanding work out there. Raptor Nine One standing by."

Chen expected a volley of applause to erupt in the OPCEN, and for good reason—after all this time, effort, and bloodshed, Project Longwing's highest-priority target had been taken off the battlefield for good. And the ground team had somehow survived the effort with all of their men intact, no small feat given where they'd conducted their raid.

But instead she was met with silence as she set down her radio mic, a chilling reminder that five American contractors from the second team remained unaccounted for. It was one thing to manage non-attributable fighting men in the context of covert operations, but actually losing them while knowing *there was nothing you could do* to get them back was another thing entirely.

The intelligence staff had been monitoring every means at their disposal for any indication of whether the missing team had been killed outright or survived capture and, if so, where they were now; the effort had been to no avail, and that presented a delicate matter for the surviving family members. Protocol for a lost CIA officer or contractor was simple: a member of the personnel department would be dispatched to notify the family and allow them to read a letter of condolence signed by the director, after which the letter was returned to the Agency. Benefits would be paid, a closed-door award ceremony scheduled, and ideally the matter would never hit the press.

But in this case, Meiling Chen could provide no conclusive evidence as to what had actually happened to those five men.

She banished the thought for the time being, focusing instead on more pressing matters.

"Priorities," she called out. "Intelligence section, your primary focus as of this moment is to detect any threats to our team's safe exfiltration with their captive. Operations section—"

"Yes, ma'am," Jamieson interrupted.

Chen fixed him in her gaze and continued, "Find out the extent to which DoD will support an emergency daylight exfil, if required. Our risk tolerance has shifted considerably now that Weisz is alive. And make sure the carrier's medical staff are prepared to receive him."

She turned to face Gregory Pharr, an Agency lawyer who was the subject-matter expert for Project Longwing's convoluted authorities.

"Legal, where do we stand on paperwork for an extraordinary rendition?"

"Fully drafted," Pharr responded. "I just need to update the specifics of his capture and we'll be good to hook."

"I want to review it fully before you submit."

"That is what I understood, ma'am."

"That will be all," she concluded, barely finishing her sentence before lifting the phone from its cradle.

Now came the best part of her job. With the team still in Yemen, it was too soon to claim total victory, but this was as close as she was going to get before the exfil was complete.

When the line connected her with an Agency switchboard operator, she spoke.

"Put me through to the office of Senator Gossweiler."

35

"Wait," I hissed. "Don't you fucking dare."

There were a few embarrassed murmurs from Reilly and Ian, currently clustered around the Iveco truck and, more importantly, around Erik Weisz, who was propped up in a seated position against the rear tire.

We'd returned to the khat farm minutes earlier, and while my teammates performed actual combat necessities like topping off magazines and water, I was relegated to the indignities of setting up satellite communications to relay our newfound status to Chen, the last person on earth I wanted to talk to.

I collapsed the telescoping rods of my mobile satellite antenna as quickly as possible, glancing back over with the fear that either Reilly or Ian would disregard my order and wake up our prisoner before I arrived.

But Weisz's face bore the serene expression of sleep or worse, the latter all too possible with the dried blood and brain matter covering his right forehead and cheek.

Once I'd successfully packed up the antenna, I checked my watch—eight hours of daylight remaining, not nearly enough time to make a run at the prison in Sana'a.

But it was more than enough time for me to come up with an excuse to delay exfil.

Strictly speaking, what I'd told Chen about not recovering intelligence wasn't a lie—there was the small matter of a million-plus dollars in US currency sitting in a duffel right now, but I wasn't about to tell that to her. Because while my team couldn't exactly take that money home unnoticed, we faced the yet-unresolved issue of four American POWs locked up in an impenetrable prison in Sana'a, 270 kilometers to our north. Rescuing them, or even remaining alive in Yemen long enough to make the attempt, would likely require financial resources that Chen wasn't about to provide.

If we hadn't discovered Munoz, this would have been a home run. Capturing Weisz was no small feat, and Chen had made her first favorable tactical decision in ordering the quickest possible pickup at a landing zone a scant two-hour drive from our current location.

I stood and turned to advance on Weisz, nearly running into Cancer in the process.

"Easy, boss," he said.

I asked, "Blowout plan set?"

"Iveco is fueled, and Baterfi's militiamen are positioned at the main gate. Exfil?"

"Osprey pickup out of Lima, quarter to one."

He gave me a hopeful glance. "We gonna make that?"

Cancer was, I knew, probing my steadfastness in pursuing the POWs—and, with the knowledge that he was scanning me for doubts, I resolved to show him none.

"Definitely not. I'm going to give it some time, then tell her we got into trouble and had to flee to a bed-down site. Plan on exfil getting rolled 24 hours to the next period of darkness."

"Think about it," he said. "Our team is alive, and we recovered Munoz. Then we managed to grab Weisz, and have the chance to get him out alive in"—he consulted his watch—"less than fifteen hours."

I drew a breath. "You know what? You're right."

His posture didn't soften as I continued, "We did get Munoz, and we did get Weisz. But I just had to waste brain cells dealing with one manipulative naysayer, so let's not make it two. My marriage has been strained to the breaking point after two years of chasing this asshole all over the globe"—I jerked a thumb toward Weisz—" and now we've got him. So please, Cancer,

I beg of you: can you find it in your cold, black, shriveled heart to let me have five minutes of fucking peace and quiet to enjoy this—"

"Fine," he conceded, throwing up his hands. "Have at it."

"Perfect."

Before I could move, however, Cancer reached into his pocket and said, "And we missed something on our first search. Weisz was wearing this."

He handed me a necklace, and I quickly examined the large, intricate silver pendant. It looked like a tree whose branches ended in various symbols: key, crescent moon, dagger, and rose. Was this from some secret society?

I turned away from him to close the distance with Weisz and said, "Wake him up."

To his credit, Reilly didn't roll his eyes at me; it was a mystery to him as much as the rest of us what level of cognitive function Weisz was capable of after his SUV turned into a high-speed centrifuge. Instead, he knelt beside the prisoner, whose back was propped up against the car, flex-cuffed ankles stretched out before him. Then Reilly grasped the prisoner's trapezius and gave a powerful squeeze.

Ian barely had time to set up his digital voice recorder before the medic completed the act; and, as it turned out, there was no need to rush.

Weisz didn't move or react in the slightest, which wasn't a good sign. Reilly could practically curl my best bench press, and if his strength didn't do the trick, there was no point in the rest of us making the attempt.

"All right," Reilly muttered, "round two."

He formed a fist with one hand and pressed his knuckles to Weisz's sternum, rubbing up and down against the breastbone with increasing force and vigor that was actually painful to watch; still, Weisz remained motionless. It was utterly impossible for any man alive to fake unconsciousness under such circumstances, and the odds were looking better and better that we'd inadvertently induced a coma from which Erik Weisz would never awake.

Reilly abandoned the effort.

"Last chance," he said, "if the salts don't work, nothing will."

He retrieved a small plastic pouch from his kit, and I exchanged a concerned glance with Cancer beside me. The outcome of this final attempt would determine whether we'd just gone to great lengths to extract a human vegetable from Al Qaeda's backyard, and I intuitively sensed that Weisz had spoken his last words before our explosive detonation at the bridge.

Reilly held his breath and squinted before tearing the pouch open, and within seconds, I knew why.

I could smell the ammonia even at this distance, my eyes stinging with the noxious fumes as Reilly wafted the packet six inches in front of Weisz's nose without result. Gradually he brought the inhalant closer, finally losing patience and stuffing the open end beneath our captive's nostrils.

That final act had the intended effect.

While the man didn't open his eyes, he was unquestionably awake, head jerking to the side as his body jolted to full muscle tension.

Reilly removed the packet immediately and Weisz's eyelids fluttered open. He cringed at the daylight before his gaze darted across the team, settling momentarily on me.

Then he looked at the medic and the open pouch in his hand, after which he spoke the first words to his captors.

Or more specifically, to Reilly.

"Let me get another hit of that."

Reilly shot me a quizzical look.

"Sure," I said.

Weisz took a few tentative sniffs at the newly offered packet, then inhaled more deeply before flinching and shaking his head, eyes pinched shut. Then they flew open with a startled glare that revealed dazzlingly bright hazel irises.

"Okay," he managed, nodding with vigor, "I am *back*."

Then his face morphed into an electrifying smile, the face of a celebrity all too delighted to greet their fans in person. He continued in an elegant Italian accent, "May I have some water, please?"

Cancer signaled the medic to join Worthy and Munoz on security; Reilly departed as I lowered myself to a seated position on the ground, settling into a casual cross-legged stance as Ian held a canteen for Weisz to take long, gulping sips until he was satisfied.

I held up the amulet he'd been wearing and asked, "What is this?"

"An Italian cimaruta," he said, "from my mother. She hung it over my crib to ward off evil spirits...until now, it seemed to work."

So much for a secret society, I thought, pocketing the talisman as the captive looked from Ian to me and asked, "And who do I have the pleasure of meeting?"

"You and I spoke," I began, "over a satphone, once. In Libya."

Weisz tilted his head, appearing as if his recollection countered my own. Then he replied, "You were in Libya, perhaps. I was not."

"Where were you?"

"At the time?" He thought for a moment, his expression brightening with the effect of recalling a particularly fond memory; or maybe, I thought, he was simply taunting me.

Then he said, "Ukraine, I believe. Yes, definitely Ukraine. Kharkiv, at the moment we spoke. Where is Matteo?"

"Was he the guy riding next to you?"

"He was."

"Still in your truck. You brought most of his brain back on your face, though, so there's that. Were you in Ukraine to support the locals, or the Russians?"

Weisz looked like he couldn't have possibly understood my meaning, going silent for the first time since awakening.

I leaned toward him and offered, "I'm still speaking English. Were you supporting the Ukrainians, or the—"

"*Supporting?*" he scoffed. "I went as a student, as I always do."

I had no idea what he meant by that, though apparently Ian did. The intelligence operative slowly dropped to a knee at my left side, taking up a seated position that mirrored my own and rubbing his temple with one hand.

I asked, "A student...what do you mean?"

It was not Weisz, but Ian, who responded, "The next generation of warfare..."

"Yes"—the captive nodded—"exactly this. The future is not about battle tanks, fighter jets, air-to-ground capabilities, not about what one man with a long-range missile can accomplish, you understand? The script, this *new* script, is only being written in a few places right now.

Ukraine is one of them, and I have made many visits to study there just as I have to Yemen."

Ian asked, "Azerbaijan?"

Weisz didn't need to reply for me to interpret his response in the affirmative; the terrorist leader closed his eyes and inhaled as if we'd just asked about a particularly relaxing vacation, before finally responding with breathless enthusiasm.

"Yes, Azerbaijan...drones versus main battle tanks. It is incredible what they have accomplished. I try to remain objective, of course, but it is one of my favorite places to visit."

Weisz blinked as if all this information should have been obvious. "It takes a network to defeat a hierarchy, after all. Anywhere that has occurred over the past ten years, I have been there."

I became aware that Ian had a notepad in his lap, jotting annotations with surprising speed as a backup to his digital recorder.

His response was far more composed than mine—I felt like I was in a trance state, suddenly channeling some vastly superior alien intelligence that would answer any and all questions to the limits of my imagination. Was Erik Weisz simply in shock, I wondered, or always this forthcoming? I suspected the latter, but I forged ahead in case I was wrong.

"Cigarette?" I asked.

"I never smoke."

"Then tell me what terrorist plots are in the works right now, starting with America."

"Plots?" He smiled, delighted at my naivety. "This thing has grown much larger than me. I no longer concern myself with the tactical, or even operational. Only the strategic."

"Then why," I asked, intending to test him on this declaration, "did you attack Cairo?"

"The answer to that is quite simple: I didn't."

"Bullshit. You can't tell me you had no connection to—"

He cut me off.

"Obviously. As I said, my concerns are strategic. I supplied a small quantity of the total VX, along with some funding, to Islamic State in the Sinai Province. Both the target selection and method of attack for Tahrir Square, however, were theirs alone. The rest of the VX, as you are aware, went to Khalil Noureddin along with a target assignment not in Egypt but Italy."

Ian supplied, "Naval Air Station Sigonella."

"Indeed."

Then the intelligence operative continued, "That's what we thought. But why strike Sigonella? You could have killed a lot more civilians in any number of cities within range of those missiles."

Weisz considered the question for a brief moment.

"I knew the hostage rescue elements would operate from there, along with the most exotic drones employed to locate a senator's daughter facing imminent execution in Libya. It seemed poetic, so..." He gave an ambivalent shrug. "I suppose I ordered it...for fun."

Jesus, I thought, this guy wasn't lying.

I asked, "What other WMDs are in play right now?"

"How would I know?" he shot back. "The process of acquiring VX began years ago, as I am sure you are well aware. But I anticipated my capture long before this point, and so rather than demanding subservience, I provided the connections between organizations, along with seed money and guidance, and culled a portion of the ensuing financial gain for reinvestment only when connections became profitable."

"Why?"

"I did these things in the name of progress. Guns, drugs, human beings, diamonds, precursor chemicals, aircraft, explosives, cash...all are now changing hands without any limitations of national borders or, indeed, even continents. In this way each organization retains independence and self-determination, is insulated from the setbacks of government interference against the others, yet operates in concert with the whole—so a victory for one node is a victory for the entire network. My role has never been to control, but to delegate authority, allow self-organization, and empower those organizations with the greatest potential. The result is far more adaptability on an international scale, as I am sure you can imagine."

"Tell me what happened to Duchess."

I saw genuine confusion in his eyes. "I'm very sorry. But I have no idea who that is."

So her death really was random, I thought. Then, realizing my mistake, I clarified, "Kimberly Bannister."

"Ah," he gasped, appearing for all the world to be happy that he could finally illuminate some of my more primitive understandings. "The woman in charge of Project Longwing. I had her killed, of course."

"Why?"

"Because I could not reach you."

"Reach me?" I asked, suddenly feeling an upswing of rage concerning the impact of my professional activities on the lives of my wife and daughter.

But that rage was countered by an equal portion of confusion as I replied, "I go shopping for fucking groceries. What do you mean you couldn't reach me?"

"My apologies. I misspoke. What I meant to establish was that I could not *identify* you. *Reaching* is simple enough, if one has a name. I did not."

"Then how did you get Kimberly Bannister's name?"

He thought for a moment, then said, "Natalie Keaton."

Ian was furiously scrawling on his notepad as I asked, "Who the fuck is that?"

"She works in the CIA's personnel department. Pay grade of GS-12, I believe. She had access to the program's title and director, but beyond that, well, the program is quite well compartmentalized."

Now I was the one in shock, unable to comprehend the extent of his candor as I spoke my thoughts aloud.

"And you don't mind giving her up."

Weisz gave an easy shrug. "I have no further use for her. And I must admit that you have bested me quite soundly. This is quite embarrassing to say, but...well, I thought you were already safely in custody in Sana'a, and that I could pay for you upon the conclusion of my visit to Al Qaeda. I had no idea there was a second Project Longwing team."

"Yeah," I offered, "well, if it's any consolation, until a couple days ago neither did we."

"As I said, the program is quite well compartmentalized."

His expression brightened, giving the appearance that he viewed this entire exchange as an intellectual exercise that he was more than willing to continue. "What else would you like to know?"

"Your end goal," I said firmly.

He chuckled heartily at my ignorance, eyes tearing up before he gave me a sad little frown—a master of his craft tutoring a new pupil. Then he asked compassionately, with a professorial tone, "What do *you* think my end goal is?"

"As best as I can tell, it's anarchy."

"Anarchy?" he said, sounding surprised. "That is already upon us, though the civilized world has yet to realize it."

"Explain."

"More water, please."

Ian complied at once, eager to keep Weisz speaking, and once the terrorist leader had drunk his fill, he said, "Thank you. Where were we?"

"Anarchy," I said.

"Ah. Of course. Look no further than the population crisis. It holds all the answers you seek."

"Overpopulation holds the answers?"

Weisz grew frustrated with me, cutting his eyes to Ian and, with a forced expression, imploring him to inject some intelligence into the proceedings.

Ian cleared his throat and said, "*Under*population."

"Yes." Weisz nodded. "Excellent. Let us first consider China, whose one-child policy has utterly devastated their ability to maintain current production levels over the next few decades. All but a few countries in the world face equally devastating consequences of voluntarily reduced childbirth, which means international trade as we know it will soon break down. The global labor force is shrinking rapidly, my friends, and all available demographic statistics indicate that any opportunity to alter this outcome came and went decades ago. Both China and Russia will be superpowers no more —merely two extreme examples of what will occur across the vast majority of countries."

"So?"

"So? The world, my friend, is operating on a false construct of maritime security and fair trade established by your country after World War II. This house of cards relies on imports and exports to be generated at levels necessary for each country to survive, and when one domino falls, the rest collapse as well. A single factory shutdown in the supply chain causes a chain reaction that can take a year or more to remedy, and such shutdowns will occur on a global level in the not-distant future. And mass famine will be only the first beginning of this coming wave."

Ian knew well enough that I was ignorant about such nonsense, and he hastened to take the lead.

"I'm familiar with what you're saying, and there are people a lot smarter than either of us who would agree with you. What I don't understand is what connection, if any, you make between massive geopolitical shifts and your actions in linking various terrorist actors around the world."

"Ah." Weisz nodded. "Consider the fall, the imminent collapse. What will become of your governments then? When the global order implodes— and it shall—the ruling elite will flee to the luxury bunkers their stolen wealth has provided."

I said, "If you're right about all this, I don't disagree. But terrorism isn't going to solve any of that."

"Terrorism," he said coldly, spitting the word back at me, "is nothing more than a means to mobilize the people, to unite them under a banner of resistance. To get them off the rancid teat of corrupt governments that will not stand for much longer. They do not need to go to war against the world order any more than your country needed to go to war with the Soviet Union; instead, they just need to hold fast until their opponent collapses from within. And not even a global superpower can defeat a peasant army of true believers—just ask the Vietcong or, better yet, the Taliban, as unsophisticated a group of cavemen as God ever saw fit to allow into the twenty-first century. You know there is truth to what I am saying because you've kept my name out of the mainstream media. No government, after all, wants to risk creating a martyr for self-determination.

"The fact that the movement has succeeded thus far is all the evidence you need to know it comes from a place of truth. False motivation can be suppressed, but the real desire for change...nothing is powerful enough to put out that fire. I simply connected the dots to build a coalition of world-wide resistance—reprogramming the system, you see, so that some will survive the inevitable fall into chaos. Doing so requires security, security requires guns, and when the militaries of the world dissolve, there will be a new order of local power ready to lead the way out of darkness."

This guy was either completely insane or a startling genius, I thought, though I couldn't discern any middle ground between the two possibilities.

"Well," I replied, "we've got you now. Who's taking your seat at the table?"

"Table? This is not the military, my friend. Not a government, not a hierarchy at all. Quite the opposite, in fact. It is instead a network, and one that you grievously misunderstand."

Ian began, "You're saying that—"

"There *is* no succession, you see? No mantle to replace. The web exists; my endgame is complete, and how I operated for so long and with such impunity is a testament to the fact that my services were desperately needed. For years I forged alliances and connections while your country battled dirt farmers in the desert to maintain dignity in avenging two thousand civilians, an action which occurred as a direct result of the uncontested Western slaughter of hundreds of thousands of innocents all over the world over the past century, all of which you chose to sweep under the rug by saying that your enemies hate your freedom."

He looked from me to Ian and back again, speaking now with strained emphasis.

"What freedom, my friends, what freedom? Your population is held captive by mass incarceration and a twelve-hour news cycle during which you are fed the views of a handful of family dynasties running media conglomerates that dictate your every opinion, with just enough political, racial, and sexual noise mixed in to keep you divided.

"Your puppet masters think they consolidate power, but the only true power lies in a *cause*. America has lost sight of what that word even means, and so she resorts to pointing at monsters abroad. For twenty years you chased terrorists in other lands, you vilified immigrants, without recognizing that the greatest threat to your nation's continued existence is her own citizens."

I interrupted, "America has been doing just fine for the last couple centuries. If 9/11 didn't bring us down, I don't think anything will."

Weisz looked profoundly disappointed at my conclusion.

"You are only reinforcing my point."

"How?" I asked.

"Let us call a spade a spade: Bin Laden was an idiot. A well-intentioned idiot, but an idiot nonetheless. He could only conduct a strike with the brains of Khalid Sheikh Mohammed. And consider that strike, if you will: economic and military targets of the World Trade Center and Pentagon, which succeeded. What of the missing airliner?"

"The passengers overcame the terrorists, which contradicts everything you're saying."

A pained look flashed across his face.

"Well, I do not mean to quibble on details—the flight was actually shot down, a fact that is well known to many in your government and military who lied about it to their people as they always do. But what I am asking you is, what was the target of that plane?"

Ian answered, "The United States Capitol."

Weisz bowed his head gratefully, a prophet whose message was finally understood. "Correct, and with it the political component of the attack."

"Which failed," I noted. "Al Qaeda didn't succeed."

"Yes, and that is precisely my point. Extremist Muslims couldn't strike your Capitol Building. And yet, your own so-called patriotic citizens were able to attack and overrun it—quite successfully, I might add—less than twenty years later, on January 6th. Do you see the contradiction? Do you understand? *Your own people did what Al Qaeda could not.* And this occurred in a country that was as peaceful and prosperous as any on earth in the course of human history...all while debating which of two political puppets should sit in a chair in your Oval Office to serve the real ruling elite, who pull the strings via campaign financing, lobbying, and revolving-door politics. So tell me, how will those 'civilized' people react when the world order falls?"

I was rendered speechless, unsure where to take the interrogation and hoping Ian would fill the gap.

He didn't.

Instead I assumed a tone of total confidence in Weisz, playing the role of disciple as I said, "So what happens now that you're off the battlefield?"

"Think back to the days before I established a global network. That was the closest you will see to terrorism being kept in check in this lifetime. Killing me will be like stepping on a pregnant spider."

Ian asked, "Meaning?"

I sighed. "Look up a video. The babies go everywhere—fucking horrific."

"It is," Weisz agreed. "And as a matter of fact, my disappearance is at this very moment achieving the same effect. The network is now far bigger than any one man, least of all me. So good luck with the fallout. You are going to need it."

Finally, I couldn't take any more; I was used to interrogations against fearful men gripped by capture shock, where the mere possibility of torture induced them to spill their guts. With Weisz, I got the impression that torture would, if anything, give him a certain degree of erotic pleasure.

"Well," I said, "you can have fun explaining that to your real interrogators. Because you've got the rest of your life to do it."

"No," he said dismissively, "I most certainly will not. I am already dead, you see."

For a moment, I wondered if Weisz had anything so crude as a fake molar loaded with poison.

Suicide pills were famously *de rigueur* for high-ranking Nazi officials, although similar methods of hasty self-destruction were carried in an imaginative number of ways by members of various international secret services. The CIA had, upon request, provided a pen with a cyanide cap to a Soviet diplomat who made ready use of the device when the KGB arrested him for spying on behalf of America.

But no sooner had the thought occurred to me than I dismissed it out of hand: whatever Erik Weisz meant by the comment, it was nothing so obvious.

Or easy.

"Why," I asked, "do you say that you're already dead?"

"You forget where you are, my friend. I am worth too much for my capture to go uncontested—"

An explosion erupted from the khat farm's main entrance, the blast followed by volleys of unsuppressed gunfire from the guard posts.

Ian and I leapt up, looking toward the noise and unable to see anything beyond a dust cloud rising lazily over the khat fields.

Cancer ran to my side and said, "VBIED at the gate, let's go."

Weisz shrugged.

"I told you. You may as well kill me now and get it over with."

Cancer drew his pistol, suddenly looking very young—it was the expression of a child who'd formed an instant bond with a pet store puppy, and now turned hopeful eyes toward the parent in the hopes of prevailing through the sheer magic of the moment.

"Hard no," I said. "Get his ass in the van. He's coming with us."

Though crestfallen, Cancer's response to my order was immediate. He holstered his Glock and forcefully dragged Weisz toward the Volkswagen.

Ian started to move out, too, until I grabbed his shoulder, leaned in, and whispered in his ear.

He listened, absorbed my order, then recoiled. "Are you sure?"

"Positive."

He looked at our vehicle. We had no time left, but Ian still made sure he got in a last shot. "You're going to do what Erik Weisz couldn't. You're going to get us all killed."

36

Reilly struggled valiantly to keep his HK417 level from his seated position in the Iveco's jostling cargo area, watching vigilantly for any signs of pursuit as Munoz sped beyond the farm's back gate and onto a dirt trail.

Worthy was seated at the opposite corner of the tailgate, wielding his Galil to lock down an intersecting field of fire across the road behind them but nonetheless serving as a backup shooter: he'd restrict his shots to anything that Reilly couldn't handle alone with his more accurate weapon.

The truck sped past a road intersection between the sandy hills around them, the first of many dirt roads that crossed their exfil route. None of them, however, would help the team in the least. Once the khat farm's meager defenses were overwhelmed—which wouldn't take long, judging by the quantity of incoming gunfire when they left—Weisz's rescuers wouldn't be long to arrive. If Reilly's team hadn't reached the paved roads of the nearest town by the time that occurred, the enemy could easily follow the dust trail, much less vehicle tracks, and the men in the khat truck would be spotted and relegated to the impossible task of fending off what was presumably an incredibly well-resourced pursuit.

If that happened, there were only two possible outcomes and neither of them good: the team could cut Weisz loose and survive, however temporarily, or they could be slaughtered to a man.

Whatever the case, Reilly thought at the first sight of a Kia sedan sliding around the bend behind his truck, they were about to find out.

He opened fire at once, struggling to keep the vehicle in sight through the perpetual cloud of moondust churned up beneath the khat truck's tires. His shots were only as accurate as the minefield of divots and potholes in the dirt road allowed, but the medic succeeded in landing enough hits from his bouncing platform to cause the Kia to brake and disappear from view.

Worthy transmitted, "One vic down, how long until the hardball?"

"*Paved road in sight,*" David responded from the lead van. "*Less than a minute.*"

He'd barely finished the message before the next enemy vehicle appeared, this one a truck of unknown make and model. Reilly saw only a vague shape of it through the rising sand, but that was sufficient for taking aim and delivering a five-round salvo. Judging by the sudden disappearance of the truck, his bullets had shattered the windshield and caused the driver to second-guess his dedication to the cause.

"Two down," Worthy announced over the radio, "frag out."

Then the pointman hucked a grenade over the tailgate, the projectile sailing out of view to serve as a deterrent to anyone else wishing to test their luck by following. Reilly felt the clap of its detonation a few seconds later, hoping that it would be followed by a secondary explosion from some hapless vehicle that had driven over it but hearing none.

No matter, he thought, the blast alone should do the trick.

David's voice came over the net, asking, "*You see anyone else?*"

"We can't see shit," Reilly replied. "Our truck is kicking up a sandstorm out here."

"*Should clear up in a second, we're hitting gravel now.*"

Judging by how long it took to feel the rumble of loose rock beneath the tires, Munoz was trailing the van by a decent margin. Reilly's visibility cleared as the Iveco sped away from the dust cloud, revealing desert slopes that sailed past for a full five seconds before his next indication of enemy pursuit.

He took aim at a Subaru blasting forth from the wall of sand, getting three shots downrange before registering that the car was merely the first of three in a procession that included a Toyota sedan and an Isuzu pickup.

Worthy opened fire as both men continued shooting until a turn in the road broke their line of sight, providing a reprieve for a hasty reload. Reilly couldn't be sure if their shots had served to end the pursuit. On the plus side, they didn't need to kill everyone or, indeed, anyone at all; the real goal was to stop them from following long enough to abandon the khat truck. Whether or not they'd succeed came down to the enemy's determination and number of available vehicles more so than Reilly and Worthy's marksmanship, which had thus far seemed sufficient to the task at hand as the pointman transmitted their next update.

"Three vics in pursuit, we're not out of the woods yet."

David replied, *"Hang in there, paved road in sight."*

The announcement would have been a source of comfort if the Subaru didn't appear a moment later. Reilly fired five shots in quick succession—this time he was certain of a few hits as the car swerved violently before the khat truck thumped onto a relatively even surface and veered around a bend. A strip of pavement appeared beyond the tailgate as buildings swept into view on both sides of the road, his first indication that they'd finally reached the only population center of significance within miles and, with it, the make-or-break point for ending the chase while they still could.

Owen Al-Down wasn't exactly a bustling urban metropolis; Reilly had studied the satellite imagery and found the town's only real significance was its location at a strategic T-intersection of highway junctures. None of the highways, however, represented a viable escape route until the team had eliminated their pursuers before committing to a direction of movement, and they were soon going to run out of real estate in which to maneuver.

Then there was the very real possibility that they'd encounter a roadblock at any moment.

The situation went from bad to worse as a pair of motorcycles followed them around the bend, darting into view ahead of a sedan fishtailing past the corner.

Reilly ignored the assholes on bikes—Worthy would make short work of them—and focused his fire against an emerging car instead, spiderwebbing the glass with a cluster of bullet impacts and forcing the driver to veer wildly around the next bend and out of sight.

By then the two motorcyclists were out of the fight, one laying down his bike and the other, having braked too sharply before or after the first bullet impact, catapulting over his handlebars. His body made a shockingly graceful arc that ended when his vertebrae turned to dust with a horrific impact that would've caused him to bounce if his own vehicle didn't slam into his ribs and crush him beneath its weight a moment later.

"Cars and bikes," Worthy transmitted, "they're still coming at us."

Maintaining a stable shooting position was a challenge when the Iveco was traveling over rough concrete, and that complication had tripled with the addition of Munoz braking, wheeling the truck around a turn, and accelerating again before repeating the process as he chased after the team's lead van.

And he wasn't the only one attempting to do so. Reilly saw a veritable parade of enemy cars and trucks cresting into view as Owen Al-Down turned into an urban street race between two sides trying to either gain or maintain control of Erik Weisz.

The medic opened fire once more, joined by Worthy as they stitched their fire across every windshield they could make out amid a convoy jostling for position to take the lead. Whatever they were being paid, it wasn't enough: a Toyota sedan drifted sideways at the hands of a driver who was now incapacitated or dead, only to have its rear quarter panel blasted out of the way by a pickup that forced its way to the front, enemy fighters in the bed firing wild bursts of automatic fire. By the time Reilly fired his first rounds at the driver, however, a Nissan pickup swerved alongside it in the narrow street, planting its passenger-side tires atop a short curb as civilians flung themselves out of the way. More shooters were struggling to aim over the cab, blasting away at the fleeing Americans.

Reilly reloaded with the dawning realization that for every pursuer he and Worthy vanquished, two more seemed to appear in their place. Both men were knocking this out of the park, hitting their targets mercilessly and effectively between magazine changes, and it wasn't making a difference in the least.

He heard the *thwacks* of bullet impacts in the Iveco's rear bumper and fired another half-dozen rounds before pausing to transmit, "We can't shake them."

"*Figure it out*," David replied without sympathy.

Reilly considered whether to shoot or radio back, and sided with the latter.

"We cannot," he said, "fucking shake these guys. They're not going to stop coming at us, and if you keep pushing it, we're all going to run out of ammo. I know you don't want to lose Weisz, but I'm telling you—*we've already lost him*. The only question is whether the rest of us make it out or not."

"Go time!" Cancer shouted, looking over from the steering wheel of the Volkswagen van.

"Hold on." David turned in the passenger seat to face the rear. "Angel?"

The intelligence operative was in the van's cargo area, seated beside a restrained Weisz and across from a terrified Baterfi, and he didn't respond immediately.

Ian had considered the situation, of course, and as usual had a response prepared for the inevitable decision point that faced them now. Two things caused him to hesitate, with the first being the obvious fact that there was no guarantee his prediction would prove accurate.

Second, and far more paralyzing to him at present, was what he unquestionably knew would occur within seconds of offering his opinion. Over the course of his career, Ian had carried out many orders that he didn't want to follow. The worst such cases involved the fear that he'd die as a result of his compliance, and that possibility had never felt quite so real as it did right now.

But his job was to deliver an objective assessment to the best of his abilities, no matter the personal cost; and within two seconds of David's inquiry —the span of time it took for yet another bullet to thunk into the van's frame—Ian responded with the truth.

"They're being paid to recover Weisz dead or alive. If they know he's dead, they're not going to risk their lives by chasing us further. At least, for now."

Despite his conviction that he was right, Ian regretted the words as soon as he'd spoken them; Cancer was already working his pistol out of its holster, a difficult effort when seated in a moving vehicle but one that he appeared to be negotiating with enthusiasm until David placed a hand on his arm to stop him.

"There's no time. Angel, do it now."

Ian drew his Glock with one final thought.

Fuck it, he decided—orders were orders.

"Ah," Weisz said, "I see…"

Ian placed the barrel of his pistol into Erik Weisz's jowls, aiming upward. To his credit, the terrorist mastermind held still to assist him, his lips morphing into a wide grin that would be his final expression as David shouted his next command.

"Now!"

"No," Cancer cried, "*NO!*"

Ian pulled the trigger, the bark of his pistol deafening in the confined space. Baterfi flailed wildly to shield himself from the outcome, though the majority of Weisz's brain matter was ejected upward, slapping into a greasy stain on the van roof that fanned out like a gruesome inkblot test around the single bullet hole now perforating the surface.

Weisz's head lolled backward on his shoulders, and Ian wrestled his Glock back into the holster as he fought for words.

"Sorry," he sputtered to Cancer, "it wasn't my choice, I'm sorry—"

"Yeah," David agreed, "not your choice. Got it. Now get rid of him."

Ian grabbed Weisz's shoulder and attempted to push him sideways on the bench seat; the corpse instead fell to the floor in a heap, leaving the intelligence operative to try pulling it toward the rear as an ever-lengthening smear of gore spread across the vehicle. It was like trying to haul a 200-pound sandbag.

"Help me," he yelled at Baterfi, who flinched as a pair of bullets impacted near the roof.

The Yemeni shook his head in revulsion, appearing mortified at the carnage this otherwise polite American had just inflicted.

Ian shouted, "You want to be next?"

This inquiry succeeded in rousting Baterfi into action. He rose and added his strength to the dragging effort, both men sliding Weisz's body until Ian could reach the rear cargo door handle and yank it with one hand.

The door flew open to reveal the street flying by below, and Ian straddled the body to pull it between his feet. Weisz's head rolled sideways and Ian glimpsed the face of madness, a vestige of the terrorist's final grin remaining like a horrid death shroud. He had died as he had lived, Ian thought—stark raving mad, and with both a violence and brilliance that made the intelligence operative shudder at the thought of his prophecy at what was to come in the wake of Weisz's ungraceful exit from the world stage.

Then Weisz's shoulders cleared the rear bumper and gravity took over, tipping his corpse to the point of no return until it slammed into the concrete road.

The khat truck swerved erratically as Munoz tried to dodge the body rolling toward him now, succeeding only partially as the passenger-side tires ground Weisz's legs to a pulp amid sporadic bursts of automatic fire from the pursuing vehicles.

Ian pulled the cargo door shut and fell back onto the floor in the process, coating his ass in Weisz's blood and brains before Baterfi helped him up and both men made their way back to their seats. His next action was to peer tentatively into the cab with the fearful expectation that Cancer would be aiming a pistol at him with the full intent to use it in a not-misguided murderous rage.

What Ian saw was far worse—the sniper was instead a model driver, icily silent with a 10-and-2 grip on the wheel.

"I'm sorry..." Ian managed.

David backed him up, assuring Cancer, "It was my decision. It'll take you a few minutes, or decades, but in time you'll laugh about this along with the rest of us."

At that moment Reilly transmitted, "*Pursuit has ended, let's ditch the khat truck while we still have the chance.*"

Then, with the most well-intentioned but nonetheless disastrous of congratulations, he continued.

"*Well done, Cancer. Looks like the next case of beer is yours.*"

37

The sun was low in the sky by the time Cancer braked the Volkswagen van to a halt and killed the engine.

David looked over from the passenger seat and asked, "Are we okay?"

Cancer said nothing; by now, he was getting used to maintaining silence.

He hadn't spoken a word since that nerdy little douchebag Ian had stolen his kill; it wasn't that he'd lost the power to offer an opinion, merely that he knew himself well enough to understand that the rage boiling inside him needed an outlet that was not tactically feasible while operating a motor vehicle.

But now he was free from that constraint, exiting the van along with his teammates and surveying his surroundings.

The remote cemetery lay in ruins, lined by rectangular slabs so weathered by the elements that any writings were impossible to make out; some ancient tribe or another had established it long ago, probably back when the surrounding area was viable for agriculture. Now the village itself was little more than a cluster of ruins they'd passed on the way in, and the graves stood as the most organized evidence of human presence.

That fact was, in a way, ironic; between the foreign airstrikes and internal conflict that had been tearing Yemen apart for prolonged intervals over the past few decades, a cemetery was as representative of the nation as anything else. The less civilized alternative was one of the countless mass graves that had been established in every region throughout the land—if the killing continued for much longer, Cancer thought, Yemen would run out of places to lay her dead.

He flexed his back, then rolled his neck and rotated his shoulders to ease the muscle tension that had been mounting for the last two hours of driving. They were off the grid now, no security apart from themselves unless Baterfi summoned more men, which would bring with it the very real possibility of a betrayal from their own partner force.

And in the meantime, they had to accomplish the impossible.

Drawing a final inhale of dusty desert air, Cancer walked to the rear of the vehicle where his team had gathered along with Baterfi to discuss the way ahead.

David began, "All right, first let's clear the air—"

Cancer pivoted toward him with blinding speed, using all the momentum of his sudden twist to drive his right arm to full extension.

The sniper's outstretched hand didn't form a fist—when one shot was all he'd get, something as crude as a punch wasn't an effective way to administer either pain or justice. Instead, his palm was open, the web between thumb and forefinger impacting the base of David's throat in a pummeling yet momentary contact.

The team leader stood as if nothing had happened, but only for a second.

Then his mouth opened like a fish gasping for air, one hand moving to his neck before Cancer stepped away to make room for the inevitable: David fell to his knees, then dropped forward to plant his free arm against the ground in a tripod position before collapsing on one side.

Ian managed a relieved sigh, ending his exhale with the words, "I was afraid you'd blame me—"

It was as far as he got before Cancer turned and threw a right cross so quickly that Ian's attempt to dodge the blow would've failed even if he'd anticipated the punch, which, judging by appearances as well as his words, he most certainly did not.

Cancer's fist impacted his cheekbone in the most merciful concession allowable under the circumstances—namely, that he could've instead delivered a left jab that would've shattered the intelligence operative's nose in the time it took him to blink. Ian spiraled sideways before falling in the dirt, leaving Cancer to shake out his now-stinging hand as he whirled to face the others.

"Who else knew?" he said, voice on the brink of insanity as he jabbed a finger at Reilly, then Munoz. "You? *YOU?*"

Both men held up their hands as if at gunpoint, leaving no doubt as to their ignorance as Cancer squared off with Worthy and spoke in a growl. "*You*, motherfucker..."

The pointman alone had managed to maintain his composure in the wake of the sudden assault, wisely keeping his hands down as he met Cancer's eyes and spoke in a peaceful drawl.

"Brother, if anyone else would've known, it'd be me."

Cancer's eyes widened, scanning the redneck for any indicators of deception, however subtle, as Worthy continued, "And I had no idea. If I did...well, I'm a lot of things, but not suicidal. Not sure I could've gone along with that plan."

Only then did the sniper relax somewhat, pausing his tirade to assess the status of his victims: Ian sitting up with a hand over his face, while David writhed on the ground making a staggered series of choking noises as he tried to restore oxygen to his bloodstream.

"I'm okay," Cancer said at last.

Reilly lowered his hands and moved to David's side with the words, "You really need to switch to microdosing psilocybin. That LSD gets you too amped up, man—"

"Leave him," Cancer said, the two words succeeding in halting the medic's progress toward their writhing team leader, still gasping for breath on the ground.

Reilly made a theatrical show of retracing his steps as Cancer popped the knuckles of both hands in succession.

Then Cancer felt his adrenaline crash—from their hasty exfil from the khat farm, the attack against Weisz's convoy, from the entire goddamned mission in Yemen.

He looked up at the sky and released his breath, proclaiming his next statement with equal parts relief and resignation.

"Oh, God...we finally got that son of a bitch."

Worthy nodded, sounding solemn. "Two years and twelve missions in as many countries across five continents, including the illegal job we had to do to stop his first attack. And yeah, we finally got him."

Reilly giggled to himself, then said, "It doesn't seem real, does it? Like, that this could all be over."

"Or not," Ian croaked from the ground, where he'd wisely chosen to remain in subservience to Cancer's previous display of rage, "considering what he said about what's going to happen."

The sniper glared at him. "I don't care what he said, we got him. Plucked his ass off the face of the earth. This feels good, man. I mean, *real* good."

Then he looked at David, who was still on his side and trying to manage gasping fits of air. "How's it feel for you, you piece of shit?"

David gagged, then sucked a partial breath.

"That's what I thought," Cancer said, feeling his momentary elation descend to a boiling sense of anger once more. Ian had stolen his kill, David had ordered it, and now it was up to the sniper to take charge of the way ahead.

Rolling his neck on his shoulders to release some of the tension now mounting, Cancer snapped, "Let's talk about these POWs. I voted against going after them because I didn't want our guys getting killed. Now, I'm hoping that happens, especially for these two fucks on the ground. Racegun."

"Yes, boss," the pointman replied.

Cancer fixed the man in his gaze. "Let's pretend you're half as good at coming up with mission concepts as you are at fucking your sister in whatever backwater swamp you call home. You sure your part of the op will work?"

Worthy nodded.

"I am sure. I've been thinking it over, and yeah, if nothing else, it'll pay off because no one will see it coming."

"Good. Doc."

"Yeah?" the medic asked.

"You sad, stupid roid monkey." Cancer shook his head. "You wouldn't even be on this team if you hadn't injected enough badger juice to give you a clitoral enlargement that would make Ron Jeremy avert his fucking eyes."

"Sure." Reilly shrugged. "Yeah, I know."

"But you had a thought bouncing around that walnut-sized brain of yours that Racegun might be right about this. Still think so?"

"I do. It's dumb enough to work, and the proof is that I can actually understand the plan."

"All right then."

Munoz blurted, "What about me?"

Cancer swung his gaze to him, eyes narrowing. "What about you, dipshit?"

"I mean," Munoz began, "what you said about them was hilarious. Do me now."

"You've got to *earn* the right," Cancer said in a low, even tone, "to be insulted by me. And so far you haven't done shit on this mission but abandon your guys without firing a shot, miracled your ass into getting a free meal ticket because we found you, and guilted us into going after your team with your sad fucking puppy dog eyes."

"Shit," Munoz muttered, blinking quickly, "that stung a bit more than I thought it would."

Cancer looked at Ian, who was finally rising from the ground with his left cheek swelling in what was, he sensed with satisfaction, the beginnings of a catastrophic bruise.

"Angel, what do you have to say?"

The intelligence operative shook his head.

"I voted against it then, and I'm voting against it now—"

"It was a rhetorical question because I don't take advice from anyone who jerks off to Princess Leia past the age of twelve, you miserable little jizz rat. And unless you want your jaw broken, don't you even dream of making eye contact with me until I give you permission."

Ian looked away, and Cancer spun to jab a finger at Baterfi.

"You."

"What did I do?" Baterfi asked, throwing up his hands in surrender.

"It's not what you did, it's what you're going to do. To pull this off we're going to need a lot more guys and not your gang of misfits, because word about Weisz has gotten out and they're going to sell us up the river at the first opportunity."

He dropped his hands and conceded, "I offer no argument."

"Who do you know that'll help spring a prisonbreak in Sana'a?"

Baterfi considered the thought, then answered reluctantly, "The Khawlan Brigade has many men imprisoned there. They would support this, but—"

"But what?"

He made an uncomfortable expression, as if pained by the very thought.

"The leader, Jamaan, and his men, are all a bit...well, you would say, crazy."

"Perfect," Cancer said, nodding. "Crazy is exactly what we need right now."

38

I was stiff, sore, tired, and pissed off as I followed Baterfi beneath a darkening sky, approaching the doorway to a building flanked by armed guards. My men had been ordered to remain with the vehicle and, seeing that we were devoid of options, it was there they'd remain until my present business was complete—or until I was shot inside the structure during one double-cross or another, a possibility that at this point I would've almost regarded as a mercy killing.

My job as a globetrotting covert soldier could be construed as glamorous, but only to those who'd never encountered combat themselves; barring such experience, it was simply impossible to comprehend how much the warrior profession positively sucked balls.

I was going on three days with minimal sleep, multiple gunfights, had been struck in the face by a spotter scope, struck in the throat by a teammate, and very nearly crushed by the truck containing the highest-ranking target I'd ever have the chance to pursue. Cold-bloodedly executing a hapless and probably concussed personal assistant was the only reprieve and a brief one at that, which was as good an indicator as any that my team and I were truly "in the shit," and we had a long way to go before there would be any chance of making it out.

The fault for that last detail, however, was mine alone.

My last communication with Meiling Chen at CIA Headquarters had succeeded in shifting our exfil 24 hours to the following period of darkness, a feat that had required no small amount of moral compromise on my part.

I'd readily admitted to Chen that we'd been attacked at the khat farm, as well as the fact that we'd successfully evaded pursuit and were currently evading enemy contact, unable to reach our exfil grid for the time being.

What I hadn't reported, however, was that Weisz had been shot in the head and unceremoniously dumped out the back of our fleeing vehicle to save our team. If Chen had received intel reports that countered my version of events, she made no mention of it; as far as I knew, she believed that our former captive was alive and well in our care, and I wasn't about to contradict that perception with anything as paltry as the truth. If I abandoned four American POWs, especially members of a sister team, I'd never be able to look at myself in the mirror again—nor would Cancer and Ian, though they had yet to realize that fact. Worthy and Reilly seemed well enough aware, and now our fates were tied with the missing Project Longwing contractors.

I steeled myself with that thought as I followed Baterfi through the doorway, entering a room lit by a few light bulbs suspended from the ceiling.

The cinder block walls were held together by a crude mortar job, the room's floor littered with plastic water bottles along with sleeping mats, prayer blankets, and pillows atop which sat three men who didn't bother to get up.

Two of them were clearly lackeys, one in jeans and a polo and the other in more traditional attire.

They flanked the one I'd come to see, a gnarled old man with a henna-dyed beard who wore a blazer over a dress shirt, belt with a tribal dagger, and headscarf along with a wrap-around skirt called a futa. He smiled at the sight of me, revealing a grin that was short of more than a few teeth.

It took a bit of discipline to return the smile as I said, "As-salamu alaykum."

He and Baterfi exchanged a lengthier Arabic greeting, after which my guide turned to me and said, "This is Jamaan, commander of the Khawlan Brigade. Please, have a seat."

I complied while bracing myself for the Arab norm, where a lengthy and often trivial conversation over a tray of tea and sugar cubes preceded any mention of actual business. To most Americans it seemed like a waste of time—but to Arabs, it was about building trust, establishing bonafides, and sharing a human connection in an otherwise unforgiving desert.

But I'd never been to Yemen, and whether what followed was normal or some protocol that Jamaan devised for his guests, I had no idea and didn't particularly care either way.

He procured a produce bag stuffed to the breaking point with leaves and stems, and collected a wad of the contents before passing it over to me.

It wasn't an offer so much as a demand, and not one that I was willing to reject on three grounds: one, I desperately needed to establish rapport; two, the rest of my team was microdosing mushrooms and/or LSD so fuck everything; and three, I was so exhausted that I would've guzzled horse urine if there was even a slight chance that it would lift my spirits.

I took the bag and emulated what he did now, picking the leaves from the stems, rolling them in my fingers, and then stuffing the resulting wads in my mouth in ever greater quantities.

He said something in Arabic and Baterfi translated, "He says chew, chew. Like a goat."

"Right," I said, already displeased by the bitterness, "sure."

I started chewing and found the bitterness multiplied tenfold—it tasted like a mix of banana peel and grass mulch.

Baterfi said, "He wants to know if you like it."

I bleated like a goat, the noise drawing a howl of laughter from the toothless Yemeni and his cronies as a man appeared bearing a tray that he set before us. On it were three small cups filled not with tea but a liquid whose blackness explained why it was being served in such small vessels.

My first sip confirmed my suspicions—the scalding liquid was brewed at what must have been triple the strength of the average American coffee.

Nor, I soon found out, would just two stimulants do for the proceedings: Baterfi pulled a pack of cigarettes from his jacket and presented one to each man, followed by a cheap lighter that we used to spark up in succession. Which was just as well, I thought, because Cancer would probably never let me bum a smoke ever again.

Jamaan spoke, followed by Baterfi.

"Now we may discuss business."

I nodded, finding the folded map in my pocket and spreading it on the ground between us. Then I pointed to the red dot at the southern fringes of Sana'a.

"This is the target," I began, speaking slowly so that Baterfi could keep up. "*Funduq 'Aswad* prison. It's got guard towers and iron gates blocking access to the front and rear entrances. A few dozen guards on duty at all times, from what we've heard."

After Jamaan heard the translation and replied in Arabic, Baterfi said, "He knows this place. Thirty-seven of his men are imprisoned there."

"Along with four Americans that I need to get out alive."

Another exchange, after which Baterfi relayed, "And he says there are rooftop fighting positions that will be reinforced at any sign of an attack or escape."

"Excellent," I said, taking a pull of my cigarette followed by a sip of coffee. "*Shukran.*"

Jamaan spoke again.

"How will you get in?" Baterfi asked, correcting himself for clarification. "Possibly. How will you *possibly* get in?"

I tried to give Jamaan a resolute stare, probably looking absurd in my filthy state and not being helped in the least by the enormous wad of leaves currently stuffed in my face. And whether due to the khat, coffee, or my cigarette, I was starting to feel upbeat if not invincible.

So I told him the plan, watching his expression closely as Baterfi translated my words.

Jamaan's face morphed from curiosity to confusion, then concern, and finally, elation.

I waited for a response, and got one not in the form of return dialogue but laughter.

"*Na'am, na'am,*" he cackled. "*Jayid jiddaan.*"

Baterfi started to translate, and I cut him off with the words, "I get it."

The man had just said *yes, yes, very good*, a phrase that even my elementary grasp of Arabic allowed me to comprehend.

What I didn't know, however, was if Jamaan actually believed I'd succeed in accomplishing the feat I'd just described, or was merely happy to watch me and my men die in the process. Everything prior to the prison break attempt would be accomplished by my team alone, and he wouldn't have any skin in the game unless we delivered as promised.

Undaunted, I continued, "My men lead the way into the prison. We go inside first. This part is important—we find our guys before you release your own. Once we get the Americans back to the vehicles, you get your boys out. After you drop us off, you keep all the hardware we find in the process. Do we have an agreement?"

Jamaan chewed his khat thoughtfully, then chattered away in his native tongue before Baterfi conveyed his thoughts in English.

"Certainly," he said. "Yes, he agrees."

39

Worthy's heart pounded as he knelt beside the building, scanning behind him to survey the lucid green panorama of a desert countryside glowing in his night vision.

The effort served as a distraction more than anything else; there was no movement between the various structures he'd been progressively bounding between to reach his current location, and if there was any threat to speak of to his rear, surely one of his teammates would have warned him by now.

He'd barely completed the visual sweep before Cancer's voice came over his earpiece with the next transmission.

"Go, now—run."

Worthy rose to his feet and darted around the corner with his Galil, charting a deliberate straight-line course for the next piece of cover along his route: a large, tin-sided building that he assumed to be a mechanic workshop.

He broke into a run, trying to thread the needle between being too slow and getting spotted, and moving with such speed that his thundering foot-falls would carry across the night air to alert his team's quarry for the evening.

It was a delicate balance, and added to the mix was an odd sense of detachment, a very tangible warmth and euphoria that pervaded his every movement; no combat high, this, but rather the lingering effects of Percocet he'd taken to counter the otherwise distracting spinal pain that remained ever since concluding his freefall out of a Houthi pickup.

As he ran, Worthy resisted the urge to venture a sidelong glance at his team's objective for the evening, keeping his gaze resolutely fixed on his destination and, just as importantly, the ground that remained before it—if he stumbled now, he could blow the entire operation.

But he cleared the edge of the structure and slowed to a stop, reversing course to take up a kneeling position at the corner in preparation for his next move. As he panted for breath, his nostrils were immediately filled with the thick stench of a caustic cocktail: diesel, engine grease, dirt, and rust. Definitely a mechanic's paradise inside.

"*Stand by,*" Cancer transmitted, "*you might be able to get another bound...*"

Please, the pointman thought, don't let that be the case.

A moment later the sniper concluded, "*Negative, hold in position. Bogey One is turning around.*"

Worthy gasped with relief, suddenly grateful for the nauseating fumes if it meant a reprieve, however slight, from the bounds he'd been performing with increasing speed and frequency for the better part of the last half hour.

He lifted his left hand from his rifle, using it to key his radio.

"How's it looking?" he asked, releasing the transmit switch and tugging at his water hose to bite the nozzle and suck down a few mouthfuls as he awaited a response.

Cancer's voice was casual over the net.

"*Let's see...Guards One, Two, and Three are still heads-up, Four is barely awake. Bogey One has stopped along your corridor, he's trying to figure out how to stuff more khat into his face. Bogey Two is static at the northwest corner, fucking off on his phone without a care in the world—must mean he's in charge.*"

The slight didn't go unnoticed by the main assault element of Ian, Munoz, and David, the latter of whom responded in kind.

"*At least he's not fighting his teammates.*"

Worthy felt like he was eight years old again, pretending to watch TV with his brother as they listened to their parents fight in the kitchen. He held his breath in anticipation of a response from Cancer, who wasted no time in making a return transmission.

But it wasn't what the pointman had been expecting.

"*Racegun, go go go. Move.*"

The sudden order caught Worthy off guard. He pushed himself to his feet and began his next loping bound, the last one he'd make before the raid commenced.

First he aligned himself with the final position of cover and concealment ahead, this one a large shed whose entrance must have been on the far side.

Once he confirmed that not a footstep would be wasted in charting a direct course to his destination, he focused on gaining speed while searching for obstacles in his path and finding instead an unobtrusive expanse of sand that had been packed flat by countless tires.

By then he was a scant five meters from the shed, and with the remaining distance closing fast, he risked a quick glance at the objective itself.

The four mine-resistant ambush-protected vehicles appeared much as they did the first time he'd spotted this depot, an event that had been seared into his memory for the past two and a half days since he, Reilly, and Munoz had set off to meet their source to pay for information on the missing POWs.

So exact were the parking locations that he would have doubted the MRAPs' serviceability, save one glaring detail—the last time he'd set eyes on this location, there had been two Oshkosh M-ATVs, a BAE Caiman, and an International MaxxPro. Precise identification was a cinch when the vehicles in question rose ten feet off the ground, weighed in the neighborhood of fifteen tons, and looked like they'd been engineered for marauders in a post-apocalyptic wasteland.

But as the team's initial reconnaissance confirmed, the BAE Caiman was now gone, possibly off to maintenance while in its place rested a second MaxxPro; perhaps, Worthy thought, the very same one that had passed him on Jihanah Road while he was on his way to the source meeting. Between that and the fact that two other vehicles had swapped positions since his last viewing, the odds were good that he was now looking at four perfectly operational MRAPs and, with them, the only solution for getting in and out of Sana'a proper with a prison break somewhere in the mix.

He'd scarcely redirected his gaze to the shed, now ten meters distant, when Cancer transmitted again.

"*DROP.*"

Worthy complied without hesitation, pivoting toward the MRAPs and lowering himself into the prone as stealthily as he could manage with his heart hammering. He took up a firing position and aligned his night vision with his holographic rifle optic—the bad guys had night vision too, and Worthy couldn't exactly blaze his infrared laser without notifying the turret guards to his presence.

He could, however, engage whatever threat was about to appear quietly enough to keep his presence uncompromised and accelerate the assault accordingly. Worthy caught a flash of movement to his right and adjusted his rifle, shifting his aim to track a man who sauntered out from behind a building with his rifle at the ready.

Cancer continued, "*Bogey One reversed course, take him if you need to.*"

A cascade of thoughts crashed through Worthy's mind as he prepared to be spotted and react: exactly how high was this guard who'd been switchbacking in nonsensical changes of direction like a drunken fisherman, how good was his night vision, would he look left and, if so, how good was Worthy's camouflage against the vehicle tracks below. But for the time being, the man continued his stroll without looking down the corridor representing the single greatest blind spot in the Houthi's slapdash defenses.

The problem with a blind spot, however, was that it worked both ways. A fleeing enemy could manage to run between any number of structures that Worthy had leapfrogged between on his way to the objective, and if that happened, they'd be out of view from both Cancer and Reilly on overwatch, as well as the main assault element.

Someone had to make sure that didn't happen, and the task had fallen to Worthy for two reasons. For one, they'd reasoned that Worthy on Percocet was still a better close-range shot than anyone else on the team dead sober, and so what should have been a small matter of bragging rights for the

Georgian pointman had instead become a cause to incur tremendous personal risk yet again.

And second, Worthy had earned his singleton position in the lion's den for the simple fact that he alone had proposed this entire plan.

No one else on the team had seen the MRAP depot except for Munoz, who was in no position to propose a remotely unbiased tactical suggestion, and Reilly, who, bless his heart, wouldn't have thought of this in a million years. Since Worthy had proposed the idea, its success or failure now hung heavy on his psyche. This was the hinge point from which the rest of the POW rescue attempt would unfold for better or worse, and it may well be wrecked from the start if he didn't accurately engage the guard now in his sights.

But that wandering target didn't seem to consider the possibility of an American lying in plain view between the buildings; he instead marched out of sight behind the shed that Worthy had been trying to reach all along.

"*Hold,*" Cancer said, "*Bogey One proceeding south, waiting for him to get some distance. Stand by.*"

Worthy was left with the unenviable view of the four MRAPs parked side-by-side and ass-to-ass, their turrets oriented on the road to the south in both directions, as well as the open ground to the north—they were anticipating a vehicle approach, and for good reason. The MRAP depot was so deep within Houthi territory during a government ceasefire that the immediate security effort wasn't in place to hold the terrain for any considerable period of time, nor, he thought with dismay, did they have to.

For one thing, a dismounted assault on this position was more or less inconceivable; for another, all the defenders needed to do was manage a single radio call for support, then hold their own until an army of responders arrived. Neither task was particularly difficult considering that each guard position was set in the next best thing to a main battle tank, and unless the team could manage a near-simultaneous takedown of every Houthi fighter in one fell swoop, the POW rescue effort would be dead before it began, and with it, Worthy and his teammates.

"*Go,*" Cancer transmitted. "*Be quick and be quiet.*"

Worthy pushed himself to a knee, then to his feet, and jogged the remaining distance to the protective cover of the shed.

Then he crouched at the corner and transmitted in a whisper.

"In position, need SA on my bogey."

Cancer was quick to provide the situational awareness he'd asked for. *"He's still drifting southbound, too far from the trucks. Suicide, advise we wait until Bogey One cuts north and initiate when Racegun has a clear shot and straight line to the MRAPs."*

"Agreed," David said. *"Main assault is set. Cancer, you have control."*

"Copy, all elements stand by."

Cancer and Reilly were on a desert ridge three hundred meters to the north, which held the only elevated vantage point from which they could reliably engage the guards in turrets. Bogey Two would fall to the main assault element of David, Ian, and Munoz, who were currently sheltered in a ravine to the northeast that they'd spent an hour traversing on their elbows and knees. Judging by their radio transmissions, the effort had been complicated considerably by dragging Weisz's duffel bag full of cash along for the ride; but to leave that money alone at their vehicle staging area with Baterfi or his counterpart, Jamaan, was a guarantee they'd never see it again, along with any possible militia support.

That left Bogey One to Worthy—and that was, regrettably, before he considered the possibility of anyone else who happened to be waiting unseen.

Because while they'd surveyed the objective long enough to identify six and only six defenders, it was entirely possible that more men waited inside the vehicles, sleeping between guard shifts. Considering no one in their right mind would risk leaving such an armored haven when salvation was just a radio transmission away, and that the MRAP combat locks were just as unbreachable as the armored doors that held them, the initial take-down was just the first part of tonight's raid.

Cancer transmitted, *"Bogey One northbound. Racegun, you've got about thirty seconds before he clears the corner."*

"Copy," Worthy replied in a whisper. He stood up straight to flex his back, feeling the dull onset of pain that signified his last dose of painkiller was fading fast.

Then he took up a kneeling position, readying his rifle in a two-handed grip. A final mental rehearsal ticked through his head: wait for Cancer's next call, pivot left around the corner to peer west toward the MRAPs and, if all went well, Bogey One sauntering across the open ground. Drop his target while Cancer and Reilly took out the turret gunners, and then make the final run toward his designated vehicle, the M-ATV in the southwest slot of the vehicle formation. Everything after that point would occur on sheer instinct and moment-by-moment reaction, which left him to draw a few deep breaths to steady his nerves while he still had the chance.

"*Twenty seconds,*" Cancer said.

A sense of total and absolute calm descended over Worthy, who found himself entering a realm of centered focus not uncharacteristic of the final seconds before a raid commenced, but particularly profound—maybe the Percocet was still functioning as advertised, he considered as he awaited Cancer's ten-second call.

But that call came far too soon, and when it arrived it was anything but routine.

"*Shit,*" the sniper hissed, "*Bogey One cut east behind the shed, I can't see him. Racegun, check your six.*"

Worthy's options boiled down to confirming he'd received the message or reacting as quickly as possible.

He sided with the latter, rising to spin in place and dropping to a knee again, rifle raised and aligned with the far corner in anticipation of the roving guard's appearance as he once again married his night vision with his daylight optic to aim without heralding his position with an infrared laser.

It didn't take long for the man to appear; Worthy anticipated shots against a perpendicular target, and was dismayed when his bogey instead cleared the building with an oblique approach that meant they saw each other at the exact same instant.

The guard stopped with the jolt of a child suddenly encountering a spider, his abrupt halt coinciding with the first of three subsonic rounds impacting his torso.

But it was far harder to aim with the combination of night vision and optic than it was with night vision and laser, and Worthy's target emitted a startled and bloodcurdling yelp before the next trio of bullets caused him to spin a quarter turn sideways before falling forward.

Everyone else on his team was too far distant to hear the cry, though the Houthi guards manning MRAP turrets were sure as shit looking in his direction. At least one would be able to identify a fallen comrade who may or may not be dead, which left Worthy in the unenviable position of needing to confirm his kill and initiate the raid before a radio call went out to Houthi reinforcements.

He keyed his mic and said, "Execute, execute" as he rose, breaking into a run toward the fallen opponent as he moved his left hand from the transmit switch to the lower receiver of his Galil. He continued shooting on the move—at this point, he'd have to reload anyway and was, as ever, reluctant to get shot in the back.

So Worthy dumped as much of his current magazine as he could with rapid-fire single trigger squeezes, the last occurring with the rifle held in a near-inverted position as he passed the body. Slowing only to execute and emergency reload and slam his bolt forward, he pivoted right around the building corner and accelerated.

It was a gamble under the best of circumstances. If Cancer and Reilly hadn't heard his transmission or had time to react, Worthy could find himself at the receiving end of a .50 caliber heavy machinegun burst from the same truck he was supposed to enter and clear. And if he hesitated—maybe even if he didn't—that same gunner could just as easily send a radio SOS.

But his first racing steps around the corner assured him that thus far, the plan had been salvaged as well as could be hoped.

Cancer and Reilly were firing subsonic rounds from suppressed rifles; the combination was phenomenally effective at reducing the noise of each shot, but there was no concealing the *thwack* of a bullet against the MRAP armor, regardless of whether or not it had passed through a human skull, or the blazing sparks of metal-on-metal contact around the turrets.

He cleared the building at the fastest pace he could manage, and registered a three-man formation sprinting into the clearing to his right: David, Ian, and Munoz, who had more ground to cover and were probably even more taken aback by Bogey One's sudden departure from his patrol route than Worthy was.

The bullet impacts amid the MRAP turrets came to an end, and Worthy managed three more racing footfalls before Cancer transmitted again.

"Guards down. Assault, assault, assault."

By then Worthy was less than ten meters from his designated truck, an Oshkosh M-ATV. As he closed the remaining distance, he scanned the windows for any presence of interior light. Seeing none, he abandoned the effort for his next task, slowing to a stop as he brought his weapon vertical with one hand.

Planting one boot on a D-ring shackle mounted on the front bumper, he hoisted himself atop the dusty hood, rising to a crouch and moving toward the twin sloping panes of ballistic glass that served as a windshield.

The turret loomed above them with an M2 .50 caliber barrel angled slightly skyward—how sad it would be, Worthy thought, if a new gunner appeared to man it faster than he could react. Leaping atop the MRAP roof, he aimed down into a blood-splattered semicircular hatch.

Activating his infrared floodlight revealed a collapsed figure below, and Worthy fired twice before crouching to a seated position, swinging his legs over the edge, and leaping inside.

Reilly led the way downhill at a run, scanning the objective as he approached.

His and Cancer's role thus far had been relatively simple: a pair of turret gunners at three hundred meters for each man, which wasn't exactly pushing the bounds of long-range marksmanship when there was plenty of time to set up prone firing positions with bipod-supported weapons. But that wasn't to say things wouldn't get a hell of a lot more interesting in the coming minutes.

Cancer was now in hot pursuit as Reilly led the way toward the target site, both men prepared to stop and provide precision gunfire against any threats that appeared as their teammates cleared the MRAP interiors.

Instead, the only movement Reilly saw were his teammates emerging in succession amid the four armored vehicle turrets, popping up like as many meerkats as the team frequency came alive.

"*Truck One clear*," David transmitted. "*Report in sequence.*"

Ian was next.

"*Truck Two clear.*"

Then Munoz, sounding astonished at their good fortune, "*Truck Three clear.*"

Worthy was last, his voice unusually strained—and for good reason, Reilly considered, given the poor bastard had been thrust into the hot seat with a back injury and an uncooperative roving guard.

"*Truck Four,*" the pointman gasped, "*clear.*"

So there hadn't been any slumbering guards inside the MRAPs, the medic thought as he continued his charge downhill. The lack of further enemy fighters, however, was both a blessing and a curse. Because while that fact had spared the assaulters from eating a close-range pistol shot as they entered through the turrets, it also spelled the arrival of one or more trucks bearing a second shift of Houthi fighters that could appear at any time.

David continued, "*Assemble on me to clear the west-side sheds. Cancer, check in.*"

Cancer responded, "*Me and Doc are inbound to clear the east-side sheds, thirty seconds out.*"

The time estimate was pessimistic; Reilly reached the flat ground moments later, by which time the assaulters were scrambling to form a unified four-man element and flowing toward the nearest structure to the right of the MRAP formation.

Reilly cut left, altering his trajectory toward what appeared to be a small, three-sided shed, slowing his pace to allow Cancer to close the distance behind him. They didn't have time to search every outbuilding around the objective, but the closest ones were of paramount importance. They held the greatest possibility of hidden fighters, and that counted for a lot given that it would take time to hide the bodies of the two roving guards, much less man the vehicles per their pre-appointed load plan.

He felt Cancer slap his shoulder from behind, slowing further as he neared the shed and fanning out to the right of it to establish a field of fire inside before entering.

As he visually cleared the nearest wall, however, he saw that entry wouldn't be necessary. Within the open-fronted structure were stacks of crates, an ammunition resupply point for the heavy weapons atop the MRAPs and nothing else.

Reilly dropped his barrel and spun right, taking aim at the final shed without breaking stride.

As with the previous one, it was a three-sided building, though far too large to be another ammo point. If any Houthi fighters had been sleeping in there, they were surely awake now. He instinctively decided to make entry and clear the structure as if it were a single room, reasoning that his greatest advantage as ever lay in speed, surprise, and violence of action—and sure, if he was being honest, superior training and equipment never hurt anything.

Reilly slowed when he was a few steps from the corner, signaling his intentions to Cancer.

Then he dipped his barrel before pivoting left and flowing inside.

He brought his rifle up and activated his infrared floodlight, both to illuminate his surroundings and to blind any night vision-equipped opponents inside, as he moved to his point of domination at the far corner. The walls were lined with tools, though most of the interior was taken up by a pickup that had been reversed into place. Seeing no threats ahead, he quickly panned his aim right to confirm there was no one inside the truck, though he noted an aberration in the shape of its windows: they were crude rectangles, not normal autoglass but bullet-resistant.

Shifting his aim to the pickup bed as he moved, he saw no one and accelerated to the far corner, clearing behind the truck before slipping along the back wall to confirm that the opposite side was free of threats.

Cancer had dropped to a knee to scan beneath the vehicle, which left Reilly to clear the final blind spot.

He set a foot atop the rear bumper and pulled himself up the tailgate, aiming his HK417 into the bed with one hand.

It was both abnormally short and empty, ending with an odd metal overhang; beneath it, a fixed chair was positioned.

Reilly lowered himself to the ground and moved along the driver's side to re-establish security at the front of the shed, facing out toward the MRAPs.

He was halfway there when something caused him to stop in his tracks and piece together the two disparities he'd noticed in his hasty clearance: the ballistic glass and the covered area of the pickup bed.

For the first time, Reilly looked up. His team was far from safe and had the most deadly portion of their entire mission in Yemen ahead, but what he saw riveted him with a sense of awe and caused all other concerns to fade from his mind.

David's voice came over his earpiece.

"*West side clear, east side check in.*"

Reilly transmitted back before Cancer could.

"East side clear," the medic said, "and Suicide?"

"*What?*" David replied.

By then Reilly was stroking the pickup hood, taking in the vehicle's details in their entirety.

The chassis belonged to a Toyota Land Cruiser, and the welded panels of armored glass were the least of its distinguishing features—someone, nay, some *genius*, had first conceived and then actually managed to retrofit the roof and bed with metal panels to support the immense weight of the turret from an armored personnel carrier.

From this turret protruded an unmistakable barrel too powerful to be wielded by brute force alone, hence the controls in the pickup bed: it was a 14.5-millimeter KPV machinegun, the stuff of armored personnel carriers and anti-aircraft guns.

Reilly keyed his mic again and continued breathlessly, "We may need to make one tiny, *eensy*-weensy change to the plan."

40

Ian piloted the International MaxxPro down the highway, taking in his first impressions of the outskirts of Yemen's capital city.

Dawn was growing brighter by the minute, revealing a haze of sand—or was it smog?—that painted the sky over Sana'a in a flat beige monochrome. Streetlights whipped past on the lane divider to his left, while the right side of the road held a paved strip with perfectly spaced shrubs rising out of circular cutouts in the cement. It was an oddly civilized path leading into the heart of Houthi power, complete with repetitive billboards for Arabic Pepsi.

Worthy's voice transmitted from the radio speakerbox to Ian's right.

"Guard tower on the right, we're blowing past."

Ian saw the structure a moment later, a small building suspended ten meters over the ground by a metal framework crossed with stairs. Three armed men were clustered at the balcony rail, looking down at the convoy of armored vehicles cruising toward them with headlights blazing. One of the guards held up a hand in greeting, which served as the intelligence operative's first confirmation that the MRAP theft hadn't been reported yet.

And until it was, the team had the best camouflage they could possibly get: their faces were impossible to distinguish at a distance through ballistic glass, and the trucks themselves had all the appropriate flair of Yemen flags and turrets spray-painted with the Houthi slogan proclaiming death to America and Israel, with "Curse on the Jews" thrown in for good measure and, Ian presumed, redundancy.

The guard tower swept out of Ian's sight, and then the view changed considerably.

Gone was the row of trees beside the highway, replaced by neatly spaced heaps of stone and concrete blocks—crude fighting positions for cannon fodder armed with rockets, he imagined, in the gaps between government ceasefires. All appeared unoccupied, and were soon replaced with blocklike buildings rising to either side of the highway as the convoy slipped into Sana'a.

Worthy transmitted, "*One kilometer to traffic circle, left turn onto 50 Meters Road.*"

Ian lifted a hand mic to reply over the new convoy net—they'd tuned all vehicle and personal radios into the team's alternate frequency in the interests of seamless communications once the raid began.

"Angel copies, one klick to left turn."

He accelerated the MaxxPro to remain within twenty meters of the armored pickup ahead. Worthy was serving as pointman from the driver's seat, and while the turret controls were unmanned at present, they'd be occupied on the way out by an uncharacteristically exuberant Reilly.

To his credit, the team medic had made an admirably logical case for stealing the truck: they were navigating a heavily trafficked civilian thoroughfare so IEDs weren't an issue, and by virtue of the raid ahead, they were going to lose at least one MRAP and maybe more. Extra seating wouldn't hurt, and while the short journey to the prison would likely go uncontested, getting out would be a bitch. And so, Reilly had reasoned, what was the harm in taking along one extra big gun?

Worthy said, "*Eyes-on left turn, two hundred meters—the National Bird of Yemen is out in full force.*"

The pointman was referencing the countless plastic produce bags that drifted over the streets, carried by the early morning breeze; all had once comprised retail packaging for khat, and the sight of them was perhaps the only reassuring factor for the team right now. Those bags, along with the sparse vehicle traffic, provided a stark indication that most of the city was still sleeping off their khat hangover.

Lopsided poles suspended phone lines over the sidewalks before rows of unoccupied storefronts, and Ian caught his first glimpse of pedestrians in the form of two men striding across the street between him and the point vehicle. In America it would have been considered suicidal, but in third-world nations the populace seemed to have the act of crossing thorough-fares with the minimum survivable distance between bumpers down to an exact science.

Ian slowed regardless, as much out of concern for the upcoming turn as for the civilians, and felt the air brakes engage as 38,000 pounds of metal decelerated. The men crossed without incident, leaving him to begin a right-hand turn in pursuit of the point pickup as it carved a path around the traffic circle.

Stealing the MRAPs was a cinch, at least once no enemy fighters were left to defend them—no hot-wiring required.

Instead Ian had simply turned the power switch on, watched the cluster gauge come to life, and found the push button gear selector to shift the vehicle into drive.

The good thing about the MRAPs was that, as with most general-purpose military hardware, they were built for the lowest common denom-inator. An endless succession of eighteen and nineteen-year-old Americans had piloted such trucks across the deserts of Afghanistan and Iraq, and judging by the depot they'd just raided, the Houthis had no trouble doing just the same. These vehicles had a tremendously complex integration of electronic countermeasures, ballistic armor, and heavy weapons systems and could withstand unbelievable explosions while keeping the occupants alive; as an engineering feat, they were true marvels of the military indus-trial complex.

But once Ian got used to the air brakes and rigid suspension, operating one from the driver's seat bore precious few material differences from driving a truck.

A big, dumb, and exceedingly top-heavy truck.

His biggest issue thus far had been avoiding ditches deep enough for him to drop a tire into and cause this tall beast to tilt more than thirty degrees sideways. After that, gravity would take hold and roll the armored leviathan onto its side, a possibility that had also been achieved by countless eighteen and nineteen-year-old Americans driving MaxxPros across the deserts of Afghanistan and Iraq.

As a result, piloting the vehicle through a 270-degree turn across the traffic circle was a hair-raising venture, the body roll evident despite his low speed, though he reversed the steering wheel to emerge on 50 Meters Road without incident by the time Worthy transmitted again.

"1.5 kilometers to left turn on A31."

Behind him, David and Munoz fared considerably better as they manned the pair of M-ATVs, the acronym designating them as MRAP All-Terrain Vehicles. And while that may have been a slightly optimistic term for their off-road capabilities, they were light years ahead of the far larger and heavier MaxxPros; Cancer drove the other as he brought up the trail of the formation.

Or more properly, Ian thought, the trail of his team's formation.

Because following Cancer were eight civilian vehicles concealing 29 members of Jamaan's Khawlan Brigade, all of them armed to the teeth and frothing at the mouth at the possibility of killing Houthis and freeing their own men.

That latter part of the mission was supposed to occur only after they'd established and held perimeter security long enough for Ian's team to locate and free the missing Project Longwing members. After that, the militia would have free rein to release as many prisoners as they liked—but Ian knew working with untrained host nation fighters was like herding cats under the best of circumstances, and what would actually transpire at the prison remained to be seen.

50 Meters Road was a four-lane divided highway with ample room for the MRAPs, though the pickup slowed behind an enormous cargo truck piled high with burlap sacks; Worthy could easily negotiate it in what remained of the left lane, but the MaxxPros would have a hell of a time. Particularly, Ian thought, considering that his view out the oblong pentagon side windows was obscured by armored slats that almost completely blocked a line of sight to the inherently useless sideview mirrors.

Cancer transmitted, *"Truck Five cleared the turn."* Then, a moment later, *"Any second thoughts?"*

David answered from the driver's seat of the third truck, *"Say what you want about him, but Weisz didn't strike me as a dishonest man."*

"Me neither," Ian agreed.

The team leader continued, *"And if he was right about what will happen now that he's gone, then getting those boys back might be the most important thing we accomplish this mission."*

Reilly's voice rose over the backdrop of wind as he manned the turret of the second M-ATV.

"If he was right," the medic said ominously, *"rescuing them will be the* only *important thing."*

For all his reluctance to mount a rescue attempt in the first place, Ian now had a hard time arguing in opposition.

Chen had thrown them into the fire, and by extension, the Agency itself. No one on the team cared about doing right by either any longer. Both had sold them out, and in the end the eight American contractors in Yemen, regardless of which team they'd been assigned to, didn't have anyone else to save them.

They only had each other.

"Well," David said, *"that settles it. We're on."*

Ian adjusted his grip on the steering wheel, frustrated at the delay incurred by the cargo truck ahead. In other circumstances, raiding an objective at first light could be considered an act of tactical prudence; here, however, they'd simply driven toward the prison as fast as they could because they had no alternative.

The four slain gunners were still in the back of their respective vehicles, and the two roving guards had been added to the tally in the hopes that there would be even a minute of confusion that the quartet of MRAPs and an armored pickup had been dispatched elsewhere as the result of an administrative mix-up.

So Ian was just as eager to initiate the raid in the interests of beating the APB as he was in getting out of a truck with an enemy corpse inside. And with Worthy's next transmission, he realized he wouldn't have to wait much longer for either outcome.

"*Two hundred meters, left turn onto A31.*"

Ian slowed the MaxxPro in anticipation of the point vehicle's next move, watching the pickup mount the median curb and cross into the opposing lanes, stopping to ensure all incoming traffic had come to a halt before proceeding.

By then Ian was steering his MRAP through an identical maneuver, feeling the massive tires thump over the lane divider before the pickup pulled forward again, leading the way down a wide side street at a crawl until Cancer transmitted that he'd made it across.

Then the pickup accelerated, and Ian's MaxxPro along with it; he was operating on autopilot amid an ever-rising sense of fear not that the real raid was about to commence, but rather that he bore the sole responsibility of ensuring that it began without a hitch.

Things began moving faster, Worthy transmitting route instructions and Ian not bothering to reply as he followed the armored pickup deeper into a labyrinth of commercial and residential side streets. The prison's main entrance was far more accommodating to receiving vehicle traffic, but the team had no intention of fighting their way through the most established defenses when the proverbial back door was wide open for what they had in mind.

The streets were claustrophobically tight now, civilian vehicles crammed into every available space from sidewalk to street. His MaxxPro grazed a row of cars on the right without losing speed; they jostled sideways like building blocks as he corrected course, occupying whatever free space there was to be had.

Worthy transmitted, "*All right, boys, this is it—final turn ahead. I'm going to let you guys pass so I can block the road from our militia boys.*"

Ian felt the mental resistance that this couldn't be possible—the seven-minute drive from 50 Meters Road had swept past in the blink of an eye, and for a moment he thought that the pointman had to be wrong.

A rush of fear jolted him to his senses; Worthy wasn't mistaken, it was just the eerie parabolic shift of time perception for someone who was being shoved into an inferno from behind.

The pickup veered to the side of the road and came to a stop in front of a T-intersection between buildings, and Worthy spoke over the radio.

"Angel, take that right and you'll see it straight ahead."

Ian steered left of the stationary pickup, braking harder to negotiate the upcoming turn as David transmitted his final commander's guidance.

"You got this, brother. Don't think, just GO."

A lump was forming in Ian's throat as he rounded the turn and took in the sight before him. The street proceeded fifty meters to a concertina-topped iron gate flanked by a small building, a guard tower rising on either side amid a tall stone perimeter wall.

Ian reversed the steering wheel until his MaxxPro straightened out, confirming all four tires were pointed in the same direction before he depressed the gas pedal gradually. He let the vehicle gain initial momentum before his right boot dropped further.

A man in fatigues emerged from the small building beside the gate, holding an AK-47 in one hand as he lifted the other in a fist to signal Ian to stop.

Not today, Ian thought as he felt the vehicle building up speed. Any semblance of empathy he might have held for the guard was quelled by the anti-Semitic portion of the Houthi motto—Ian had been on the receiving end of every imaginable Jewish slur when he was growing up, and years of suppressed rage boiled within him now.

He saw the guard's face flash from annoyance at an unannounced prisoner transfer, to confusion that the enormous Houthi MRAP wasn't braking as ordered, to horror that it was actually accelerating, and did so all in the span of three protracted seconds. Then the man abandoned his post entirely, darting sideways as Ian focused on the gate growing larger in his field of view until the moment of impact erased it altogether.

The iron doors blasted apart like tinfoil as the 15-ton MaxxPro soared beyond the compound walls, leaving Ian to glimpse a row of staff vehicles sporadically parked along a windowless two-story brick building. He corrected his course for the building's exposed corner and floored the accelerator as far as it would go, hearing his teammates' voices on the radio and bursts from Reilly's .50 caliber machinegun over the rush of blood in his ears and the whir of a 9.3-liter engine giving everything it had to give.

There was, in a sense, a supreme irony that Ian's vehicle was making the breach; he alone had contested this entire attempt until the bitter end, and that, as much as his inflated degree of aggressiveness, should have rendered him the last person to lead the convoy.

But his lack of shooting ability was the real reason for the current assignment. He was an adequate marksman, to be sure, but nothing compared to the rest of his team.

And when the viability of an interior clearance effort would be determined in the opening seconds of putting boots on the ground inside the prison, he was the lowest-priority shooter and thus relegated to the role of vehicle breacher.

Or, to put it more precisely, high-velocity battering ram.

The final moments stretched into an eternity as Ian second-guessed his chosen destination: ideally another vehicle would be in front of him to confirm the breach point. In this case it wasn't an option, because after the speed required to ram the gate, there was no room for an MRAP driver to come to a safe halt without rendering his vehicle completely inoperable—which was, of course, exactly what Ian was about to do.

His MaxxPro's sheer momentum would likely blast through two or more prison cells and crush whoever was inside, all victims of unavoidable collateral damage in the effort to rescue the missing Americans.

And if they were in the cells he was about to pummel through, well, this was going to be an exceedingly short and embarrassing Project Longwing raid.

The thought evaporated from his mind as his senses became suddenly godlike, vision registering the finest details in the wall before him even as he considered it impossible to delineate the tiny cracks and pittings in the brick surface without standing mere inches away—impossible because his front bumper hadn't yet struck the building. Instead he observed the sand-crusted mortar patterns with a fascination that bordered on psychedelic awe until they fractured and then collapsed all around him.

Then time was thrown into an impossibly fast vortex, and Ian found himself in the center of a violent storm of flashing images: first interior lighting, then darkness, the sensation of an earthquake swallowing him whole and somehow the perception that a second and possibly third wall had fallen before he was thrown against his harness so hard that it knocked the wind out of him.

His mind was one continuous ringing bell, the onset of physical pain transcending his adrenaline's best attempts to suppress it. Blinking his eyes clear, he saw flickering lights through a wall of dust beyond the windshield before they were eclipsed by the haze of swirling concrete dust, a portion of the building's decimated wall that had fallen through his open turret.

Ian put the vehicle in park and killed the engine, then undid his harness by feel before repeating the process on the unoccupied passenger seat to free the Galil rifle he'd strapped down.

Noxious fumes filled the cab then, choking him in a white cloud that further obscured his view—whether jarred by impact or triggered by the dust cloud, the MRAP's fire suppression system was discharging halon gas from red canisters mounted throughout the vehicle. Waving the fog away from his console, he pressed and held two buttons on the radio to initiate a "zero out" procedure that would wipe all frequencies. The truck would be examined at some point, and the last thing they needed was to compromise their convoy net before they'd made good on their escape, if they made good on it at all.

With that complete, he triggered a switch to his left, leaning over to hold it as the powered driver's door swung open with a comically absurd degree of slowness before he had enough space to wedge himself out.

Ian halted his exit mid-effort upon seeing a flash of movement along the MaxxPro's left side. David Rivers was inexplicably dropping to the prone with his rifle before slithering beneath the truck.

I hit the ground beside the MaxxPro's rear tire and began crawling forward on my belly, exploiting the highest section of ground clearance to overcome the disaster I'd encountered upon exiting my own MRAP and racing on foot toward the breach.

The building's facade had been punched clean through, which was no surprise; but it was only after I'd negotiated a heap of rubble and human remains in the nearest cells that I found the true problem.

Ian's melee had shot clean through two adjoining cells, and the vehicle was currently lodged between the hallway and the cells of the opposite side. Since he'd struck the building at its corner, the only direction I could move was blocked by either the breach vehicle or the standing walls that stood flush against its right side. So I was forced to go left only to find that if I proceeded any further past the MaxxPro driver's door, I'd enter another cell.

So I crawled perpendicular to the MaxxPro's scorching-hot undercarriage now, following the axis of what I hoped was a hallway. But there would be no way to tell until I reached the passenger side and peered beyond the shattered remnants of wall and ceiling chunks that blocked my view.

I reached the pile in seconds, holding my rifle in one hand as I clambered atop it and took aim with a single decision point looming: whether to call in the rest of my team, or order another MRAP breach and strip our exfil of a second vehicle and its attendant heavy weapon system without any guarantee of success.

But that latter option was stricken from my thoughts at the sight that met me atop the pile. I'd just hit paydirt.

The hallway was choked with dust and lined on both sides with cell blocks that were, judging by the sound of coughing and shouts in Arabic, filled to capacity. I aimed toward the end of the hall, seeing a T-intersection that remained free from any sign of enemy response amid bursts of .50 caliber and small-arms gunfire outside.

"I'm in," I transmitted. "Crawl under the MaxxPro driver's side, there's hallway access."

A voice called out behind me, "I've got your back—go."

I recognized it as Munoz, which was oddly poetic: if anyone was going to die in the opening salvo, it may as well be the guy who ordered the mission along with the one who'd brought it to my team's attention in the first place.

"Moving," I said, starting to crawl again before stopping to take aim at a Houthi guard skidding to a halt from the left side of the hallway intersection. His face was priceless as he appraised the sight with a stunned expression as if he couldn't make sense of what he was seeing—the poor bastard was either in severe denial, or he hadn't heard the machinegun fire outside and thought the blast to be a Saudi airstrike. I pumped three rounds into his chest.

He dropped as I pulled myself up the rubble and moved to the wall, now desperate to clear room for Munoz and get a second barrel into the fight. Even then, we weren't going to get very far on our own, and had to establish a foothold for the rest of the team to enter; as things stood, the space beneath Ian's MaxxPro was a "fatal funnel" much worse than any doorway could be. If we didn't secure the T-intersection ahead in the coming seconds, the next Houthi guards to arrive could well prevent us from ever doing so.

"I'm up," Munoz said, my signal to begin moving down the left side of the hall as he took the right.

And while staying close to walls was a staple of close-quarters battle, it had no place in a prison filled with desperate inmates on the brink of starvation, insanity, or both.

Hands clutched at me through the bars, grabbing my sleeve as I wrenched my arm away and continued the clearance amid the stench of mold and sweat, urine and feces, a nauseating blend that assaulted my nostrils as I shouted the callsigns of the missing Americans.

"Talon, Lucky, Outlaw, Patriot."

No response—not in English, at least, though the inmates continued crying for help—and I came to a stop before the corner of the T-intersection, pulling security down the opposite side. Munoz mirrored my position, both of us holding cross-clearance until backup arrived, and while I couldn't make out anything beyond a turn in the adjoining hall, Munoz apparently had a more eventful view.

He began firing in rapid single shots, his suppressed AK-47 emitting rounds that passed less than a meter from my left shoulder. Maintaining my shooting position without flinching took balls of steel that I didn't have right now, but I couldn't relinquish my sector of fire and risk getting shot in the back unless Munoz desperately needed support.

But his rifle went silent, lowering slightly in his grasp as he announced, "One down."

"Three up," Ian called out to my right, slowing to a halt beside me.

His arrival preceded Cancer by mere seconds—the sniper jogged to Munoz with the words, "Four up."

"Three," I said loud enough for everyone to hear above the shouts of inmates, "two, one."

I lowered my barrel and dropped to a knee, spinning around the corner to take aim as Ian assumed a standing position overhead.

And while I saw no enemy—either the prison was minimally staffed or the guards in that direction had yet to react—I waited for a second to confirm there was no gunfire from Munoz and Cancer, now performing an identical high-low clearance on the opposite corner.

Their rifles were silent, though I could hear the fight continuing to rage outside the prison.

"Go," I shouted, rising to advance as our two elements divided to continue the search.

For me that meant slipping down the dank hallway, sweeping my rifle's taclight to compensate for the flickering overhead bulbs and identifying a juncture to my left. As I approached it, I heard Reilly over my earpiece.

"I'm in the hall, where do you want me?"

Things must have been quiet outside the prison for the medic to leave Worthy alone in favor of reinforcing the assault—a .50 caliber machinegun against the guard towers at the back gate seemed to have that effect. Before I could answer him, Cancer did it for me.

"Go left at the T-intersection, you're with Suicide and Angel."

It was a judgment call that he made without input, and probably the right one; Ian was both the weakest shooter and probably still reeling from a mild concussion. And regardless of Munoz's sub-par weapon, the fact remained that Cancer had thus far proven himself to be more or less unkillable.

I knelt at the next corner and spun around it to see a hallway lined with cellblocks that, apart from an International MaxxPro M-ATV embedded in the far corner, appeared identical to the previous one. No guards in sight.

"Talon," I yelled, "Lucky, Outlaw, Patriot."

The cacophony of overlapping Arabic shouts continued without any English piercing the noise—at least, until Reilly called out breathlessly behind me.

"Three up."

"Swap with Angel," I said, shifting to face the hall in our direction of movement.

Footsteps shuffled behind me as Reilly replaced Ian as the number two man, leaving me to rise and sweep past the cellblock corridor, scanning for threats ahead. We had to penetrate deep and fast while we still could, and with the surprise of our vehicle breach and insertion in the prisoner area fading by the second, every meter of covered ground mattered.

My next danger area was an L-shaped turn in the hall ahead. I aimed at the edge of the corner as I moved, and no sooner had I fixated on it than a figure scrambled around the side, rifle raised.

Untrained fighters were a real joy in close-quarters combat, I thought—the man spilled into the hallway as he took aim, centering himself for an easy volley of subsonic fire that didn't even require me to slow my walking pace.

But bad guys tended to move in pairs, and I broke into a run to get my barrel angled around the corner before another Houthi fighter could beat me to the punch. Skidding to a halt, I dropped to a knee and rotated around the edge with Reilly doing the same from a standing position.

The first thing I saw was another uniformed guard, first standing in shock at the sight of his fallen comrade and then raising his rifle in a frantic motion that sent a short automatic burst into the ground by his feet.

Reilly and I had better results with our suppressed shots, and the man fell to reveal a reinforced door swinging open on the opposite wall. I needed to reload but didn't have the time, waiting instead for a new threat to appear as I noticed a chair on either side of the threshold. The two men we'd just slain must have been fixed guards to account for any loose prisoners, which meant we were staring at the entrance to some administrative wing where prisoners were processed and their fates sealed.

And, apparently, where the remaining guards spent their time between rotations.

The men now spilling forward had been delayed by the time it took to don their gear, emerging with flak jackets and helmets in addition to assault rifles.

I lowered my aim and seeded rounds at pelvis height, scoring wounds that served as "mobility kills" as surely as blowing the tracks off enemy tanks. Once they fell, they were far more vulnerable to fatal shots through the head and neck, and together Reilly and I stacked bodies outside the doorway until my weapon went empty.

"Reloading," I said, conducting an emergency magazine change as Reilly continued to fire.

By the time I sent the bolt home and took aim once more, Reilly returned the favor with the same announcement, leaving me to the sight of a muzzle flash at the edge of the doorway. Someone was trying to angle his rifle around the corner without fully exposing himself, though my return fire succeeded in extinguishing the gunfire; then, as the wounded shooter jolted from the pain of getting shot in the arm, I took aim on his shoulder and fired again.

He retreated from view, though the sounds of men shouting beyond the doorway assured me our fight was far from over. Reilly, apparently having completed his reload, began taking precision headshots against the four men who'd fallen immediately after charging outside the door, and I transitioned my rifle to a left-handed firing position before tucking myself tighter against the corner.

Our position here was both good and bad, bringing us no closer to the missing American inmates but allowing us to isolate the prison interior from reinforcements. Remaining in place would be dangerous, but far less so than allowing a flood of armed fighters into the prisoner area uncontested.

When the wave of incoming fighters abruptly stopped, I keyed my radio.

"Cancer, we're pinned on defense at the admin entrance. You and Bulldog are going to have to find them."

I'd barely initiated my reload when the sniper responded, irritated.

"Hold your horses, I'm working on it."

Cancer swept his barrel across the room as he moved to the corner, at first relieved to find no enemy fighters and then dismayed by what he discovered instead.

The stinging scent of acid hung heavy in the room, so strong that he considered departing along with Munoz to head back the way they'd come. But there was a door on the far side, and reaching it would yield access to another part of the building they had yet to see.

He led the way down a wall covered with mounted chains and shackles, shifting his rifle to shine a taclight on the chipped and blood-stained tables bearing an array of torture implements designed to elicit compliance.

Cancer saw car batteries, cables and alligator clamps, metal rods and blindfolds, and a pile of what appeared to be human fingernails. The ceiling held iron bars over which chains were draped to suspend prisoners' arms behind their back, and the corner he approached held the source of the smell in the form of a cylindrical container bearing the red skull and crossbones of a hazardous substance.

Munoz approached from the opposite side as Cancer took up a position beside the remaining door, hearing the distant bursts of Worthy's M2 machinegun while waiting for his counterpart to arrive.

Between growing up around his dad and his uncles, Cancer had spent enough time hearing prison stories to fill an entire book. He needed to find the solitary confinement area for high-value prisoners, and this torture chamber wasn't it—but he was certainly getting warmer.

Cancer waited for his teammate to come to a halt, then gave him a nod.

Munoz flung the door open and Cancer flowed through it, his first glance at the corridor beyond revealing a corner and only one way to go. He cut right and aimed down the hall, seeing a one-way intersection to his left followed by a final turn farther ahead.

He moved toward the first juncture as David's voice came over the radio.

"*Cancer, we're pinned on defense at the admin entrance. You and Bulldog are going to have to find them.*"

"Hold your horses," he replied, "I'm working on it."

The solitary confinement wing had to be nearby, though when Cancer cleared the next corner from a kneeling position, he saw only another cell block, this one with an open door on the far side.

It was eerily quiet until he shouted, "Talon, Lucky, Outlaw, Patriot."

And while no voices rose in response, he saw the glint of human eyes in his taclight beam—the cell occupants were lining up to peer at him, though none of them spoke. Whoever these prisoners were, they'd borne the worst of Houthi interrogation as evidenced both by their silence and the proximity of their living quarters to the torture chamber.

"Lock down that door and don't move until I call you."

"Got it," Munoz replied, and Cancer rose to move toward the final turn in the hall, bracing himself for a solo clearance and all the reaction time that could require.

As he moved, he detected an odd series of rustling noises beyond the corridor turn ahead, the echoing and indistinguishable murmurs of men. No standard cell block, he presumed, though he was equally unable to accept that sound could travel so well from the rooms of solitary confinement. Whatever the case, Cancer was about to find out; he knelt and glanced around the corner before committing, momentarily confused by what he saw.

The hallway extended past rows of solid doors with slots at eye level, which was a promising development.

Twenty meters further, however, the entire passage was blocked by a row of transparent panels that he realized were riot shields held by crouching guards in helmets and body armor—the first rank, as it turned out, because behind them was a row of men in identical attire wielding shotguns and assault rifles over the heads of their shielded counterparts.

He ducked his head behind the corner as gunfire rang out, the ricochets from bullets and buckshot representing his most immediate threat as he nonetheless felt himself delighted at the challenge ahead. Whether the approaching Houthis were trained as a correctional emergency response team or were merely utilizing the equipment available to them was and would forever remain a mystery—a tightly grouped mass of targets was a rare thing in close-quarters battle, and Cancer intended to make the most of it.

He didn't throw the grenade overhand, instead lobbing it low around the corner where it struck the floor and began a skittering series of rolling bounces toward an inevitable detonation.

"Frag out," Cancer shouted, knowing the words would be meaningless to anyone but the missing American POWs who, if they were in earshot, would be flinging themselves to the ground behind whatever cover they had.

The grenade blast shook the hallway, a thunderclap of sound and concussion hitting him even around the corner. The echo receded, predictably, to shrieking wails and moans from the decimated response force.

Cancer pulled the pin on a second grenade and repeated the process, effectively running the same play because from the sound of it, the first had worked out quite nicely.

He waited for the next explosion to subside, flinching at a wave of dust that carried with it the sickly sweet scent of roasted pork that was, he knew from experience, the result of scorched human flesh.

Then he angled around the edge with his taclight, now illuminating a partially shifting mass of bodies and protective gear that he laced with subsonic rounds until he was satisfied that no threats remained.

Reloading, he shouted one word.

"Talon."

A muffled cry arose from behind one of the doors, followed by the pounding of a fist on metal.

Cancer transmitted, "I found 'em. Bulldog, stand by to receive." Then he moved to the source of the noise, the second door to his left. He located a speakeasy window at eye level, flipping the latch to pull it open and shifting his taclight to see the hollow eyes of a gaunt face.

"Brent Griffin," the man said, sparing Cancer the trouble of confirming his name by way of standard hostage rescue protocol. "The other three—"

The statement ended in the shriek of rusted metal as Cancer muscled the enormous slide bolt lock sideways, then cranked the handle and wrenched the door open.

The inmate took care of the rest, shouldering his way out of the cell in a sight that, despite his anticipating it, caught him off guard.

Griffin was tall and had probably been quite lean at the moment of his capture; days in a Yemeni prison, however, had rendered his frame skeletal, and the team leader was now an emaciated shadow clad in loose pants and a T-shirt that was little more than a rag. He was barefoot, and his lower lip was swollen, split open and caked with dried blood.

The sniper processed the sight for a half-second before taking a knee against the wall and aiming over the bodies of the riot squad to center his sights on the open doorway beyond. No movement yet, but that wouldn't last long.

"Send them to me for assignments," he said over his shoulder, "then push everyone back down the hall and to the right to link up with Bulldog."

"Who?" Griffin asked.

"Munoz."

"He's *here?*"

"How do you think we found you?" Cancer replied, the rhetorical question eclipsed by Griffin's voice as he yelled, "Lucky."

A knocking sound echoed in the hallway, followed by the screech of metal as Griffin pulled open another slide lock bolt and called out again.

"Outlaw."

A second man's voice boomed, "Patriot."

More pounding and rusty wails from the bolts, the urgent murmurs of men behind him followed by a figure stiffly kneeling to Cancer's right and declaring in a hoarse voice, "JTAC."

With pale skin and red hair, Quinn Kendrick looked exactly as Irish as his callsign implied. Cancer responded, "MaxxPro gunner, your truck is right of the breach point."

The man vanished then, replaced by a man with Asian features whose muscled body didn't appear to have suffered in the least from his incarceration, though his eyes were blackened and nose askew from a recent break. Judging by Munoz's descriptions of his teammates, the sniper took him to be Logan Keller and received his confirmation when he said, "Intel."

Cancer said, "You're riding shotgun on the Franken-pickup."

"The fuck is a—"

"You'll know it when you see it. Right of the breach."

Keller rose and left, making way for a black man who said, "Medic."

No explanation needed for this man's callsign of Patriot, Cancer thought—his name was AJ Washington.

"M-ATV gunner—"

"No-go. They fucked up my shoulder too bad."

"Then you drive and I'll gun. Truck is left of the breach."

The two men stood in unison, though Cancer remained in place as Washington departed with a series of running footfalls that faded to Griffin's voice.

"We're good."

"Walk me out," Cancer said, waiting to feel the tug of Griffin's hand on the casualty recovery handle on the back of his kit before he began walking backwards while keeping his barrel trained on the open door.

They only had a few meters of ground to cover before reaching the corner, and Griffin spoke as he continued guiding Cancer backwards.

"What's my assignment for exfil?"

"M-ATV gunner, your truck is right of the breach point."

"Corner."

Cancer slipped around the edge, finally dropping his barrel to spin left. The other three men from the second team were against the wall behind Munoz, who was still pulling security down the corridor of cell blocks.

Griffin ran to join his newly freed teammates without being prompted, and Cancer followed in short order. Slapping Munoz on the shoulder, he said, "Lead them out the way we came."

Munoz rose without response, tears streaming down his face as he wordlessly departed to lead his team toward the torture chamber.

Cancer trailed the formation, taking up a rear security position as he transmitted, "Jackpot times four, making our way back to the breach, ETA one minute."

"*Copy,*" David said, "*let me know when you make it into the breach hallway and we'll break down our blocking position.*"

Worthy came over the net before Cancer could reply, his voice frantic.

"*Net call, you guys better move fast—Jamaan's men are flooding into the breach.*" Panting, the pointman continued, "*It's about to get a hell of a lot busier in there.*"

Worthy lifted the empty ammo can from its mount, hurling it off the MaxxPro's turret as Cancer responded to his last transmission.

"*Well stop them, asshole.*"

The pointman dropped inside the vehicle, kneeling on his gunner platform and shouting, "Tell him to get his guys out of the building!"

Baterfi gave a helpless shrug from the passenger seat, waving his phone impotently. "He still is not answering."

Wonderful, Worthy thought as he retrieved a full ammo can and hauled the heavy box back into the light, emerging through the turret hatch to drop it into place beside the gun. Ripping the metal crate lid open with one hand, he used the other to transmit, "Jamaan is off the grid. Find a back door and open it from the inside."

The snaking belt of ammo consisted of linked rounds almost four inches in length. He grabbed the running end to perform a speed load, keeping his head low as he pushed the first bullet through the open cover of the feed tray until he felt it click into place.

A bullet clanged off the armored plate in front of his gun, leaving Worthy to think, *You're going to pay for that, fucker*, while racking the retracting slide handle rearward and pushing it forward twice in rapid succession.

Spinning the turret required him to operate a manual crank—the electric drive was nonfunctional—and he spun the handle counterclockwise to rotate his gun to the right, seeing a figure drop out of sight on the prison's rooftop by the time he did so.

Worthy ducked slightly and elevated the machinegun's barrel toward the position, both hands gripping twin vertical spade grips with his thumbs resting on either side of a C-shaped slab of metal. When the fighter reappeared, he was five meters to the left; Worthy compensated for the adjustment with a quick pivot of his elbows before pressing both thumbs against the butterfly trigger.

The M2 roared to life with a satisfying *thunk-thunk-thunk*, requiring all his upper body strength to control as he watched the edge of the roof explode into dust and brick fragments while working his fire back and forth over the course of an eight-round burst. He detected traces of pink mist and flying body parts amid the fray, releasing the trigger and visually scanning for his next target—in this case, a head popping up from the previously decimated guard tower beside the gate. Wheeling the turret left, he opened fire again as Cancer transmitted.

"Breach corridor is packed, no way we're making it out. Suicide, consolidate and we'll find a rear entrance—"

Judging by the militiamen racing toward the breach point now, it was inconceivable to think that this entire operation had actually started according to plan.

While driving the point vehicle, Worthy had stopped to let the four MRAPs pass before blocking the street with his pickup. That had succeeded in ensuring the militia convoy didn't block the getaway route, so all the team needed to do on exfil was re-man the MRAPs, reverse out of the prison access road, and be on their way with a clear route ahead.

Worthy had barely dismounted and locked the pickup amid sounds of Reilly's .50 cal chewing through ammo when he heard a cracking explosion and saw an avalanche of building materials that could only be Ian's MaxxPro striking the prison—so far, so good. He ran along the access street to see David racing into the cloud of debris, followed in short order by Munoz and Cancer as they abandoned their MRAPs.

Only Reilly remained, the medic slinging a few more bursts of heavy machinegun fire at the eviscerated guard towers before the big gun went silent and he completed a 360-sweep for further threats.

Worthy leapt into the cab of the remaining MaxxPro, scrambling past Baterfi in the passenger seat to occupy the gunner turret and man the fully-loaded M2. By then Jamaan's men were running down the access street, engaging any and all ground-level opposition while shrieking nonsensical battle cries—that was one interpretation of perimeter security, the pointman considered as he rotated his turret to search for enemy fighters. But without those fighters, he'd be unable to man the .50 cal and secure the parked convoy without getting shot from below.

Reilly had already more or less destroyed both guard towers, and if there were any Houthi fighters willing to race into militia gunfire that felled the first wave of resistance, they had yet to muster up the courage to do so.

"I'm going in," Reilly transmitted, ducking out of his turret to reinforce the breach.

No problem, Worthy had thought. Between the "Ma Deuce" machine-gun's power and range to engage elevated targets and Jamaan's militiamen cleaning up anyone who resisted from street level, he could hold his own out here for a few minutes.

And then everything had gone to shit.

His first indication was the sight of civilian vehicles appearing at the end of the side street, and from the wrong direction. He took aim in antici-pation of a Houthi response, only to find more militiamen leaping from the cars and trucks to join their comrades. And since they weren't part of the approved convoy trailing the MRAPs toward the prison, Worthy could only assume that Jamaan had alerted some local resistance network who had come to join the fray and, in the process, blocked the only exfil route available.

From there, things had gone from bad to worse.

It had only taken one hooting asshole to shout something in Arabic and run toward the breach before the rest followed like as many lemmings.

Both his team and Munoz's men now faced not only an influx of armed lunatics but also the mass of Yemeni prisoners about to be released in the process...and Worthy was more or less out here alone, relegated to the perimeter as a result of his injured back.

He fired another short burst into the guard tower's observation plat-form, then spun the turret right toward the prison to scan the rooftop for any more brave souls who dared to challenge him. They'd been popping up like flies since shortly after the raid commenced, and Worthy was pleas-antly surprised to find that, for the moment, no more were visible.

But the sight that greeted him instead was actually worse. Rail-thin men in varying degrees of clothing appeared in droves at the breach point, the liberated inmates emerging from the hole punched by Ian's MRAP and scrambling onto the side street. If the team didn't make it out soon, their exfil was going to be complicated by a factor of ten, Worthy thought.

And then, just as he spotted another rooftop fighter and clacked off another burst from his M2, David came over the net.

"Racegun, we made it out. Moving to the trucks now."

Worthy didn't avert his eyes until he was certain his target was down, then glanced right to see a group of men racing from a back door being held open by Reilly. All of his teammates were in the mix, along with four disheveled Americans partially clad in ratty civilian clothes.

Worthy swept for further targets as the Americans divided themselves among the team vehicles, with Munoz, Reilly, and a man from the second team running past on their way to the pickup.

"Yo, Bulldog," Worthy shouted.

Munoz came to a stop, looking chagrined that he'd forgotten the one thing he needed. Worthy reached into his pocket and then tossed him the keys to the armored pickup, which he caught before resuming his run.

Then Worthy heard the thump of a man scrambling atop the MaxxPro's hood, and a moment later an angular face with a shock of red hair appeared at the side of the turret.

"Kendrick," he said by way of introduction. "Thanks for coming."

"Take the gun," Worthy replied, ducking down and clearing the gunner platform as the former Air Force Combat Controller lowered himself into position.

Worthy wedged himself into the cab and past Baterfi, awkwardly clambering into the driver's seat and firing the engine as he called over his shoulder.

"Ammo cans at the nine o'clock, along with an AK-47 for you."

Kendrick replied, "Okay, I see them. And...you know there's a dead guy back here, right?"

"The last gunner," Worthy explained, recovering his encrypted Android phone for navigation and putting the MaxxPro in reverse. "Try to do better than he did. I can't see shit from here, so you need to talk me out. We need to back out to the left side of the access street, stop before we T-bone the pickup, and I'll take it from there. Got it?"

"Sure thing."

Worthy grabbed the vehicle hand mic. "MaxxPro up."

David spoke next. *"M-ATV Two up."*

Then Cancer.

"M-ATV One up. Doc?"

"Still running," Reilly said, *"but we'll stay out of the way. Racegun, you can start backing up."*

The team now applied the "Mother Duck" theory of partner force operations: it was virtually impossible to order a large group of host nation fighters to exfil in anything resembling a timely fashion. But the second the Americans started to withdraw along with their armored vehicles and big guns, the militiamen would follow in the most expeditious fashion possible.

Lifting his foot from the brake, Worthy mashed the accelerator.

"Slight left," Kendrick announced, and Worthy made the steering correction amid the thump of a militia vehicle being smashed out of the way.

"Slight right—straighten out."

Another metallic crunch that barely rocked the MaxxPro on its enormous frame, followed by a third, and then Kendrick was shouting at him.

"Hard right, *hard* right, ninety degrees."

Worthy whipped the steering wheel sideways, seeing the prison access road flash out of sight as Kendrick screamed, "Stop, *stop!*"

Slamming the brakes had the effect of a train wreck inside the Maxx-Pro, ammo cans clanging against one another as the suspension groaned in protest, but it had apparently prevented him from reversing into the armored pickup he'd parked minutes earlier. Reilly transmitted, "*Shit, that was close—Franken-truck is up, ready to roll.*"

The transmission brought a rush of exhilaration to Worthy. In the span of the brief mission they'd gone from five vehicles and six Americans to four vehicles and *ten* Americans, which boded well for their escape plan provided he could get them out in the first place.

But the sight beyond his windshield revealed a haphazard array of civilian vehicles blocking the path ahead, presumably belonging to the militia and/or resistance fighters still occupied with ransacking the prison.

With the two M-ATVs still reversing toward him from the access road, he faced a brief flash of panic before remembering the obvious.

I'm in a fucking MaxxPro.

Worthy reached for a panel beside his right knee, using an index finger to push a button marked by a capital *D*.

Then, replacing his hand on the steering wheel, he accelerated.

The vehicle lurched forward in compliance, building speed as Worthy swung the bumper as easily as he'd swing a broom, dusting cars out of the way in sideswiping motions.

The effect on the parked cars was catastrophic, though Worthy could barely hear the smash of metal and shattering glass from his position in the driver's seat; to him, this felt like playing a video game. *Grand Theft Auto*, he thought, *Yemen Prison Break Edition*.

It took him less than thirty seconds to negotiate the stretch of parked cars, after which he came to open city streets. From here he could take a right and proceed immediately to the highway, but doing so in the most expeditious fashion would bring him alongside the prison's main entrance and, with it, whatever defensive fortifications remained.

He continued straight for another block instead, then made the turn and caught his first glimpse of the highway.

"Taiz Road in sight," he transmitted. "Bulldog, how's the rear?"

Munoz answered from the driver's seat of the pickup. "*All trucks in convoy, militia cars are starting to follow.*"

Cancer added, "*Get us the hell out of here.*"

Worthy accelerated toward the four-lane divided highway ahead, and the fact that he needed to take a left past two rows of incoming traffic bore precious little obstacle to a convoy of armored vehicles.

He throttled the MaxxPro out from between the buildings gradually at first, giving the civilian drivers a chance to stop before committing fully to entering the highway at a perpendicular angle. Worthy veered right around a billboard rising from the median, thumping over it with two tires before slowing to allow southbound traffic to stop. Then he carved the steering wheel counterclockwise to cut them off in full.

Rolling on the gas, he tried to look left and appraise the convoy's progress before realizing the armored slats made that nearly impossible.

Instead he transmitted, "Three kilometers until left turn on 48th," and then called out behind him, "How are we looking?"

Kendrick replied, "Two up...three up...four is making the turn—all right, we're good. Hit it."

Worthy was all too happy to comply, flooring the gas pedal to gain distance from the shattered remains of their prison raid.

Reilly jolted in his seat as the pickup cleared the highway median, bumping his head on the edge of the covered turret.

"Fuck," Reilly cried, "take it easy, would you?"

The driver was unapologetic.

"You want to get out of here," Munoz called back, "or you want it to be comfortable?"

"Preferably both."

The third man in the vehicle scrambled under the metal overhang where Reilly's front-facing gunner seat was situated, his voice grave with concern.

"There's a whole lot of vehicles following us, man."

Judging by his features, Logan Keller was half Asian at least, and he was built like a brick shithouse. Reilly immediately wanted to inquire about the specifics of his best deadlift, but he suppressed the impulse.

"Those are militia cars," he said. "They're on our side—more or less. You see anything with police or military markings, consider them bad guys."

"Check. What else do you need from me?"

"Two things. First is to spot my targets—I'm not exactly looking at an HD screen here."

Keller adjusted his grip on the AK-47 in his hands, a generous donation from one of the slain Houthi MRAP guards. "And the second?"

"Don't get shot," Reilly concluded. "It'd be pretty embarrassing if we came all this way just to lose you on exfil."

"I'll try not to let you down. You have a plan to ditch these vehicles or what?"

"Yeah. Sure. Not much of one, but a plan. Let's take this one step at a time, though."

"Cool."

"And here—take these. Might need them."

The medic procured a set of foam earplugs from a pouch on his kit, a backup to his radio earpieces with a decibel cutoff. David and Cancer were already half-deaf as a result of irreversible hearing loss, and Reilly had no intentions of joining them.

Keller inserted the plugs and took up a seated position at the edge of the covered area, wisely remaining clear of the two-meter barrel swinging over the truck bed. Reilly scanned for targets along the buildings on either side of the militia convoy.

The retrofitted turret was, in a way, like the Great Pyramid of Giza; Reilly had no idea *how* the Houthis had managed to move it from a Soviet armored personnel carrier onto a reinforced pickup, and regardless of whether or not that involved alien intervention, he was impressed.

Less impressive, however, was the primitive turret itself.

On the plus side, everything was fairly intuitive. Within a few minutes, Reilly had accustomed himself to operating the hand crank to rotate the gun, the foot pedals to adjust its elevation, and the control handles to fine-tune the point of aim.

But the speed of those adjustments in response to his inputs left much to be desired, and judging from the extent to which the crosshairs floated within the grainy screen before him, it was far from a precision weapon when operated from a moving vehicle.

That being said, he still wanted to use the damn thing, feeling conflicted between relief that his team had made it out of the prison with the POWs in one piece, and disappointment that he might actually make it out of here without firing the 14.5mm. The latter emotion faded entirely, though, at the arrival of Cancer's next transmission.

"*Cop car, three o'clock.*"

Judging by the fact that the .50 cal atop the sniper's truck hadn't yet fired, Reilly presumed the police vehicle was an emerging target the gunner had just missed his opportunity to engage.

Panning his joystick left, he traversed the turret and its corresponding autocannon as Keller shouted, "He's coming onto the road alongside us."

The medic's first thought was that couldn't possibly be true; what self-respecting cop would willingly barrel his patrol car toward an armored convoy?

But a moment later he saw an SUV that looked like a small, outdated jeep crest into his screen, light bar twinkling as it turned onto the highway and accelerated.

Maybe the Houthi officer was overzealous or, more likely, he was attempting to provide a courteous police escort to what he presumed were his own people.

Whatever the case, he had a radio, and that was all the justification Reilly needed for his next action. He maneuvered his joystick until the bouncing crosshairs were more or less centered on the hood, and depressed the trigger for exactly half a second before releasing it.

A wave of heat and light blasted across his backside, along with the smoking stench of gunpowder-infused smoke. The five shots that ensued were sufficiently close together to present one undulating blast that sounded like the sky being torn apart by a thunderbolt, and while Reilly was unsure of how accurate his fire had been, he was certain that at least one round connected with its intended target.

Each MRAP was equipped with .50 caliber machineguns whose bullets dwarfed those of any assault rifle in the team arsenal, and even *they* looked like tinker toys compared to the 14.5x114mm rounds from an autocannon that had taken down helicopters the world over.

The police vehicle vanished in a flash of smoke before skidding out of the haze, a charred and flaming hulk that spun sideways before flipping on its side and rolling as the lead cars in the militia convoy swerved to avoid it.

"Got him," Reilly transmitted.

"Holy shit," Keller shouted over the wind and echo of an SUV grinding itself to a pulp behind them.

The medic resumed his panning scans and asked, "Why's your callsign 'Outlaw?'"

Keller was quiet for a moment, then admitted, "Accidentally punched a cop trying to break up a barfight."

"You get away?"

"Barely."

"Damn, man," Reilly said in astonishment. "You're a lot cooler than our intel guy."

"Well he managed to find my team, didn't he?"

"No—that was me and our pointman."

Munoz loudly cleared his throat, coughing for emphasis.

Reilly raised his voice to announce, "AND MUNOZ."

Worthy transmitted then, "*Convoy of technicals headed toward us. We're going to need Doc's gun to range it.*"

David replied, "*MRAPs, shift right. Bulldog, take the left lane and push forward. Doc, start shooting these fuckers.*"

Munoz complied at once, swinging the vehicle sideways and accelerating as fast as he could manage while Reilly scanned his screen for the incoming threat.

His autocannon's effective firing range was nearly twice that of the .50 cals mounted atop the MRAPs, and that was only the second most important consideration: while his teammates were manually controlling their machineguns from a pintle mount, Reilly had a mechanized turret and corresponding optics capable of greater precision at a distance.

"Hold it steady," he shouted to Munoz, who steered as straight as he could manage as he accelerated to the front of the convoy.

Reilly panned his sights down the incoming lanes in an ever-further glide, seeing nothing but sporadic civilian cars amid mostly empty road that stretched toward the horizon for so long that he thought Worthy must have been mistaken.

How the pointman had spotted the pickup convoy was anyone's guess. Reilly could barely see it until he zoomed in his optic almost as far as it could go, the view on his screen now a trembling blur that nonetheless revealed the grainy apparition of a pickup truck with a bed-mounted machinegun, trailed by a row of similar vehicles.

The lead truck's gun flickered with a sudden muzzle flash a half-second before Reilly returned the favor.

His 14.5mm cannon came to life with a sky-splitting roar once again, and he sent a short burst before releasing the trigger to appraise his results, which took some time: the inbound convoy was probably two kilometers out, not worth the team's M2 gunners wasting the ammo while on the move but well within Reilly's effective range.

The rounds blazed a smoking trail of flame and debris fifty meters behind the last vehicle, which was all he needed to put his next burst on target.

This was "Kentucky windage" at its finest, he thought as he offset his crosshairs from his initial point of aim to compensate for the movement of his target before firing again. This time he held the trigger for a full second before releasing it to let the recoil subside, then repeated the process before coming up short mid-effort for two reasons.

For one thing, the impact of his second burst was impossible to determine in the wake of the first—the entire pickup convoy disappeared amid a smoking fireball through which any further targets were concealed, if they continued to exist at all.

And for another, the great 14.5mm autocannon had stopped firing.

"Looking good," Munoz called back from the driver's seat. "Hit them again to be sure."

Reilly tried, finding that his pull against the joystick trigger resulted in a mushy resistance with no discernible breaking point.

He broke his focus on the screen to scan his turret controls for some kind of warning light located next to an easily flippable switch, but everything appeared as it had before—he'd activated the firing system, and there was nothing left to fix.

"My gun's down," he transmitted in disbelief, feeling shattered that his prize from the depot raid had failed him just as he'd warmed up to employing it.

David replied, "*Bulldog, fall back to the third slot. Racegun, you're on point.*"

Reilly scrambled out of his gunner seat, grabbing his HK417 from a rifle mount as he took a seat under the metal overhang opposite Keller and, after a moment of stunned silence, said, "We've got some straphangers, huh?"

"Yep," Keller agreed, watching the scene outside the pickup bed as Munoz braked to let the first two MRAPs pass.

The Franken-truck had been the farthest from the breach point, and Reilly had spent the entirety of the exfil so far stuffed in the turret, scanning for targets on a video screen. Now that he was seeing the fleeing MRAPs for the first time with the naked eye, he realized his teammates weren't the only passengers.

Worthy's MaxxPro sped past with a former Yemeni prisoner holding onto the side-view mirror mount for dear life, his feet braced against the armored wheel well cover. At least three more were crouched on the roof behind the turret, and the lead M-ATV had two starving inmates surfing the driver's side running board while clinging to locked door handles. More were on the roof, and as it passed, Reilly saw another three perched on whatever exposed metal they could grip along its backside.

Munoz glided the pickup to the right lane in front of the second M-ATV with Cancer at the turret, presiding over a mix of prisoners and militiamen flattened against the side of the vehicle and clustered on the roof, all of them looking like shipwreck survivors.

Reilly glanced over at Keller to assess his broken nose, then yelled, "I'll set the bone once we make it out."

"Cool," Keller shouted back.

"So what's your deadlift?"

Keller was taken aback. "Huh?"

"Max deadlift. What do you got?"

"440. Why?"

Reilly's face flushed with embarrassment. "Doesn't matter."

"What's yours?"

"It's not important," Reilly said, growing impatient. "Just focus on security—"

He went silent as Worthy shouted over the team frequency.

"*Bail out to the left!*"

The American convoy responded immediately, each driver whipping a 90-degree turn as quickly as he could manage without causing a rollover. The vehicles thumped over the median amid a screech of brakes while civilian cars swerved to avoid them—Reilly scanned outside the truck bed to see what had alarmed Worthy, and found his answer in the form of a T-72 tank rolling onto the highway ahead. Its tracks rolled to a halt as the turret completed its turn with the main gun angled toward his team.

The MRAPs were now seconds from converging with various side streets and disappearing amid the protective cover of buildings, but the tank crew had them dead to rights.

A wall of flame emerged from the tank's main gun, and Reilly's last thought was to wonder which of the team vehicles would pay the price.

Cancer's last act before the tank fired was a feverish spin of his turret, attempting to bring his M2 to bear in order to open fire.

His .50 caliber rounds would have about the same effect on a T-72's armor as throwing rocks would, but that wasn't about to stop him. Getting rounds downrange at least afforded the possibility of destroying the tank's optics and rendering its gunner blind, and if that failed, he would go down shooting.

Because if what he saw now was any indication, everyone in or on his truck was about to die no matter what he did.

The tank cannon's final adjustment had brought it directly on line, so much so that all Cancer could make out of the six-meter cannon in the final millisecond before it fired was the gun barrel view of a black circle.

His attempt to fire the M2 was futile; there was no time to take aim before the tank vanished behind an eye-searing flash of white that transitioned to blazing orange. His M-ATV was about to turn into a million-dollar paperweight. The team's biggest gun at present was a 14.5-millimeter autocannon—now nonfunctional, thank you very much—while the tank's smoothbore had just sent a 125-millimeter projectile into supersonic flight.

Time slowed sufficiently for Cancer to see a speck of darkness that grew in size with impossible speed, the round ringed by a shimmering haze of heat that distorted the air against a backdrop of smoke and sand. It was on a collision course if not with his vehicle then with his head; what a death, he thought, to be decapitated by a tank round. For his team, it would be the war story to end all war stories.

But the black streak flew past his turret instead, striking a building and exploding as Cancer was showered by a tidal wave of dust and debris. Glass fragments sliced through his fatigues as every window blew out at once amid a deafening shockwave that caused the entire truck to shudder on its frame.

Then it was over—the M-ATV was speeding down a side street, Cancer's head ringing as he appraised the Yemeni prisoners on the roof behind his turret.

They were cut and bleeding from glass shards, and probably deaf without hearing protection, but alive.

David transmitted, "*Everyone make it?*"

"Not by much," Cancer replied, "but yeah."

Now their once-united convoy was scattered as individual vehicles plowed through the streets, with the militia vehicles God-knew-where in the process.

David continued, "*All drivers, take the side streets southeast until you hit 48th Street eastbound. We'll regroup there. Racegun, have Baterfi relay that to Jamaan so he can radio his convoy.*"

"*On it,*" Worthy replied. Then he added, "*Funny, Jamaan's actually answering his phone now.*"

The pointman had barely finished the transmission when Cancer's truck braked and whipped sideways to make a 90-degree right turn with a meter to spare before scraping the nearest building.

"The fuck?" Cancer shouted, struggling to remain upright.

His driver didn't respond to him, instead transmitting through his hand mic.

"*Lead M-ATV, this is trail M-ATV. I just saw you go by, moving to pick up the rear.*"

The speaker was AJ Washington, the other team's medic; Cancer had been about to reprimand him for the sudden driving maneuver and remained quiet instead, thinking the man had been well justified in his actions. Linking up with David's truck would be a huge play; when operating solo, an MRAP gunner faced the mutually exclusive possibilities of covering the direction of movement or leaving his backside exposed.

Once they'd joined forces, however, Cancer could cover 180 degrees to the rear while ceding forward security to Munoz's commander, Griffin, currently operating the other .50 cal.

"*Copy,*" David replied, "*we'll go straight until you reach us.*"

That outcome occurred after another spirited turn, this one to the left. Cancer glanced over his shoulder to see David's prisoner-strewn M-ATV ahead and, down the street, a swath of hillside that left a very finite number of turns remaining to reach the highway. Satisfied, he redirected his focus to rear security as his team leader transmitted.

"Both M-ATVs linked up, should hit 48th in a few mikes."

The transmission was followed in short order by Munoz, who said, *"Pickup still scrambling, we'll meet you there."*

Then Worthy, *"MaxxPro copies, already southbound."*

All that remained was to hit 48th before re-assembling their convoy and leaving Sana'a for good, and hope to God that no more enemy vehicles spotted them in the meantime. The trip would be infinitely more comfortable for him than the three poor bastards holding on for dear life to the roof behind the turret—they were prostrate against it, heads down, having by now experienced the effects of an M2 firing directly over them.

Cancer shouted to the driver, "Yo, Patriot, you listen to rap?"

"I'm black," Washington yelled back. "What do you think?"

"Then I got one question for you—"

Washington cut him off.

"I like Tupac better than Biggie Smalls, and I don't want to fight beside any man who thinks otherwise."

The sniper remained silent for a moment, then replied, "Is it too late to take you back to your prison cell?"

"Come on, man—consider the lyrical flow."

"It's all about the storytelling. Tupac's smooth, yeah. But Biggie raps like a fucking machinegun on full auto—"

Cancer ended his counterpoint then, and for the worst possible reason.

He adjusted his M2's aim and thumbed the butterfly trigger, firing at the turret of an RG-33 MRAP that appeared around a corner behind him, now four blocks distant. It was the first of two such vehicles, he saw at a glance.

Ian must have reacted almost immediately to the sound of gunfire; before Cancer could appraise the accuracy of his shots, Washington swerved the truck in pursuit of the lead M-ATV.

"Two RG-33s," Cancer transmitted, "coming in hot."

David responded, *"Last turn toward 48th Street is coming up, and it's a long straightaway. Even if we lose them, they'll spot us on the highway."*

If that occurred, they faced the unfortunate reality that visibility worked both ways as much as heavy weapons systems did; by the time the team could spot and engage the enemy MRAPs, they'd be getting shot at as well.

What a pickle, Cancer thought—they were both escaping on, and chased by, lethal hardware produced in the good old US of A. Between Yemen and Afghanistan, he was left to wonder how much of America's military exports actually remained with their intended recipients long enough to do more good than harm.

He keyed his mic and responded with annoyance.

"Sure, Suicide. I'll save your ass, as usual. Patriot, once we turn onto the straightaway you pull into the first side street with a building big enough to hide us. I'm on tire duty and the lead M-ATV is the rabbit, shooting for turrets while speeding away. We hit 'em in a two-way crossfire and leave them stranded with dead gunners. Questions?"

Whether or not there were, Cancer didn't know—the first RG-33 crested into view again, leaving him to open fire once more. This time, however, the enemy gunner was shooting back.

The cracks of supersonic bullets speared against the armored plates to his front as both gunners traded shots. Cancer struggled valiantly to keep his stream of tracers aligned with the RG-33 turret, his vision momentarily obscured by a spray of blood and bone as two of the three inmates behind him disintegrated amid the incoming fire, rolling off the roof as the M-ATV made a right turn at maximum speed.

Cancer released the trigger and conducted a momentary assessment of his remaining rounds, seeing that he'd be able to sustain precious few bursts before needing to reload. Doing so was a protracted process that he didn't have time to conduct before the RG-33s rolled into view one way or another, and he suddenly felt as helpless as the sole remaining Yemeni prisoner gripping the edge of his turret, now blood-splattered and looking to him with sunken eyes that were wide with horror. In a way, the enemy vehicles represented a far greater threat than the T-72 they'd just dodged on Taiz Road: there was no danger of a tank keeping pace, but the MRAPs trailing them now could match their speed if not exceed it.

Washington veered the M-ATV onto a side street before braking to a sudden halt. Apparently Cancer's plan to shoot out the RG-33 tires had been accepted, though now he wasn't entirely certain he had the ammo remaining to make good on it.

As soon as the truck came to a full stop beside a building, the man on the roof along with whatever prisoners and militiamen still clung to the sides began loudly protesting in their native tongue. Rather than rely on either the sternness of his voice or his limited Arabic, Cancer responded in a universal language.

Grabbing his M110 from the turret beside him, he swung it toward the man in front of him—he went quiet, and then, for the benefit of everyone out of eyesight, he racked the bolt.

A single round flew out, wasted in the process, though the unmistakable metallic clack of a rifle bolt cycling over the idling engine served to silence all remaining dissent in a split second.

With that intervention complete, he set his sniper rifle down and replaced it with the twin grips of his M2, lowering his barrel toward the street ahead as he spoke to Washington.

"When I say 'go,' you floor it and get us off this street as fast as you fucking can."

"You got it," the medic replied.

Taking out the RG-33 tires was a gamble, but a calculated one; puncturing the reinforced sidewalls would take either armor-piercing rounds or something with a suitably impressive high caliber, and Cancer had both in his M-ATV turret.

As long as his current box of ammunition held out.

By then the groan of RG-33 engines was audible around the corner to his front, and he received his indication that they'd made the turn onto the straightaway when the deafening blast of a heavy machinegun opened up. It was followed by the more distant fire of the M2 in David's truck, and crisscrossing streams of red tracers whizzed in either direction down the street of his kill zone.

Cancer rested his thumbs on the butterfly trigger, opening fire when the first RG-33's front bumper crested into view.

The enemy driver tried braking at the sound of this new gunfire, but instead skidded past the intersection on two functional tires far too late for the gunner to alter his point of aim. The second RG-33 fared better as its driver attempted a full stop before entering the kill zone, but the vehicle's momentum carried it into the intersection as Cancer blasted .50 caliber bursts at its tires, churning great clouds of sand and chipped asphalt that prevented him from gauging his success.

Then the M2 went dead in his hands, the sound of its gunfire replaced by him yelling as loud as he could.

"*GO!*"

Washington floored the gas, leaving Cancer struggling to lift his M110 and bring it to bear on the stationary gunner before him, now wheeling his turret to close the final degrees remaining before full alignment with the fleeing M-ATV. The weapon in question was nothing so simple as a standard-issue M2, Cancer saw as he took aim, but an SPG-9 recoilless rifle that fired 73-millimeter anti-tank rounds.

The sniper began firing with the crosshairs bouncing wildly in his grasp, bracing his weapon as best he could from a moving vehicle as he drilled the trigger again and again, multiple times per second. He didn't need to kill the gunner, just prevent him from firing until Washington had succeeded in clearing the next turn. After the close call with the tank round, Cancer knew there was no way his luck would hold out a second time against such a devastatingly large munition.

But whether due to his marksmanship or the bumps in the road determining his point of aim, he saw a puff of brain matter shoot out above the RG-33 turret.

It was a chance headshot, plain and simple, though Cancer didn't end his fire until his M110 went empty and his emergency reload was interrupted by Washington wheeling the M-ATV down a side road, out of sight, on his way toward 48th Street.

41

Ian pulled his truck to a stop behind the MaxxPro, leaving the engine idling as he swung his door open.

Griffin ducked out of the turret and hoisted an enormous duffel bag toward Ian, who took it with him as he and David climbed out of the vehicle. His boots had barely hit the ground before a militiaman confronted him, eager to assume the driver's seat until one of his comrades shouldered him out of the way and clambered up on the running board.

Glancing left as he pulled the duffel strap over his shoulder, Ian saw a similar scene playing out among the other team vehicles now being relinquished—militiamen were streaming out of the civilian cars behind the convoy, each vying for their preferred position on the newly inherited military trucks as the Americans departed. Whatever prisoners and militia fighters had survived the wildly careening ride while clinging to the MRAP exteriors now clambered down, seeking less deadly seating options for the ride ahead.

The convoy's plan to reunite on 48th Street had succeeded, after which they'd barreled out of Sana'a and into the suburbs of Bayt al Hadrami. A vast majority of the remaining threats would come from the city, not toward it, and now they needed to distance themselves from the military vehicles as quickly as possible.

Ian's first move wasn't to race toward the safety of the three long build-ings beside the road, but rather to jog toward the MaxxPro, where he grabbed Baterfi by the arm and led him toward the one man who could get this entire mess of men and vehicles moving again.

Jamaan had probably lost as many men as he'd freed, but the chance to kill Houthis in their stronghold had apparently offset that fact. The militia leader was grinning ear to ear, chuckling merrily as he loudly congratu-lated his men, pumping his M4 assault rifle up and down in one hand.

David appeared beside them, carrying his own rucksack as well as Ian's, and addressed Baterfi. "Tell him he's got ten seconds to get moving before I start shooting people, and he's the first to go."

Baterfi relayed the message, sugarcoating the contents from the sound of it, but Jamaan clearly got the point. He barked an order and then strode to the passenger door of the MaxxPro, and once he'd boarded it the vehicle pulled forward.

Its sudden departure caused the remaining men to scramble into the other MRAPs, the armored pickup, and the civilian vehicles before they too accelerated, the entire motley procession roaring down the road as they sped away from the Americans. That road would soon be occupied by Houthi aggressors chasing the convoy, and Baterfi along with nine Project Longwing contractors broke into a run in unison, following the tenth—Worthy—as he led the way around the nearest building.

It was Ian's first time seeing this place in person—only Worthy, Reilly, and Munoz had been here before, and he desperately hoped their assur-ances on its suitability for remaining undetected were accurate. After all, they were now ludicrously close to the very MRAP depot they'd raided earlier that morning.

A voice beside him asked, "What is this place?"

Ian looked over to see the other team's medic, Washington, his confused gaze flittering around the cluster of three long, low buildings as they moved.

Then he responded, "Chicken farm."

I followed Worthy through the dusty confines of the poultry shed, stopping when he knelt beside a floor hatch and threw it open.

The pointman was the first in, blazing his taclight in a hasty clearance as I followed him down a rickety metal staircase and into the basement chamber. The only objects in the space were unlit propane lanterns in each corner, and I hustled to the ground to make way for the rest of the Americans to enter.

The men poured down the steps, and I plucked the one exception from the stack as he stepped off the staircase.

"Call your drivers," I said to Baterfi, "and get me an arrival time."

"I already have," the Yemeni man responded, holding his cell phone in my face. "The first cars will arrive in fifteen minutes."

I announced, "Fifteen minutes until exfil. My guys, put your radios back to primary frequency. Our medic will treat anyone who's injured, and everyone else keep it down because the team leaders need to have a powwow."

Griffin appeared at my side then, though I directed my eyes toward the hatch to confirm that Ian had pulled it shut behind us. I watched him struggle to make his way down the stairs with the weight of the duffel bag on his shoulder.

Baterfi eyed it greedily and I let him, walking to a corner to set my ruck down. I activated my rifle's taclight before setting the weapon atop the pack to provide sufficient illumination for what was about to occur. Griffin and I had exchanged the basics on our drive to Bayt al Hadrami—namely, that our mutual boss Meiling Chen hadn't ordered their rescue or even informed us that a second team existed—but the next few minutes would contain the real meat of what needed to occur going forward.

I took a seat cross-legged on the ground as Griffin did the same.

He leaned forward to match my eye level, a tall, lean, and intense ground force commander whose lower lip was busted apart and almost comically swollen. I met his piercing gaze as he whispered, "There's no way we can keep this from Chen."

"Make no mistake, Griffin, we're not going to tell her shit. As far as she's concerned, your entire team got rolled up, including Munoz. And as far as she's *going* to be concerned, you were all imprisoned and successfully escaped when the Khawlan Brigade miraculously acquired Houthi MRAPs and initiated a prison break. Then you stole vehicles and made your way to the Emirati base in Aden, because that's exactly where Baterfi's men are going to take you. And you've got the entire drive to make sure your team tells the same story."

"So we never met?"

"As far as the official record goes, neither of our teams are aware of the other. So we keep it that way. Both of us lie to headquarters, but today binds our teams together until the end of time."

Reaching into a pocket, I removed a slip of paper and held it before him. "This is the number to my burner phone back in the States. Memorize it, then hit me up from your own burner once you're back. We're going to establish our own comms plan, and it's going to extend to undeclared satphones on future deployments. You just became the undertaker in the opening act of *The Godfather*, and I'm Vito Corleone telling you that I may call upon you to do a service for my team. If you're in a position to act on it —if we end up in the same country at the same time, and it's my guys hung out to dry—then you return the favor. Agreed?"

Griffin looked astonished. "So we just lie our fucking way out of this? To Chen, to the Agency?"

I smiled at him.

"Welcome to Project Longwing."

He took the slip of paper.

I continued, "If Chen isn't going to look out for us, then we look out for each other—however we can."

"Agreed," he said.

Then I procured a cell phone from my pocket, handing it to him with the words, "When you make it to safety, you call me on this. I'm the only number that's programmed. And you're going to have to hurry—the drive takes eight and a half hours minimum. My team has exfil at quarter to one, and I need to stay within cell phone coverage to get your message before heading to the open desert. The brevity code to assure me you're safe..." I paused, looking up to see Baterfi standing over the duffel, staring at it like a man entranced, before lowering my voice to go on, "Is 'gold mine.' If I don't hear that, I'll assume you've got a gun to your head. And I carry out my insurance policy."

"What's your insurance policy?"

"Baterfi," I called out.

He broke his gaze with the duffel, squatting down beside us.

I reminded him, "You agreed to stay at my side until every man on that second team makes it to the Emirati base in Aden."

"Yes," Baterfi agreed.

"They arrive without a scratch, you get the duffel bag full of cash and we go on our way."

He nodded eagerly, eyes aglow with the prospect of such newfound wealth; leaving Weisz's money behind had been a somewhat contentious decision, but just barely.

It wasn't as if my team could keep it, nor did our country have any need for such a paltry sum amid almost a trillion dollars in annual military spending. We'd already stripped a bill from each stack for financial analysis of serial numbers on the off chance that information could uncover ongoing terrorist financing, but that was where our concern began and ended.

I went on, "But if anything happens to those men—a car crash, an arrest, if they get hit by a fucking asteroid that falls from the sky—then we put a bullet in your head and set the money on fire."

Baterfi gasped.

"Kill me if you must, Suicide, but do not burn that money."

Redirecting my gaze to Griffin, I concluded, "*That's* my insurance policy."

Reilly finished packing his medical equipment and shouldered his ruck, then plucked his rifle from the ground to proceed up the stairs as the last man.

By the time he reached ground level of the poultry shed and closed the hatch, the remaining men were speaking in low murmurs as they clustered around the door. Reilly's team was in full kit with rucksacks and Munoz's men looked like shipwreck survivors in tattered civilian clothes with whatever local weapons had been waiting for them in the MRAPs. Baterfi stood off to the side, appearing serene now that the conclusion to this entire nightmare was close at hand.

Cancer stood at the cracked door, peering through an inch-wide space as he waited for the vehicles to appear.

Reilly made his way through the assembled men to find Logan Keller, the intelligence operative he'd shared a pickup bed with on their way out of the prison.

"Hey Keller, how's the nose?"

"Hurts a hell of a lot more after you set the bone. But pain is beauty and beauty is pain, am I right?"

Nodding vaguely, Reilly considered that his medical intervention only did so much to offset the horrendous appearance of Keller's twin black eyes.

"Sure. Right. So let me ask you...who's the most gangster dude on your team?"

Keller didn't have to consider the question for long.

"In a gunfight? Washington. No idea why he became a medic, because—"

"Not combat," Reilly corrected him, clearing his throat before whispering in a conspiratorial tone, "*Chubbing.*"

The man's eyes brightened over the dark purple half-circles ringing them. "Well shit, man. Why didn't you say so? That's me by a mile."

"Cool. When you make it to Aden, do me a favor."

He nodded. "You guys just saved my bacon, along with my team's—anything you need."

"You're going to be debriefed by an Agency case officer named Declan. Little nerdy fucker, looks like he should be wearing a pink polo and a braided belt."

"Chinos and boat shoes." Keller nodded. "I know the type."

Reilly agreed, "Right, exactly. You can't miss him. He almost got me killed fucking up a power shutdown on our first target."

"So what's the mark?"

"His coffee thermos. I want you to figure out a way to slather your nuts all over the rim—if possible, all of your nuts. Bonus points if you can manage a full submersion."

At this Keller hesitated, his eyes ticking back and forth between Reilly's as he considered the implications of heat dispersion in a contained liquid.

Then he flashed Reilly a reassuring grin, placing a hand on the medic's shoulder and giving it a shake.

"I thought you had something challenging for me. Sure, man, I've chubbed plenty of assholes in my day. Consider it done."

"Thanks," Reilly said, the last thing he had a chance to say before Cancer spoke.

"Team Two, your ride is here. Safe travels, boys, we'll catch up with you in the States. Burner phones only from here on out."

With that, the sniper flung the door open to reveal blinding sunlight, the glare soon blocked by a black sedan that rolled past before stopping, containing the top security talent that Baterfi could muster. A panel van filled with food, crates of water bottles, weapons, and ammo braked to a halt directly outside the doorway.

Griffin announced, "Thanks for the save, gentlemen," and vanished outside.

Washington was next, addressing Cancer with the words, "You better have fixed your taste in rap before we meet again."

Then he was gone, leaving Keller to advance while loudly whistling a tune that Reilly recognized as Lynyrd Skynyrd's "Free Bird."

Kendrick followed, holding up a fist to tap each man's knuckles in turn as he said, "Thanks for coming for us."

Munoz was the last man to exit, eyes glazed with tears as he embraced every team member in quick succession.

"What are you doing?" Reilly asked when it was his turn, squeezing Munoz in a great bear hug nonetheless. "Get the fuck out of here."

The team watched from the open doorway as their counterparts loaded the panel van. Munoz waved one last time before pulling the cargo doors shut behind him.

As the van pulled forward, Reilly saw another sedan follow it as the convoy made its way forward on a long trip to Aden. Their trip was going to occur in the fashion of Stateside drug smugglers with a spotter car in the lead calling out possible threats, the team vehicle in the center, and a trail car tasked with causing a traffic accident to draw attention in the event the authorities tried to flag down the panel van.

If all went well, the journey would be as uneventful as the one that hopefully awaited Reilly's team: two hours to a bed-down site to wait until nightfall, then a three-hour drive to a drop-off point, followed by a six-kilometer walk to their exfil point. All a piece of cake, he thought, provided there were no complications.

Reilly cleared his throat and said to his teammates, "So Cancer pretty much saved the day, and we all agree that rescuing these cats was the real mission."

Worthy said, "Yeah. What's your point?"

"Well, I'm just saying..." Reilly said uneasily before posing the real question. "Does that mean he gets the case of beer?"

"Fuck no," David objected. "Team rules are very clear—primary target kills only. Case goes to Angel."

Cancer's face turned to stone, a grim tension taking hold in the poultry shed until the sound of approaching vehicles could be heard over distant traffic.

"And these," Baterfi said, "these are ours."

Ian hoisted his duffel and slung it over his shoulder as Cancer activated his taclight and made a hasty sweep of the ground to confirm no equipment had been dropped or forgotten. Reilly saw an Isuzu pickup roll to a stop outside, followed by a cargo truck, and after Worthy, David, and Ian had swept out of the doorway, he made a move toward the sunlight. He stopped when he saw Cancer, who stood by to depart as the last man.

"Don't sweat it, man—*I'll* buy you a case of beer. You earned it."

42

Cancer completed a thermal scan with the optic atop his M110, then let the buttstock rest on the ground as he flipped down his night vision.

The undulating desert hills of the Shabwah Governate appeared largely as they had during the team's infil: the green silhouettes of sand dunes and rocky peaks converged and separated to form a desolate landscape whipped by periodic gusts of wind, existing beneath a cloudless sky blanketed by stars.

There were, however, two notable exceptions; for one thing, his team was now firmly in Houthi territory rather than operating in a contested frontline region, and for another, they had yet to spot a single enemy fighter.

After everything they'd been through in Yemen thus far, the lack of significant complications seemed almost unsettling. Jamaan and his Khawlan Brigade must have had a plan before accepting the MRAPs, though as to what the specifics of that plan were, Cancer hadn't a clue and didn't want to know. What he *did* know was that the Houthis had their hands full trying to track down their missing vehicles and the militiamen who'd stashed them God-knew-where among their network of resistance safehouses and cover businesses.

It was that very reality, however, that provided his team with a viable excuse why they no longer had a living captive. Shortly after the prison break, David had sent a transmission to Chen stating that their bed-down site had been attacked by a Houthi raiding party, after which they'd had to flee overwhelming enemy fire to ultimately reach an alternate location.

Erik Weisz had been killed in the crossfire.

Now the team's exfil was assured, or very nearly so—they'd been waiting on this hilltop for over an hour, having found it to be the farthest point on their route with a trace of cell phone reception.

He turned to orient his night vision toward David, who waited alone near the peak.

The team leader had conducted periodic calls with Griffin, now leading his team ever-further toward the Emirati base in Aden. As of the last update, they'd made it to the city's outskirts, but that had been ten minutes ago, and now everyone was on pins and needles waiting to find out whether the convoy would be successful in negotiating the home stretch.

The other team's lives, as well as Baterfi's, now depended on it.

But if they did make it—if they actually pulled this off—then Cancer's team was a scant three-kilometer foot movement away from their exfil point.

Cancer rose abruptly, lifting his sniper rifle from its resting position atop the bipod and jogging over to the man at his right flank.

"Ian," he said, kneeling, "cover my sector for a minute."

"Yeah, all right," Ian said, adjusting his seated position to obtain a broader vantage point.

Turning in place, Cancer marched uphill toward David.

The team leader noted his approach, his night vision swinging over as he asked, "Something wrong?"

Cancer took a seat beside him and spoke without preamble.

"Why'd you do it?"

"Do what?" David asked innocently.

"That bullshit move with Ian. Having him kill Weisz."

A pause.

"You want the truth?"

Cancer's anger flared. "Would I be asking if I wanted you to lie? I get enough of your mouth during our day-to-day, I don't have to beg for more."

"Two reasons," David replied. "One, it was for your own good."

"How do you figure?"

Drawing a breath, the team leader responded, "Think about it: if you got a primary kill on this op, *especially* Weisz, what would happen? You'd sit back on your haunches, get complacent, tune out on future missions. That's a threat to yourself as much as the team. I need you sharp, on the edge. Because it's you that brings our boys home, not me."

"I don't even know what 'complacent' means, and you know it. I do bring our fucking boys home, though. What's the second reason?"

A longer pause this time, and then David said simply, "You're not going to want to hear it."

"I just said I do," Cancer fired back. "So tell me."

"I mean it. Let this one go."

"You want to get punched in the throat again? Because I'm warming up to the idea—"

"You hide it well," David cut him off, speaking quickly, "but deep down you've got a profound instinct for preservation—not for yourself, obviously, but for your team. The only thing that gets you past that is anger, and for once I didn't have the enemy to provide that. You weren't angry enough to get behind a POW rescue when we had Weisz in the bag, and I had to give you a reason to get pissed off. So I had Ian take your kill. And then what happened? Suddenly you were leading the charge to save that entire team."

Cancer was silent for a long time after that, staring off into the night sky and the desert hills below. David had played him like a fiddle the only way he could—not with logic, not by asserting command, but by channeling an ever-present rage in the direction he wanted it to go.

Finally, the sniper looked down and spoke.

"I hereby tender my resignation."

"Well, I don't accept it," David shot back.

"I quit. I'm through with this bullshit."

"You wouldn't know what to do with yourself *without* this bullshit. Let's face it: you're too damn old to do anything else, and so am I. What else are we going to do, sell insurance?"

Considering the thought, Cancer replied, "Used cars, maybe."

"I'd love to see you try and do that. Or even work for another team leader, one who doesn't vibe with your particular brand of sociopathy quite like I do."

"There you go with the psycho-babble again."

"You know I'm right."

"Doesn't mean I have to like it."

"No," David conceded, stretching his back with a groan, "it doesn't."

Cancer found his cigarettes and lit one, taking a drag before David spoke again.

"Hey man, can I bum a smoke?"

"No."

"For old time's sake."

After taking another puff, Cancer thrust the cigarette in the team leader's face, and David delicately pried it from his fingertips before taking his first inhale.

Cancer lit another one for himself, pursing his lips to blow a long, wispy stream toward the stars.

"I fucking hate you," he said wistfully. "You know that, right?"

David filled his lungs with the aromatic carcinogens of a multi-billion-dollar industry bent on addiction before he replied.

"Love you too, brother. I love you too—"

He went silent amid the buzz of a phone in his pocket, recovering it as Cancer ordered, "Put that shit on speaker."

David did, answering with, "*Salun hilaqa.*"

There was a moment of silence before Griffin replied.

"Gold mine," he said, repeating for emphasis, "gold mine, gold mine."

Then, ecstatic, he went on, "We're at the front gate, Emiratis are getting the Agency rep now. We're home free, now see to it that your team does the same."

"Will do. You've got my number memorized?"

"By heart. I'll give you a call next week once we make it back. And don't forget that our boss is a snake—be careful with her. Good luck with your cover story."

"Good luck to both of us," David replied, ending the call as Cancer stood and transmitted.

"Net call, get ready to move. Team Two made it. We're heading out now."

"*Thank God*," Worthy replied.

Reilly countered, "*Don't you mean al-hamdu lillah?*"

David was rising when Cancer realized his team members weren't the only ones to receive the news—someone must have notified Baterfi, who came bounding up the hilltop with sheer exuberance in his voice.

"They are safe?"

Baterfi didn't give a shit about those men, but the prospect of Weisz's money was an undercurrent beneath every word of his question.

"Yeah," Cancer responded, "they're safe. Thanks for your concern. But you've still got to stay at our side until we're gone. Think you can carry that bag for six kilometers?"

"For this money," Baterfi replied proudly, "I would gladly walk a hundred."

43

Ian knelt beside David, listening as the team leader spoke into his radio.

"Copy, Warhammer Six Two. This is Suicide Actual. LZ is secure and marked by IR rope." He snapped his fingers to cue Ian, who activated his infrared laser and began tracing the beam in a circle on the flat ground fifty meters away.

David continued, "Five Eagles standing by in PZ posture. Be advised, we've got one-by local guide co-located with our team, he's staying behind —try not to shoot him."

A moment later he continued, "Roger, Suicide Actual standing by."

Then he transmitted over the team net, "One minute."

That time estimate seemed excessive to Ian, who could already make out the MV-22 Osprey's profile as it emerged through the inky green darkness of his night vision, a dark shape blotting out the stars as it roared over the desert at two hundred feet.

There was no getting used to the sight of such an airframe, he thought, watching the tilt rotors transition from horizontal to vertical. The Osprey was half plane, half helicopter, and all ugly, although the sight of it brought him immeasurable comfort as the aircraft began gliding toward the landing zone. It represented a one-way ticket out of Yemen, hopefully forever, and after everything his team had gone through over the past six days since snatching Faisal Haidar as a defecting source, it couldn't arrive too quickly.

Ian's team—and Baterfi—were currently kneeling in a single staggered row. While Ian and David faced the landing zone, the remaining three shooters were oriented toward the rocky slopes they'd traversed to get here. If any enemy fighters were waiting to make their presence known, this was where they'd reveal themselves.

But the Osprey made its approach uncontested, the eerie whoosh of its rotors echoing across the desert during a final descent that caused Ian to narrow his eyes and look away, anticipating the inevitable.

Seconds later the formation was blasted by a vortex of sand and grit, the wind subsiding somewhat after the Osprey's landing gear made contact with the desert.

His team rose in unison, moving out in a file as Worthy led the way to the aircraft.

Ian shouted at Baterfi as he passed him.

"Spend it well. And thank you."

Whether the Yemeni man had heard him or not was anyone's guess. Baterfi was shielding his eyes—and his beloved duffel bag—from the sand, a reminder that those unaccustomed to working in close proximity to military aircraft tended to find the experience a bit more overwhelming than they'd been prepared for.

The file of men jogged in a semicircle until they were aligned with the ramp, which Worthy darted up a second later, followed by David and then Ian himself.

A stench of fuel pervaded the cabin as Ian unshouldered his rucksack and lowered himself into a jumpseat beside his team leader. He looked over to see Reilly and Cancer doing the same, the latter man shouting something to the crew chief standing beside the ramp as David transmitted to the pilots.

The roar of the engines reached a deafening crescendo as the Osprey lifted off, the cabin shuddering before tilting at a forward angle and gaining speed. Then the bird tilted right and climbed, leaving Ian to feel the slap of David's hand against his thigh.

"That wasn't so bad, was it?" the team leader asked. "And here you were afraid the POW rescue wouldn't work."

Ian summoned a resolute breath.

"Yeah," he agreed, "and now I've got something new to worry about."

"I'll handle Chen."

Raising his voice over the sound of the engines, Ian replied, "She's no idiot, David. There's no way you're convincing her, and at this point it's all about damage control so she doesn't stuff us into a woodchipper on our next mission."

"Which was more or less my specialty with Duchess," David pointed out.

"Duchess would never have approved the mission we just got sent on. Chen's a different animal. You need to handle this very delicately."

"Questioning my diplomacy?"

"I am," Ian huffed. "If there's two things I need to be concerned about with you, diplomacy is the second. And judgment is the first. So don't fuck this up—our entire team's future is riding on it, not just yours."

David considered that a moment, his expression inscrutable behind his night vision device.

Then he lifted both hands to rotate the device upward on its mount, his face beaming in an exaggerated smile.

"Come on now, Ian," he said. "When have I ever let you down?"

Ian was silent as the Osprey banked a hard right turn, the first of many navigational checkpoints on their multi-hour, nap-of-the-earth flight back to the USS *Harry S. Truman*.

44

Charlottesville, Virginia, USA

Laila and I sat on a park bench overlooking the playground, nursing our coffees as we watched our daughter race around the obstacles. We had the park largely to ourselves: with morning temperatures in the mid-50s, most adults of reasonable mind would stall their kids until the afternoon sun arrived.

But there was no dissuading Langley, who at the tender age of eight was unwilling to hold off for more reasonable temperatures. She'd wanted to go to the park, and who was I to refuse? No matter that my blood was so thin after a week in the desert that I'd had to wear a fleece, jeans, and coat just to stomach the thought of remaining outdoors in what was, to me, arctic conditions—my daughter had spoken, and she had me wrapped around her finger.

So after a late-night return home, my first morning back in America with my family was spent freezing my ass off.

The visit also brought with it a strange sense of déjà vu; this was the same park I'd brought Langley to after retiring from my mercenary career, and I was sitting on the very same bench where I had been when Duchess first approached me with an offer of employment for the Agency.

Now I sat where Duchess had, while Laila occupied the seat that formerly held a younger, very naive David Rivers who thought that his gunslinging days were over.

Laila sighed and said, "I booked a dinner reservation at the Ivy Inn tonight."

"Fancy," I noted. "What's the occasion?"

"You're home. Isn't that enough?"

"Works for me."

She hesitated before speaking again, green eyes scanning the playground to ensure Langley was gainfully occupied before continuing.

"And...I've got something to tell you."

"Go ahead."

Laila fixed her eyes on my face as she asked, "Are you sitting down?"

"You can see that I'm sitting down—"

"I'm pregnant."

The words hung in the air between us, my mind going blank, suddenly drained of the racing thoughts and constant hypervigilance that characterized my sober state.

"You're—" I began.

"Pregnant," she affirmed, her eyes watching mine closely.

A surge of reckless, delirious joy welled up in the center of my chest, and I pulled Laila into an embrace with hot tears stinging my eyes.

"Oh," I began, "my God...we're going to be parents...*again*."

Releasing her from my grasp, I kissed her cheek and asked, "You're sure?"

"I missed my period right after you left, and took three tests since then. I'm pretty sure."

"We need to get you to a doctor," I said, wiping away the tears now running down my face.

"Appointment is already scheduled. First we need to tell Langley."

"Okay," I agreed. "We should do something fun for her, like a cake or a T-shirt—"

"I've got a gift-wrapped box filled with blue and pink balloons hidden in our closet. Before we go to dinner tonight, she's going to open it."

I nodded eagerly. "Good idea. Better than mine. As usual."

Then I noticed Laila's face took on a curious, if not concerned, expression.

"What's wrong?" I asked.

"Nothing," she said. "I've just never seen you cry before."

I sniffled and wiped my face before replying, "Well get used to it, because I dare say I'm not going to make it through the delivery with dry eyes."

Laila paused, running a fingertip thoughtfully across her lower lip.

"You know what this means."

"Yeah," I said breathlessly. "It means everything."

She shook her head, her voice stern.

"Your job, David. I can barely raise one kid with work and you being gone all the time. There's no way I can do it with two."

This brought me up short.

When this discussion had previously occurred—and occur it had, with ever-increasing frequency as the duration of my Agency employment drew on—quitting had seemed utterly impossible. On the surface, there was simply no career that could match the ones I'd had whether military, mercenary, or paramilitary, and after what I'd done in the service of all three, every remaining job choice seemed meaningless to the point of oblivion.

But if I probed deeper into that thought, the real issue was one of identity, of Self with a capital "S." I'd been a warrior since I was eighteen, and my entire psyche now rested on that tenuous foundation. If I stripped that title away, what would remain?

Learning that a new life resided in Laila's womb, however, changed everything. I no longer cared what I did, or didn't do, to earn something as absurd as a paycheck. Being a father was enough.

I said, "I've got a year left on my contract. When the baby's getting closer, I'll quit. What are they going to do, sue me? I've pissed off enough people and know enough of their secrets that they'll probably be thrilled I'm gone. Hell, after my meeting with the boss tomorrow, the decision might be made for me."

"Slow down," Laila said, placing a hand on my thigh. "You don't have to quit. I just can't...I don't want you to renew your contract."

In a way, I thought, this was fitting: I was sitting on this very same bench when I retired from life as a criminal mercenary and was recruited into the Agency. Now, my CIA career would die here as well, left behind for bigger and better things.

"I won't," I replied, surprising myself with the ease with which the words left my mouth, and the fact that I felt not a shred of remorse for saying them. "When my time is up, I'll never sign up to fight for them, or anyone else, ever again. I'm done."

"Thank you. David, thank you."

She knew from my voice that I meant it, though before I could respond or even know what to say, Langley came bounding up from the playground.

My wife and I assumed our responsible adult countenances, smiling and greeting her as if nothing had changed since we entered the park. In reality the entire world had shifted on its axis, for us as husband and wife, and for me as a professional warrior, but there would be plenty of time to inform our daughter about both.

"Hey," Langley announced, "do we have any water?"

Laila groaned. "Darn it, I left your bottle in the car."

"I'll get it," I volunteered.

"No," Laila said. "You stay here with Langley. I'll go."

I gave her the keys and she left us then, heading back to the parking lot as my daughter pulled herself onto the bench, looked at me, and, once her mother was out earshot, asked, "So why were you crying?"

My heart swelled with pride with the news that had melted any vestige of the battle-hardened freedom fighter that I used to consider myself, but I settled for relaying a simple, "It's nice to be home."

"How was your trip?"

"Good. Great, even."

She didn't look convinced. "Did you get a bad guy?"

"Buddy," I said, leaning toward her with a conspiratorial raise of my eyebrows, "we got *the* bad guy."

Instead of looking impressed, her face flashed disappointment.

"Then why don't you sound happy about it?"

"I am happy. I'm with you and Mom, and..."

I almost blurted out that Langley would soon have a new sibling, and brought myself up short. After all, a surprise was a surprise, and I wasn't about to spoil it for her.

Instead I looked from her to the playground and back again before concluding, "This is as good as it gets. Right here, right now."

Langley didn't buy it.

"If you got *the* bad guy," she said, "you should be doing backflips right now. You're not. So what's wrong?"

There was something profoundly disconcerting about having a daughter who was an old soul. Langley could read me like a book, and had been able to do so from the moment I'd first met her when she was five years old.

And if I was being honest with myself, she was right. I'd almost forgotten about Erik Weisz in the wake of rescuing the second Project Longwing team, and now faced the prospect of an extremely irate boss who took no issue with sending my men to their deaths long before I'd orchestrated the elaborate series of lies I now found myself immersed in.

But we'd gotten Weisz, plain and simple. So why wasn't I doing proverbial backflips?

I certainly would have been if he was killed in the ambush. Actually speaking to him, however, cast my team's future in a far more uncertain light; he didn't remain silent, spit in my face, or declare he'd never divulge his secrets, all of which I'd encountered with other captured enemy combatants.

Instead Weisz was open to dialogue if not outright enthusiastic to answer all of my questions, and his words near the end of the interrogation continued to haunt me.

The network is now far bigger than any one man, least of all me. So good luck with the fallout—you are going to need it.

There was no bravado in his statement. If anything he'd been sympathetic, and if Weisz truly believed what he said—and I had no doubt he did —his opinion certainly wasn't coming from a place of being ill-informed. Judging by my team's history of frantically trying to follow intelligence threads however we could find them, he knew a hell of a lot more about the current state of worldwide terrorist affairs than the CIA.

Things were about to get busy, I sensed, and considering that Chen was now running the show and that trust between us had plummeted below rock bottom, it couldn't have come at a worse time.

"Langley," I said, looking over my shoulder to be certain her mother was well out of earshot, "you know how some people suck?"

"Sure."

"Like, they're only concerned about themselves, and will trample over whoever they can to get ahead, with no regard for other human beings?"

"Mm-hm."

I looked at her and shrugged.

"Well, sometimes those people are in charge."

She gave a knowing nod. "So your boss sucks."

I put my arm around her and pulled her close, redirecting my gaze to the playground.

"That's exactly it, buddy. Daddy's boss fucking sucks."

45

CIA Headquarters

I stood alone in the conference room with seating for eight, the empty chairs lined up on either side of a glass-topped table whose surface I studied now.

Beneath the glass was a faithful reproduction of a vintage map displaying the world in a symphony of watercolor pastels; I'd seen it before, stood in this very space awaiting Duchess's arrival, though now as I glanced across the panoramic vista, the stakes were considerably higher for myself, and for my team.

In some ways the world had changed infinitely since the map's production in 1898, and in other ways, not at all. Colonial power had transitioned to proxy wars and puppet regimes, and the Industrial Revolution was long forgotten in the wake of artificial intelligence. The US, Russia, and Japan remained global powers, along with Great Britain, France, and Germany—though China had since entered the fray, and India's and Brazil's fortunes were rising. The human race remained mired in a cycle of endless conflict, with the Spanish-American War replaced by rebellions, secessions, coups, and invasions spanning four continents and a number of countries I'd need three hands to accurately count.

And while the places on that map that I'd led my team to had only increased since the last time I saw it, I now knew that a very finite number remained to be tread before my time with the Agency was up. We generally had a few months of training cycle between missions, so how many deployments remained in my dwindling career? Three? Four, at most? The answer, I supposed, depended on whether or not I got fired before my contract's end, potentially in the coming minutes.

I heard the door open behind me, and turned to face Meiling Chen as she entered.

"David," she said, sweeping into the room and allowing an aide to close the door behind her, "it's good to see you. Welcome back."

I shook her hand cordially, noting that she held a file folder as I nodded to the wood-paneled walls surrounding us. "Beats the produce section at Wegmans."

She smiled warmly, at ease in her kingdom. For Chen, business attire and a neck lanyard displaying her blue government employee badge was the norm; for me, however, wearing a suit and tie along with my green contractor badge was a rare event reserved for such meetings at CIA Headquarters. I felt as out of place here as Chen would have if I'd forced her to don fatigues, armored plate carrier, night vision, and assault rifle, then brought her into the sandbox with my team.

"How's your family?" she asked.

I grinned. "Growing."

"A new baby—congratulations, that's wonderful. When's the due date?"

"First appointment is coming up," I replied, "but it looks like November."

This was very different from our first encounter in the grocery store, I thought.

I'd since found out firsthand what Chen was capable of. And that was to say nothing of learning, through Munoz and Griffin, of her hard-earned reputation for getting people killed. I tried to keep that knowledge out of my expression as she continued, "And how is your wife doing?"

"She's over the moon about it. We both are. You've got three kids, right?"

"I do," Chen sighed, "though it seems more like five at times."

"And how is your wife?"

She gave a helpless shrug.

"Trying to stay sane, the same as me. Managing kids can be quite a handful. Especially when they lie, you know. Try to hold onto their secrets when you're already well aware of the truth."

And with that, I thought, the conversation had swiftly pivoted course.

"Yeah," I said, "I hear you. Just be grateful your kids are bad liars, because my daughter...she's very convincing." I gave a dramatic sigh, raising a hand and snapping my fingers for emphasis. "She can pull the wool over my eyes like *that*."

Chen replied dryly, "Clearly it doesn't run in the family."

I gasped, twisting her insult into both a compliment and an accusation.

"God, no. I'm an Honest Abe, myself. And if I was any good at lying, I wouldn't want to meet the person who could call me on it—takes one to know one, am I right?"

"Indeed. Have a seat, David."

I stepped aside to make room for her before pulling out a chair for myself, though she rounded the table to assume a power position facing the door. She was treating this like a source interrogation, I considered, and unquestionably held the upper hand in terms of brains. I, however, bested her in terms of plausible deniability and a resolute, ironclad will to never crack under pressure.

We sat down in unison, and she placed her file folder over Greenland on the map. I knew she wouldn't let me peek inside because Duchess never had, and I wouldn't bother asking about the contents.

Instead I took a final glance at the table, thinking this was how she must see the world: a tidy overhead view of satellite imagery or UAV feed, far removed from the sand, the smoke, the flying bullets that represented a second-by-second reality for the men she sent into the fray.

Setting her hands atop the table, she asked, "Are you aware of the prison break that occurred in Sana'a?"

"Sure," I casually replied. "I read the report once we made it back to the carrier. Scoured all the intel I could, trying to see if anything had burned my team. Thankfully it looked like we came out relatively clean."

"Intelligence reporting doesn't tell the whole story, of course. And just because your team hasn't yet been burned, as you put it, doesn't mean it won't happen in the future."

Her tone sounded strangely like a death threat. Was I reading too far into this, or was there actual menace in her voice? Either way, I wasn't about to speak my suspicions—what went unsaid in this exchange bore far more relevance to my team's fate than words ever could.

Instead I responded, "Absolutely. Every mission is a roll of the dice, and this one was no different. I'm just glad you and your staff have my men's best interests at heart. Khawlan, right?"

"Excuse me?"

"The prison break. It was the Khawlan Brigade?"

"That's right," she said cautiously. "And the timing corresponded with several unanswered radio checks when I tried to reach you."

"One hundred percent. We weren't close enough to hear the fireworks, but Baterfi kept getting calls that something big was going down. Not exactly prime time to stick my head out in the interests of making a satellite connection, and I turned out to be right about that, because our bed-down site got raided shortly thereafter. If it hadn't, Weisz would be alive and in custody right now."

I could tell from her neutral gaze that she didn't believe me in the slightest.

The capture of Houthi MRAPs followed by a prison break in Sana'a was a far more sophisticated affair than any Yemeni militia could conduct, and if that were even theoretically possible, the safe arrival of five Project Long-wing contractors in Aden removed all doubt.

I met her stare with casual ease, a process I'd become quite familiar with in my early interactions with her predecessor. My mind was resolute: *you know I did this, I know I did this, but you can't prove it...so let's move on.*

Besides, I thought, we'd deceived each other. But unlike her, my lies hadn't resulted in Griffin's team being cut loose in Yemen, nor in immediately filling that void with my own men when all indications showed there was no better possibility of success.

And before she could probe further into my version of events, I tossed her a greater devil than myself to highlight my virtues by comparison.

"What about the CIA officer who leaked Duchess's name and got her killed? Natalie Keaton, I think it was."

Chen eyed me levelly, gaze matched by her even tone.

"Her employment has been terminated." Her voice assumed a deeper note, as if she was trying to imply that what she now said could well apply to me. "Along with her freedom, and any meaningful civil liberties. Aside from her husband's appeals, it's like she never existed."

"Wonderful," I said cheerily, then distanced myself from the double agent by declaring, "Traitor's justice."

I waited for Chen's next attack, assuming the same professional veneer I had during my interactions with countless toxic leaders in the past.

She watched me intently, the way Duchess used to when scanning for signs of deception. I braced myself for the inevitable, and Chen asked in an accusing tone, "When's the shower?"

"The—*shower*?"

"Yes, David. The baby shower."

Now she was throwing me off balance, alternating between scathing contempt and warm familiarity.

"Oh," I said, "well, we haven't planned one yet."

"Let me know when you schedule it. I'd love to send over a gift."

"You'd do that?" I asked. "For me?"

She corrected me, "For your wife. As for you and your team, David, I believe you'll find there is nothing that I am not willing to do."

I did my best to look grateful. "That...is immensely reassuring. Things get pretty nerve-racking out there, as I'm sure you can imagine. It's no small comfort to know that a dedicated professional is running the ship here at headquarters. After all, we wouldn't want to turn my kids into orphans, now would we?"

"No," Chen said, smiling once more. "No, we wouldn't."

Steering the conversation into more pragmatic issues for her career, I went on, "And if Erik Weisz was telling the truth about what's going to happen now, you're going to need my team."

Her smile faded.

"You have no idea how right you are."

"Oh?"

Chen's face was stone cold now; I could tell she would offer no more pleasantries, deceptions, or passive-aggressive barbs.

"It's quite clear," she began, "that you understand the tactical realm. So let me give you some insight into mine at the strategic level for Project Longwing. The first thing you need to know is that counterterrorism casts a wide net: close to three-quarters of known foreign terrorist organizations now have symbiotic relationships with drug trafficking organizations. Transnational organized crime plays both sides, in some cases with the support of the state. It takes an immense intelligence effort from our country and her allies to monitor the never-ending list of connections, then follow the threads to sift out rising terrorist leadership that represent the greatest long-term threats. That's how we build our targeting matrix. Do you know what the end result looks like?"

"No," I said, waiting for her to continue.

She lifted her folder, and instead of opening it spread her hands to indicate the world map on the table between us. "It looks like this, David, with exactly three exceptions. First I want you to imagine that all international borders have vanished, and second, that the entire world is dark, with every continent as black as night. Are you with me?"

"I am."

"Now picture seventy-six candles flickering across the globe, each representing a rising star of terrorism within Project Longwing's authorities. Some are just beginning to glow because all we have is a name, others are burning bright after we've amassed enough intelligence to determine their current location, activities, and network. Can you see it?"

"Yes," I replied impatiently, wishing she'd get to the fucking point. "I can see the candles. So?"

"So within 24 hours of your team capturing Erik Weisz in Yemen, every one of those lights went dark."

The hair on the back of my neck stood on end with her last word. I waited for her to speak again but was instead met with her watching me as if to confirm I'd grasped the full intent of her statement.

"Dark," I echoed, "as in..."

She set the file folder between us and opened it, narrating the first page by way of response.

"Dominic de Lange, terrorist financier par excellence. We've tied him to a vast network of shell companies, cryptocurrency dealings, and off-the-books gold and diamond trades in Africa and the Middle East. Last seen in Singapore when Weisz was alive and well under Al Qaeda protection. Now he's disappeared off the face of the earth."

Chen slid the page toward me, though by the time I could scan the photograph of a man with a distinguished salt-and-pepper beard, she was already narrating the next.

"Mordecai Friedman, Israeli nuclear engineer. Went missing last year, and has since turned up twice in Iran before multiple asset reports placed him in Oral, Kazakhstan."

She sent that page my way—in addition to a copy of his passport photo, there was a single surveillance picture of Friedman moving toward a car parked at the curb.

"That photograph," Chen continued, "was taken one week ago, the first confirmed sighting in eight months. He got into that taxi with a backpack, and the FIS staked out his apartment after receiving our tip. Friedman never returned, abandoning all his physical possessions except, presumably, his digital media and electronic devices, less than twelve hours after Weisz's capture."

I set the page down, wondering how many personalities she was going to brief me on before conceding that I'd gotten her point.

"Katarzyna Zajac, Polish cybersecurity specialist turned hacker. She worked for the Chinese and gained mastery over the dark web before taking her skills freelance, and has since been tied to major data breaches in the DoD and DoJ. Last seen in Jijel, Algeria." Chen thrust the page my way. "Gone."

I didn't even bother lifting the paper this time, merely glancing down to see an attractive young blonde woman staring back at me before Chen was onto the next.

"Adrian Müller, German private military contractor who spent a decade fighting bush wars in Africa before parting ways with the mercenary community and turning to terrorism for hire. He was the tactical planner for the convention center seizure at the World Economic Forum, among others. We've also tied him to the Norwegian Cruise Line hijacking, which he appears to have masterminded. We'd placed him in Caracas as of last week, and now he's vanished."

That page, too, came my way, and Chen declared, "Last but not least: Kamran Raza, former Pakistani general implicated in selling uranium enrichment technology to the North Koreans. We had a very strong lead placing him in the Urak Valley of Balochistan Province, and the trail went cold the day we captured Weisz."

She didn't bother handing me that profile, instead flipping the folder shut and pushing the entire packet my way before concluding, "And those were just our top five. There are a dozen more of mid-to-high priority in there who disappeared along with the rest."

I left the folder untouched and rubbed my jaw, momentarily lost in thought.

Finally I managed, "You're telling me these people are all underground, waiting to see what happens next? Because Weisz's death left a power vacuum?"

"A power vacuum," she agreed, "at the global level. Now we're waiting to see who steps up to fill it. And when that next candle sparks, I'll need your men to go snuff it out. Because it's going to be followed by a hell of a lot more. Someone is coming after the power and influence that Weisz had, we just don't know who."

"Or how," I pointed out.

"Or how."

Swallowing, I offered, "We stepped on a pregnant spider, just like he said."

"We most certainly did," Chen said quietly, a sad smile playing at her lips. "Killing Erik Weisz wasn't the end, I'm sad to say. The way the winds are turning now, it's the beginning of an entirely new war."

CONGO NIGHTFALL:
SHADOW STRIKE #8

When elite CIA operative David Rivers and his paramilitary team are dispatched to the heart of Africa, their mission is clear: eliminate the notorious terrorist warlord, Chijioke Mubenga, before he can unleash chaos upon the world.

But fate has other plans.

A streak of anti-aircraft fire lights up the night sky, turning a covert parachute jump into a nightmare descent. Stranded miles from their rendezvous point and deep within a hostile jungle, Rivers and his team are cut off, hunted, and desperate.

In their quest for survival, they uncover a web of treachery that extends far beyond the Congo's borders. As they close in on Mubenga, Rivers uncovers a conspiracy that threatens to reshape the very fabric of global security.

In a land where trust is a luxury and every path holds potential danger, Rivers must navigate his team through a maze of betrayal, drawing on every ounce of his skill, leadership, and instinct to outwit an enemy that always seems two steps ahead. The hunt is on...but in the Congo, nothing is as it seems.

And the cost of failure is unimaginable.

Get your copy today at
severnriverbooks.com

ABOUT THE AUTHOR

Jason Kasper is the USA Today bestselling author of the Spider Heist, American Mercenary, and Shadow Strike thriller series. Before his writing career he served in the US Army, beginning as a Ranger private and ending as a Green Beret captain. Jason is a West Point graduate and a veteran of the Afghanistan and Iraq wars, and was an avid ultramarathon runner, skydiver, and BASE jumper, all of which inspire his fiction.

Sign up for Jason Kasper's reader list at
severnriverbooks.com

jasonkasper@severnriverbooks.com